BRIDE TAKES A CHARMER

Highland Vows & Vengeance
Book 3

by Kara Griffin

Dragonblade Publishing, Inc. is an imprint of Kathryn Le Veque Novels, Inc.
P.O. Box 23
Moreno Valley, CA 92556
ceo@dragonbladepublishing.com

Produced in the United States of America

First Edition August 2025
Trade Paperback Edition

ARE YOU SIGNED UP FOR DRAGONBLADE'S BLOG?

You'll get the latest news and information on exclusive giveaways, exclusive excerpts, coming releases, sales, free books, cover reveals and more.

Check out our complete list of authors, too!

No spam, no junk. That's a promise!

Sign Up Here

www.dragonbladepublishing.com

Dearest Reader;

Thank you for your support of a small press. At Dragonblade Publishing, we strive to bring you the highest quality Historical Romance from some of the best authors in the business. Without your support, there is no 'us', so we sincerely hope you adore these stories and find some new favorite authors along the way.

Happy Reading!

CEO, Dragonblade Publishing

**Additional Dragonblade books by
Author Kara Griffin**

Highland Vows & Vengeance Series
Bride Takes a Scot (Book 1)
Bride Takes a Laird (Book 2)
Bride Takes a Charmer (Book 3)

About the Book

Laird Shaw Mackintosh disbelieves the king betrothed him without consulting him. The situation is intolerable, but no one repudiates the king's command. With his neighbors' constant fracases over land rights and the homecoming of his sister and her husband, Shaw is somewhat bothered by the inconvenience—until he learns that Sorsha of Clan Chattan is an offered bride.

Sorsha was forced into a loveless marriage to Rodick Chattan. When she witnesses his murder by one of his family, she requests aid from the queen. The king adds her name to the brides being offered to Highland lairds for her protection. Sorsha accepts her destiny, especially when Shaw Mackintosh, a charming laird, offers her marriage.

Infatuated with Lady Sorsha, Shaw remembers their brief encounter at the king and queen's feast many years before. When he learns of her dreadful situation, he cannot stand aside and allow her to marry anyone but him. With his busy life as Laird of the Mackintoshes, he doesn't think his happiness or a family is possible—but when Sorsha opens her heart to him, his love for her becomes more than infatuation.

Unforeseen enemies threaten to squash the happiness he's found and he seeks vengeance. Petty wars among his neighboring clans prevent him from finding out who aims to destroy him. Shaw doesn't suspect his foe is closer than he thinks until he uncovers a traitor within his clan.

Will these Highland vows and vengeance hold the promise of love and redemption for Shaw and Sorsha?

Character List

MACKINTOSH CLAN
Shaw Mackintosh – Hero
Maven – Mamo/Grandmother
Trey – Commander-at-arms
Walen – Comrade/High-ranking Soldier
Niahm – Walen's sweetheart
Clovis – Gate watchman
Henny – High-ranking Soldier
Donald, Gordon, Craig – Soldiers
Corliss – Sister
Idris Dunbar – Brother-In-Law
Edra – Servant
Enid – Servant's daughter
Louis – Healer
Luthor – Orphaned lad

HEROINE
Sorsha d'Avranches Chattan – Heroine
Gillian (Gilly) – Daughter
Rodick Chattan – Husband
Geoff Chattan – Brother-in-law
Richard d'Avranches – Father
Lucia d'Avranches – Mother
Aela – Maidservant
Lister – Stable lad

CHAPTER ONE

Blarmacfoldach, Inverness
Highlands, Scotland
Late December 1259

THE COMING NEW year offered everyone the possibility of prosperity. With good fortune being prayed for and the rituals enacted for the coming year's goodwill, Lady Sorsha should have joined the faithful in their pleas. But she wasn't superstitious and considered the appeals and omens absurd. Life would unfold as it would regardless of prayers or faithfulness. If only she knew what awaited her, she might have spent an hour or two on her knees like the others. Instead, she found the sights in the village quite comical and entertaining.

Winter had taken a respite, for the day was pleasant with only a few clouds to blemish the bright blue heavens and a slight chill. The Yule festival took place in the village of Blarmacfoldach with its thatched-roofed, white-washed cottages and busy lane. Almost every clan in the area attended the festival except for those whose rivalries were too ingrained to allow them to join in the celebrations.

Most clans tended to stay in groups with their brethren and kept to themselves. Some clans knelt on the sacred ground outside the kirk in deep prayer, some raised their cups in *slàinte* to offer their appreciation for God's goodwill, and some sang songs of sorrow, forgiveness, and devotion. The sights, sounds, and smells engulfed her senses and brought a wide smile to her face. Now, Sorsha held the small hand of her daughter, Gillian, and delighted in the revelry around her.

She walked on the lane, past the tents and carts decorated with colorful banners and pennons. How she wished her husband, Rodick, had come with them for their daughter's sake. Alas, he was too busy and couldn't get away. He rarely spent time with her or their daughter but that suited her well because Sorsha cared not for his company.

She did her duty as the laird's wife and did her best to please him. Rodick wasn't a loving husband but he cared for her in his way by offering shelter and protection. In return, she performed her wifely duties with no objections. She hadn't wanted to marry Rodick but she was given no choice. Her parents had made a treaty with Clan Chattan and her hand was included in the alliance. At the time, she was devastated to marry the unknown, staid man, whose lands were far from her home. Yet in the years that she'd been with Rodick, her feelings had grown to acceptance.

With the return of the sun, the days began to grow longer. Fires lit that night signified everyone's jubilation as they commemorated the dead by offering sacrifices for fertility, the harvest in the coming year, and the ideals of rebirth. An uneasiness came when she spotted men nearby who had drunk to excess and were now drunk. Most sipped mulled wine or wassail, the warm concoction that brought on good cheer with songs sung. Others gorged themselves with meat and other foodstuffs. All were in a mirthful mood since work was put aside and even most quarrels were forgiven for the short time during Yule to keep holy.

Sorsha shared the cup of mead she'd purchased at the brewer's tent by handing it to Gillian. Her daughter took a small sip. "'Tis awful," her daughter said and used her tongue to try to rid herself of the taste.

Two men shoved each other, fell to the ground, and landed in a leftover puddle from the prior day's rain. A splash of the filthy water splattered her and Gillian. Sorsha gasped soundly and yanked Gillian back, and showed her displeasure by scoffing at them. They paid her no heed though and continued to wrestle on the ground. She gripped her daughter's shoulders, guided her around the ruffians, and hurried away.

"I agree, this is foul-tasting." When her daughter handed the cup back, Sorsha poured its contents on the ground and set the cup on an empty table nearby. "Oh, look, bun, there is a soothsayer here." Sorsha smiled lightly when her daughter narrowed her eyes at her for calling her the silly name. She likened her daughter to the squirrel in Gillian's favorite verse that she'd told her each night at bedtime.

It somewhat saddened her that the meaning of the story was lost on her daughter. She hoped to convey that every person and creature was important, that all were useful, and that no one was smaller than anyone. The endearment didn't gain a smile from her sweet lass. Instead, her daughter peered ahead with an unamused gaze on her face.

"Shall we go and find out what our future holds?" Sorsha pressed a gentle hand over her daughter's brown hair that hung below her shoulders. She laughed when her daughter scrunched her small face and added a pout.

"Do we have to, Mama? They are all tricksters. 'Tis all falsity. Lister told me so."

Sorsha wished her daughter wouldn't take life so seriously or listen to the stable lad, Lister. Gillian was the most serious child she'd ever beheld. Only five summers in age, her daughter found no enjoyment in life. That her sweet Gillian didn't smile or laugh or even play as the other children did within their clan often concerned her. But her daughter was too clever and didn't appreciate humor or revelry.

"Come along and let us have a wee bit of fun." She tugged Gillian's hand and entered the fortune teller's tent.

The inside was dark except for a lone candle that sat on the table. "Och, milady, have ye come to seek your destiny?" The seer was thin-bodied with long, curly black hair covered with a kerchief tied at her nape. She waved them onward and her wrinkled face welcomed them with a smile.

Sorsha sat in the chair at the cloth-covered table and nodded. "Aye, I would like you to tell me what my future holds, madam."

Gillian stood by her side and peered at the woman with a blank expression. She said nothing and appeared disinterested. But Sorsha always adored getting her fortune told at festivals and gatherings. She thought it entertaining because most often the teller got it wrong. Not once had the seers told her one thing that had come true.

"I shall tell ye your destiny. Do ye have payment, milady?"

Sorsha removed a coin from her overdress seam and slid it across the fabric of the tabletop with her finger. "What say you? Does my future behold greatness or shall I despair?" She wanted to laugh but with her daughter's serious mien, she kept her voice devoid of mirth.

The seer reached behind her, took a thick candle from the sideboard, and set it in a pot atop a small fire on the ground near her. While the seer awaited the melting of the candle, she took her hand and peered at it. With Sorcha's palm face up, the woman traced her finger along the lines of her skin and it tickled.

When the candle completely melted, the seer poured the melted wax into a crudely made glass bowl. The wax's motions in the water were supposed to foretell what would transpire in her life as shapes formed. Sorsha was enthralled by the carromancy ceremony and watched the mesmerizing movement of the candlewax floating in the water. The formation of the wax was beautiful, but she smiled to herself knowing that the resulting shapes alluded to nothing—not her past, future, or any essence of her life. They were just clumps of wax moving gracefully in the water.

"Hmm." The fortune teller straightened and peered into a round-shaped glass orb that sat upon the cloth of the table. "This is…interesting. Your life is about to change direction, milady."

"What do you read?" Sorsha shifted closer to the table and tried to keep herself from laughing outwardly.

"'Tis darkness but also light. Something dreadful will happen before this day is through. I must use another method to reason it." The seer unfolded a deck of cards from a tattered, worn cloth and muttered to herself. After fanning them on the table, she chose a card and said, "Ah, the six-of-cups card. Do not despair, Milady, for ye shall rekindle a relationship with someone from your past." The seer glanced at Gillian and smiled.

Sorsha pursed her lips at the absurdity because she could think of no one she would be reunited with. "What relationship do you speak of?"

The fortune teller clucked her tongue and sat back. "Och, 'tis gone." She raised her hands as if it eluded her. "I am sorry, Milady, but I cannot answer your question. All I can offer is that you take heed for there is some unpleasantness afoot this day for ye. Ultimately, ye will be reunited with someone from your past."

Sorsha rose and thanked her. She grabbed Gillian's hand and led her back outside the tent. "You were right, bun, that was rather silly. I promise you, the only unpleasant thing to happen to me on this day was drinking that foul-tasting mead. Now come along and we shall purchase a piece of sweetened bread to eat on our ride home."

After they visited the baker's tent, Sorsha led her daughter to the cart where her husband's soldiers awaited. Four Chattan soldiers: three horsemen and one cart driver sat by the hostelry but hastily got to their feet when she approached. She hoisted Gillian onto the cart and then crawled onto it. She almost fell to the side when the cart rolled forth. Next to her daughter, she took hold of her hand and smiled.

"'Tis cold," Gillian said when the wind pressed against them. Fortunately, they had worn their winter cloaks even though it was somewhat warmer earlier in the day.

Sorsha pulled the tartan blanket stored in the back of the cart over their laps and handed the lass half of the sweet bread. Gillian held the bread but didn't take a bite. "Are you not hungry?" she asked Gillian but her daughter shook her head. Sorsha ate hers and when Gillian handed her piece back to her, she ate that too.

The sun dissipated and the wind grew brisker. Fortunately, the ride home wouldn't take too long. She wrapped her arm around her daughter's shoulder and hugged her closely as the soldiers rode ahead. That Gillian resembled her in appearance with her long brown hair and honey-colored brown eyes often brought a sense of pride to her heart. She was grateful that her daughter didn't resemble her father.

"Did you have fun at the festival this day?"

Gillian shook her head. "I liked it not."

Sorsha sighed dejectedly. There seemed to be no pleasing her sweet lass because she found little merriment in anything. Gillian squeezed closer to her when they reached the road that led to Tor Castle. There were rumors of the lane being haunted by a powerful spirit. Yet as long as she'd lived there, no spirit had ever shown itself to her.

Thick pines and hefty-needled trees darkened the area, shading it to almost obscurity. The lane had towering trees on both sides which cut off access, and with the roadway set lower, the hillocks beside it were steep. She'd always disliked the thought of being on the road at the darkest part of the night. There was a sense of spookiness about the lane.

"Do you think the spirit is close, Mama? Can you feel the sadness here?"

Sorsha's chest tightened at her daughter's questions. "There is no spirit, lass, and no sadness. 'Tis just a dark and lonely road. We'll pass it soon."

By the time they reached the gates of Tor, a duskiness set the sky in its early-evening haze. Sorsha thanked the soldiers for their escort and lifted Gillian from the cart. As she entered the castle, she continued to the upper solar. Sounds came from her husband's bedchamber, but Sorsha needed to get Gillian settled for the night and passed by his door. She wondered who her husband argued with because their voices rose with ire.

Gillian's nursemaid had been given a day of rest and was nowhere in sight. Sorsha didn't mind having to look after her daughter and enjoyed the quiet moments with her. After she put her daughter in her night garments, she tossed back the bed cover, lifted her, and settled her in the center of the bed. "Do you wish for a cup of water?"

"Nay, Mama."

"Are you hungry? You hardly ate any of the food at the festival."

Gillian shook her head and shifted to lie her head on the pillow at the top of her bed. "Will you tell me the story again?"

Sorsha smiled and pressed her hand on her daughter's small cheek. "Of course, I shall. I always do, do I not?" She tucked the covers beneath Gillian's chin and smiled. "The great mountain and the wee squirrel quarreled. The bun said, 'Little prig, you are doubtless very big and I am but a small creature.'"

Her daughter snickered lightly at her saying "prig", and Sorsha pressed a kiss on her forehead and continued, "'Aye, but you are mighty, and 'tis no disgrace to occupy my place. For I am not as magnificent as you and you are not as uninspiring as I…and not half so spry. I shall not deny that you make a pretty squirrel track for my wee feet to run upon. We differ, we certainly do because I cannot carry forests on my back but neither can you crack a nut.'"

Her daughter sighed and blinked as sleepiness overtook her.

"Sleep sweetly, bun." Sorsha pressed her palms over her daughter's brown locks and rose.

Gillian closed her eyes and appeared to drift off to sleep. Quietly, Sorsha left the chamber, closing the door behind her as she approached her husband's bedchamber. Rodick continued to argue with whoever was with him. Sorsha wasn't sure if she should interrupt but her interest piqued and she took hold of the latch. As gently as she could, she pushed it and opened the door slightly to see who was within.

When she spotted her brother-in-law, Geoff, she shifted the door wider. Her gasp echoed in the chamber at the sight of Geoff pressing his dagger into her husband. Sorsha rushed forward and pulled Geoff's hand away, but it was too late. He'd aimed true at her husband's chest. Rodick's eyes widened and he drew in a tortured wail and fell to the floorboards next to his bed.

Sorsha knelt next to her husband and the horror of what she'd witnessed burned her throat and eyes. She removed Geoff's dagger and tossed it away from her. A sound by the door drew her gaze and she spotted Gillian standing there. Her daughter's eyes broadened with fright. A tormented scream came from her mouth and Sorsha rose to go to her but Geoff blocked her way.

"Let me go to my daughter," she said in a strained voice full of pain.

"Ye should not have come in here," Geoff said tersely.

"What have you done?" Sorsha yelled, "You stabbed him." A sob tore at her throat. Rodick whispered something and she knelt again and leaned closer to hear. "We shall get help. Fetch the healer, Geoff. Hold on, Rodick."

"I…am…sorry." Rodick panted and moaned, "I could…not show ye affection." His eyes shifted to Geoff and his breath came heavier.

She turned and shouted at Geoff. "Help him. Get the healer." Her brother-in-law stood aside and made no move to get aid, but watched her with his hooded dark eyes. She turned back to her husband. "Please, Rodick, don't leave us."

"Sorry, I…did…not…love ye…" Her husband's whispered words ceased when his harsh breath fell from his lips. He closed his eyes and his chest stilled.

Sorsha kissed his lips knowing there was no breath there. Covered with his blood, she wept for him and the thought of losing him. She faced Geoff. "Why…? Why would you kill him?"

Geoff approached and took hold of her arms. He pulled her up to stand near him. "He was weak and I needed to rid our clan of him. Rodick was a danger to us. What care ye? He wasn't an attentive husband. Ye will not speak of what ye witnessed this day. I will have your vow."

"The hell I won't. I shall tell all what you did. You murdered your brother and won't get away with it." She tried to yank herself from his hold but couldn't.

Geoff wrenched her body closer and held her in a tight embrace around her waist with her back to him. His breath rasped in her ear. "Speak one word, Sorsha, and ye will never see your precious daughter again. I mean it, lass. Your daughter is now in my care and if ye ever want to see her again, ye will keep your harridan mouth shut."

Sorsha's eyes darted to the door where she'd last seen Gillian, but the wee lass wasn't there. She gasped and tried to dislodge herself from his hold. "You are vile and a cosh—"

He squeezed her face, pinching her cheeks, and shook it. "Keep your vulgarity behind those bonny lips."

She managed to wrench herself free from his hold and turned to slap his face. Her palm burned with the sting of it but she continued to glare at him. "You are a murderer."

He shoved her away and Sorsha stumbled backward toward the door, intent on escaping the knave and getting to Gillian.

Geoff marched to her, gripped the long strand of her braid, and forced her to the adjacent room. Once inside her bedchamber, he pushed her farther into it.

"I need to think. Until I figure out what will befall us, ye will be quiet. I will have your agreement to keep what ye witnessed to yourself. If ye do not, I will be forced to keep Gillian from ye. Her life is in your hands, lass, remember that." Geoff closed the door behind him as he left. The sound of the door's lock came and then silence.

"I want my daughter," she shouted and pounded the door with her fist. "Bring her to me. Bring her now!" Sorsha yelled, fell to the floor, and wept. Anguish filled her and with her fist, she continued to pound the door and shouted for Geoff, but he didn't return. "Gillian. Gillian, my sweet lass. Oh, God, help us."

When her sobs and wails lessened, she rose and stepped back until her legs came in contact with the bed. Sorsha sat and clenched her shaking hands. She raised them and covered her eyes, dejected at what she'd seen and what the knave had told her. She had no doubt he would keep Gillian from her.

Only the cruelest of men would keep a child from her mother. Somehow she had to figure out what to do, how to gain aid, and keep Gillian safe. If Geoff was capable of murdering his brother, the Good Lord knew what he'd do to her and his niece.

Men's voices sounded in the hallway. Sorsha hastened to the door and pressed her ear to the cold wood to listen and to hopefully glean what was happening.

Her brother-in-law's voice sounded through the door. "We know not who attacked my brother. Have him prepared for burial and set the guard to ensure no one leaves or enters our gates. We need to find the intruder."

Footsteps thumped on the floorboards and then it grew quiet again.

Intruder, ha. What a knave and liar. Sorsha was gladdened, at least, that he hadn't accused her of murdering Rodick. He could have done so, and if he had, she would've been in a worse predicament. She wondered why he hadn't. There was no adoration between them because she'd never liked her brother-in-law but had stayed away from him. How Rodick felt about his brother was unknown to her because her husband never shared his view with her on any matter.

With that, she scurried about the chamber and found parchment, ink, and a quill. Sorsha wrote to her dear friend, the only person who might offer help—Queen Margaret was her only hope. She didn't divulge that Geoff murdered her husband, but only that her husband had died. She added that she was in peril and that the queen should send for her.

As the night passed, she awaited the morning. The night's darkness subsided, and finally, she heard the sound of the latch on the door being undone. She stood and waited to see who had come. She prayed it wasn't Geoff but then she reconsidered. If Geoff came, then she could plead with him to free her and allow her to see Gillian.

Instead, Aela entered and approached. The short, stout woman ambled toward her. Her brown eyes beheld fear and they widened at viewing her. "My Lady, are you harmed? You are covered with blood. Oh, I should get my satchel and tend to you."

Sorsha hadn't changed out of her overdress and peered down at Rodick's blood staining the front of her. Her throat thickened with despair and at the wretchedness of her situation. She shook her head but said nothing.

The maid retrieved a clean gown for her and handed her a cup of mead. Aela had attended to her since she'd been a young lass. When she'd first married Rodick, her parents allowed the maidservant to travel with her to her new home. She was grateful to the woman for her care. Aela went about her chores and checked the chamber pot which was empty. She tidied the bed covers and fluffed the pillows.

While Aela worked, Sorsha washed at the basin and changed her overdress. Afterward, the maid returned to her and used her fingers to detangle her hair. She wound the strands into a long braid then pressed a finger on Sorsha's lips and kept her voice low, "Geoff has proclaimed himself as the laird. He told me that he had you removed to your chamber when you found the laird killed. Were you harmed, my lady, in your husband's attack?"

"It was not my blood on my overdress but Rodick's."

"Oh, my lady, I am so sorry. There must be a way to help you."

Aela was aware of her distaste for Geoff. Many times, she and Aela had shared looks whenever Geoff was present. He was a demanding man, unmannerly, and never thanked the servants for their attention. Now she wondered if the maid suspected that he alone was guilty of their laird's murder.

"I am well enough but am worried for Gillian. Is she safe?"

The maid lowered her chin. "I know not, my lady. She is not in her chamber and the keep's servants will not speak to me about whatever happened."

Sorsha snatched the missive she'd written from the bedside table, leaned close to Aela, and whispered, "I know a way to get help. Will you have this message delivered to Queen Margaret? Ask Lister to take it for me. His absence won't be noticed by Geoff. 'Tis important that he leave posthaste."

Aela agreed with a nod. "I will tell Lister to make haste." She tucked the missive inside her frock and pressed an errant strand of her dark blond hair behind her ear. "The laird said you are not to leave this chamber for your safety. He says that he means to protect you, *bah*, but we know the truth of the matter. He means to keep you prisoner, my lady. I worry for you. I shall come with food soon and we will figure out what to do. For now, I will have Lister deliver your message. Take your rest. You look tired."

"Will you ensure that Gillian is safe?"

"I shall try to find her. Worry not." Aela approached the door and turned to look at her before she left. "All will be well. We must have faith in that. I promised your dear mother that I would look out for you and protect you if I could—"

Sorsha couldn't allow Aela to despair. When she had married Rodick, her mother insisted that Aela go with her and sent Lister too. Aela and Lister were devoted to her care and she hadn't felt so alone. They had gone beyond their duty to aid her throughout the years. She couldn't put them in danger though because Geoff would not care a whit about a maid or a stable lad.

"You have been so kind to me, Aela. But you must promise me not to put yourself in peril. I could not bear that. I do not know what I would have done without you."

"My lady, 'tis you who have been kind to me. I have faith that God will aid you." Aela nodded with vigor. She quietly closed the door behind her and shifted the latch.

Sorsha was beyond the help of prayers and in her faith that God would aid her. She was at Geoff's mercy at least for the moment. Would he accuse her of Rodick's murder? Or would he continue with the farce that someone snuck into the castle and murdered her husband? Until the queen sent men to rescue her, Sorsha realized that she had to pretend to support the knave. For now, she would be docile and make no complaint. As long as she got to be with Gillian, she would tell Geoff whatever he wanted to hear.

She wished that she'd prayed for good fortune at the festival, but alas, it appeared she and her daughter would suffer for the foreseeable future. The coming new year offered everyone—*but her*—the possibility of prosperity.

CHAPTER TWO

Castle Moy, Eilean Nan Clach
Inverness, Highlands Scotland
Mid-March 1260

S HAW MACKINTOSH STRETCHED and crawled from his bed. He ambled to the window casement and threw open the shutters. Silence abounded in the predawn morning over the foggy, heavily wooded land in the distance. Cold winter air streamed into his solar and he took a deep breath. Shaw always enjoyed the time of morning when the day held such promise and *solitude.*

His solar was the only place that gave him peace. His gaze roved to the door of his private domain and he was dejected that soon, he'd need to leave the tranquil place. Outside his door, his clansmen awaited instruction and guidance.

Shaw listened to the quiet. Except for the wind that whistled at the three-story structure of his home, Castle Moy, and the lapping of the water against the rocks that protected the small island, there was no noise. It was early; dawn had yet to make its appearance over the mountains in the distance. None of his clansmen or women had risen yet. Before long, many would be about the land they called home. Soon the sun would rise and glisten over the waters that surrounded the stony island and a new day would bring what it would.

He scratched his chest and then took hold of the shutters

when a knock came at his door. Shaw turned away from the bonny view, latched the window casement enclosure, and crossed the chamber in a quick stride. He didn't open the door wide because he hadn't yet garbed himself. The door slightly ajar afforded him to see who dared to awaken him—not that they had—but they didn't know that.

"Laird, Clovis sent for ye. Milady Maven has left the grounds again. Ye must come at once," Enid, a young maid within the keep, whispered.

"Aye, I will see to her. Go on to the kitchens, Enid, and tell Mistress Edra that I want the morning fare on the table by the time I return. Give her my thanks as well." Shaw closed the door and hurried to dress. He pulled on a heavy tunic and covered his waist with his tartan. After, he secured his belt and positioned his sword in the scabbard he'd strapped to his chest. There was no time to waste because he had to get to his grandmother. Given the chill of the morning, she had to be freezing.

Shaw rushed from the room and when he reached the door to the keep, he stopped and grabbed his grandmother's cloak, the one lined with thick fur. He folded it over his forearm and bounded toward the gate. When he reached it, Clovis, the watchman, opened it.

"Fair morn to ye, Laird." Clovis pressed a hand over his mouth, covering a quick yawn. He must've been at the watch through the night for he appeared disheveled and unkempt. His light-colored cropped hair stuck up and his beard curled in small knots on his face. He cleared his throat and explained, "She was later than usual this morn and only left a short time ago."

Shaw nodded to his soldier, muttered his thanks, and continued onward. He crossed the wooden bridge and with quick steps, he reached the isolated location of the Mackintosh burial grounds. There amid the cold stones of the dead, he spotted his grandmother. Her body was curled up on the ground before the mound where her husband, his grandda, was buried. He sighed and approached. With a gentle hand, he pressed his grandmother's shoulder.

"Mamo, ye need to awaken," Shaw called to her and then three more times before she opened her eyes.

"What are we doing here?" Confusion crossed her face along with a myriad of expressions.

Shaw drew a resigned breath. His aged grandmother had no awareness that she slept walked each night. He'd given orders to the gate watch to allow his grandmother to pass through the gates and not to awaken her. The few times someone had tried to roust her when she'd been in such a state, she'd become violent and hurt herself more than she had those she'd attacked.

"Ye were sleepwalking again."

Her long gray hair tussled in the wind but she made no move to tame it. She gazed at him with cornflower blue eyes that had long ago faded with her age. Maven was still bonny though, even with the many wrinkles on her face. She accepted the cloak that he held out to her.

"Best get ye warm." Shaw helped to pull the cloak around her. "One of these days, Mamo, I will not be able to awaken ye."

She raised her saddened eyes to him. "'Tis what I hope and pray for each night. Why has God left me here when He has taken all those I love…"

Shaw reached out to help her rise, took her hand, and gently squeezed it with affection. "Not all that ye love were taken."

"True, ye are still here, my bonny lad."

Shaw didn't like the forlorn sound of her words or the sorrow that welled in her eyes. "And Corliss needs ye, too. We both need ye, Mamo."

His grandmother scoffed a *ha* under her breath. "That lass… Your sister needs no one, save for herself. Definitely not me. Aye, for she's a wily cat to land on her feet. Still, I should have died long ago. God surely punishes me by keeping me here. Mayhap I am cursed, aye, because I just want to be with my dear Fergus." Maven squeezed his hand and raised her face to the sky.

"Och, it seems that day is not this day."

"I'm gladdened, Mamo, that it is not. Come, let us get ye back to the keep. 'Tis freezing this day and we should get ye near a warm fire." Shaw was pained by the despondent mood of his grandmother of late.

Over three scores in age, she had lived beyond most of those she cared about, longer than anyone he knew. He did his best to watch out for her but his grandmother was headstrong and never listened to his commands or heeded his cautions—especially his warning about going to the graves in the middle of the night.

"I fear that I shall never be with my Fergus."

He set his arm around her shoulder and guided her back toward the keep. "God has his reasons for keeping ye here, Mamo."

"Aye, aye, He does. Perhaps my sins prevent our Good Lord from taking me? Do ye deem that I am cursed?"

He chuckled lightly. "Who would ever want to curse ye? Nay, whatever the reasons, ye will remain here until God calls ye home. Besides, what sins could ye have committed?"

She lowered her gaze and didn't answer his absurd questions.

Shaw kept hold of her as they meandered over the small hills of the forest and the wooden bridge that led to their home. When they reached the gates, she walked ahead of him and Shaw grew grim at the thought that one morning she would be with her husband. He suspected he would find her gone to the hereafter, her cold lifeless body a mere remembrance of the woman she'd once been. How he dreaded that day.

"Laird, missives came for ye." Clovis held out the sealed parchments.

He took the missives and scowled at them because he hadn't received so many messages in quite a while. "My thanks, Clovis. Has the sentry gone out this morn?"

"Not as yet, Laird."

"Close the gates after they leave." Shaw ambled forward and shoved the parchments inside his tunic. He'd read them later while he ate his morning fare.

On his approach to the fief, he saw glints of the morning sun shining on the waters. He spotted several of his clansmen just starting their day. They headed off toward where they practiced arms.

A shadow passed by the tree near him and he steeled himself, ready to face his adversary. He chuckled to himself, knowing who approached. His comrade jumped out from behind and grabbed him. Shaw took hold of the assailant and flung him over his shoulder. The man's body thumped on the ground. Shaw used his knee against Henny's chest to hold him on the ground and the man groaned.

"Do ye give?"

Henny grunted and ceased trying to gain his release. His bulky body stilled and then he chortled. The soldier's dark eyes, as black as night, peered at him with mirth. "Bollocks, ye saw me coming, did ye not? Aye, aye, I give."

Shaw shoved his soldier's black-haired covered head against the ground, released him, and bellowed, "I admit that I saw ye coming. Go on, ye best get on the field before Trey reprimands ye for being late."

His soldier trotted off and passed his commander-in-arms. Trey shouted at Henny but waved him onward and approached.

"Did he attack ye again?" Trey asked and shifted his hands through his blond locks as he side-eyed him with his green eyes and had a smirk on his face.

Shaw nodded. "Aye, as he does every morn. I am beginning to think Henny has something against me. Och, I know what he is up to and cannot fault him for it."

Trey cackled. "Och, ye do? What might that be, Laird? Ye mind telling me because I have yet to figure out why Henny attacks ye and our soldiers."

"He means to keep me and the soldiers on our toes. I appreciate his effort." Shaw laughed to himself because Henny was a devoted soldier. On a night when they'd both imbibed too much potent ale, his soldier confessed why he'd battered his clansmen.

Henny maintained that he did so to keep him and his soldiers from losing the skill of awareness when there was the possibility of imminent threats from foes.

"What are we going to do about him? Several soldiers complain that he sneak attacks them. He needs to be stopped before he hurts someone." Trey walked alongside him, but he kept his gaze ahead. "Or someone wounds him."

Shaw pressed his hands to his face and then lowered them. "I do not want him to cease. Truth be told, he is keeping all of us aware. There may be a time when having such skills is beneficial. For now, we will put up with his attacks. Tell your men it's for their good and part of their training. But, best warn them that they may defend themselves but they are not to do irreparable harm to Henny."

Trey grimaced. "The men will be displeased by your order. Och, ye are the laird, so I suppose we will have to put up with him."

Shaw turned to his commander. "Aye, I am the laird and ye will learn to appreciate what Henny does. Our soldiers will gain valuable experience from this, as will I. So nay, I do not want him to cease his attacks. We will let him continue to strike when we least expect it." He reached the keep and turned to Trey. "Was there something else?"

"I should get back to the field." His commander turned. "Do ye want me to come and meet with ye later to go over the training regimen?"

"If I have time, I'll come to ye. See that the men train hard."

Trey turned back to him. "Why, Laird? We are not warring with anyone and the weather is still cold. I do not see the importance of it."

Shaw didn't appreciate the disrespectful tone in his commander's voice. He reached out and gripped Trey's tunic. "Whether we are warring with anyone has no bearing on our readiness. We are surrounded by clans that would overtake us. Along with that, how many of them fight over land rights? Too many to count. If our men cannot handle a wee bit of briskness, then they should find another clan to follow." Trey tried to pull himself away but Shaw wouldn't release him. "I'm not finished. When I want ye to see what is important and what is not, I will tell ye. Get back to the field and train our men as is your duty."

When he released Trey, his commander gave him a defeated look and turned away. Shaw detested that he had to be coarse with his leader, but it was necessary. He needed his men to follow his orders without question. Although he might have agreed with his commander, he couldn't accept his defiance. Trey was stubborn and hoped to lead the men without his interference. Yet he hadn't proven himself yet, at least since Shaw had taken over as laird.

Shaw entered the keep and ambled down the hallway until he reached the great hall. He found his grandmother having her morning fare, sat next to her, and poured himself a cup of ale. As usual, there was no one else in the hall besides the two of them.

He had no siblings besides Corliss but his sister had married and lived with her husband. He had cousins, most of whom resided with Clan Chattan. Even though he had few blood-related clansmen, his clan's followers were closer to him than his relatives.

Thoughts of his family brought on the memories of his parents. Shaw missed his father and mother. They'd been taken from him five years before when a strange malady brought on fits of coughing and fever. They'd perished before he reached his majority.

He leaned back in his seat and continued to hold the cup of ale. When he raised it to his lips, his grandmother shot her gaze at him.

"When are ye going to let me go?" Her words came low, saddened.

"I would gladly let ye go, Mamo, but it is not up to me."

"God does not want me to leave ye alone. When are ye going to marry and bring bairns into the world? I deem that is what holds me here. Have ye no guilt for that?" She lowered her chin.

"That is not what holds ye here, Mamo, and well ye know it. When ye do go, it will be hard for me to accept. I want ye to be happy though, and I pray that God hears your plea."

She nodded and said nothing further. There always seemed to be an easiness between them. They often ate their morning meal in silence, which was somewhat of a blessing since his clan was rather needy and he rarely got a moment's peace.

Edra, the keep's maidservant, entered and carried a pot of pottage which she set near him. "Good morn, Laird."

"My thanks, Edra, for the fare." He pulled a hollowed-out trencher toward him and filled it with the delicious-smelling pottage. "What have ye made for the morn meal? It smells good."

"Oh, 'tis naught but vegetables and some spices. I'm afraid there was no meat left in the stores so…the pottage be light." She shrugged. "Eat your fill, Laird."

"Trey says 'tis too cold to train. Perhaps I'll have the soldiers hunt instead. They will refill your stores, Mistress, within a sennight."

"I should have told ye that we were running low. Och, there is much to do this day. My thanks for allowing my daughter to help me. Enid is capable and does my heavy lifting."

Shaw nodded to the sweet woman. Though she was aged, she still had a head full of thick brown hair with no streaks of gray as yet. Her likewise brown eyes often gazed at him with motherly affection. Edra was devoted to him and had been caring for his parents before they passed. He was grateful for all that she did for him and their clan.

He spooned in mouthfuls of pottage and wished there were pieces of rabbit in it. As he ate his morning fare, he pulled the missives from his tunic that he'd received from Clovis earlier and set them on the table. There were four in all. He spread them out and noticed the one with the king's insignia pressed into the wad of wax in the center.

Shaw opened the missive and scanned the lines. His king

wanted his attendance in Edinburgh. He didn't indicate why but only ordered that Shaw needed to make haste. Shaw sighed because the last thing he wanted was to travel. Yet he could not reject an order from his king. Alexander hadn't completely taken the crown but had a short amount of time before he would claim it outright. Shaw supported him, as he had Alexander's father. That decided, he folded the missive and set it aside. He would leave for the king's residence later that day.

The next missive was from his sister, Corliss. He read the brief message and grew grim at her words:

Brother, our home was besieged by the dastardly Cummings and was all but destroyed. Idris, my dear husband, and I shall stop at Tor on our way to ye. I look forward to seeing ye and Mamo. Pray for our safe journey. Ever your devoted sister, Corliss.

Idris Dunbar, his sister's husband, had many rivals, the Cummings Clan being one of them. The Cummings were a crafty lot and since their foiled attempt to usurp the king's father when he'd held the crown, they tried to influence others to usurp Alexander as well. Fortunately, their king married the daughter of England's king and there seemed to be a peace betwixt the nations. That, however, did little to quell the Cumming's control which was the cause of many alliances against them in the Highlands. Shaw looked forward to seeing Corliss but he wasn't pleased with his sister's news. Hopefully, the situation would de-escalate.

He reached for the next missive which was from Geoff Chattan, his cousin. Shaw barely made out the words with the way his cousin scratched his message. He perceived that Geoff wanted him to come and that they needed to meet. He'd stop by on his return from Edinburgh and perhaps meet his sister there.

The last missive, hopefully, brought better news than the previous one. Shaw cracked the seal and saw that it was from Tom, the owner of *The Tavern* in Fassiefern. He hadn't seen Tom in some time, but he was a good comrade and one that he trusted. His friend wrote that a young lad was begging for food in the town and needed a good home.

Shaw appreciated his friend reaching out. Since he'd become laird, Shaw often brought home any misbegotten lads and lassies who needed a home. His clan was smaller than most in the north and he'd gained followers by increasing their numbers with the unwanted children in nearby towns and villages. The lads were always gladdened to join the ranks of the fledgling soldiers. The lasses were allowed to work or to become the wards of his clansmen and women. All benefited from his altruism.

On his return from Edinburgh, he would have to stop in Fassiefern and find out about the lad who needed aid. If he were agreeable, he'd return with him. If not, the poor lad was subjected to misery because hardly anyone was willing—or able—to feed the needy. Late winter often left stores empty as well as coffers. Many children left orphaned through the winter suffered famine and unfortunately, death, if they were unable to gain aid.

Shaw finished his sparse meal and spoke a farewell to his grandmother. On the way out of the keep, he spotted Enid and called her to him. "Mistress Enid, I need your favor."

"Aye, Laird?" She set the basket she held on the floor and curtseyed to him.

"I am leaving the keep and need someone to look after my grandmother. If she sleepwalks during the night, ye will find her at the graves. Take her cloak for she oft forgets it. Guide her back home when she awakens. Do not try to force her for she can be violent if jarred awake."

The maid frowned at his request. "Ah…Laird, ye ask such an…important task of me."

"I trust ye to be gentle with her. Will ye see to it?" Shaw waited for her answer and the maid appeased him when she nodded.

"Of course, Laird, worry not for I shall see to her." She curtseyed again and left him.

Shaw retreated from the keep and ambled toward the opposite side of the island. The island was small but afforded enough room for a three-story stone-built home. Behind it, there was a small kitchen and a few wooden huts that belonged to his commander-in-arms and higher-ranking soldiers. Next to that sat a barracks, also built of stone, for the unwed soldiers or those without family. The training field sat beyond it and its grass was worn down to the dirt.

Across the bridge, many of his clansmen and women stayed in cottages speckled on the hills and valley, and several merchants had set up shop in wooden structures at the far end of the lane through the little village.

He reached the training field and stood watching his men wielding their swords. Clinks and clashes sounded and when Trey spotted him, he left the field.

He spoke hesitatingly, with an attitude of obeisance. "Laird… I should…*apologize* for my earlier insolence—"

"Nay, there is no need, Trey. I should not have been so…stern. I know ye are only looking out for the men and me. But I remind ye that we should always be ready for war. Ye never know when a clan or ally might call us to arms."

"Ye are right, Laird. The men will continue to train this day. I am going to have the quintains set up soon for their archery practice."

Shaw nodded his acceptance of this plan. "I am leaving for Edinburgh later this day. Whilst I am gone, I will leave ye in charge. See that the men continue to practice arms and set the sentry schedule. Have the men hunt in the mornings. Mistress Edra needs her stores refilled and has run out of meat."

"Aye, I'll see to it. Ye are headed to Edinburgh? That's a long way to travel, Laird. I will pick a few men to travel with ye."

"There is no need. I'll be taking your brother with me." Shaw realized he hadn't seen Trey's brother, Walen, all morning, which was strange. "Know ye where he is?"

Trey hunched his shoulders. "Probably still abed with his latest lady-love."

Shaw bellowed a laugh. His closest comrade, Walen, was always happy to oblige women who wanted company during the long, cold night. "If ye see him, tell him to find me."

"Aye, I shall, Laird."

He turned and left the field and headed toward the village. Across the bridge, he spotted his longtime friend walking toward him and laughed at his disheveled appearance. Walen resembled Trey with his long light locks of hair and his green eyes. Yet Walen was stockier in the body than his brother. Both were hardened soldiers and devoted Mackintosh clansmen.

"I do not have to guess where ye spent the night."

Walen laughed and moved to walk next to him when he turned back toward the gates. "Nay, ye do not. I would've returned sooner but the lass is too damned winsome for her own good."

"Ye are getting serious with the lass and have enjoyed her company this past fortnight. Will ye be offering for her hand?" Shaw chuckled because he doubted that his comrade would ever offer marriage to any woman—not since he'd been cuckolded by the woman he loved. "Will there be a marriage at Bealtuinn?"

If that was the case, he might bear witness to another joining at Bealtuinn or what the church called "The Feast of the Finding of the Holy Cross". Their May Birching rites, where men collected and fastened garlands and boughs on the windows and doors of their ladyloves symbolizing natural rebirth. On the night of Beltane, the fires lit embodied ancient courtship rituals that led to the negotiations and courting of their clans' maidens. Perhaps Walen's maiden would be selected to represent the May Queen, the virgin mother, or Goddess Flora.

But now his friend scowled hard at him and shook the locks of his tangled hair. "Bollocks, nah, och she is sweet. I am not one for marriage, as well ye know. I do not see myself taking the plunge anytime soon."

Shaw grinned at his friend's words. "Me neither. The last thing I want is an overbearing bride." A memory flashed in his mind of a lass he'd once hoped to marry. Her image had stayed with him many years after he'd lost her. There were nights when the softness of her brown eyes haunted him, of her sweet lips begging to be kissed, and her alluring body longing to be held and loved. Shaw shook away his memory and almost chastised himself for holding on to dreams that had ended so long ago.

His friend shoved his shoulder. "Are ye still love-sick over your lost lass, wee laddie?"

Shaw scoffed. "Nay, and I was never love sick."

Walen chortled. "Aye? Ye never got over her, admit it. One day, Laird, ye know ye will need to marry for the sake of heirs. When that time comes…"

"When it does, I shall do my duty." He quickly told him about the missives he'd received that morning. "I am onward to Edinburgh because Alexander requires my attendance."

"Ye must go then," Walen said.

"Aye, and I want ye to come with me. Geoff wants to meet with me as well but he didn't say what he wanted. 'Tis the truth, I detest going to the Chattan's fief. If we were not related, I vow I probably wouldn't maintain our alliance. The Chattans cause strife over their petty land rites and may become troublesome."

"Aye, especially with the Camerons. Ye seek to keep the peace, aye, and it has been so of late. Whatever trouble the Chattans are brewing, we will be prepared. Spring is upon us and the knaves will soon crawl out from under their rocks. I'll ride along with ye and could do with an escape."

Shaw tipped his head quickly at his comrade's acquiescence. What was Walen trying to escape—the winsome lass, or the boredom of the peace that had settled amongst the north? "Along the way, I need to stop in Fassiefern too. There's a lad there that might need a home."

"What do ye think Alexander wants?" Walen asked and ignored his concern for the lad, but kept his gaze ahead.

Shaw was somewhat concerned about why his king wanted his attendance too. It wasn't like Alexander to be so secretive in his missives. He hoped whatever it was, wouldn't take up too much of his time. "What do I know?"

"I'll meet ye at the stables then," Walen said and left him.

Shaw returned to the keep and collected items to take with him, giving thought to the arduous journey. In one satchel he placed a flint, flasks of water and ale, arrows, a sling with a handful of rocks, two daggers with a sharpening stone, and a small ax. In the other went his best tartan and two clean tunics, two pairs of thickly woven stockings, and a heavy cloak. The rest of the day, he handled a few unimportant clan matters and ensured all were informed of his coming absence.

By the time Shaw reached the stables, dusk had set on the land. Fortunately, there was a bright moon to guide the way on the lanes toward Edinburgh. As he rode through the gates, he peered back at his home and at the solitude he'd be leaving behind. He'd hurry and meet with the king and on his return, he'd visit with Geoff and stop in Fassifern. Soon enough, he'd return to the peacefulness of the Highlands and the serenity within the walls of his solar on Eilean Nan Clach. He didn't plan to be gone longer than a fortnight—or so he hoped.

CHAPTER THREE

Castle Tor
Inverness, Highlands Scotland
Mid-March 1260

IN THE GREAT hall, Sorsha stood by the hearth, tense and wary about meeting with Geoff. She'd been summoned and when she arrived, he wasn't there. Dread filled her. Since Rodick's death, she'd been forced to stay within her chamber. The hardship of it wasn't the loneliness or fear of Geoff, but the terror of what had happened to Gillian. Geoff hadn't visited her chamber once, for if he had, she would have pleaded with him to return her daughter.

"Milady Sorsha."

Sorsha nearly jumped at the sound of his voice. She hesitated before turning to look at the man who had murdered her husband and abducted her daughter. For months, she had despaired at what would become of her and Gillian but now was her opportunity to change their circumstances.

"Laird Chattan." She kept herself restrained as she took him in. His height, brawniness, and severity showed the warlord manner he was renowned for. Garbed in black garments, most of which overshadowed the Chattan tartan, did little to lend to an amiable mood.

His dark wavy hair and full beard were damp. She assumed he'd recently bathed. Geoff's dark eyes peered at her in return and he neither smiled nor frowned at her.

Sorsha was uncertain why he'd called her to him. Her only hope was that he intended to free her and allow her to see Gillian. "You wanted to see me, Laird Chattan? Here I am."

He grunted softly and approached to stand next to her. Before the fire, she held out her hands and remained silent. When he was ready to explain why he'd asked her to attend to him, he would tell her so. A long moment passed and she sighed slightly because her fate rested in his hands. The hearth waved before her eyes as she continued to stare at it. Above a wooden mantle, the Chattan's coat of arms, awarded to a previous war chief was sewn with the images of a ship, whortleberries, and a wildcat on richly dyed fabric.

"There are matters we need to discuss."

"Aye, indeed. When might I see my daughter?" Sorsha continued to face the hearth and tensed in wait for his answer.

Geoff turned and walked to a nearby table. He snatched up two cups and filled them with wine. When he returned to her, he handed her a cup. "Drink, Milady, for I have much to say."

"I shall listen," she said and took the cup from him and held it but didn't drink.

"I apologize, Milady, that ye witnessed what happened that night. Ye returned earlier from the festival and… My brother and I argued most of the day about clan matters. I had to act or our clan would be in ruin. Rodick was a spineless laird and was fearful of confronting our enemies. If ye had not born witness to what…happened…" He took a swig of the cup and was quiet for a moment.

Sorsha listened and understood the struggle of the clan and that Rodick was pathetic. Still, that gave no cause for Geoff to murder him, keep her imprisoned, or abduct Gillian. She took a breath and waited for him to say more.

"Rodick ignored ye and his neglect was intolerable. If I'd been married to ye, I would not have treated ye so inattentively. 'Tis the truth, I always thought ye too good for him." Geoff took another drink from his cup.

"I do not understand why you are telling me this. I vow to speak not of that night or what I saw. You have my pledge to keep secret what you did. All I want is the return of my daughter." She turned to look at him briefly but he kept his reaction shielded by facing the fire.

"Until I trust ye to keep the details behind your teeth, I cannot allow your daughter's freedom. I shall permit ye to leave your chamber but I warn ye, Milady, one word of that night and ye shall never see your beloved child again."

Sorsha swallowed at the anguish his words brought to her. "For how long? Do you deem to keep her from me for a year or more…forever? I cannot bear it. Might I at least see her to ensure she is well?" Moisture threatened to burn her eyes with more tears of despair. Remarkably, she resisted the urge to weep.

"There is a way for ye to free her and to secure your protection," his gently spoken words caused her to gaze at him. "Agree to marry me. As my wife, ye will be unable to make accusations against me. In return, I pledge my fealty to ye and will never neglect ye as my brother did."

Sorsha stiffened her shoulders. The last thing she'd ever do was marry him but he offered her a chance to regain her daughter. It mattered not what pledges he made and she cared not for his attention. Still, the offer was there and he awaited her answer. "I am taken aback…"

Aela entered the hall and in a quick stride, approached them. "My lady, Laird… The king has sent a missive along with an envoy. The messenger awaits to speak to you, my lady." She handed the parchment to her and fled.

With the king's missive in her hand, she turned away from Geoff and neared the table. Her hand shook as she opened the parchment and read:

Lady Chattan, your hasty presence is required in Edinburgh. My envoy awaits and will escort you at once. It was simply signed with an *A*.

Geoff stood behind her and reached to take the missive from her. He read it and frowned. "What does the king want of ye? Why would he send an escort for ye? Tell me. Ye cannot have gotten word to him to beg for aid. I had ye carefully watched."

Sorsha almost fell to her knees. When she'd first been imprisoned in her bed chamber, she'd known she had to act fast. Thankfully, she had sent a message with the stable lad to Margaret. That Geoff had her watched didn't surprise her. "I know not why he's called me but I must go. Aela," she called.

The maidservant reentered the hall. "My lady?"

"Pack a valise for me. I am off to Edinburgh." Sorsha folded her hands, pressing her fingers tightly together, fearful of what the answer to her next question might be. "Laird, may I take Gillian with me? I have vowed not to speak a word of—"

His brows furrowed as he cut her off. "Nay, ye cannot take your daughter to Edinburgh. Ye deem me a fool? If ye think the king will give ye aid, ye are most mistaken about that, Milady." Geoff set the missive on the table and pressed his hands on her shoulders.

Cold fear sent a chilling tremor through her. Sorsha raised her eyes and prayed that he would have the smallest bit of mercy within him.

"Ye will go as the king commanded but until ye return and give me an answer to my marriage offer, Gillian will remain in my care. As her uncle, I will see to her protection. I trust ye not, Milady, but remember that I hold your daughter's wellbeing in my hands. If ye thwart me or try to deceive me, ye will pay the price." Geoff marched out.

Sorsha flopped onto the nearby chair and willed herself not to weep. She was so close to getting him to agree to return Gillian but all was not lost. With the king's aid, she might be able to get Gillian back. But now, the king's envoy awaited and she had no choice but to leave. Her only hope was that Gillian was kept safe until she could gain her freedom. When she secured herself, she would see to it that she rescued her child.

"My lady, are you ready to leave? Your valise is packed and I placed it by the door. The king's messenger awaits you," Edra called from the entrance.

"I thank you, Edra. Please look after my bairn and protect her if you are able. I promise you that I shall return for Gillian, Lister, and you. You have been so kind to me and I detest leaving you behind." She sniffled back her despondency and tried not to weep.

Aela grabbed her hands and held them. "Be strong, my lady. I shall be here awaiting you and I will do whatever I can to help Gillian."

She released Aela's hands and walked toward the exit, saying over her shoulder, "Hopefully, Margaret will offer me sanctuary. When I get to where I am going, I shall write to you." Sorsha yanked her cloak from the peg where she'd kept it and hurried outside.

A spacious carriage tethered to two brown horses sat before the entrance of the keep. One soldier rushed forth and took her valise from Edra, while another set a crate beside the carriage. He held out his hand to assist her aboard. Within a moment, she was underway. Her chest twinged with the painful thoughts of leaving Gillian behind and the months of trepidation she'd endured.

Along the route to Edinburgh, Sorsha paid little attention to the view or the men when they'd stopped to rest or on the layover during the night. The journey was tiresome but she managed to eat, sleep, and see to her needs. Once she reached Margaret, she would be secure and with the queen's aid, she would figure out how to escape the nightmare she'd found herself in.

AT THE SIGHT of her longtime friend, Sorsha nearly fell apart. A tremble overwhelmed her insides and her heart tensed. For the last few months, she'd prayed to reach her friend, and now that she was in Edinburgh, relief brought burning tears to her eyes.

Margaret took one look at her face and then shooed everyone from her private solar. She took her in an embrace and offered comfort. Sorsha held her and sniffled back the sobs that threatened to overtake her.

"My dear friend, you are here at last. I was distraught when I received your missive and am sorry to hear that your husband died."

Sorsha stepped out of her embrace to meet her gaze and realized to her dismay that the queen was attired in a beautiful gown shaded in a golden color that made her own overdress appear to be a tattered frock. Not only was Margaret dressed as a queen should be, but she wore her brown hair elegantly pulled back with a braided gold band atop her head while Sorsha's own hair was disheveled from her travel and her gown wrinkled from the long trek.

"Gracious me, I should be curtseying before you, shouldn't I, Your Grace?" Sorsha pulled back and dipped her knee to genuflect before the queen.

"Cease that. In private, you are my dearest friend. I shall have none of that when we are alone." Margaret motioned her farther into the chamber and walked in front of her.

"I am pleased and grateful that you sent for me. Now I must form a plan."

Margaret gestured for her to sit in a seating area near the small hearth in the chamber. "Come and get warm from your travel and tell me why you must form a plan. You mentioned that you were in peril. I understand that you now must find a way to protect yourself since your husband is gone…" The queen poured her a cup of mead and handed it to her. "Drink, for you will find a little bit of solace in the cup whilst you tell me what happened."

Who knew how far Geoff's friendships reached? Although, Sorsha wasn't certain if he had befriended the king. She wanted to be truthful with Margaret but it might be better to keep from speaking Geoff's name. "I feared for myself and... some...*one* murdered poor Rodick." As much as she wished to name the murderer, she decided not to for her daughter's safety. "I find myself without protection and must somehow get Gillian from the Chattans."

Margaret sat and pressed her hands over the material of her gown. "Why did you not bring your daughter with you? I so wanted to meet her."

Sorsha couldn't reveal the whys and drew an uneasy breath. "I...I could not take her from her clan, at least not right now." She feared that if she revealed the truth to the queen, Margaret would have the Chattans besieged, leaving her daughter in a more dire situation.

"Do not despair because I have, at least, remedied the issue of protection for you."

She sat on the edge of the chair that faced the queen in awe of her friend's support. "You have? How?"

"The king has decreed that four women are to be married to Highlanders that he favors. The lairds are on their way here and shall choose a bride from amongst the women. I suggested to Alexander that he should add your name to those who will wed these men and he has agreed. Rest assured the Highlanders are more than capable of protecting you."

Sorsha tensed at hearing her speak of brides. That she added her name to the brides being offered almost sent her to a good swoon. She didn't want to marry anyone but reasoned that the only way to protect her from Geoff was if she married another. Hadn't he suggested that she marry him to keep her from revealing what he'd done?

She would never have entertained the thought of marrying her husband's brother even though many women were forced to accept such an outcome. Often when a woman's husband died, to continue the line of succession, they married their husband's younger brother. But Sorsha immensely disliked Geoff, not only because he'd murdered her husband but also because he used children in nefarious ways to gain his will. With Margaret's offer, Sorsha considered the plan and how it might serve her.

"Before you reject the king's command, know that you have no choice in the matter. Alexander has added your name to the selection of brides and I'm afraid there is no way to remove yourself from his list. But I promise you, my dear, that you will be gladdened."

Sorsha could only nod at the queen. Decorum dictated that she obey the king and she wasn't dimwitted enough to put herself in a worse situation. "Who are these grooms?"

Margaret grinned at her acceptance. "Do you recall when I was despairing with having to stay in Edinburgh after my marriage to Alexander and your father brought you for a visitation? We had a lavish feast and I caught you looking at Laird Mackintosh."

She felt the heat of her blush rise to her face. "We need not speak of that. I was young and impressionable and…foolish." She remembered the laird. He'd been very handsome to her. Was it possible he hadn't married even now? It couldn't be.

The queen chuckled. "Were we all not impressionable at that age? Aye, we were nothing but lassies whose hearts were worn on our sleeves at the sight of a handsome man. That was a difficult time for me as you well know. If it were not for you, I would not have accepted my husband so graciously. You kept me from being homesick and listened to my complaints about Alexander and that I was purposely kept from him."

"You both were very young when you were betrothed. I told you in time, you would be together, and I was right." Sorsha smiled at the memories the queen spoke of. Although it wasn't love at first sight betwixt the king and queen, there was devotion. Margaret had professed to want to lie with the king and that she was forbidden to be with him. She'd been miserable.

Margaret reached out and took her hand. "If not for you, I would have been lonely here, and you know how I detested the clime and Edinburgh. To me, it was as if I had ended up at the end of the world, a barren place full of barbarians, and lacking any entertainment. I owe you, my friend, for the joyous times we had."

She shook her head. "You owe me nothing, Your Grace. I was gladdened to help you through that difficult time and to be here with you."

"'Tis time for me to repay you for your kindness."

Sorsha pressed her body back into the chair. "How?"

"I mentioned Laird Mackintosh…Shaw. Do you remember how he looked at you as well? There was something betwixt you then, an attraction, and perhaps desire. I have never seen that look in a man's eyes, except of course, for my dear husband's when he gazes at me. Unfortunately, you were already betrothed to Laird Chattan by then and couldn't stray from your future. But now is your chance to secure Mackintosh as your husband if you so wish it. He is an offered groom."

She nearly fell out of her chair at Margaret's suggestion. "He *hasn't* married?"

"Nay, he has not. He can be yours if you want him. In a few days hence, the king is going to have a feast. All will assemble and you will cross paths with him again. The choice is yours, my friend, whether you wish to wed him or not. Of course, he is the one choosing his bride but with you in the selection, I doubt he would overlook you. I have a way of gaining his accord though if that is not so."

"I remember him being charming."

"Charming, handsome, and now, especially, brawny enough to protect you."

Sorsha remembered her encounter with the man: the tone of his voice, the sultry gaze in his grey eyes, and the gentleness in his touch when she'd danced with him at the feast. Since that night, she'd seen him at a distance on the few occasions at Tor when he'd come to visit her husband. How could such a man as Shaw be a cousin to the roguish men of the Chattan Clan? From what she knew of him, he was unlike his abrasive relatives. And again she asked herself: how in God's good grace had he remained unmarried?

The answer didn't matter. What did was that he was as available to be wed as she. It seemed as if God had stepped in to care for her. "Very well, Margaret, I shall agree to marry him if he wishes to wed me. He gave me his heart once, and sadly, I had to give it back."

Margaret patted her hand with empathy. "Perhaps, my dear, he shall give it to you again. Now, we shall have you garbed in the finest gown and I'll have my attendants make you ready the night of the feast. None of the brides will look as beautiful as you. You shall indeed win his favor."

"You are too kind, Your Grace. I profess though that none should rival your loveliness at the feast. How could we, when our queen is beyond beauty?" She'd learned from experience that the way to win Margret's adoration was through compliments.

Indeed, the queen appeared chuffed by her words.

Sorsha drew in a quick breath at the thought of seeing Shaw Mackintosh again. The vision of him flashed in her mind, that of a handsome braw of a Highlander whose face held a friendly manner. His hair had been long then, in waves past his shoulders, in the richest brown shade. But it was the intensity of his gray eyes that had stayed with her through the past years.

She recalled the sensual look on his face and in his manner, and how, at the time, she wished she could have returned the regard. With all her heart, she hoped he hadn't changed. Hopefully, he remained the charismatic man he'd been.

Sorsha didn't look forward to marrying another man for her protection, but if she married Shaw, she wouldn't be too dismayed by it, especially since she'd never forgotten him.

CHAPTER FOUR

Edinburgh Castle
Central Lowlands, Scotland
Late-March 1260

MEMORIES LONG FORGOTTEN returned to Shaw on the approach to Edinburgh Castle. He rode beside Walen and instead of taking in the view before him, he could only envision the nights when he'd joined the king in entertainment and that of a beautiful maiden whose soft brown eyes peered at him becomingly. Shaw shook the visions away because the pain of losing her was too great to consider, and yet, his chest tightened at the thought of her.

They had ridden through heavy rainfall for two days. Only by the time they reached the king's fortress, the rain had all but dissipated to drizzle. Even now, the sun was beginning to make an appearance. A wide lane led through the town's village before the great keep and castle appeared in the distance. The foot traffic, horses, carts, and merchants crowded the thoroughfare making it difficult to traverse, and so they dismounted to walk and lead their steeds to the gate.

Across the stone trestle bridge sat the gatehouse where two guards stood watch. Towers flanked the gatehouse, and beyond it, the castle itself rose in the air where battlements afforded balistrarias where men would position themselves to defend the fortress with efficient arrows. Atop the highest turret, a lone pennon flapped in the breeze with the king's emblem stitched in; it was an image of a red lion and had been created by Alexander's father, the previous king.

Shaw hadn't visited his king much since the year of Alexander's marriage, and only once thereafter so that he could swear his fealty to him after he was proclaimed the heir to the throne. Then, he'd been at the king's side. Shaw had not been much older than a lad then, but he was the king's trusted confidant and an effective sparring partner. They'd practiced arms for days on end until Alexander perfected his swordsmanship. Now years later, Shaw wondered if their relations put him in an affable position or at a disadvantage. Unsure of Alexander's regard, he'd be wary.

"Mackintosh!" a man shouted from inside the postern. He shoved his way past one of the guardsmen and clasped his arm in welcome.

Shaw instantly recognized the king's man. "Edmund, 'tis good to see ye."

"And you, my friend. Have not seen you for a long time…too long. Alexander will be pleased as well to see you. He has asked several times already if you have yet arrived. I'll take you to see him at once. Follow me. Your servant can settle the horses in the stables yonder."

"He is not my—"

Edmund didn't give him a chance to explain Walen's relation to him but hastened away.

"I should go and meet with Alexander. If ye'll settle my horse. I will return after my meeting and hopefully, we can be on our way," he told Walen apologetically.

Walen grinned as he bowed. "I am but your humble servant, Laird. Go on then. I'll probably go to the nearest tavern. Ye shall find me there." He bellowed with laughter as he strode away.

Shaw hurried forward to trail Edmund. The man moved quickly, as stout and burly as he was. A maze of hallways led to a paneled door where finally, Edmund halted.

"Before you go inside, I should warn you that the king only

desires your acceptance of what he has to tell you, so be patient with him." Edmund pushed at the door handle and shoved the door open. "I'll have our great king fetched."

He wondered what Edmund meant by *acceptance*, but the man fled before he could ask. Shaw stepped through the threshold and stood in the center of the floor. Before him sat a table with a plush chair where the king probably sat. Situated nearby were smaller tables and a few chairs. On one side of the room, a small hearth was set with fire and its warmth reached the corners of the chamber. His gaze roved the space until it fell on the young page who stood and watched him as if he awaited direction.

"Wish ye a drink, Milord?" the lad sprang to attention, ready to serve him.

"Nay, my thanks though." Shaw ambled forward and peered through the large window that afforded a view of the courtyard. When the door panel creaked, he turned and spotted Alexander entering. He bowed.

When he straightened, the king spoke not a word. Instead, he motioned to the page who hurriedly exited the room. Alexander's red hair shone brightly as the light filtered into the room from the window. He hadn't changed much, in Shaw's estimation. Even now, he behaved as he had when they were younger. Alexander passed him and reached a table laden with a jug of some kind of drink and various breads and cheeses. He poured himself a drink and lifted it. "Drink?"

Shaw shook his head. "Nay, Sire. Thank you."

Alexander drank deeply, draining the cup of its contents before placing it back on the table. Then he strolled toward him and pulled him into a brotherly embrace before pushing him back. "Lord, 'tis good to see you, Shaw. It has been some time since we parted, too long since I have laid eyes on you."

"It has. Milady Margaret, does she fare well?" Shaw purposely asked about the queen, knowing how the king had worried for the queen's health when she'd first arrived in Edinburgh. His king had stated that his betrothed wouldn't last long in the wilds of Scotland and that her tender English salubrity might not withstand the cold clime or rugged lands.

"She does well and is expecting our bairn."

Shaw smiled and bowed his head to his king. "Felicitations, Sire, on the upcoming birth of your bairn."

"Come, sit with me for I have much to discuss with you." The king moved to his plush chair.

He waited until the king sat and then sat in the chair across the table. "What is it ye wish to discuss, Sire?"

Alexander smiled and leaned back in his seat. "God, 'tis good to see you. I have missed you, Shaw, and have asked after you. Edmund has assured me that your clan prospers, there in the wild north."

"Aye, Sire, we do well enough. Though we are much smaller than most of the clans that surround us, we do our best to stay clear of scuffles."

"With those damnable Chattans, I presume… I know they are unfavorable relatives of yours. How do you get along with them?" Alexander grabbed hold of the pitcher in front of him and reached for cups on the table nearest to him. He poured a drink for himself, and a cup for him and pushed the cup across the wooden surface of the table.

"We get on, och 'tis the truth, I try to stay out of their affairs. I tire of their petty fracases with the Cameron Clan. Though I fear I might have to eventually take a side."

Alexander nodded. "True enough. You have my support if ever you should need it."

"Is that why ye have called me to Edinburgh?" Shaw took a small sip of the drink his king offered. The ale was crisp and cool on his tongue.

"Nay, there are other matters that I need to speak with you about… though I am hesitant to speak of them…which is why I sent my attendants away. I wish to discuss this in private."

"Sire, I have always and will continue to support ye. Whatever ye need, I am your servant." Shaw bowed his head and suspected whatever Alexander wanted of him might prove difficult.

"Before you object, I bid you to listen. With the armies of Scotland, I mean to take the lands Haakon holds to the north. I wish to extend our lands to the very shores. 'Twill take many men and arms to secure those lands. To do so, I thought it best to unite some of the border clans with those in the northern regions. So I have, therefore, betrothed ye."

It was as if he'd been hit with a mace. He had no words to say, and for a moment, he thought, his heart had stopped beating. Finally, he was able to suck in a breath but the silence in the chamber was palpable. Shaw tried not to frown at the king but he knew his bewilderment and displeasure sat on his face. "Sire, I am taken aback by your—"

"Hear me, Shaw, I want only your happiness. The women whom I have selected as the brides will surely gain your approval. Now there are other incentives to your agreement…" Alexander lifted his cup and drank. He continued until he drained his cup again and swiped the sleeve of his tunic across his red-haired beard.

The mention of brides indicated that there were others he intended to betroth. Shaw decided to remain silent and wait for the king to finish his explanation before he'd make his objections.

"There are four brides in all. With you, the lairds of Buchanan, MacKendrick, and Cameron clans will be afforded the opportunity to claim the women you will wed. There will be a match where you will fight in hand-to-hand combat. The winner will have the first choice of bride. Along with marrying the bonny woman you fight for, you will also forgo paying the tithe on your land for one year. The incentives are plentiful, Shaw, and all I require is your hand in marriage and the use of your soldiers when we call you to arms against Norway."

Shaw's head spun with the king's demand. He had considered the king's desire to stretch their lands to the north and west, but now it became apparent that they'd do so soon. However, the last thing he expected was to be betrothed by his sovereign. "Sire, I do not know what to say to this…"

"You cannot refuse me." Alexander pushed his barely drunk cup toward him. "Raise your cup and we shall toast to your happiness and future." The king poured more ale into his cup, lifted it, and waited for him to do the same.

Shaw raised his cup. "I am displeased to have to marry, Sire. The rest I fully agree to comply with. Surely, there is no need to wed me to a lass when ye have my sworn fealty. Have I not professed my oath, my dutiful pledge, and loyalty to ye?"

"I think, my comrade, that it will not matter when you hear the name of one of the brides."

He scrunched his eyes because it mattered not who was offered as a bride. Shaw remained unwed, and until he was ready to marry, he had sworn not to offer for a woman's hand. After his heart was crushed, the pain of giving his heart again instigated his unwillingness to subject himself to such torment unless it was absolutely necessary. But now it seemed he would be unable to offer for any bride, because the choice had been made for him. At the same time, he reasoned, he wouldn't have to give her his heart. It wasn't what he'd wanted but now it didn't appear to matter. "And that is?"

"Lady Sorsha d'Avranches…ah, Chattan."

Shaw drew his brows together at hearing Lady Chattan's name. She was married to his cousin, Rodick, and as far as he knew, she wasn't available. "She is married, Sire, and although—"

"She is newly widowed and is available for marriage."

At the last moment, Shaw was able to hide the shock of his king's announcement. His cousin Rodick was dead? So that was why Geoff had called him to the Chattan lands.

As dismayed as he was to hear of his cousin's death, he couldn't help but be gladdened that Lady Chattan was now available to wed another. He'd never forgotten her or her soft brown gaze, or the fact that she was the sweetest lass he'd ever encountered. He'd fallen in love at the sight of her. When she became betrothed to his cousin, his heart was all but defeated and full of envy. And his blood turned cold when she was forced to marry his cousin.

"How…how did Rodick die?"

Alexander shrugged slightly. "I know not how, but he is dead and the lady needs the protection of a strong Scotsman. Better yet, a Highlander and a warrior. I trust you wouldn't be displeased if such an arrangement came to pass. I recall you being enamored with the lass."

"I was, Sire." Shaw was completely astounded by his king's news. If he could marry Sorsha, he'd be more than pleased.

"Now, I remind you, Shaw, that you must win her hand in the combat. Once you have won a bout you may choose your bride. I will have you speak your agreement to our covenant."

Shaw wasn't worried in the least about the brawls. He wouldn't allow anyone to marry Sorsha but him, he'd see to it. "Of course, Sire, you have my agreement. I will gladly supply ye with soldiers when ye decide to advance on Haakon's lands. I shall reap the tithe which will aid my clan well for the coming planting season. And I heartedly accept the hand of a maiden as my bride if for no other reason than…because it pleases ye."

Alexander rose. He took his arm to seal their pact. "You only agree because it pleases you, not me. But no matter, this eve we shall have a feast where you can once again witness Lady Sorsha's beauty."

"I look forward to it, Sire." Shaw followed the king to the door and bowed to him before taking his leave.

When he exited, the king shut his door. Shaw stood in the hallway, tense and overtaken by his conversation with Alexander. He stumbled forward through the passageways and made his way to the outside of the castle. His steps hastened when he passed through the gates. On the lane of Edinburgh's village, past the dimly lit shops and homes, he continued onward until he reached the tavern where he suspected Walen had spent his time.

Almost everything inside the tavern was made from pine wood and the scent of it mixed with the stale odor of ale and the body odor of its patrons. It hit him akin to a smack in the face when he crossed the threshold. The tavernkeeper, in conversation with someone, made no acknowledgement of his presence. There were few inside the almost empty building at that time of day. Most men had made their way home for their nightly meals.

Shaw was numb and a little shocked by his exchange with the king and his change in circumstances. He found Walen sitting with his feet resting on a bench that flanked the table. His comrade grinned as he approached. When he reached him, Shaw slid onto the opposite bench, snatched a cup from the center of the table, and held it out for Walen to pour him some ale.

"Ye look like ye could use a wee drink. How did your meeting go with the king? What news did he impart?" Walen poured ale into his cup and set the pitcher in the center of the table.

Shaw didn't know how to answer that and muttered, "I am getting married."

Walen bellowed a laugh and practically fell off the bench. "Ye jest, Laird, ye do. Although I find ye humorous, ye have to be telling a wanker." His comrade swiped at the tears of laughter that came to his eyes.

"I assure ye, I do not jest. If I win the hand of Lady Sorsha, though, I vow I will not be displeased at all. Do ye remember her?"

His friend ceased his laughter, grabbed his arm, and shook it. "Well then, I suppose congratulations are in order. Of course, I remember the lass. She is the reason for your surly disposition over the past years. Shall we drink to the bride then? Our clan could use a bonny lass for its lady. 'Tis time ye begot heirs and I'm sure your mamo will be chuffed to hear this news. When is the unfortunate day?"

"I am to attend a feast this night and wed at the soonest."

Walen groaned, raised his cup, and waited for Shaw to raise his. Once he did so, his comrade clinked his cup to his. "To the groom, may ye ever be pleasured by the sweetness of your wife." After they each drank the contents of their cups, his friend poured more ale for them. "Och, not much time then to drink and get well-soddened before the end of your bachelorhood."

Shaw nodded but barely cared about Walen's words. Instead, he wondered if Sorsha was still as beautiful as he'd remembered. She had been rather young then, barely half a score plus some years in age. Not only was her beauty evident, but she'd had a tender and kind heart. The lass held beauty inside and out. She'd spoken softly to him and he'd never forgotten the silkiness of her voice, and the way her eyes shone when she looked at him.

It was as if her essence entered him and heated his blood with the need for her. Since her wedding to Rodick, he'd searched for another woman who stirred him with as much desire as she had. Shaw had never found a lass to rival her. Now, he had to ensure that she became his as he'd wanted so many years before.

He peered at his cousin and clinked his cup again to his. "Nay, not much time at all."

CHAPTER FIVE

O N THE NIGHT of the feast, Sorsha dressed in a rust-colored gown that flowed loosely at her arms and the material fanned at her feet. A gleaming belt of gold surrounded her waist and matched the slippers the queen had given her. The maids did her hair in an elaborate braid that crowned her head and the remainder of her tresses hung long in strands of smaller braids and untethered locks. She peered at herself in the glass of the window casement and almost lost her breath—unable to recognize the woman who peered back at her.

During her captivity and with the distraught of losing Gillian, Sorsha had changed. The free-spirited lass she'd once been was gone. No longer was she the winsome, laughing mother and wife. In her place, a more resigned woman stared back. Now Sorsha just wanted Gillian returned to her and to be left alone by Geoff. She had no sense of vengeance for what he'd done to her. There was no reason to put herself in further danger. Once she got her daughter back, she would find a way to stay clear of the Chattans and prayed that her new husband would cherish and protect her and her daughter.

"Are you ready?" Margaret asked.

"As I shall ever be." She followed the queen until they reached the king in the hallway outside the great hall. The king motioned her forward into the small antechamber and she entered. She dared not look at those inside, too afraid to face her past because she feared Shaw Mackintosh wouldn't remember her or the time they'd spent together.

With slow steps, she crossed the chamber and stood with the other women offered as brides. Sorsha took a breath and raised her chin. Her gaze roved from one braw man to the next as the Highlanders stood grouped across from them. Her breath about ceased and a sense of heat overwhelmed her body. A wariness flushed her skin as if she were that long-lost lass, the girl whose heart was easily won by the charming Highlander.

In spite of his relaxed expression, his muscular body stood braced and ready for the king's entrance.

Her breath increased as she viewed his stance and the way his tunic hugged the contours of his arms and chest. At his waist, a muted brown tartan was belted and fell to his knees. Her gaze lingered a little at the bare skin of his legs beneath the hem of his tartan until they reached the top of his boots in soft brown leather. Sorsha tried to slow her breathing. The sight of him was still exciting and everything she'd remembered. He was too handsome, too strong, too affecting and her heart raced at the memory of being in his arms. When she saw Shaw, every other man in the room disappeared and a sense akin to coming home settled over her. He was as she remembered. Her heart, which had been pounding with anxiety, slowed, and she was able to draw in a deep breath. At the same time, heat flushed over her, and for a moment she was not the resigned woman in the mirror, she was a girl again, infatuated by the charming Highlander.

The queen entered and gave her a raised brow as she followed King Alexander to the dais. He'd stopped briefly to say something to the Highlanders, who continued to shift on their feet, uncomfortable but apparently resigned to their fates, and then proceeded to move forward. All waited to hear what the king would say. He cleared his throat and motioned to the assembly.

"This is a moment of import, and I am pleased to see you

here. We shall now have a feast with dancing and merriment. I will give you this time to greet each other and become familiar. Before the night ends, the selections will be discussed and finalized on the morrow. I bid you to eat and drink."

Within moments of the king's speech, the double doors to the great hall opened.

Sorsha was in awe of the splendor. The glamor of the chamber was set by three large candelabras to which many candles sent a glow about the faces of those in attendance. On a platform in the corner, musicians began to play a soft ballad.

She looked around at the women with whom she stood and noticed one young woman who appeared discouraged to be in the chamber with the Highlanders and decided to approach her. Perhaps she felt alone and unsure of herself and this situation in which they found themselves, and didn't know how to proceed. Her heart went out to her, and maybe because of the wisdom she'd gained from being married to a laird, she felt responsible to help her.

Moving closer, she caught the woman's eyes with her own and said, "I have not met you before. I am Sorsha of the d'Avranches previously from Cheshire."

The lady dipped her chin. "I am pleased to meet you Mistress d'Avranches." She did indeed sound unsure. Sorsha could easily imagine her feelings. If she hadn't been married already and didn't know Shaw, she would feel exactly that same way. She tried to set the woman at ease.

"Sorsha, please. I was formerly Lady Chattan but alas, I am no longer. Are you as delighted as I am to have been chosen by the king?"

"I suppose I am," she said and bowed her head. "I am Kendra of Clan Graham." The woman gave her a slight smile.

As much as she wished to counsel the young woman further, she noticed the queen staring at her from across the room. Margaret gave her a pointed look and a jerk of her head toward Shaw. She could easily read it to mean she needed to go meet him without delay. *Very well then.* "We should go and greet the men," she told Kendra, and then set off, leaving her alone.

It was not her place to help another woman find her husband. She was expected to find her own. So she kept her gaze fixed on Shaw.

He crossed to speak to the queen. As she approached, she overheard Margaret speaking about Mistress Kendra and her aim to introduce her to Laird Cameron. *Good.* The thought that the young woman wouldn't be left to fend completely for herself made her feel better about deserting her. The queen was already planning for Kendra's betrothal and she would choose well for her.

She didn't mean to interrupt her conversation with Shaw, but she drew close to him and smiled, then curtsied to the queen as was proper, though her eyes remained on him. She knew Margaret would be pleased she was focused on him and—for once—ignored court etiquette. Shaw bowed to her in return, and when he rose, he kept his gray eyes fastened on hers. The recognition in his gaze sent warmth through her. He spoke and even his voice sent a thrill through her, though his words were anything but titillating. "Milady Sorsha, I was dismayed to learn of your husband's, *ah*, Rodick's death. How are ye faring? This must be a difficult time."

She kept her face lowered so he wouldn't see the effect his voice had on her. Sorsha had always admired his deep tone which she likened to a caress of the wind when he spoke. Her heart thudded from his nearness, hard enough that she wondered if he could hear it. She took a deep breath and said, "Laird Mackintosh, it is a pleasure to see you again. Aye, Rodick recently passed and the queen wanted to secure my protection. A woman without a husband is vulnerable to troubles."

"Indeed she is. Do ye recall when we met here in the king's castle?" His eyes stayed on hers and she was struck at how even though they were gray as cold steel in color, the expression they held was warm.

She wanted to remind him of their past. "I recall us laughing at the mishap of that servant… remember when she dropped the entire tray of cups on that poor lord?"

Shaw chuckled lightly. "Ah, the Englishman who escorted ye. I remember him well. He was overzealous in his guarding of ye. Come and let us take to the dance."

When he took her hand in his, Sorsha drew a small sigh at the warmth of his touch. She trembled and was unsure if it was from desire swarming her body or the emotions coursing through her. His touch was tender, yet strong, as if he offered so much more than his escort to the dance floor. Was it her imagination? She didn't think so.

She gently squeezed his hand and allowed him to lead her as the harpist's chords filled the chamber with a soft melody. She moved around him in steps to the dance. Each time he approached her, she met his intense gaze. The overwhelming urge to touch him caused her to clasp his hand and force him to follow her.

Sorsha didn't know where she was taking him, but she wanted to be alone. They ended up on a balcony to the right of the great hall. A short stone wall surrounded the length of the balcony and she sat upon it.

He joined her, sitting beside her, and stretched his legs outward. His muscular, hard thigh almost pressed against her softer one but she shifted a little closer, purposely squeezing herself against him. How she wanted to press her hand on his hard, muscular thigh, to caress him, and to tell him without words how much she had missed him. She lifted her eyes and saw the passion in his gaze. At that moment, it was as if they had never been separated. They didn't speak but could only gaze at each other until Shaw finally broke the silence.

"I never forgot ye, lass. When ye married Rodick, I was begrudged in my pursuit of ye. Now that ye are available again, would ye be amiable to marrying me?" He took her hand and squeezed it with his warm fingers.

She looked down at their joined hands. It felt so right to be able to touch him and she couldn't help but enjoy it. "Oh, Shaw, you do not know how disappointed I was to have to marry Rodick. My father forced me to accept him because he'd made a treaty with the Chattans. I had no choice but to obey him." Reluctantly, she withdrew her hand from his, as saddened memories brought forth the reminder of hurting him then.

Yet Shaw's tone didn't sound angry or piqued. She shifted closer to him, and briefly closed her eyes, allowing his nearness to affect her senses. He smelled of a manly scent that reminded her of rain amid a warm summer day, and the sound of his voice nearly shook her. "If you want to marry me now, then yes, I would be amiable."

"I professed my feelings for ye back then but we were so young. I thought we had time. To have to witness your marriage to my cousin was a difficult time for me…"

Sorsha reached for his hand again and this time she held it. "I wasn't told until right before my wedding that I was to marry him. It was a horrid day to be sure. I vow it was a difficult time for me as well." She lowered her chin and tried not to let the sadness of her admission affect her.

"Ye had a child, did ye not, and gave Laird Chattan a daughter?"

Sorsha smiled and nodded. "I did. Her name is Gillian."

"Is she at Tor?" he asked and caressed the tops of her fingers with his thumb.

She glanced at his hand and the sensual way he stroked hers. In all the years she'd been with Rodick, he never once touched her in such an appealing, desirous way. "She is, but I hope to retrieve her soon." She decided now was not the time to discuss how Gillian was essentially Geoff's hostage.

"I was almost knocked on my arse when Alexander told me that ye were an offered bride. Though I am sorry for your loss, lass, I am not displeased to take ye for my wife. I promise ye that ye will be held in the highest esteem by my clan and by me as well." He lifted her hand and brushed his hard, manly lips over her knuckles.

Sorsha's breath caught in her throat. She scrunched her eyes and grinned, hoping his words held the promise of a better life for her and Gillian. "There is nothing, Laird Mackintosh, that would make me happier."

"Shaw, lass. Ye used to call me Shaw, do ye remember? I was always fond of the way ye spoke it. I will do my best to win your hand before any of the other grooms can name ye. Should we return to the hall?" He stood and pulled her to stand.

Sorsha didn't know what overcame her, but once she was on her feet, she embraced him. Her arms surrounded his hard familiar body and she pressed herself against him. She lifted her face to better see him but his gray eyes smoldered with a look she well-remembered. Shaw shifted his face toward hers and he set his mouth near her lips.

"I have always been enchanted by ye." He kissed her all-too-briefly.

When he pulled away, Sorsha fingered her lips and teetered on her feet, completely captivated by him. "We shall do well together, Shaw. I vow to be a good wife for you."

"There is no other woman's heart I desire more than yours."

CHAPTER SIX

THERE WAS TRICKERY afoot. Shaw realized that when he'd been chosen to fight in the first two battles and was commanded to purposely lose. The queen had bade him to do so, and of course, he couldn't disobey her order. That the king wanted to witness their combat also led him to believe that the king was only after entertainment and used the marriages as a way to do so. Still, Shaw was more than incensed at his defeat, especially against MacKendrick and Cameron. Now, there was one last opponent and Shaw decided to take matters into his own hands. He wasn't about to be routed by Buchanan or possibly lose Sorsha once again.

"Ye look like ye got run over by a cart." Walen chortled a laugh. "I say ye can still take Buchanan even though he's a wily fighter. Your face is no longer bonny. Make certain ye protect it, Laird, in the next bout. Can ye even see out of that eye?" He made a hissing sound and grinned.

Shaw disliked his comrade's banter, but it was true that he wore the battering his adversaries doled out in the last bouts on his face. "Cosh, be quiet or I'll skelp ye. I feel like I was run over by a cart. I need ye to do me a favor."

Walen stepped toward him; his brows wrinkling, and his eyes squinting. He lowered his voice with seriousness and asked, "What do ye need?"

"Find Buchanan and tell him to come to me. I'll await him here." He pulled a golden cup from a small satchel he wore and handed it to his comrade. "After, take this and have it melted down." He told him exactly what he wanted made from the melted gold.

"I'll see to it, Laird." Walen marched off with a purposeful stride.

Since Declan MacKendrick had won Lady Isabella's hand and Magnus Cameron had won Lady Kendra's, that only left two remaining brides—Eva Scott, and Sorsha.

In Shaw's opinion, Sorsha was definitely a prize worth fighting for. As he paced along the wall by the king's garrison awaiting his opponent, Shaw considered how to sway Breckin Buchanan to agree to allow him to name his bride. He wasn't about to be further entertainment for the king and didn't want to fight in another round. He especially didn't want to be saddled with Eva Scott. Although Eva was beyond beautiful, she was rather young and from accounts, a spoiled willful lass.

Breckin walked next to Walen and when they reached him, his opponent grunted. Shaw waved Walen away so he might speak to Breckin privately. When his comrade was far enough away, he motioned to Breckin and they walked slowly along the wall.

"Ye know, Breckin, that we are being used for our king and queen's entertainment."

The Buchanan laird pressed the long locks of his blond hair back from his forehead and grunted. "Aye, I deem that is so as well, but what can we do about it?"

"I say we forsake the last bout and decide right now which brides we will choose." Shaw studied Breckin's face for a sign of his accord but the man kept his reaction in check. "If the king wants us to accept his other terms, he will permit us to marry without the last fracas." It was all Shaw could think of to get out of fighting with Buchanan. Not that he couldn't take the warrior, but he had been somewhat weakened in the last bouts and wanted no part in another fight.

Breckin seemed to be considering his proposal. He pressed his hands over his face and groaned as if he suspected the idea was worthy.

Shaw dipped his head as the queen approached. They turned to her and bowed slightly. Margaret walked regally toward them but did not smile.

"Your Grace," they both greeted her at the same time.

"Lairds Mackintosh and Buchanan, I would have a word with you. As you know, there are but two brides left. Unfortunately, my dear Alexander was called away to meet with his council and the last bout is no longer necessary."

"All is well?" Shaw asked, knowing that Alexander was still answerable to the council. He hadn't yet ruled Scotland on his own and was accountable to the lords who oversaw his rule.

"Oh, all is well. Worry not. The lords only wish to ensure Alexander's visit to England will not put them in jeopardy. They deem he might be easily persuaded by my father to concede to matters in which the lords hold interest."

Shaw dipped his head as she explained. "I understand ye will soon visit your family. Are ye pleased by this, Your Grace?"

"Our nation is humbly looking forward to the birth of your bairn," Breckin said.

"I shall be gladdened to see my family. The news of Scotland's successor will reach you within days, I am certain." Margaret waved off the chamberlain who stood afar. "Now, we should settle the matter of the brides. This night we will hold the weddings after the late meal and then have a bit of a celebration. Since you were amiable and conceded to my interference in the first two bouts, Mackintosh, what say you? Who do you choose?"

"Lady Sorsha is sweet," Breckin said.

Shaw flinched when he named Sorsha. He'd hoped the man didn't have a hope to win her hand. "Aye, she is sweet, but she was recently widowed, and lest ye forget, Lady Sorsha bore a child for her husband, my own cousin. We hope to keep the child amongst the family. I heard that she was a willful minx who oft causes discord in the home, although I had not witnessed such when I visited the Chattans." He almost detested speaking such disparaging things about Sorsha's daughter, untruths to aid him. He cared about Sorsha and her daughter but he had to do something to sway his rival's interest. Hopefully, the falsity about Gillian aided him.

"Her child is a wee terror?" Breckin moaned. "Ye know that I have younger brothers who try my patience and I have enough trouble keeping them in line…"

Shaw set his fisted hands on his hips. "Eva might be willful as well, but she's young and ye won't have to get her with child right away. Besides, she is beautiful. Have ye ever seen such a face or such bonny hair on a woman?"

"She is comely and bedding her would not be too much of a hardship," Breckin said and chuckled. "And aye, she's young enough to train to my tastes. If ye want Sorsha then I suppose I am not too put out to take Eva's hand."

Shaw glanced at Breckin who gave a slight nod. "I choose Lady Sorsha then."

Margaret clapped her hands together and squealed. "Oh, this is marvelous. She was hoping you'd choose her. Of course, there always was something betwixt you two, was there not? Since Declan and Magnus have already taken their vows, we shall commence with your weddings shortly. Make your way to the hall in a short time and I'll have the Chancellor fetched."

"Aye, Your Grace. I'll be off then so I might tell Sorsha the news." Shaw bowed to her and gave a nod to Breckin before he turned and marched away.

As he approached the castle, he saw Walen by the corral, brushing his steed.

"We will leave on the morrow at first light. Be ready."

"I am always prepared, Laird. Will ye wed this night?"

He nodded. "Aye, I will, and happily. I must make haste because the ceremony is soon to begin."

Walen grabbed his arm, stopping him from moving on. "Shaw, I know ye did not want this marriage, but since ye have been reunited with Lady Sorsha, I have not seen ye happier. I am gladdened by it. The clan will rejoice when we return. It shall be a remarkable surprise."

He didn't know why, but emotion snuck into his retort. "I never thought I would be as pleased. Lady Sorsha is everything I have ever wanted in a wife. How am I so blessed?"

"Ye are blessed and deservedly so, Laird. I shall bring the trinket ye asked for when the goldsmith has it ready. He says it shouldn't take much time to make it. Enjoy your night for I am a wee bit envious." Walen's bellow sounded and followed him as he walked away.

Shaw went back inside where he asked several servants which chamber Sorsha occupied, then walked with spry steps through the castle corridors until he reached the door of his beloved. He knocked and waited. Sorsha opened the door and smiled at him but her brown eyes held a concerned gaze.

"Shaw, I did not expect you... Is everything well? I thought the next bout was taking place. I could not stand to see another brawl and so I..." She stammered and ceased in mid-speech. "Could not watch again..."

"There will be no more brawls. The king has been called away and Queen Margaret has called a halt to the bouts. She is permitting us to marry. We will do so before the late meal. But first, I must ask ye—are ye certain ye wish to marry me?" A tenseness tightened his shoulders as he waited for her to answer.

"Of course I do. I shall get ready and will meet you in the hall shortly." Sorsha reached out to set a gentle caress on his face. "You haven't changed your mind, have you?"

He shook his head. "Nay. Ye know how much I want ye...how much I have always wanted ye." Shaw leaned toward her and set a light peck of a kiss on her soft lips. Shaw wanted to kiss her deeply, especially when he tasted the sweet honey from the mead she'd drunk on her lips. He was sure their kiss would send him to the brink and he couldn't wait until he could take her and make her his. "I shall see ye soon."

She closed the door and he ambled away, his heart lighter than he could ever remember. His future—their future—shone brightly before him.

Shaw entered the chamber he'd stayed in while he was in the castle. He shared it with the other Highlanders but all kept to themselves. Breckin entered a moment later and approached.

"How did Mistress Scott take your news?" Shaw asked him as he collected clean garments and gathered the items he needed so he could wash his body.

"Ah, well, let us say she was none too pleased. I might take a screeching bride to my bed this night," Breckin jested. "Och, it would not be the first time I have to soothe a nervous virgin. It's all the same to me; the lass has no choice. She shall do her duty."

"She will accept ye, given time. I'm headed to the stream to wash if ye want to join me. The Chamberlain gave me use of the washroom room och I cannot abide sitting in a small tub. Besides, I would rather bathe outdoors."

Breckin nodded, grabbed a change of garments, followed him, and they left the castle. Along the short walk, neither spoke. The day was chilly and cloudy, quite dismal, but nothing would hamper his happiness. Shaw couldn't cease grinning at the thought that he would marry his longtime love that day.

At the stream, he quickly dunked his head in the water and washed his hair. After he dried himself, he redressed in clean garments. "We should return."

Breckin finished belting his tartan and grunted. "Aye, to my ill-fated destiny."

He cuffed Breckin's shoulder with force. "Do not be so surly, my friend. Even if Mistress Scott is a terrible wife, she'll give ye handsome bairns. And lest ye forget, ye can always spend time away from your fief."

His comrade bellowed a laugh. "At least there is that."

The walk back to the castle took little time. Shaw returned to his chamber briefly to discard his soiled garments. He stood by the window casement and reflected on his good fortune of late. Walen entered the chamber and handed him a small cloth sack. "'Tis made as ye requested."

Shaw emptied the pouch and studied the object for a moment before replacing it inside the sack. Suddenly, the thought of his marriage sank in. In a short time, he would have a wife. Though he was gladdened to marry Sorsha, he pondered how much of his life would change. He had little family to speak of except for his mamo but now he'd have a wife and stepdaughter. In due time, perhaps he and Sorsha would be blessed with bairns. His life was about to take a turn for the better.

"I wish ye all the best this night, Laird. Ye know where to find me." Walen flung the door open and disappeared through it.

Shaw left the chamber and reached the great hall where he was met with a lively group of people who chatted and awaited the ceremonies. There were some lords and ladies present, Milady Eva's family, and Sorsha. The other lairds and their new wives had already left the castle. Shaw wanted to be on his way too but since his marriage took place later in the day, he'd await the morrow to make the trek back to the Highlands.

He sauntered to Sorsha and took her hand. "Are ye ready, lass?"

"I am but I'm also nervous."

Shaw gently squeezed her hand. "There is nothing to give ye worry. I am not uneasy about our marriage." He grinned and waited for her to smile at him. "Here, a gift for ye." With his thrust-out hand, he bade her to take the pouch.

"What is it?" She held the pouch and eyed him warily.

"Open it."

She did as he requested and removed the gold cuff from the pouch. "Oh, 'tis beautiful, Shaw. You did not need to give me a gift."

"I wanted ye to have something to remember this day. It's etched with words in Gaelic. *Gu sìorraidh is gu bràth.* Those are the words I want ye to remember this day. Forever and always, my love."

Sorsha slid the cuff on her arm and her teeth flashed as she gave him a big smile. He was pleased that she liked his wedding gift and he meant the words he'd had etched on the gold cuff. He had been enamored of her from the moment he'd seen her, forever and always.

Sorsha turned her attention from the cuff to gaze at the entry where the queen now stood. She glided into the chamber, followed by a man in vestments which he took to be a priest. When Queen Margaret reached the dais, she held up a hand and all were silenced.

"Lords, Ladies, and Gentlefolk, we are privileged to bear witness this day the marriage betwixt Laird Mackintosh and Lady Sorsha, and Laird Buchanan and Mistress Eva. The Chancellor has come down with a malady and so we asked Father Benedict to perform the ceremonies. If the brides and grooms would step forward."

Shaw led Sorsha to the dais. He stood next to her and awaited the beginning of the sacrament. Breckin and Eva stood to their left and both looked disgruntled at having to marry each other.

Father Benedict, a young priest who had probably just recently been ordained, cleared his throat. His shaven head showed little hair and his brown eyes peered at them with affection. "My good lords, ladies, and gentlefolk, I am pleased by Her Grace's request to perform these marriage sacraments." He bowed his head to them, cleared his throat again as if he were nervous, and his voice shook. He held up his hand, blessed them with the sign of the cross. "Marriage is a vow of permanence. It is a symbol of loyalty and union which will be honored throughout all the times to come. Through life's celebrations or hardships, you must stand together."

He continued, "Love is not perfect. Life may bring you pain and you may use words or actions to hurt one another. You may raise your voices or daggers but alas it is these times when you grow stronger as a couple for what you have is worth fighting for. Beside you is the one person who will be tied to you for the remainder of your life. Keep them in kindness and love and you will never be alone."

The priest's words settled upon him and Shaw bowed his head in respect to what they meant. He'd always professed to honor women but especially his wife.

Father Benedict turned and whispered something to the queen to which she responded. Their words were so softly spoken that none heard them. After, he motioned to Sorsha. "Lady Sorsha, will you take to be your husband, Laird Mackintosh, and pledge to him before all gathered here, to be his love and his defender in unrest? Will you stand by him in all things fair and foul? Will you cherish him, forsaking all others, keeping only unto him, so as long as you both shall live?"

Sorsha raised her chin and peered ahead. "I shall, Father."

The priest motioned to him and Shaw folded his hands in front of him. "Laird Mackintosh, will you take to be your wife the Lady Sorsha, and pledge to her before all gathered here, to be her love and her defender in unrest? Will you stand by her in all things fair and foul? Will you cherish her, forsaking all others, keeping only unto her, for as long as you both shall live?"

Shaw didn't hesitate to respond and reached out to take Sorsha's hand. "I vow I will."

The priest spoke then to Breckin and Eva, asking them to make the same pledge. When Benedict finished with them, he raised his voice and said to both couples, "May life's challenges be met together with courage and optimism, and may your days be filled with laughter, trust, friendship, and love. You once walked alone, but now you walk with each other, hand in hand. You now have someone to share life with, to offer refuge and sheltering love at the end of each day. With God's blessing, I pronounce you married, husbands and wives from this day forward. You may now seal your vows with a kiss."

Shaw turned to Sorsha and pulled her toward him. Before he

set his lips on hers, he smiled lightly. When his lips touched hers, he reveled in the softness of her and the pleasant way she responded. She settled her hands on his shoulders and kept her mouth firmly against his. When he pulled back, he couldn't help but chuckle.

"I have waited for this moment for years, Sorsha, and I'm pleased."

"As am I, Shaw."

Father Benedict cleared his throat, clearly uncomfortable with their signs of affection. They stepped away from one another and turned back to the priest, who then made the sign of the cross over each of the couples as he spoke a blessing. "The Lord bless thee, and keep thee. May He make his face to shine upon thee, and be gracious unto thee. May the Lord lift up his countenance upon thee, and give thee peace. The service has ended. Go in faithfulness and peace."

The assembled people murmured, "Amen," and then Sorsha turned back to Shaw., "Now what? Will we leave right away like the others did or shall we stay the night?" Shaw ignored the cheers from the onlookers and led her away from the dais. "It might be better to make the journey home on the morrow. Besides, there is only one thing I want to do this night."

"Aye, and that is what worries me." Sorsha stopped walking forward and stood beside a long table. "Promise me that you won't be disappointed."

He felt the tug of his brows but tried not to scowl. "Sorsha, ye could never disappoint me."

"I...I have been told that I am unloving."

Shaw pressed a finger to her lips. "Shhh, lass. We shall prove them wrong. Now say ye trust me." When she nodded, he set a peck of a kiss on her cheek. "Let us have our supper, and then we can be gone from this hall."

"I doubt that I could eat a bite," Sorsha said with a shaky voice.

Queen Margaret glided toward them and when she reached

them, she clasped Sorsha's hand. "Oh, Laird Mackintosh and Lady Sorsha, I wanted to offer my congratulations on your marriage. Shaw, attend to me because I want an additional vow from you."

Shaw bowed to the queen. "I would gladly offer any vow ye deem, Your Grace."

"Protect my dear friend, this sweet lady, with your life." Her voice softened but had such severity to it that alluded to the gravity of Sorsha's situation.

"I vow to do so as will my entire clan. Lady Sorsha is in good hands, Your Grace."

"You are quite noble, Laird Mackintosh, and I expect you will make my dearest friend happy. If not, she will tell me so and you will bear my wrath."

He couldn't help but smile. "Have no worry over that, Your Grace, because it is my duty to make Sorsha happy and I plan to do so for the remainder of our days."

"Then I shall take my leave of you for I long to retire. Sorsha, I shall return later in the year. I expect to have missives awaiting me telling me of your new life."

"I will gladly write to you often, My Lady."

The queen left them and in her wake, several ladies-in-waiting and attendants followed.

"I shall miss her. Margaret has been my good friend and I pray that she has an easy time delivering her bairn." She sat at a table.

"I am certain she shall." Shaw sat next to her and pulled a trencher in front of Sorsha. "Let us eat." He placed various foodstuffs on his trencher and poured them each a small cup of wine, thinking the whole time about the queen's command. Finally, he said, "Why would Margaret insist on me protecting ye? Of course, being my wife, ye are most important. But it was the way she said it that made me wonder... Is there a specific reason for the need for my protection?"

"I...every woman should be protected by her husband. I am certain that is what Margaret meant." Sorsha picked up her supper dagger and cut a piece of meat.

"It does not matter, lass, because I made certain vows this day. No one will ever harm ye. My sword will seek its vengeance if anyone deems to try to hurt ye. It sounded as if…"

She pressed her hand on his forearm. "Shaw, I made vows too, and have faith that I will endeavor not to ever cause you such vengeance."

CHAPTER SEVEN

ER SILENCE REMAINED necessary. Sorsha had to keep the happenings at Tor Castle to herself, at least for now. Somehow she had to think of a way to rescue Gillian and avoid seeing Geoff. Would Geoff be wrathful that she'd married Shaw and enact retribution for her defiance against her wee lass? She could only pray he wouldn't. But best if he didn't know of Gillian's peril. It could only make things worse.

Still, she wished she could tell Shaw what happened and have him retrieve her daughter.

For now, until she came up with a sound plan, she had to keep all to herself or risk Gillian's safety. She couldn't help but feel saddened, knowing her daughter was in Geoff's hands. With a quick prayer, she hoped Gillian fared well and that she understood why her mother hadn't come for her. She could only imagine the sorrow and anguish her young daughter must be feeling.

Now, Sorsha stood in a mostly darkened chamber awaiting Shaw. Stone walls sent a chill through the room even though the servants had lit a fire in the hearth. The flames danced, but only sent a feeble glow to the corners of the chamber, making dark shadows dance upon the stone and furnishings—a good-sized bed and a small table. There were no other furnishings within. With shaky hands, she lit two candles situated in the holder and held them high to get a better view. Somehow her valise had made its way to the room. Sorsha set the candelabra on the small table and grabbed it.

Wearily, she sat on the edge of the bed and rummaged through it until she found her sleep attire. Hastily, she removed her garments and the cold air sent a flush of bumps over her skin. Just as quickly, she pulled on a nightdress.

Near the window casement, she watched the sky turn to darkness and a tremble overtook her. She feared the night to come. Was she as unloving as Rodick had told her? When they were together as husband and wife, she suffered through the ordeal of his touches. Her husband had grunted and groaned as he'd ground against her. Usually, within minutes it was over. She hadn't suffered overlong.

But Shaw was a caring man and she suspected their joining would differ from the uncomfortable nights she'd spent with Rodick. Still, Sorsha was unsure if she should get in bed or stand awaiting her new husband. What would he expect of her?

Before she made a move to lie on the bed, Shaw entered the chamber. He appeared so handsome with his luxuriously flowing silky hair caressing the tops of his shoulders. His eyes bespoke his happiness at seeing her and crinkled at the edges. She wanted to run at him and throw herself in his embrace, but something held her back. Perhaps her nervousness got the better of her. She stood still, watching him across the chamber and the silence between them unnerved her further.

When she remained silent, he approached with slow steps until he reached her. "I had not considered how difficult this would be for ye. If ye are still mourning Rodick, we can wait…"

His patience seemed to calm her and she drew an easy breath. She set her palm on the bulge of his arm muscle and shook her head. "'Tis not that. I am not mourning him. There was never affection betwixt us." Sorsha sighed because saying such reminded her of Rodick's last words and the look he'd given her as if he'd had regrets.

Shaw took hold of her arms with a gentleness and leaned his forehead against hers. "There will be affection betwixt us. Ye must know how I felt when ye were given to him."

"That was a difficult time…for us both. I tried to find you, Shaw, and planned to abscond with you before the ceremony but I couldn't and was told you had gone." Sorsha stepped closer to him and wrapped her arms around his hard body. She breathed deeply taking in the scent of him and closed her eyes at the solace he brought to her.

"I did not know that. When your betrothal was announced, I left hastily because I could not witness ye being given to another." He touched her chin with his index finger and gently tilted her face back to look at her fully. "If I'd known that ye wanted to run away with me, I would not have left ye there."

"It does not matter now. I fear that I will dissatisfy you since Rodick often voiced his scorn when we were…together and said I was frigid. I do not want to disappoint you, Shaw." She lowered her face to his tunic and sighed, feeling weary and worn from hoping to please him. Sadness welled within her because the last thing she wanted to do was disappoint him.

Shaw pressed her back and took hold of her hand. With an encouraging squeeze of her fingers, he subtly told her all would be well. "It is my duty as your husband to ensure that ye give as much pleasure as ye receive. We will prevail together, sweet lass, and I promise ye there will be enjoyment for us both."

"This is quite embarrassing. I am not a maid, yet…I know not what to do and never participated in the…act." She couldn't continue her explanation and felt the heat on her face.

He stepped backward, putting a little distance between them. His gaze mollified her when his smile reached his eyes. "What do ye want to do?" His eyes slid from hers to her mouth and then back to her eyes.

"I want to kiss you if you want to…" She took a step toward him but he met her before she could take another. Without thought, she wet her lips with a stroke of her tongue. Her heart raced, thumping madly at the prospect of kissing him. He'd always had such an effect on her, even when they were young and unknowing in the ways of men and women or mating.

Shaw wrapped his arms around her body and pulled her against him. He said nothing but lowered his head. His lips brushed over hers twice before he forced her mouth to open by taking hold of her chin with gentle fingers. Then he swept his tongue inside her mouth and the sensation of it sent desire swarming through her. She'd never felt such longing, at least not since she'd first laid eyes on him.

As he pulled back, he moaned softly. "I cannot get enough of ye."

Sorsha pressed her hands on his chest and marveled at his strength and hardness. But surely a man such as he had been with many other women! She was bound to disappoint him. Apprehensively, she shifted away but took his hand in hers and led him toward the bed.

"Before we… we should remove our garments." His voice almost cracked though his eyes remained dark and full of desire.

"All of them? I never did so, when… Are you certain that we should?"

Shaw flashed a grin. "Aye, lass, there is naught more bonny than an ungarbed woman. Do not be abashed, sweetheart, for a woman's body is a sight to behold and I am certain yours is exquisite." He set his hands on her shoulders and pressed the fabric of her nightdress until it slid down her arms and then off her body to puddle on the floor around her feet.

She didn't move but stood frozen to the spot and lowered her head. So he had seen other women. Surely, she was lacking. At least, she wasn't sure her body was beautiful. It wasn't that she was ashamed of it, but no one had ever seen her unclothed, or even implied it was something they desired to see.

Shaw pressed his hand on her jaw and then lowered it to her neck. The sensation and warmth of his touch sent a chill through her. "Just as I suspected. Ye are lovely."

"Should I…I undress you?" Sorsha was unprepared to do something so bold. But he nodded and now she had to proceed. With as much bravery as she could muster, she reached for his belt. After undoing it, she let it fall and it clattered at their feet. Yanking at his tartan, the material fluttered to join the belt. Shaw stood in his tunic and he used his hands to shift it over his head.

His chest shone in the candlelight. There was a smattering of light hair on his chest and his musculature appeared sculpted and hard. She was tempted and couldn't resist pressing her fingers on his skin. He was brawny and warm. "You are so handsome."

"And ye, lass, are going to make this difficult for me."

She gasped lightly. "What mean you by that? Are you—"

"I only meant that I am already affected by your presence. If ye touch me again, I might enflame from within. I want naught more than to join with you and to feel your soft skin against mine."

Sorsha longed to kiss him and to press her body against the heat of his skin. She set her hand on his shoulder and her other on the side of his neck. "Shaw, I want to…" Her words ceased as she reached up to press her mouth on his.

Shaw pulled her gently and they fell backward onto the bed. Her body splayed over his but all she could think about was the way he kissed her. His mouth moved over hers and persuaded her to return the sensual lure of his tongue. Her hands pressed over his skin, taking in the curves and ripples of his musculature.

Soon, she lost herself in the depths of his kisses and she moaned at the power of him and at the height of his dizzying allure. His large hands perused slowly over her body and caressed her in return. When his fingers cupped her breast, she drew in a startled gasp—not because she was afraid, but for the intensity of pleasure that seemed to reverberate through her because of his touch. She kept her mouth against his and focused on the movement of his body and hands.

Sorsha submitted to him and any trepidation she'd had vanished. She allowed her hand to meander down his body until she reached his hip. With little effort, she drew him closer until their bodies touched everywhere. The desire that swarmed her heated her from within. Shaw tore his mouth from hers and groaned.

"Ye make me yearn for ye, lass. Aye, I burn to take ye but do not want to hurt ye." He set light kisses down the base of her neck and muttered, "Ye are a bonny woman but delicate." His lips trailed from her neck to her throat and he gently suckled.

His touches invoked bliss and his kisses sent her spiraling in a mass of emotions, and sensations that caused unrecognized twinges in her body. Sorsha tilted her head back and tried not to get caught up in the wonderment of it. She just wanted to feel this unknown pleasure and not think too much.

She swept her hand over his shoulder and tried to pull him against her. Her breasts ached, and somehow she knew only the heat and press of his chest would soothe them. Shaw drew her back into his embrace and his firm body pressed against her. She moaned as the intensity grew because she had never imagined being with a man would be so affecting.

Shaw watched her with hooded eyes. "Are ye certain ye are ready to do this?"

His words made her tremble and she reached out to pull him in for another kiss. Her lips gentled over his and when she drew back, she smiled. "I want naught more than this."

He shifted his hand over her body until his fingers pressed against her womanhood. She moaned softly at the gentleness and the allure of his touch.

"Shaw, what you are doing to me…" She couldn't finish her words but drew in an awed breath at the pangs of desire swarming inside her.

Shaw continued to stroke her while his lips wickedly entranced her to return his kisses. He forced her back upon the bed and positioned himself above her. "I will take it slow."

Sorsha shook her head. She needed him to hurry. She didn't know why, but she did. With her fingers pressing into his arms, she yanked him to her. His erection eased into her and she squeezed her eyes closed, knowing the hurt that would come. But with each shift of his body, there was no pain, only pleasure. She gasped in delight.

Whatever was happening between them wasn't enough. Sorsha gave over to the will of her body and the rule of her heart. Instinctively and without thought, she met his body as he plunged forward to enter her and then withdrew before moving within her once more. Each swift movement made her heart thud. As if she dashed madly toward unknown bliss, Sorsha tried to keep him as close and found that it was possible if she wrapped her legs about his waist, so she could meet each of his thrusts with one of her own.

As she peered at him, his beautiful, piercing gray eyes filled with a passion she'd never known existed in a man's gaze just as his manhood filled her in another way.

"Ye are so bonny, Sorsha, aye, and made for loving."

She couldn't respond to his endearing comment because her mind was trapped in the sensual aura of his touches, movement, and the enmeshing of their hearts. Sorsha had never experienced anything so incredible and she hoped it never ended. The very heat and thickness of him pressed into her repeatedly and was both shocking and exhilarating. Sorsha leaned upward and kissed his face. Her breaths came heavier the more their bodies met.

A fever seemed to ravage her and swarmed to the core of her. She wanted him to thrust harder but he continued at a leisurely pace as if he had no intention of rushing.

"Hurry, Shaw, please…" She rasped and a moan got caught in her throat when the first rivets of her culmination took control of her.

Shaw moaned a deep sound and hastened his thrusts. She had never felt anything so overwhelming and wanted to weep at the intensity of it. She lost her breath as a sweet torment pulsed within her. Her body shook and an intense climax forced her to cry out. The pleasure almost receded as quickly as it had come but her body continued to pulse and tingle.

Shaw resumed his movement, gliding his length into her and teasing her with purposeful advances. "Ye are so sweet, lass." He pressed a kiss on her cheek and moaned, "Ye are going to be the end of me."

She held him and shifted her legs to prevent him from pulling away. His moan reverberated within the chamber and he placed his forehead on her shoulder. She splayed her fingers through his dampened hair and urged him on with moans and sighs of her own. Shaw growled and stilled. His body seemed to steel and he couldn't seem to move. She caressed him and hoped he had received the same pleasure as she had.

Never had she imagined the marital act would be so affecting. The heat of his skin kept the chill at bay, but she could only focus on his body pressed so alluringly against hers. "Shaw…?"

He lifted his head and grinned, flashing his teeth and scrunching his eyes. "I knew it would be perfect between us."

"It was. I…I disbelieve it was so…beautiful, and know not what to say." She twirled a finger in his long locks and sighed.

He leaned upward and kissed her lips then nuzzled his cheek to hers. "Ye need not say anything except that ye enjoyed it."

"Of course I did. You are amazing, husband."

He shifted his body next to hers and set his arm over her torso. They quieted and she was completely caught up in her thoughts. She'd never experienced anything quite so marvelous with Rodick. Then a horrid thought came. "Did *you* enjoy it? I was not a…disappointment?"

Shaw grunted. He took her hand and pressed it to his chest. "Do ye feel that, sweetheart? My heart has never clashed so madly. Enjoy it? Hell, if I enjoyed it any more than I had, I would have been slain. Ye are not a terrible lover and do not ever think such nonsense."

She'd never heard that word used that way before, but it sounded right. She was a lover, and she wasn't terrible at it. She giggled softly. "That is good to know. I hope we do that again." Sorsha couldn't wait until their next encounter. She would have to test her theory that the sensations of pleasure would return.

"Aye, as often as we like. If I had my way, Sorsha, we would never leave our bed."

A giddiness came over her and she laughed. "Unfortunately, we must, but I shall like to lie with you often too. You are a laird and must have many duties. Now as your wife, I suspect I too have duties."

"Ye were a wife to a laird before. Did ye not have duties?"

She shook her head. "Nay, I was never allowed to involve myself in the keeping of Tor. It was as if Rodick wanted to keep me from knowing his clansmen and women, or perhaps he did not wish to have a woman control any part of the keep."

"*Allowed?*" Shaw shook his head. "As my wife, ye will have the run of my keep. It will be your home as well as mine. Speaking of home, we shall leave at first light. Let us get some sleep so we are well-rested for the long journey."

Sorsha lay in his embrace and never dreamed of being so desired by her husband. She also never felt like she belonged at the Chattan keep. Now she would go with Shaw to his home and she hoped with all her heart that she would find his home welcoming. Her life could be nothing but joyful being married to a caring and charming man. Yet without Gillian, there was a piece of joy missing from her soul. Somehow, she had to rescue her daughter, and soon.

CHAPTER EIGHT

I N HIS HASTE to get on the trail home, Shaw rose early and dressed. He peered at his wife, confounded by how he'd been fortunate to finally marry her. Even in her sleep, Sorsha appeared beautiful but it wasn't her allure that attracted him. Her spirit and manner first drew him to her. She had kind eyes, a gentle and approachable manner, a winsome voice, and a tender heart. She was everything he'd hoped for in a wife.

As he dressed, a sense of protectiveness came to him and he vowed then that no one would ever harm her. He'd make certain of it. Once they reached Moy, he would have her safely ensconced on his island and within the protective arms of his clan, where he would ensure that he kept his vow.

With a caress to her shoulder, he rousted Sorsha and she opened her eyes. "Good morn, Wife. Are ye ready to get started?"

Her sweet lips widened in a smile. "Wife…," she said with a sigh. "I am still pondering how this came to be, *Husband*. But aye, good morn."

Shaw pressed a hand over the silkiness of her locks and grinned. "I know it will take getting used to, lass, but aye, ye are my wife at last, and I am pleased. Now, we should arise, for we will leave soon. I presume ye will want to say your farewells to the queen. Meet me by the corral and we will leave posthaste."

Sorsha wrapped the bed cover around her body and shuffled

to the edge of the bed. "Margaret said they too were leaving this day for England. Perhaps she hasn't left yet. Go on and I shall hurry." She turned and waited for him to reach the door before she stood.

Shaw grabbed his satchel, closed the door behind him, and ambled outside. He'd garbed himself in his warmer tartan and heavier tunic for the morning was chilly. As he approached the corral, he spotted Walen already tacking up their horses, and one more for Sorsha. He moved to his own mount, secured his satchel to the saddle, and checked the horse's bridle, and girth.

Walen was quiet as he finished his tasks. Once done he leaned against the wooden postern with a wily smile splayed across his face. "How was your night? Pleasurable, I imagine? I had a productive night and won some coins…" his voice trailed off and he chuckled. "I suspect ye gave no thought to me, though."

"I am gladdened to hear ye were not bored in wait of me."

"Not at all, Laird, there was a group of the king's men-at-arms who entertained me and in my appreciation, I relieved them of their silver. As you can see, I secured a horse for milady this morn, as well, so she'll have her own mount to ride."

Shaw meandered his hand over the neck of the chestnut mare his friend had purchased for Sorsha. The horse was somewhat smaller than theirs but sound enough for the journey. Their horses were bred to ride amid wars and a hillier climate than the fine-boned and bonny mare. They might have to pace themselves so as not to overtax her.

"My thanks. We will depart as soon as Sorsha arrives. I get the sense that something troubles her. She has not said so, och there is a bit of sadness in her eyes."

Walen chortled. "Ye mean she is not overcome with utter joy at marrying ye?"

Shaw shoved his friend's chest. "Jest all ye like, and of course, she is overcome with joy at our marriage but something is troubling her. That is all that I mean."

"Have ye asked her what it is?"

He shook his head. "Nay, I do not want to force her to tell me. Given time, she will understand that she can speak to me of her troubles and that I will listen. Living with the Chattans, I expect she has not had an easy time of it and is untrusting."

"Best keep your ears alert then because here comes milady now…" Walen moved to untie her horse and smiled at her as she approached. "Milady Sorsha," he said and bowed. "'Tis a pleasure to see ye again. I have not laid eyes on ye since ye were last here at the king's keep."

"Is that you, Walen? I remember you. You are still following Shaw around?" She laughed lightly and his comrade's eyes shone with affection.

"'Tis naught but my lot in life, milady, to serve my laird and follow him. And I am also at your service and vow to protect ye with my life. Our clan will rejoice when they learn that our laird has finally wedded and to such a bonny woman at that."

Sorsha raised her dainty brow and scoffed. "You still have a way with words, Walen, and yet are not as charming as your laird."

Walen bellowed a laugh. "Ye only say that because ye are now married to him."

She folded her hands in front of her and a coyness brightened her cheeks. "It is good to see you too, Walen, and my thanks for your offer of protection."

"Your horse, milady." Walen handed her the reins and rounded her horse to mount his.

Shaw hurried forward and helped her mount her horse. "We shall ride a good distance this day and need to make as much ground as we can before nightfall. If ye need to stop to rest, tell me so." He let his hand linger on her thigh and glanced up at her bonny face.

"I shall, but worry not, I will do my best to keep up." Sorsha patted the mare's neck and waited for one of them to lead their procession toward the gates.

Walen rode ahead of them and Shaw rode next to her. He

was glad to be going home, but then he remembered that he needed to stop in Fassiefern and at Tor. When he'd awakened, he meant to tell Sorsha about their journey and the stops he needed to make. Once through the gates, he waited until they reached the lane on the outskirts of Edinburgh to broach the subject.

"Sorsha, along the way, I need to stop in Fassiefern. It should not take long, och there is something I need to do." He slowed his mount to be next to hers and gazed at her as their horses trudged along. She focused on the lane but nodded in response.

"What is in Fassiefern?"

He didn't want to explain but should because he didn't want her to worry. "There is a lad there that needs a home."

Walen slowed his mount to ride on the other side of Sorsha now. Shaw didn't say more and she asked for no further explanation, that is until his comrade interjected.

"Aye, our laird takes in poor unfortunates that are without and brings them home to our clan." Walen chuckled. "Our comrade, Tom, runs the tavern there and oft keeps an eye out for anyone needing shelter. 'Tis our laird's way of increasing our clan's numbers but also—"

Shaw cut his comrade off. "Our clan is small and we have plenty of room for the forgotten children in the village. If the lad is amiable then he will be welcomed into our clan."

Sorsha's eyes widened but she had somewhat of a smile on her face. "That is... commendable, Shaw, that you seek to aid those children. I am gladdened that we will stop and hopefully give the poor lad aid."

"Aye, and afterward, we will ride for Tor. Geoff sent me a missive asking me to come. My sister and her husband are expected to stop there on their way to our keep. She means to return to our clan. I expect that we might be reunited there."

His wife's mouth drew tightly and her brows furrowed. "Must we? I...cannot go there...to Tor because..." Sorsha ceased and quieted. Her shoulders slumped and she kept her gaze ahead.

Shaw called "whoa" and tightened the reins. His comrade

continued onward and didn't notice he'd stopped, or perhaps he moved forward to give them privacy. Sorsha turned her mount and faced him.

The look of pain in her eyes concerned him. Earlier, he'd told Walen that something troubled his wife and he was certain that it had to do with the Chattans. Perhaps Rodick's death plagued her but he wasn't privy to how his cousin had died. Until he knew, he was in the dark. Whatever happened to Rodick had to be at the root of his wife's troubles. He needed answers to his questions, but he wouldn't force her to speak of her former husband if it was too painful for her. He waited to hear what she had to say.

"I apologize, Shaw, but if you need to go to Tor, I...I cannot." She lowered her chin and wouldn't look at him.

"My visit to Tor can wait if it distresses ye."

"It does."

"Why does it? Is it because of Rodick's death? How did he die? Ye have not spoken of it with me and should. Mayhap the troubles ye deem that follow ye are not as worrisome." He reached to take her hand and she clasped his fingers tightly.

"'Tis not Rodick's death that troubles me... I just... There was much heartache there and I never want to step foot on that land again. Promise me that you will not force me to go there."

Her voice strained with each word and she seemed to be flustered. Whatever the reason, Shaw understood that she'd had a difficult life with the Chattans. Hell, he was their cousin and couldn't count the number of times they'd caused him grief. Still, it had been her home and her daughter was there. "What about Gillian, your daughter...? Should we at least not retrieve her so ye can be together? If ye are worried that she will not be accepted by my clan—?"

Sorsha shook her head with vigor and gazed at him between the ears of her horse. "Nay, 'tis not that. It's just that I fear Geoff will not let Gillian go so easily. She is his brother's child, after all, and I suspect that he had hoped to marry me, but with the king's demand..."

"He hoped to marry ye?" Shaw didn't like hearing that. Geoff was a belligerent man and a bully who forced others to accept his will.

If Alexander hadn't compelled him—or even any of the other Highlanders—to marry her, her life would have been a living hell. "Did he intend to force ye to marry him?"

She continued to peer at the spot betwixt her horse's ears when she answered, "I know not. He…asked me before I left for Edinburgh and I had not given him an answer. I suspect though that he might have because he made certain threats. It matters not now. Please…do not make me go there, Shaw. We can figure out a way to retrieve Gillian later."

Shaw glanced at Walen and tipped his chin as a signal for his comrade to move on. "We will continue onward to home after we visit Fassiefern. I do not want ye to worry."

Sorsha nodded then and nudged her horse forward to follow Walen's. Shaw took up the rear of their procession and couldn't help but wonder what happened at Tor. His wife had not only appeared reluctant to speak of Rodick's death, but almost afraid to go into any depth at all. Had Geoff proposed marriage to Sorsha, or was there more to it? And why was she so lax about retrieving her daughter? Sorsha wasn't the kind of woman to forgo her motherly duty, at least, he didn't think she would. Her demeanor alluded to her being a capable mother, one who cared for her child. Whenever she spoke her daughter's name, an affectionate shine came to her eyes, followed by a depth of sadness and even distress. She had to be missing Gillian.

Patience, he reminded himself. Sorsha needed his support, not endless questions that would only remind her of what he suspected was a torment of some kind. Soon enough she would tell him what bothered her, how her former husband had died, and they would find a way to recoup Gillian from the hands of his nefarious warlord cousin and away from Tor.

THE VILLAGE OF Fassiefern lay ahead on the lane. Its location on the north side of Loch Eil afforded many travelers to stop on their way northward. It was a good resting place with a tavern, a kirk for the pious, and various shopkeepers and merchants. All sorts of foodstuffs were made ready for purchase: meats, meat pies, and a good assortment of breads.

A fishmonger shouted, haggling over the price of a crate of fish with an elder man. Another merchant sold sacks of wheat, barley, oats, and rye, stacked in rows before the stall. To the one side of the lane, a small corral held goats, sheep, pigs, and one rather large cow. Not only did the hawkers sell food goods and produce, but there were all sorts of items for sale: wool, hides, furs, pots, candlesticks, cloths, horseshoes, and nails. Market day was a busy time for the merchants and both peasants and wealthier clientele crowded the lane.

Their procession was hampered by the flurry of activity and when they reached a small hostel that offered a place to secure their horses while they visited the village, Shaw dismounted. He helped Sorsha from her mare and together they waited while Walen secured their horses and paid a hostler for a small helping of feed and water. The weather had improved on their approach to the village and he was gladdened because it would aid in locating the lad.

At the far end of the village sat a whitewashed stone building. Called *The Tavern*, the inn and mead-house was owned by his comrade, Tom, who welcomed all within its walls. His friend made a good fortune by offering a place for people to rest.

"Let us get sustenance at the tavern. I will ask Tom for news of the lad, and then you will stay here with Walen while I go in search of him." Shaw opened the door for Sorsha and followed her inside. Walen trailed after them. He found an empty table at the back of the establishment which gave them a bit of privacy.

A woman wearing a wimple and a stain-covered apron approached and took their order. Shaw requested a pitcher of ale, a basket of fresh bread, and a trencher of cooked chicken. They would have a good supper before they took to the trail again later that day.

"Should we not help you look for the lad?" Sorsha asked.

His gaze shot to Sorsha. "If ye want to help, I would welcome it. Walen, ye will stay here and keep our table. The lad will need a meal before we set off for home."

"Aye," Walen agreed almost too eagerly. Shaw gave him a look that told him not to imbibe too much ale. Fortunately, their food arrived a moment later. Walen would have food in his stomach before he could drink much.

In silence, they ate. Shaw was anxious to search for the lad before evening fell. He spotted Tom at a high table where he served drinks to a group of men and went to speak to him.

"Tom, ye be busy this day."

"Market day is always busy." The man wore his dark hair pulled back and his beard trimmed short. He was stout yet nimble for he stood on his feet for many hours throughout the day. "Och, I was wondering when ye were going to darken my door. Here for the wee lad, are ye?"

Shaw nodded. "Aye, what does the lad look like and where might he be found?"

"Last I saw 'em, he was holding up by the wall of the kirk's sacristy. Ye will probably still find him there unless he's gone to thieve amongst the people at the market. Luthor, that is his name, has light hair and blue eyes. He's about yay tall," he said, and held his hand at his waist. Tom picked up a cup and set it beneath the wooden surface of the table. "Can I get ye a drink?"

"I've supped, but it grows late, Ye might ask Walen. I know he'd like a drink. But not too many." Shaw shook his head and struck the tabletop with his palm. "My thanks, Tom. I will go in search of him near the kirk then." He motioned to Sorsha. Together, they shuffled through the mass of patrons and left the tavern.

Outside, he took hold of her hand because so many had crowded the way. Along the lane, he protected Sorsha from knaves and pickpockets. His glare alone told those bent on thieving that it wasn't a wise idea.

At the kirk, he moved around the wall until he reached the back. There, by the sacristy, he found the remnants of a makeshift bed of hay. It had to be where the boy slept at night. On the wall above was a wooden awning of sorts which probably kept the lad dry while he slept. The sight of the poor conditions disheartened him.

"He is not here and must be about the village."

Sorsha released his hand. "We shall go in search of him. Know you what he looks like?"

"Tom said he has light hair and blue eyes. The lad is called Luthor. He's about as high as my hip. Just keep an eye out for an unkempt lad—probably a thieving one—and we will find him." Shaw took hold of Sorsha's arm and was about to round the kirk to venture onto the lane in the quest of the lad when he spotted someone walking forth. He scrunched his eyes and discerned that it had to be the lad. "Luthor!" He shouted a greeting but the lad's eyes widened before he turned tail and fled.

"Stay by the kirk. I will go after him." Shaw left Sorsha by the kirk's entrance and sprinted off to trail the lad. Luthor was fast but Shaw kept a view of him as his small frame meandered through the market crowds.

At the end of the lane, the lad seemed to disappear. Shaw stopped and shifted his eyes about the area, searching for any movement. Beyond him, crates and bales of hay stacked high sat yonder. It was the perfect place for a lad his size to hide.

Before he reached the crates, Shaw heard his name being called. He turned and saw Sorsha approaching as she ran forth holding the hem of her overdress above her feet. "I told ye to await at the kirk."

"I could not stay there when you might need my help. Where

is he?"

Shaw tilted his head toward the crates and pointed ahead. "I think he might have hidden in there."

"Let me go. The poor lad is probably frightened. He might not be so fearful if I approach him." Sorsha passed him and crept toward the crates. She called out, "Good day…be not afraid. I am Sorsha, a friend…and this is Laird Mackintosh. He is a friend of the tavern keeper. Come out, lad, I promise you are safe. We just want to talk to you."

Shaw noticed the lad's head move upward from behind a stack of crates. Only his blue eyes showed as he assessed her, and Shaw beyond. Apparently deciding they were safe to approach— or perhaps to pickpocket—he emerged. As the lad cautiously rounded the stack of crates, Shaw noticed how grubby his face appeared. Indeed, his garments were tattered with tears and stains, and the boots on his feet not only looked too small for him but were worn to the soles. His wide, fearful eyes stared but he didn't speak.

Sorsha held out her hand and waved. "Are you Luthor?"

The lad nodded and rubbed his forearm across his face.

"We were told that you are alone. Is that so? Where are your parents?" She knelt near but not close enough to chase him back beyond the crates.

"Taken away, aye, by the sheriff."

"Oh, I am sorry to hear that. You *are* alone! We want to help. Are you hungry?"

Luthor nodded. "Aye."

"Then come along and we shall get you food to fill that stomach of yours." She held out her hand and Luthor stepped forward. Sorsha clasped the lad's hand and led him to the lane.

Shaw remained quiet lest he scare the lad. He followed Sorsha as she walked back to the inn. Aye, his instincts had been right. She was a good mother. He could tell by her soft, comforting chatter. Now, the lad seemed in awe of his wife, probably as much as he was.

Once at the tavern, she entered and approached the table where Walen sat. She motioned for the lad to sit on the opposite side of the table. Without hesitation, his big eyes on Walen's half-finished meal, he slid onto the bench. Sorsha took the space beside him and Shaw sat across from them, next to Walen.

"Luthor, how old are ye, lad?"

He didn't look away from the food as he held up five fingers. "Mama said I was born in a great summer storm."

"You will soon be six years, then," Sorsha told him. "You are far too young to be out here alone."

The lad nodded and swiped at his lips with his forearm. The poor boy was so hungry, he was drooling. And Shaw wasn't the only one to notice it. Walen pushed the trencher of food toward the lad and nodded to him. "Eat your fill, lad, help yourself."

Luthor pulled the trencher closer, took the largest piece of bread, and eyed the chicken as if unable to believe that, too, was included in the invitation.

Walen gestured to the chicken with his eating knife. "Laird Mackintosh helps lads by providing them with a home on his clan's land. Would you be amiable to coming home with us? You will have a roof over your head and food and will not have to beg or scrounge for a meal. That sounds good, does it not?"

Luthor fell onto the chicken, cramming it into his mouth with both his dirty hands. Finally, with grease on his chin, he answered, nodding vigorously but still eyeing them warily. "Aye, och I will not be here when Mama and Papa return."

"You expect them to come back?" Shaw asked.

The lad lowered his head, and then after a pause shook it. "Nay, they been gone long," he said softly and sorrowfully. Then he lifted his face to stare directly at Shaw. "Will ye make me a slave? I heard some lads are slaves for—"

"Of course not," Shaw spoke up. His heart was full of sorrow for the lad. He'd often heard similar tales. It was one reason why he'd decided to help orphaned or abandoned boys. "When a lad comes to stay with us, he is given a choice of labor. Some opt to take arms training. Some find farming more suitable. Others work with the smith or in the kitchens, or in the stables, or with other servicemen within the clan. The choice is yours, lad."

A smile widened over his small, but dirty face. "Do ye mean that I could wield a sword?"

Shaw chuckled because Luthor was akin to most lads, aspiring to be a warrior. "Not right off, lad, but aye, when ye are strong enough to do so. Is that what ye wish, to be part of the regiment of soldiers?"

"My papa fought for the king, he did. The sheriff took my mama and papa away." Luthor lowered his face, sniffled, took a handful of chicken, and shoved it into his mouth.

"I am sorry to hear that, lad. Maybe in time we can find out what happened to them and help you reunite. Until then, we can offer a safe place to live."

Luthor snatched another piece of bread and ate it. "I will work hard at arms training, Laird."

Shaw reached across the table and patted the lad's shoulder. "I know ye will."

CHAPTER NINE

IT TOOK OVER a sennight to reach the outskirts of Mackintosh land. Days had passed since they found Luthor in the village of Fassiefern. Along the way home, they found a stream of water where Luthor was able to bathe. Shaw produced some boys' clothes he'd found somewhere in the village—or perhaps he'd kept them in his pack—and he insisted the lad take a bath. Since Luthor was to ride with her, Sorcha was grateful. After his life on the lanes in the village, he was understandably filthy.

As he led the boy away from their camp, carrying a pot of heated water, she held back a giggle when she heard Shaw tell Luthor that he wouldn't let Sorsha treat him like a bairn.

"After all, lad, ye are nearly a man och, soon to be a warrior, so ye can wash yourself. But ye have things living in your hair. The wee pesties must go."

For the rest of their journey, the men stopped their mounts each night to rest before continuing. Not only did they travel slowly but had to make frequent stops because the lad insisted he needed to seek nature's call. Sorsha felt for him when he squirmed and moaned until they agreed to halt but unlike most lads his age, Luthor was a quiet lad and rarely spoke except for moments when he needed to seek a tree.

Sorsha held Luthor between her thighs atop her horse and wrapped her cloak around him. As they rode, he frequently held out one leg and then the other, admiring the shiny new boots Shaw had given him. She knew they were probably the nicest—and newest—things Luthor had ever been given, at least that he could remember, and he was obviously proud of them. It made Sorsha laugh to see him pointing his toes, and sometimes spitting on his fingers to rub away a mud-mark on the toes or heels.

The air cooled considerably the more northerly they rode. She prayed they would reach Shaw's home soon because she was exhausted and ready to end the journey. Shifting her body sideways, she peered at Shaw and gave him a questioning gaze as if to ask, *How much longer?*

He chuckled low. "I know what ye are thinking, lass, and aye… Our home is yonder beyond those trees. We will reach the bridge to the island in a short time."

"Praise God," she mumbled.

As they rode past the trees, some of which rose high into the sky, the land opened to spectacular beauty. The view of the cottages that dotted the hills and land beyond was enchanting. Smoke wafted from chimneys in the late day's sky and people moseyed about, greeting each other and conversing. The Mackintosh clan's people appeared friendly and kind. A woman waved to them from afar. From a distance, Sorsha could tell that she had long flowing locks shaded in red. She wondered who she was waving to—Shaw or Walen.

Whistles sounded as they crossed the bridge toward the gates. Men scurried from their posts and greeted Shaw with rambled words. He signaled to them and dismounted when a man approached.

"Clovis, all is well?"

The guard's dark eyes shifted from Shaw to her, to Walen, and then to Luthor. "Aye, Laird, nothing to report except… We received a missive from Mistress Corliss. She wrote that she would be here within a fortnight or so. I told Edra so she could prepare her chamber."

Shaw tugged the reins of his horse and motioned for her to

follow. "My thanks, Clovis. Come and see me later when ye are off duty to give me your report."

"Will do, Laird," he said readily and returned to his post.

When they reached a corral near the main keep, Shaw helped her down from her horse and then she pulled Luthor from the horse's back and set him on his feet. As she waited for Shaw, she glanced around and regarded the main keep. It was different from her former home. Here, a rectangular stone building sprawled yet, it had no turrets or adjacent towers. A rocky walkway led to the door that had been painted white.

She decided that his home was as charming as he was and resembled an oversized cozy cottage. Thick thatch made a handsome roof with two chimney stacks set equally one on each side of the domain.

"Walen, take Luthor to the garrison where he can stay with the other fledglings. Get him settled in." Shaw was about to turn but she stepped in front of him.

"Must he stay there? He is young and perhaps he would feel better if he stayed within the keep with us?" Sorsha flashed an appeasing smile, hoping Shaw would agree.

"What say ye, Luthor? Do ye wish to stay with the other lads in the garrison or at the keep with us?"

Luthor stepped away from her but turned and looked up. "I...in the keep...with Milady," he answered in a soft voice that rendered her heart. As much as Shaw wanted to let the lad act the man, in truth, he was still very much a youngster who needed a woman's touch. She hoped that Shaw understood. And when she looked at her husband, he met her gaze with his own. The corner of his mouth quirked with a secret smile, and his eyes danced. He understood Luthor's needs. Truly, she was a blessed woman to marry such a man.

"Very well then. Never ye mind, Walen. See to the horses and visit your brother. He must be itching to see ye," Shaw said and as if to answer her questioning gaze, added, "Walen's brother is Trey, our commander-in-arms." He opened the door to his keep and gestured for her to go, following closely behind them.

Sorsha smiled in appreciation of the information. She took hold of Luthor's small hand and guided him inside.

Immediately upon entering, she noticed a long corridor that ran down the center of the structure and a set of stairs that led to the upper floors. On each side of the hallway, ornately carved wooden doors led to other rooms. Shaw marched on and she followed.

"Let us get a drink and I will have Mistress Edra bring us food."

As soon as they entered the great hall, a woman rushed forward. She bowed to Shaw and awaited instruction. The aged woman, Edra, wore her thick brown hair pulled back tied at her nape. Her soft brown eyes seemed to peer at Shaw with motherly affection. Sorsha envied him a little because it had been a long time since she'd received such a caring look. That made her think of Aela and how much she missed her.

"Laird, 'tis good to have ye home."

"Edra, ye are looking well. This is my wife Sorsha. We could do with some food. Our journey was long."

Sorsha smiled and gave a slight nod to greet the woman.

"Oh, what wonderful news. Welcome, Milady, welcome. I'm afraid ye missed the mid-day meal but I will hasten and ready an early supper for ye. And, Milady, I shall be gladdened to aid ye in any way. Let me know if ye need anything…" Edra bent at the waist to peer in Luthor's face. "And who is this wee laddie? Is he your son?"

"Nay, he is a lad Laird Mackintosh found in Fassiefern." Sorsha removed her cloak and set it on a nearby chair. Luthor stood by the table and kept his gaze on his feet, quiet as usual. Sorsha filled the space where a small boy would usually chatter. "I am thankful for your gracious welcome, Mistress Edra."

As they'd spoken, Shaw had strolled away. Now he'd returned with two cups filled with ale for them. He'd gone to the buttery, Sorsha realized. She'd need to get a tour of the keep right away if she were to be in charge. "My thanks, Edra, for the welcome. If you haven't yet met, this is Luthor and he shall be staying with us. Is there a chamber within where he can sleep?"

"There are no other children here, but och there is a small chamber near yours that we can settle him in. I shall see to it after I bring food." Edra curtseyed to her and stopped at the threshold when an elder woman appeared.

The elder woman spoke quietly to the maid at the doorway and left her, entering the hall with a smile and hastened steps. "My dear lad, ye have returned," the woman said with a smile.

Shaw set the cups of ale on the nearby table. "Ah…here she is. Sorsha, this is my grandmother. We call her Mamo. Mamo, this is my wife Sorsha. We were married in Edinburgh." Shaw pulled a chair away from the table for his grandmother and she sat, never moving her eyes from her. Then he shifted a chair back for her and Sorsha slid onto it. He sat at the top of the trestle table in what appeared to be a larger chair probably meant for the laird while Luthor walked around the hall, gazing at some of the weapons that hung on the wall and at the tapestries. He seemed to be enthralled and very much occupied, so she turned her gaze back to the woman Shaw had called Mamo.

Sorsha had never seen such a beautiful elder woman. Her shiny white-gray hair flowed over her shoulders and her face reflected love for Shaw. She instantly liked her but she was uncertain if the feeling was reciprocated. "'Tis a pleasure to meet you, Lady Mackintosh."

"Come, lass, ye may call me Maven, or Mamo if it suits ye. Tell me how ye persuaded my grandson to marry ye because he swore never to marry, I despaired that he meant to remain unmarried for all his days."

"Very well, Mamo." Sorsha eyed Luthor to be sure he was all right before turning back to her. "I am afraid that it was not I who persuaded Shaw to marry me. King Alexander commanded that he take a wife and I just happened to be there as one of the choices."

Shaw chuckled. "Aye, he did, but ye fail to mention, Sorsha, that we'd met many years before. I knew her, Mamo, when I went to serve the king before his marriage to Queen Margaret."

Mamo's mouth hung open slightly before she righted herself. "Oh, pray tell… Is *this* the woman ye professed to care for all those years ago? The one who married the Chattan laird?"

Shaw nodded. "Aye, she is. She was widowed, and now I am fortunate to be married to her." He reached across the table and took her hand. She gripped his fingers tightly, so grateful to be his wife now.

"I am the fortunate one, Mamo. Your grandson is a worthy husband and I cannot be happier." Remarkably, there was no coyness in the way she spoke. Sorsha meant every word she spoke, and once Gillian was returned to her loving embrace, her heart would be completely whole.

"Ye belong together now, aye, for fate has played a hand in your coming together. It does this old woman's heart good to see ye both happy. Forgive me," Mamo said and pressed her eyes. "I cannot seem to cease weeping. My tears are joyous. I want to hear every detail of what happened in Edinburgh."

Shaw released her hand, pressed his chair back, and stood. "I shall take that as my leave then. Ye will be all right here until I return? I will not leave ye if…"

Sorsha shook her head. "Nay, go on. I am sure you wish to meet with your clansmen. Luthor needs to be settled and then I will make myself at home."

He pressed his hand on her cheek. "Aye, 'tis your home, lass, do not forget that. Just know I might be a while and need to hear my commander's report. Mistress Edra will find you some supper as promised, and help both you and Luthor to your rooms, and I will see ye later." He lifted her hand to his mouth and pressed a kiss to the base of her palm that promised a warmer homecoming just between them, later. She felt her cheeks heat.

As soon as Shaw cleared the doorway, Maven reached across the table and patted her hand. "I am gladdened ye were given to

Shaw as a bride. He never forgot ye, lass, ye know that?"

"He has said as much." Being alone with Shaw's grandmother brought on a shyness; Sorsha didn't retort but kept her gaze on Luthor, who continued to amble around the chamber. She smiled when he pretended to fight with an imaginary sword, talking to a pretend foe and finally behaving like a normal little boy, unafraid and well-fed for once. This made her almost as happy as being Shaw's wife.

"Shall we take the lad to the kitchen and get him some food?" Mamo asked.

"I should like to bathe him as well and handle some other matters. Aye, let us to the kitchen."

Sorsha called Luthor, and Mamo showed her the way to the kitchen. It was located in a small building behind the back of the fief. From the outside, the building appeared small, but once she entered, she realized it was quite spacious.

Edra set a pot on the hook above the fire and turned to her. "Oh, Milady, I was about to bring the foodstuff."

"Shaw had to meet with his men. Would you mind if we ate here, in the kitchen?"

Edra bobbed her head. "I shall serve ye as soon as the stew heats."

Sorsha approached the worktable that sat before the hearth. "Can we have some water heated for a bath for the lad? And might we find some more garments that would fit him better than the ones he's wearing?"

"Oh, is not Grace's lad about his size? She has three lads so she'll likely have something to fit the wee lad," Mamo said to Edra.

"I am certain she would have garments for him. I can go when I finish warming the water for his bath."

"Nay, ye are busy attending to the clan's new lady. I shall go and will return soon." Mamo smiled, bowed to her, and left the kitchen.

Edra pulled a large tub from the antechamber and set it near the fire. She poured heated water into the bath and continued to do so until it reached halfway to the top, then plopped in a big bar of rough soap.

"Luthor." Sorsha gestured to him, and he trudged forward as if he were going to his death. She almost laughed because while he accepted his bath in a stream, now—like most lads—he apparently abhorred bathing. With a gentle push to his back, she pressed him forward and pulled at his garments until he was free of them.

Luthor was shy and kept his head lowered. Without much ado, she lifted him and set him in the tub. He sat down and swirled the water with his hands. A film of white froth from the soap began to form, distracting him from his distaste for bathing. He giggled a little as his small body slipped around the bottom of the tub.

"You will feel much better once you've bathed and then we will have a good meal," Sorsha told him, trying not to laugh at the surprise on his face when the bar of soap slipped from between his hands. She imagined he'd never seen anything like it in his life. So as not to embarrass him with her laughter, she turned to the housekeeper. "What are you serving, Mistress Edra?"

"I made a hearty pottage with plenty of venison for supper." Edra tossed the garments outside the kitchen next to the entrance.

"Well, it smells delicious." As she waited for Luthor to finish bathing himself, she sat on a stool near the table and watched him. He seemed to enjoy the tub, and Lord knew, he needed to wash away some of the road dust that stuck to him. Little boys seemed to attract more dirt than girls. Or at least, more dirt than Gillian had ever collected. "Do you have parchment and ink?"

Edra hastened to the antechamber again and returned with pieces of parchment, a quill, and a small bottle of ink. "Here, Milady. Will this do? I use it to make lists for market day."

"'Tis perfect. My thanks, Edra." Sorsha scrawled a message to

Aela letting her know that she would send for her as soon as she was able. She didn't disclose where she was for fear that Geoff might intercept her message. Instead, she wrote that she was safe and not to worry about her. When she finished the missive, she glanced at the lad and sighed. "Luthor, I am going to write to the king's chamberlain to ask after your parents. What are their names?"

The lad peered at her and shrugged his shoulders. "Mama and Papa."

He was young, and she should have realized that would've been his obvious answer. She laughed because he sounded so sure of himself. "Of course you would call them that but what did your ma call your da?"

"Father."

Sorsha wanted to groan because getting the answer was going to be difficult. "And I assume he called her Mother?"

Luthor nodded.

"What is your family name? For instance, I was part of the d'Avranches family before I married and then I became part of the Chattan clan. Now, I am a part of the Mackintosh clan."

"Oh, aye, Milady, Papa said that we belonged to the MacWilliams clan."

Finally, she got her answer, although it was almost as difficult as pulling a tooth. She set the parchment in front of her and wrote to the king's chamberlain asking if he would look into the matter of Luthor's parents. She added that they were now in possession of their child and hoped to find out where they were. When she finished, Edra set a candle near her so she could seal it. Sorsha held the candle over the folded parchment until enough wax dripped onto it and did the same to the message she'd written to Aela.

"Will you ask for this to be delivered to Edinburgh? To Edmund, the chamberlain in the king's castle?" Sorsha held out the missive for her to take.

"Aye, I am sure Clovis can arrange it. He's the gate watchman and oft receives missives which he can give to the messengers to take back with them."

She held out the second missive. "And this one needs to be handled discreetly. It is meant for the maidservant at Tor Castle."

Edra glanced at it but then nodded. "I can have one of the stable lads take it. Tor is not too far from here."

"You are so helpful, Edra." Sorsha approached the tub and took the soap from Luthor to apply to a washing cloth left lying over the edge of the tub. She lathered the lad as best she could, including his hair, and then used the cup that Edra had supplied to rinse him. When she finished, she helped him from the tub and wrapped the drying cloth around his bony body. It made her happy to think that before long he'd have flesh and sinew covering those bones, from good food, good rest, and plenty of wholesome activity. Again, she thought about how grateful she was to be married to such a kind man. Too many people ignored the plight of orphaned urchins; the thought that he might not have survived his ordeal on the lanes twisted her heart and stomach.

He stood watching her while she used a basin to scoop out some water to wash her face and hands. How she longed to have a bath as well but first, she needed to get the lad settled.

Edra came into the anteroom with two heaping bowlfuls of a hardy stew and they ate while waiting for Mamo to return.

"There, how does that feel?" She dressed him and used her fingers to comb the locks of his hair. He appeared so much younger now than he had when he'd been covered with grime.

Luthor raised his face. "I like being clean, milady."

"I am sure you do. So do I. Now, come and let us get you settled for the night. The journey was long and exhausting. You will probably sleep until the morrow."

She thanked Edra again for her aid, grabbed her cloak from the chair, and followed Mamo back into the keep. On the second level, Mamo opened a door. "I had one of the soldiers help me ready the chamber since Edra was busy."

The room was small and only fit two small beds made of straw-stuffed mattresses. Atop the beds lay a cover woven in the likeness of the Mackintosh tartan. There was one small trunk near the little window on the outside wall but other than that, there were no other furnishings.

"It is much better than sleeping outside of the sacristy, is it not?" she asked Luthor.

He nodded enthusiastically. "Aye, 'tis, milady, and warmer." Luthor crawled onto the bed.

"Sleep well, wee lad." Mamo turned and left them.

Sorsha was hesitant to leave Luthor. Being so young, she wondered if he would be afraid during the night or if he feared the dark. Before she closed the door, she heard him speak.

"I miss my mama and papa," his little voice came.

Sorsha's heart hurt hearing the desperation in his tone. She approached the bedside and clasped his hand. "They must miss you as well. Worry not, because we will find them. The king's chamberlain will know where they are. While we await word from him, I want you to consider yourself part of this family. I won't let anything happen to you, Luthor." She knelt next to the small fire in the hearth and stoked it to make it warmer in the chamber. Then she lit the stub of a candle on the little table near the bed. At least if he awakened during the night, he wouldn't be so fearful. "I will check on you during the night and will stay close, so do not be afraid."

"I am not afeared, Milady."

She knelt next to his bedding, tucked the covers around the courageous lad, and pressed her hand on the soft locks of his hair. "I know you are not. You are the bravest lad and spent a good many nights by yourself. You are safe here, remember that. Now, close your eyes and sleep sweet, and I shall see you on the morrow."

Before she left the chamber, Luthor rolled onto his belly and closed his eyes.

Sorsha closed the door and turned to leave the hallway when

she spotted a woman entering a chamber next to Luthor's. She wasn't sure where she would sleep or if Shaw intended to share a chamber with her. Rodick never had.

At the top of the steps, she almost bumped into Edra, who carried her valise. "Milady, I wanted to show ye where the laird's chamber is. And the men brought your belongings." She ambled down the hallway and stopped at the door where she'd seen the woman enter. While it was good that she wouldn't be far from Luthor as promised, something struck her about the woman who had gone into Shaw's room, and instead of entering, Sorsha turned away.

Her heart felt crushed. He was like all husbands, unfaithful, and had a roving eye. How many times had she witnessed Rodrick taking his mistress into his bedchamber? Too many to count. Not that she had mattered because Sorsha had been grateful she did not need to spend the night with him. Still, a woman hoped for a devoted husband and she thought that Shaw would be so.

"I need some air and wish to walk about before I seek my rest."

"Very well, Milady. I shall put your belongings inside your chamber."

She couldn't leave fast enough, certain that she would have interrupted Shaw with the woman. Certainly, that was something which she didn't want to see!

When she reached the outside, she pulled her cloak around her and fastened it with its tie. Sorsha walked along dejectedly, without a purposeful direction. She wanted to cry at the thought that her husband had a mistress. An even worse predicament before her was what she should do about it. Should she confront him? Should she demand that he send the woman away? Or should she say nothing?

She'd always thought she wasn't woman enough for Rodrick but she hadn't loved him so it hadn't mattered. But for Shaw to have a mistress was unbearable. She loved him, she realized, and didn't want to share him with any woman. She would fight for him, she decided, but first she'd need to confront him.

"Ye look like ye have the weight of a crag on your shoulders, Milady." A woman stood before her, the one she'd seen when they first approached the Mackintosh village. "I am Niahm. Walen told me that our laird had married and I wanted to meet ye."

Sorsha took in the beautiful woman who stood before her. Her glorious reddish locks hung in waves about her face. The woman had bluish-green eyes, rosy-hued skin, and pretty pink lips. She was absolutely lovely. Compared to Niahm, Sorsha was as comely as a field mouse with her drab brown hair and similarly-colored eyes. "Good eve, Niahm. It is a pleasure to meet you."

"Are ye all right, Milady?" Niahm bowed her head, smiled, and moved to walk beside her.

"I am," she lied. Sorsha wasn't about to speak of her heartbreak to a stranger.

"Would ye like me to show ye around?"

Sorsha nodded and allowed the woman to lead her forward. "You mentioned Walen. How do you know him? I became acquainted with him many years ago when Shaw visited the king and we recently met again in Edinburgh."

Niahm's cheeks brightened. "We…*ah*, he comes by occasionally and visits."

"Visits? Oh! By that, I suspect you mean that you and he are—"

"Pray, do not speak it, Milady, but aye I mean…*that*."

Sorsha hid her smile because it was nice to have a woman to speak to and she hoped to befriend Niahm. "Are you close? Might he want to take you as his wife?"

Niahm's gaze lowered and she looked at her feet. "I know not, Milady, but I hope he does. It has been my fondest wish that he notice me and he has. But 'tis well-known that he does not want to marry. I will not have false hope."

They were sisters in mistreatment at the hands of men, Sorsha decided and she linked her arm to hers. "Niahm, call me Sorsha. I deem you are a friend and as for Walen... we shall endeavor to inspire him to offer marriage since you desire it."

"Do ye think we can influence him?"

"Why not?" She took a deep breath. Now that Niahm had confided in her, and since she felt a camaraderie with the woman, Sorsha felt ready to share her worries. "Now tell me, does Laird Shaw visit many women in the clan? I am newly married to him and confess I do not know much about him."

Niahm stopped her from moving forward. "Laird Shaw, as far as I know, has never visited any of the women in the clan. Why do ye ask?"

It seemed impossible. A virile man like Shaw had to have some kind of mistresses. *Didn't he?* "Do the women visit him? I thought I saw someone entering his chamber and..." Sorsha hoped that her summation was unfounded. Did Niahm tell the truth? "Perhaps I was mistaken."

"I know not if they visit him. But if ye are bothered by it, ask him. What is the worst that can happen? If he says *aye*, then at least ye know the truth. If he says nay, then ye can make him explain why the woman entered his chamber." Niahm nodded confidently as if she knew firsthand what she spoke of.

"I do not want there to be discord betwixt us especially with us being so newly married. Perhaps I shall ask him...If I am not cowardly."

Her new friend scoffed. "I doubt, Milady, that ye are cowardly."

Sorsha reflected on her conversation with Niahm and chided herself for caring whether Shaw was interested in other women. With the years of marriage to Rodick, she had learned her place as his wife was not as important or as coveted as much as that of being his mistress. And she knew that Geoff Chattan would have been much the same, if not worse.

Now, even if her marriage to Shaw was less than what she

expected or hoped for, at least she was better off than being married to Geoff Chattan.

CHAPTER TEN

S HAW RETURNED TO the fief to retrieve another tartan to drape around himself. As the night crept onward, the air had cooled and he wanted to keep warm whilst he went about getting his reports from Trey and others. He needed to find out how the training sessions went and if they had filled the stores as he'd bade for Mistress Edra.

Inside his bedchamber, he quickly found the tartan he sought. Before he retreated, the door opened and Enid, Mistress Edra's daughter, entered.

"Laird, I heard ye were home and I wanted to let you know that your mamo only went to the graves twice whilst ye were gone. I awaited her and kept her warm until she awakened as ye had instructed. She did not put up much of a fuss when I returned her to the keep."

Shaw bobbed his head as she spoke. It was good to know that Enid took her duty to heart and that his mamo was in safe hands. "My thanks, Enid. Will ye have a tub sent to my bedchamber soon? I am sure Sorsha would appreciate a bath after our long journey."

"I would be happy to see to it, Laird." She bowed to him and hastily left.

He was gladdened that his grandmother remained safe while he was gone. With a quick motion, he flipped the tartan around his shoulders, fastened it with his belt, and hastened his steps to leave the fief. Outside, he breathed deeply, taking in the pristine air of the Highlands, rejoicing at being home. He met with Trey by the field and there was little to report. The men had trained and the stores had been replenished.

Clovis shouted a greeting as he approached. "Laird, a messenger came from the MacPhersons." He handed the small enclosed parchment to him and bowed. "I am still on duty, och there is naught to report. No missives came whilst ye were away and only the one from Mistress Corliss. It were quiet."

"No messenger came from the Chattans?"

His guardsman shook his head. "Nay, Laird, only your sister's message, but naught from the Chattans."

"My thanks, Clovis. Go on then and seek your rest when ye finish your duty." Shaw held the missive and pondered why the MacPhersons would contact him. They weren't aligned with them but it was rumored that the MacPhersons had recently sided with the Chattans against the Camerons. He'd read the missive when he had time to consider the ramifications of their contact and tucked it into the small sheath that held his dagger at his waist.

He spotted Sorsha walking with Niahm way down the lane. How lovely she looked. Seeing her here was akin to a dream he'd often had. Only this wasn't a dream and she was truly there on Mackintosh land. Sorsha appeared as if she belonged to the Mackintoshes as if she was meant to be the lady of their clan.

Shaw kept his focus on his wife. His steps slowed because she seemed to be enjoying herself and she smiled. Her mood lightened him because he was concerned about her embracing his clan as hers. He didn't want to intrude on her conversation with Walen's woman and waited for her to reach him.

A sound behind him drew his interest. Footsteps alerted Shaw that someone was advancing. He knew well who it was and before he could attack, Shaw whipped around and grabbed hold of the soldier. He shoved him back, but Henny wasn't easily thwarted. Henny clasped his body and tossed him to the ground. Shaw landed with an *oomph* before he rolled to the side and tripped Henny. The soldier fell next to him and Shaw removed his dagger, holding it effectively above the man to instill the rebuff of his attack. When his soldier held up his hands, Shaw allowed him his freedom.

Henny got to his knees with a wide smile on his face. "Bollocks, Laird, your hearing is sound. Aye, ye foiled me again, ye did. 'Tis good to know ye are ready for anything."

Shaw laughed but then sobered when the women shrieked and came running. Niahm continued to cry out but Sorsha gripped Henny's tartan to pull him back. He quickly re-sheathed his dagger, got to his feet, and pressed his hands over Sorsha's to give aid to Henny. "Release him, Sorsha. He means no harm."

When she did as he bade, Henny roared with laughter and sauntered away. He called over his shoulder, "Until next time, Laird. Mayhap then ye won't need your bonny woman to save ye." His chortle sounded and others walking nearby stopped to observe the fracas.

"Bloody hell, Henny. I did not need my wife to save me now and well ye know it." Though he shouted his retort, Henny continued to bellow.

Shaw was appalled by his soldier's blatant remark and at the grins on the faces of his men. Henny was intent on winning one bout with him but he'd do whatever he could to ensure that didn't happen. He owed it to his soldiers to be ready to face any threat that Henny or anyone else threw his way. He meant to be the example his soldiers needed, and doing so meant he needed to accept and be ready for Henny's sneak attacks. Hopefully, it would prepare his men for whatever fracas they faced.

"Are you hurt? Why did he attack you?" Sorsha stood close to him but had a delightful, confused expression that wrinkled her brows.

"Nay, he did not hurt me." He took his wife's hand and tried to lead her away.

Niahm shook her head but giggled low and then she walked away.

"I do not understand..." Sorsha withdrew her hand and peered at him.

"He uses sneak attacks on me, and others, in order to help us hone our hand-to-hand combat skills. 'Tis annoying and he takes far too much pleasure in it, but it is helpful," Shaw admitted.

"Oh, that is clever. I shall leave you then," she said and tried to step away.

But Shaw wasn't ready yet to let her leave. He pulled her against him and clasped his hands behind her back. Lord, he wanted to kiss her but with so many onlookers, he withheld his urge to do so. "I am through with my reports and long for my bed. Come and we will seek our slumber together. Ye must be tired after the long ride home."

"I am and...*um*...wanted to...ask where *my* chamber is..."

Sorsha kept her gaze over his shoulder when she spoke but he noted her voice was low and somewhat hesitant as she stammered. He leaned toward her and grinned to help alleviate any worry she might have. When she wouldn't look at him, he raised her chin with a slight touch. "Ye shall stay in my bedchamber. I want ye by my side during the night."

"But I...I do not wish to...to interfere with... Ah, what I mean to say is..." Sorsha pulled back and turned away.

Shaw pulled her close once more, perplexed by her evasiveness. He kept his hands on her hips to keep her from leaving. "What is it ye are trying to say? Ye may speak freely, Sorsha, because I want honesty betwixt us...always. What is bothering ye?" He retook her hand and squeezed it affectionately.

"I saw a woman entering your chamber. If you are intent on entertaining others there—"

"A woman?" Shaw pursed his lips as he thought of whom she saw. "Oh, ye mean Enid. She is Edra's daughter, a maidservant within the keep. She only came because she wanted to tell me about Mamo. I asked her to ensure my grandmother's safety before I left on the journey to Edinburgh."

Sorsha's brow crinkled once more with worry and he fought the urge to kiss the creases over the bridge of her nose away. "Why would your grandmother need to be protected? Is there danger afoot?"

He shook his head vehemently. "Nay, all is well here and ye need not worry. Our walls are protected and a sentry rides out at all times of the day. But Mamo sometimes sleepwalks and goes to the burial grounds at night or early morn. If anyone tries to roust her, she can sometimes be violent. So I asked Enid to look after her in case she went there whilst I was away. Mamo does not realize she does this and often goes without care for cold or anything else."

So Niahm had spoken the truth. Shaw took no women to his bed. She would be the only one. It was almost too good to be true. But now she needed to respond to his concerns about Mamo. "That is a scary situation, Shaw, and I am sorry for thinking the worst. I shall not make such a mistake again."

"I understand, Sorsha, why ye did. But I want there to be trust betwixt us, and soon enough, ye will have faith in me enough not to question such matters. I could not leave without ensuring Mamo was kept safe and I asked Enid to watch over her. I worry that one day I might find Mamo gone for she wants to go to the hereafter because she longs to be with my grandfather."

Sorsha took hold of his other hand and clasped both his hands with sympathy. "Oh, that is terribly sad, Shaw. I hope she knows how much you care for her."

"She does and now she has ye too. Together, we will look after her."

"I will be gladdened to help you."

He turned her back to the fief and was in no rush to enter it. Being with Sorsha lightened him and he was glad to be able to tell her of his worry about his grandmother. When he was gone, which was more often than he liked, he now had Sorsha to ensure his grandmother was cared for.

They entered the fief and then he led her to the upper floor. In the hallway, he stopped her before they entered their chamber. "Where is the lad sleeping?"

Sorsha pointed to the door in the hallway next to theirs. "I settled him some time ago. No sounds are coming from his room. I shall check on him to ensure he has settled for the night."

"Aye, he is young, which is why I agreed to let him stay with us but eventually, he will be moved to the barracks with the other lads who foster."

She nodded in understanding before she pressed her finger to her lips and opened Luthor's door to peek into the darkened chamber. The lad's soft snores reached Shaw's ears and he smiled as she quietly closed the door once more. "He is asleep."

"Good." Shaw reached behind her and pressed her back toward their door. He opened it, shuffled her inside, closed the door with a thud, and then pulled her against him. His lips sought hers and he gave her the slightest peck. Then he leaned against the closed door and pulled her back against him. Her body rested against his and his hands roved over the front of her body until he was able to cup her breasts.

"I have been thinking about doing this all day. 'Tis the truth, I like touching you." He pressed his hands over her bosom, the curves of her hips, and her sensitive torso. She giggled slightly when he touched her there which drew his smile.

"I like you touching me," she said with a raspy breath.

Shaw set his cheek next to hers and whispered, "I like ye touching me too."

Sorsha set her hands on his forearm which kept her against him. His need grew and the hardness pressed against her buttocks. Shaw moaned softly at the prospect of loving her again.

"Is that bath for me?"

He nodded. "Aye, I thought ye would want to wash away the travel dust. Go on. The water should still be warm."

Sorsha undid the tie of her cloak, then the bodice of her over-dress, and removed it. Beneath her garments was a thin chemise, an undergarment that showed more of her body than it hid. He thought her sweet when she shyly removed the garment and stepped into the tub trying to hide her body with her hands. With her lovely backside to him, she craned her neck to peer at him. Shaw sat on the bedside and watched her. Her movements were graceful and unbeknownst to her, she carried herself in a seductive way.

When she finished bathing, she reached for the drying cloth set on a nearby stool. He considered her abashment and stood. To distract himself, he approached the window casement, opened a shutter slightly, and gazed at the star-filled night sky. There was nary a moon to give any light about the land. Night obscured the waters that surrounded the island. The waters were still and no lapping of their waves sounded on the banks.

Shaw shook his head at his simple thoughts and wished she'd hurry.

"Shaw?"

He turned and found her standing close. Shaw pressed his hands to her waist, loving the soft, silky feel of her skin against his calloused palms, hastily lifted her, carried her to the bed, and set her in the center. With care, he removed his sword and sheath and placed them by the bed's headboard. He removed his layered tartans and then his tunic. His belt clanked on the wooden floorboards but he cared not and shifted it under the bed with his foot. Then he knelt on the bed and used his hands to crawl toward her. As he lay next to her he tilted her chin so she would look at him.

"When we married, Sorsha, I made certain vows to ye. Ye are the only woman who will ever occupy this bed and the only woman I will lie with. Always remember that."

"I was foolish for thinking—"

"Nay, I understand why such a notion would come to ye. This is a new situation for us both and I want us to be faithful to each other." Shaw's voice held a little emotion as he spoke. He hoped she felt the same.

"'Tis just...Rodick did his husbandly duty but he often bedded others. I...I was nothing but a burden to him, a chore he detested. I want us to be faithful too." She sighed and he pressed his hand on her face, causing her to close her eyes.

"He was a fool, not ye. Any man that cannot see your worth, Sorsha, is an arse. Now kiss me, wife, because I need to touch ye and..." Shaw ceased his thought and pressed his lips to hers. He couldn't get enough of kissing her and turned his mouth to the softness of her lips.

Sorsha joined her hands behind his neck and kept him close. His chest caressed against her breasts and brought forth a light groan from him. He wanted to take her and be joined as one. They'd had little opportunity to be together on the trek and had only coupled twice. If he had his way, he would have taken her each night. But though he desired her, he wanted to please her and show her that a man could be gentle, caring, passionate, and loving. He wouldn't have been able to do so on the cold, hard ground so close to Walen and the lad.

Now she tried to shift him to lie beside her and he complied with her unspoken demand. Sorsha rose to kneel beside him and pressed her hands over the top of his thigh, his stomach, and chest. Her touch ignited a passion within him and his heart increased to a fevered pitch. Being with her was everything he'd ever envisioned, wanted, or needed. Shaw let her take her time exploring him. He wanted her to be comfortable with touching him.

Sorsha set her mouth on his chest and kissed her way to his mouth. The way her lips pressed against his throat along the way caused him to take in a heavy breath. Lord, he wanted her and his patience was threadbare and unraveling quickly.

Without giving her a warning, he grabbed hold of her and flipped her onto her back. His body spanned hers and he willed himself to go slow. But Sorsha urged him on with sweet moans and touches that spurred his lust. The desire between them flowed effortlessly and uncontrollably. He was about to enter her then realized that he needed to be gentle with her.

"I want ye badly and cannot resist—"

"Take me, Shaw. I need you too." Her words came in a sweet whisper against his mouth.

Shaw pressed his lips against hers as his erection found its way into the warmth of her being. Her heat and tightness caused him to rasp in delight. He shifted slowly at first, trying to maintain control and to give her pleasure. Her body easily accepted his and when she wrapped her legs around his thighs, he was lost in a peril of extreme infatuation. Shaw continued to propel his body and as their movements increased, so too did their surrender.

He was barely hanging on and forced himself to withhold the need to expel his seed. His wife was more important than his instinctual need and he wanted her to experience the ultimate pleasure. With effective thrusts and powerful strokes, he couldn't withstand the impulse to delve into her sheath. She clasped him tightly and called his name in besotted shouts of sensuality. Her culmination tensed her body beneath his, and still, he waited. But his restraint was short-lived when his body deceived him and thoroughly abandoned him.

Every muscle within him clenched with the agony of his surrender. His seed gave way and his shout nearly rendered him incapable of movement. He pressed against her and drew in rasps of breath. For a long moment, he leaned his head on her shoulder and tried not to crush her. But he realized her hands were entwined within the locks of his hair. Her fingers caressed his head as if she were trying to soothe him, but she, too, seemed to have trouble catching her breath.

"Sorsha, ye are bonny and have me besotted." He shifted back but kissed her softly before he completely withdrew.

His wife lay back with a bonny smile on her face. She pressed the tips of her fingers over her eyes and sighed. "What just happened?"

He grinned as multiple answers came to him, but when he noted the shine in her eyes, he smoothed a hand over her hair.

"Are ye weeping? Did I hurt ye?" Shaw thought he might've been somewhat rough with her.

"Nay, it was…wonderful. Really, Shaw, I never felt anything so perfect."

Perfect…Perfection…Transcendent.

Their encounter led Shaw to realize that he might be more than infatuated with her. He lay next to her, yanked her body closer to his, and smoothed a hand over her torso. "I cannot wait until ye are carrying my bairn. Ye want more children? I know ye must be missing your wee lass, but it got me thinking that I want bairns and soon. Do ye?"

She set her hand atop his. "I had not thought about it…until now. Aye, I do want more children, yours… And of course, I miss Gillian and pray that she is well."

Shaw couldn't begin to understand the woe that must be in Sorsha's heart over being separated from her child. He intended to wait until she was ready to retrieve her daughter, but something prevented her from doing so. If they were going to collect Gillian from the Chattans, it should be soon. That decided, Shaw leaned his head against hers and sighed.

"I will be gone most of the day on the morrow but should return by nightfall."

"I am sure I shall be well while you are gone. Where are you going?"

He cleared his throat and told a bald-faced lie. "I plan to meet with my allies." Well, no, that wasn't necessarily a bald-faced lie, but it wasn't the truth either. He intended to meet with his allies in case he needed them when he confronted Geoff Chattan. Though his wife wouldn't share her reluctance to retrieve Gillian, he intended to retrieve their wee lass as soon as possible.

For now, he was content to hold Sorsha all night if only to remind himself that she was finally his—the woman he'd been infatuated with since he'd first held her.

CHAPTER ELEVEN

IN THE PRE-DAWN, darkened morning, Shaw left his bed and hastily prepared to leave. When he picked up his belt, he remembered placing the missive he'd received from the Mac-Phersons in his dagger's sheath. But after removing his dagger, he found no missive. It must have fallen out, but he couldn't recall when or how. It mattered not because he wasn't ready to face the MacPhersons, and currently, he was more worried about his own clan and the Chattans.

He snatched a loaf of bread on his way out of the fief and shoved it into his satchel. On the journey to Tor, he'd appease his hunger. When he reached the postern of the bridge, someone grabbed him from behind and held his head in a grip. *Henny!* Shaw wouldn't be deterred and gripped the forearm of his assailant and used his foot to dislodge the man. The soldier fought to keep his balance and gripped him, and Shaw fell back against the wall before he was released.

Henny swayed on his feet but managed to remain standing. "Good morn, Laird, ye be alert this day. Are ye leaving the keep?"

"Aye, I am. Go and prepare my horse...and yours. Roust Trey if he hasn't awakened and meet me back here shortly."

Without a word, Henny sprinted off toward the barracks.

As Shaw stood there awaiting Trey and Henny, he whistled for Clovis. His gate watchman resided in a small cottage near the gate and within a moment, his door opened. Clovis meandered toward him with sleep still evident in his gaze. The man groused and rammed his spread fingers through his mangled hair. His eyes narrowed and his mouth taut in a slightly irritated pout.

"'Tis ye, Laird. I thought one of the soldiers whistled. I will have the gate opened for ye." He motioned to two of the soldiers who approached at his signal.

"I need ye to keep our gates closed this day. Allow no one within the keep or on the island."

Clovis flapped his hands at the guards and they shuffled back to their positions. "Ye be off, Laird? Will ye be gone long?"

"Aye, I am going to meet with Geoff Chattan and I do not want to worry about my clan whilst I am gone. None are to know my destination. Keep it to yourself." Shaw shifted his gaze as Trey and Henny walked toward him, holding the reins of their horses and his.

"I will see to our protection, Laird, whilst ye are gone," Clovis said and walked off toward the soldiers that guarded the gate.

When his commander-in-arms reached him, Shaw pulled him aside. "Send our fastest horsemen to our allies. Have them relate to the Campbell and the Mackenzie lairds that I might need their support. Ask them to meet me at the great glen later this morn."

Trey released the reins of his horse and turned, but stopped. "How many Mackintosh soldiers do ye want along, Laird? Should I roust Walen?"

"Clear the barracks. Leave ten men behind to help guard the gate and to watch over my family. The rest will ride with me to the glen. Walen can stay behind. I am sure he would appreciate some time to settle back before I take him on such a mission." Shaw took the reins of his horse from Henny and led him through the gate. As he sat waiting for his followers, he considered his plan.

A legion of riders called their call to arms as they rode past him on their mission to gather his allies. Shaw was unsure what to expect when he visited Geoff Chattan. He certainly wasn't about to set foot on his cousin's land without a well-embodied army at his back. If Geoff threatened him, he'd be prepared to face any peril. Though the Chattans were distant allies at present, in the past, they had been closer but that was when his father lived. His father had agreed with the political stances of the Chattans. Shaw did not, but he wouldn't interfere with his cousin's turmoil unless it was absolutely necessary.

Not only did the Chattans try to encroach on other clans' lands, but they also tried to forge alliances against the king. Since he'd given his fealty to Alexander, he couldn't abide by such a traitorous act. Shaw hadn't been approached by Rodick or his brother on such causes but they knew too well his friendship with Alexander. When his sovereign was made king, Shaw took a vow and swore his loyalty to him and there was naught to persuade him to abdicate his pledge.

When his men finally gathered beyond the gate, he led the procession toward Chattan land. Horses' hooves thundered on the dry ground and wafted dust into the air. He didn't stop but continued to ride hard and fast. He wanted to finish his chores and return before dark. With him, he hoped to bring home Sorsha's wee lass. If his cousin refused his request to return Sorsha's daughter, there would be hell to pay.

Along the route, his soldiers rode in sets of two and took up a long length of the roadway. On the approach to the Great Glen, Shaw slowed his pace. The Northwest Highlands opened to the Great Glen and its hillsides allowed rain to drain into the River Loy. Spring had yet to show its full effects and no buds had sprouted yet. The wind rolled over the tops of the hills and created a brisk chill but at least it wasn't raining. Still, it was a serene place and the optimal meeting place for his allies to congregate.

They dismounted and took a rest while they awaited the Campbells and the Mackenzies. No fires were lit, no camps were made, and all remained on alert. The Chattans were too close and their stronghold sat yonder behind the tallest hill. Hopefully, their sentry wouldn't take notice of them until Shaw wanted them to.

As soon as his allies arrived, Lairds Colin Campbell and Kenneth Mackenzie left their men in the flat land of a nearby field and marched toward him.

Shaw stood at the forefront of his brethren and welcomed his comrades with a smile and a slight wave. "I am gladdened ye came."

"Of course, ye called and we hauled our arses to get to ye. Here we are," Kenneth said, nodding the wavy locks of his reddish-brown hair. "What goes? Are we to war? My sword is at the ready."

"Possibly. Geoff Chattan asked for a meeting but he gave no reason. Did ye know that Rodick died recently?"

"Aye, we heard about his death. How did he die? Was it an accident?" Colin asked.

Shaw shrugged. "Hell if I know, but I will ask Geoff about it. I am gladdened ye came because I am unsure if I will be welcomed by my cousin. Two men will go with me but if there is trouble… Keep a lookout on the pennon by the rampart. If it falls, ye will be fair warned that I am in danger."

"Aye, aye. We will keep watch," Colin said, and held out his arm to stop him from leaving. "Why do we not just go in with ye? Better to be close at hand if he means to cross ye."

"I do not want to show force. There is something precious that I must retrieve from the Chattans and cannot endanger it." Shaw suspected that Geoff had a duplicitous reason for keeping Sorsha's daughter from her. Not only did he hope to fetch Gillian, but he hoped to glean information on what happened to Sorsha's husband. If Geoff had anything to do with his brother's death, Shaw wasn't sure how it would impact him, his clan, or his allies. "Keep alert and watch for the signal."

Kenneth pressed a hand on his shoulder. "Worry not, Shaw, we are here if ye need us and ye have our protection, as always. How long do ye plan to be?"

"Hopefully not long at all. But who knows what Geoff is up

to? I trust him not. I will meet with him and if he makes any threats, I will signal to my men to lower the pennon."

Colin shook his arm and grinned at him with shining blue eyes. His light hair was pulled back, making it easier to see the delight that shone on his comrade's face. Colin wasn't fond of the Chattans and he'd often voiced his abhorrence of Rodick and Geoff's leadership. He had no qualms about keeping them as rivals and longed to take his sword against them. "When the pennon drops, Shaw, we will come with haste."

He nodded, signaled to Trey and Henny to follow him, and retrieved his horse. On the short ride toward Tor's walls, Shaw kept quiet and remained alert in case of an ambush. The pathway that led to the gates of the castle always gave him an eerie feeling as if someone was watching them. Perhaps it was the Chattan sentry or someone more sinister. He shook the creepy sensation away and focused on the closed gates in the distance.

"Ye know, they say there is a benevolent spirit that resides here on this stretch of land," Henny said and chortled. "Mayhap we should offer up a prayer to God for our safe passage."

Trey laughed but then sobered. "Do ye believe that nonsense?"

"All I am saying is that there's a tale about the murder of a great king and witches… Ye have to admit there is a strange aura here. I am a wee bit superstitious when it comes to such things," Henny said gruffly.

Shaw quieted them with a scoff. "Let us stay focused, men. We near the gate." He strove to appear indifferent so the Chattans would not make more of his visit. At the gate, he stayed on his horse and called out to the watch.

"Shaw Mackintosh to see Geoff Chattan."

A man shouted, "Ye mean Laird Chattan."

"Aye, I suppose I do now. He bade me to come and should be expecting me."

The guard shuffled forward and directed others to help him. They unlatched the wooden beam securing the entrance and shifted the iron gate wide. "Aye, he told us to expect ye. Make your way to the castle. He should be within."

Even his horse seemed affected by the menacing atmosphere of Tor and slowed its pace. Shaw pressed its sides a little to encourage his horse to move forward. With his men riding on each side of him, he glanced at them to silently command their duty. Henny would leave him once they entered the castle. He would make his way to the rampart where the pennon hung to await the signal from Trey. His commander-in-arms would stand guard by the great hall's entry where Shaw's meeting with Geoff would take place.

Now to enact the plan.

In a short time, he entered the hall and found no one within. His boots thumped across the rush-covered floorboards until he reached the hearth where a fire had been banked. The peat sent warmth to him as he waited for his cousin's appearance. He didn't wait long for Geoff. His cousin crossed the hall and he stopped near him.

"Shaw, ye finally came, and 'tis good to see ye." He set a hand on his shoulder and smiled. "How long has it been since I laid eyes on ye? Too long. Come, sit with me for I have much to tell ye."

He ambled to the long table and sat on a bench. Geoff poured him a cup of ale and set it in front of him before taking the bench across from him. "Ye have my condolences on the death of your brother. I confess that I was shocked to receive such news. How did he die?"

Geoff grunted and sipped at his drink. Then held his cup and shook his head. "It is a sad affair, but och…someone entered the castle and murdered him in his bedchamber. His poor wife found him… We are still searching for the culprit but I am also trying to put to right our clan's wealth and stores. Rodick was a terrible leader. I hope to reconfirm our alliances, which is why I asked ye to come. The Chattans have long since been connected to the Mackintoshes. We wish to maintain our relations. After all, we are family, blood, and have always been."

Shaw stole a glance at the door to ensure Trey stood in view then reverted his gaze to Geoff. "There is no cause for us to end our alliance, so aye, if ye wish to reconfirm it, we shall continue as we have."

Geoff banged his cup on the table and grinned. "I am glad-dened to hear it. Now, tell me what took ye so long to come? I sent my missive ages ago."

"I, *ah...*" Shaw had to tread carefully and swallowed hard before he spewed out his news. How would Geoff take the news that he'd married his former sister-in-law? "I was called to Edinburgh by Alexander."

"And ye ran off to do the king's bidding? I'm not surprised to hear that, since ye always were Alexander's pet." Geoff scoffed and eyed him warily.

"We Mackintoshes support the king as well ye know. Of course, I left with haste when he called." Shaw hesitated in the telling and his shoulders tensed.

"What did he want?" Geoff picked up the nearby pitcher and refilled his cup. He offered to do the same for him, but Shaw shook his head.

"He wanted me to marry."

Geoff snorted a laugh and then bellowed with mirth. "Bol-locks, the king betrothed ye? Tell me that Alexander is not playing matchmaker for his followers now. No man should ever allow another to make such an important decision for him. A man's wife is sacred. Tell me ye did not agree to such a farce."

"I did... Sorsha and I were married over a fortnight ago."

"Sorsha?" Geoff's brows furrowed as the news rendered him shocked. "*Our* Sorsha? Lady Chattan? My own brother's wife? Tell me that is not so, Shaw." He struck the wood of the table with his fist and rose slightly.

Shaw noted his aggressiveness and pushed back the bench should he need to defend himself. With a quick glance at Trey, he waited to give the signal. In moments, the army that awaited beyond the Chattan walls would advance, if need be. "I cannot tell ye that because aye, the Sorsha that I married was the former Lady Chattan. Now she is Lady Mackintosh, my wife. I hope, as my ally, that we have your support." He purposely alluded to the fact that if Geoff didn't support them then he could forget any pact between them.

"Are ye telling me a wanker? Ye skelp me in the face with this news. Aye, for I am well galooted." Geoff straightened and set his hand on the hilt of the sword hanging by his side.

Shaw didn't retaliate by showing his willingness to fight with the man. He kept his hands on the tabletop and peered at his cousin. "I wish to keep our alliance, Geoff, and pray ye do not give me reason to retract it. If ye do not support my marriage to Sorsha then perhaps we should part ways now. Maybe ye do not need the Mackintosh army at your back, and have enough allies should ye be faced with war."

Geoff snatched his cup from the table and raised it high. "Then I shall offer my heartfelt *slàinte* on your marriage."

Shaw rose and lifted his cup and his cousin clinked his. "My thanks. Sorsha tells me that her daughter is still here in your care. I have also come here not only at your summons but to collect her. My wife misses Gillian."

"She is here. Has Sorsha shared with ye what happened the night she found Rodick murdered?" Geoff raised a brow but otherwise didn't show much regard for their conversation.

"Nay, she has not spoken much about it. About our marriage... do not hold it against her, Geoff, because Sorsha had no say in her marriage to me. The king commanded that she wed and she did her duty. Now, I mean to make her happy and the foremost thing I can do is to return her daughter to her."

"Aye, her daughter misses her and it is only right that she be returned to her mother. Speaking of family... Your sister is soon to arrive. She nears and should be here within a day or so. Will ye await Corliss? Ye are welcome to stay. Surely, ye wish to be reunited with her."

Shaw wasn't about to spend more time than necessary at the Chattan castle. He pressed his lips and considered Geoff's invitation. "I am beholden to ye for your offer, och I was away for some time recently. I should return to my land this day. Not only because I want to take Gillian to Sorsha, but there are clan matters I should attend to—as a laird now yerself, ye'll understand."

Geoff bowed his head. "Understandable, Shaw, for I know what ye mean. Since my brother's death, I have been called to remedy many clan matters. Very well, I will have the lass fetched for ye. Convey my greetings to Sorsha and remind her of what we spoke about before she left for the king's castle." He twitched a finger at a servant who lingered by the buttery. "Have Gillian brought to me, as well as her belongings. She will be taken to her mother."

The maidservant's mouth hung open and she nodded vigorously before running off to do the laird's bidding.

"I shall, and Sorsha will be happy to see Gillian again." As Shaw waited for the lass, he sipped his ale and found himself somewhat perplexed at Geoff's words. What did he want Sorsha to be reminded of? What had they spoken about before she left? He wasn't about to ask Geoff to elaborate on his baffling comment though. "If ye will, convey to my sister when she arrives that we are looking forward to her visit. Tell her to come home and not to dally."

"Ye know Corliss. She shall come when she is ready to and no sooner."

"True enough. My sister is stubborn. Och, I have missed her. She wrote to me about some distressing news of her home being burned out by the Cummings." Shaw studied his cousin's face for some recognition of his knowledge of the matter but Geoff remained aloof.

"She only relayed that she was stopping here on the way to your keep. Idris is a close comrade of mine and an ally. I suspect that he means to visit for a time since he is now landless. The poor man was routed from his land and his clan all scattered. But no matter, for I will send Corliss and her husband along as soon as possible."

It seemed that Idris was in league with Geoff. He'd been unaware of Idris Dunbar's close association with the Chattans and it gave Shaw pause. He wasn't overly fond of Idris, but his sister coveted their marriage. Her happiness meant a good deal to him and so he'd agreed to the betrothal. Now, realizing Idris's relations to the Chattans, Shaw needed to be mindful of his brother-in-law.

Shaw shifted on his feet and grew weary with waiting for the lass. The awkwardness of having to blather with Geoff made him uncomfortable and nothing more came to mind of what to say to him. He kept quiet and when sounds came from outside the great hall's entry, he turned and was stunned at the vision before him.

Gillian resembled her mother in her looks from her long, flowing brown hair to the rosy hue of her skin, to the shade of her bonny brown eyes. But Gillian was wee and couldn't be as high as his waist. Her wee steps drew her closer and her movement was graceful.

She quite enchanted him so much so that he'd almost forgotten to take a breath. Sorsha's daughter was beyond beautiful.

As she walked forward, she folded her hands in front of her and kept her gaze on Geoff. There was something in her gaze that drew his interest. Her brown eyes were widened and unblinking as if she tried to see everything around her. Gillian was afraid. Worse, as she drew closer, her fear was evident, not only in her eyes but also in the rigidness of her shoulders and gait. That a child of her age would fear Geoff suddenly angered him. Shaw wanted to chastise his cousin for scaring the lass.

When she reached them, she stopped and continued to keep her gaze fixed on Geoff. Shaw waited to hear her voice, knowing she'd sound as beautiful as the angels in heaven, but she said naught.

Geoff's voice was as gruff as if he addressed one of his men, not at all as gentle as one would use when speaking to a wee lass. "Gillian, this is Laird Mackintosh. Ye will go with him now."

That was all the explanation his cousin imparted. *What an arse.* The terrified child had to wonder why she'd go with him or who he was. Shaw knelt on his knee before her and she returned her gaze to him.

"I am Laird Shaw, lass, and am your ma's new husband. She wishes for your return to her and I am here to take ye…" For a brief moment, Shaw thought he noted a twitch of her lips as if she wanted to smile, but she remained staid and still.

"Ye be a good lass and listen to Laird Shaw," Geoff instructed. To him, he said, "The lass oft tells falsehoods so do not listen to her if she tells tales."

Shaw disbelieved Geoff would say such, especially about someone the man deemed insignificant. He was certain his cousin held no regard for his niece. Shaw motioned to the lass. "Come, Gillian, we shall leave. I am certain ye wish to see your mother and I know she is anxious to see ye too." He held out his hand but she made no move to take his. With a sigh, he took her hand and gently forced her to walk with him.

Before he left the hall, Geoff called out, "Remember our pact, Shaw. If I need your support, I expect ye to come and give aid."

He nodded but didn't retort. As quickly as he could, he left the castle and his men met him in the courtyard. Shaw mounted his horse and motioned to Trey to lift Gillian to sit before him. He set his arm around her small body to protect her and to keep her from falling.

"Your ma was worried for ye, lass. Are ye happy to be going to her?"

Gillian said nothing, but her wee body tensed.

Shaw wondered why she didn't reply but then he realized the lass didn't know him. Perhaps she was shy and rarely spoke at all. In time, Gillian would come to trust him. He'd make certain that she did, and one day, he hoped that she would be her winsome self.

CHAPTER TWELVE

B Y THE GREAT Glen, he slowed his mount and waited for Trey to approach. Shaw handed him Gillian before dismounting. When his feet hit the ground, his comrade thrust the wee lass back to him. Gillian's eyes remained closed, and she appeared to be sleeping. He held her and walked toward his allies who camped a short distance away. A fire lit the tree canopies and sent warmth to him as he neared.

"Set a tartan here for Gillian," he told Trey. His comrade complied with his request and grabbed another. Shaw set the lass on it and then covered her. He hoped to reach home before night completely darkened the sky but he had to give the account of his meeting to his allies.

"Someone get Laird Mackintosh a wee dram," Kenneth Mackenzie said.

Colin Campbell motioned to one of his men who handed him a cup and Shaw took it. He sat next to the lass and kept his voice low. "I am afraid that I called ye here for naught."

"Och, so your meeting went well then?" Colin asked.

"Aye." Shaw wasn't sure how much to divulge because he was sure Geoff spoke falsely about his brother's death and why he'd kept Sorsha's child in his care. There was definitely something amiss about both situations.

"What did he say?" Kenneth asked.

"He claims that someone entered the castle and murdered Rodick." Shaw took a sip of the drink and the weight of his meeting with Geoff eased. Now that he had Gillian, there were no more ties to the Chattans for Sorsha. His one wish was that he could retract his alliance with them, but it hadn't been the moment. His main focus had been to get away with the child. Instead, he'd bide his time and if or when he was called to honor it, he'd decide whether a war was worth his pact with his mother's relatives.

Colin scoffed and blew a harsh breath. "'Tis unbelievable. How could someone enter Tor without being noticed? What did ye witness when he rode through? Was his keep secure? How many guards were there?"

"None could get past the watch that I noted but that is not to say that they could do so easily when Rodick was laird. Who knows what the situation was then? Mayhap their security was lacking? Still, I am skeptical about it because Geoff did not explain except to say that someone stole inside and murdered his brother. He didn't seem unnerved or anxious for vengeance."

Trey grunted. "Surely the watch would have been alerted before the wrongdoer absconded after the deed. They would've easily apprehended the culprit."

"Och perhaps they did not discover Rodick's body in time and the assailant had already fled?" He shrugged. They may never know. "It matters not now. I thank ye both for coming," Shaw said to Colin and Kenneth. "And for giving me aid and awaiting me. I am beholden to ye. Should ye need me, just send word. I will always honor our pact but I cannot say the same of the Chattans. Something is amiss and I am not able to trust Geoff even though he is my kin."

His comrades inclined their heads. Colin said, "Then we shall be off."

"I want to get home afore the night grows too dark," Kenneth said, "Back to my warm bed."

His allies assembled their men and set off on the lanes in the direction of their lands. Shaw appreciated their support. They'd been allies for a good many years and he trusted them, not only in the face of war, but as comrades, and men.

"Will we leave right off?" Trey asked.

"Aye, I want to get home too. My wife is anxious to be with her wee lass, who needs to be put to bed. Get the men ready and we will leave shortly." Shaw was about to rise when he noticed Gillian's eyes were open and that she was staring at him. "Are ye hungry lass?"

She lowered her chin to avoid his gaze and didn't answer.

"'Tis time to go." Shaw rose and held out his hand to her. The moment was taut with apprehension as her gaze widened with fear but then she finally placed her hand in his. He helped her to rise, then took up the tartan from the ground and handed it to Henny.

Shaw kept his pace slow as he approached the horses. Gillian followed meekly and silently, carrying the tartan Trey had covered her with and with which she'd wrapped herself. When he reached his horse, he pulled the leftover bread he'd wrapped and saved from earlier that day. Without asking her again if she was hungry, he turned to her and pressed the bread into her hand. "Eat."

His men were ready to make for the lane and he could delay no further.

He quickly mounted his horse and shifted back to make room for the lass. Trey handed her to him and Shaw adjusted the tartan she held around her shoulders. "That will keep ye warm whilst we ride home."

As they began to ride, he let some of his men ride ahead and kept his distance from them. He whispered to Gillian, "I met your mother when she was a young lass. Now I am fortunate to be married to her. I vow, lass, to be a good da to ye. Ye may not understand what that means yet, but one day ye shall be happy."

For the next league or so, Gillian leaned back against him. Shaw was pleased because that meant she was letting her guard down. Suddenly he realized that he was now a father. Shaw wanted to be the kind of father that he'd had, an honorable man who held love in his heart for his children. He wanted his children to have as much faith in him as he had in his da. With a silent vow, he promised that Gillian would never go without—without care, love, or attention, and be secure in the knowledge that her new da would always take care of her.

With the motion of the horse, he thought perhaps Gillian had fallen asleep again but when his men shouted, she craned her head and he noted she was awake. She hadn't eaten a single bite of the bread and that sunk his shoulders a little. But the lane that led to the gates of his home lay ahead. He was never more gladdened to arrive. Sorsha was in for a surprise, one that might make her heart burst with joy.

Trey rode back from the front of the procession. "Riders sit outside the gate, Laird."

"Who are they?"

"'Tis the MacPhersons, Laird." This came from Henny.

Shaw passed by his soldiers and rode to the front of the procession, not stopping until he reached Laird MacPherson. His steed whinnied and pranced, as the lane was crowded with horses. The moment was rife with tension as his men pulled their swords free from their scabbards. His gates remained closed but the men who had remained at his home while he went on his excursion, assembled, and appeared ready to take up arms.

Alan MacPherson leaned forward in his saddle which shifted the long strands of his red hair over his shoulders. The man resembled a fierce warrior with the ornate plate of a shield across his chest and the bands of leather surrounding his arms. His beard was done in various knots and braids and though kempt was unruly at the same time. His blue eyes darkened with the man's forwardness when he grunted before saying, "I thought I would have to await ye forever."

"I just returned to my holding. Why are ye here?" Shaw wasn't pleased by the MacPherson's visit, especially when his eyes shifted to the lass on his lap. "Ye dare to come on my land without permission?"

"I had to come, Mackintosh. Who's the wee lass?"

Shaw ignored his question and didn't respond. With a glare, he expressed his ire at the man's brazenness. "As ye can see my soldiers are not pleased by this…foray."

"Ye gave me no choice since ye ignored my request for a meeting, I had to come. Can we meet now?" Alan grunted and tipped his head at the Mackintosh soldiers. "I see your men are ready for a fight, but I do not wish to appease them."

"There are things I must see to since I have only arrived. Ye may make camp in yonder woods and await me there. I will come and see ye when I can." Shaw motioned to Clovis, who opened the gate. He rode through and didn't look back.

His main concern was getting Gillian to her mother and then he'd probably have some explaining to do. After, he'd see to the MacPherson and find out why he'd come. Shaw had forgotten the missive he'd misplaced and wondered now if it indicated what was so important that Alan risked his soldiers' lives in coming without an invitation.

Shaw crossed the bridge and continued riding until he reached the keep. There, he slid from his mount and held out his arms to Gillian. She set her hands on his shoulders as he lifted from the horse. He didn't want to set her down and carried her inside. Her wee body was light and barely weighed as much as a goose. She held on to him tightly and Shaw supposed she was still fearful. "Now, let us find your mother. She will be overcome with joy when she sees ye."

Shaw entered the fief. Through the long hallway, he listened for voices but didn't hear any and hoped Sorsha hadn't retired for the night. At the great hall, he stopped by the entrance and saw her sitting in a chair by the hearth. Across from her, his mamo seemed to have fallen asleep.

"Sorsha…" Shaw hurried to her and kept his eyes trained on hers. "There is someone here to see ye." He set Gillian on her feet and gave a light nudge to her shoulder to press her forward.

She gasped and stood hastily. "Gillian!" Sorsha glanced from him to her daughter then back to him. "How? Gillian!" She hurried forth, fell to her knees, and took her daughter in her arms.

Shaw knelt next to them and set an arm around his wife's shoulder. She visibly shook and tears streamed down her cheeks. The moment tensed his heart at witnessing the anguish Sorsha must have felt in missing her daughter. Now she couldn't speak and swayed with Gillian in her hold. Gillian's little arms wrapped around her mother's neck and tears shimmered in her beautiful brown eyes.

He pressed a hand over Sorsha's back. "I shall give you a moment to be together."

He rose and moved to the hall's entrance, where he stopped and looked back at the scene before him. He wasn't an overly sentimental man, but the sight of a mother holding her wee lass nearly buckled his knees with emotions. As he traversed the hallway, he was now gladdened that he'd retrieved the lass. Gillian belonged to her mother and him.

Back outside, he ambled toward the gate and noticed none of the MacPhersons remained. He whistled for Walen who stood afar speaking with his brother near the training field. His comrade trotted to him but said not a word when he moved to stand next to him.

"I am going to meet with MacPherson and thought ye might want to come."

"Damned right I would. So would Trey and Henny. There's a group of our soldiers who insisted they come along too because we trust not the MacPhersons."

Shaw nodded and motioned to Trey. His overzealous soldiers barreled off the training field and boisterously whooped as they marched on the lane. He found it almost comical and he didn't want to be the one to break the news that there probably wasn't going to be a scuffle. If the MacPhersons wanted to fight, they would have already used their swords by the gate.

The thumping of his soldiers' footsteps rumbled behind him as he made his way into the woods. About half a league away, the MacPhersons had made camp and various fires lit the woods. Dusk had come and gone by the time he found them. Shaw wanted to hurry and get the meeting done so he could return to Sorsha.

Alan MacPherson signaled to his men to stay back when Shaw approached. They stood before the encampment with hostility in their gazes, their swords drawn, and with a show of intimidation in their stances. Shaw realized he needed to send the MacPhersons on their way at the soonest before blood was shed.

"Alan, come, walk with me, and ye can tell me why ye have come all this way."

Alan gave a quick look at his men and shook his head before he stepped forward. "There is to be no arms betwixt ye and the Mackintosh soldiers," he said to his men and then hurried to catch up to Shaw. "So ye did not get my missive?"

Shaw decided to be honest with the man. "I received it, och, I misplaced it before I could read what you'd written. Why have ye come? We are neither rivals nor allies…"

"Nay, we are not but that can change… Nevertheless, I have come to tell ye that the Chattans have been up to no good. I know ye are related and aligned, och ye may want to be made aware that—"

He couldn't allow the man to continue. "Ye are allied with the Chattans, so explain to me why ye have come to tell me about your rift with them?"

"We are no longer allies. There have been rumors and with Rodick now dead, I trust not Geoff." Alan seemed to hesitate about telling him what the problem was.

"For Christ's sake, Alan, spit it out. I do not have all day." Shaw's impatience caused him to fist his hands and scoff at the man.

Alan narrowed his eyes, apparently assessing his words carefully before speaking them aloud. Finally, he shrugged, as if satisfied with how he decided to explain. "As ye know the Dunbars' land was ransacked by the Cummings recently."

"Aye, my sister wrote to me and told me so. What has the Cummings to do with the Dunbars?" Shaw ceased walking when he reached a small clearing beyond the hearing of the soldiers who stood in wait for them.

"The Cummings detest the Dunbars but that is not what concerns me. Ye see, the Cummings had no reason to attack the Dunbars—unless they were bidden to do so by the Chattans."

Shaw drew a resigned breath. The fact that the Chattans might have been behind the Dunbar Clan attack did not sit well. Geoff was supposedly allied with the Dunbars. Why would he have the Cummings attack his ally? It made no sense. "And ye now worry that your clan will be next? Is that it?"

Alan nodded his head vehemently. "What is to stop them from taking over the area completely? I am not aligned with many clans but am reconsidering an alliance with the Camerons. I thought it best ye knew."

"Why the Camerons?" Shaw had his own reasons for wanting to forgo his alliance with the Chattans but he wanted to know what troubled Alan.

"The Camerons have made it known they will go against the Chattans if they try to overtake their land. We must band together if we need to confront Geoff. He is far more brazen than his brother ever was. Have ye heard whether he wants to invade us?"

Shaw understood Alan's concern and that of the Camerons. The Chattans were ruthless when it came to land and territory. "I spoke recently with Geoff and he made no mention of an alliance with the Cummings clan. Besides, his comrade, Idris Dunbar's home was recently sacked by the Cummings. If this is true then I believe Geoff would've been ireful with the Cummings for attacking one of his allies."

Alan groaned. "'Tis something to consider... Perhaps the

Cummings are not aligned with the Chattans as is rumored. Still, the Camerons have vocally proclaimed they will not suffer any slight by your family and I would do well to think of that when and if the time comes to pick a side."

Shaw suspected that might be a situation that warranted thought but for now, no decision had to be made. "I will let ye know if I hear any news about Geoff's plans or of his involvement in using the Cummings to overtake the Dunbars. We shall see if he retaliates against the Cummings for their ill-fated deeds against the Dunbars."

"Aye, we will indeed. I shall leave ye then. Send word when ye have any news."

Shaw stopped Alan from walking away by grabbing his arm. For as aged as Alan was, his arm was solid and firm. "I bid ye to remember that just because my mother was related to the Chattans does not mean that I am in league with them. I may or may not take a side when the time comes, och that does not mean that I am against anyone. I seek to maintain peace if such a thing is possible."

Alan chortled. "Peace, bah, there will never be peace here in the Highlands as long as the Chattans make idle threats and use other clans against their own allies. Why, 'tis sacrilege."

Shaw marched away and whistled for his men. They walked with haste back to their gates and dispersed, some walking to the barracks, some to the fields, and some toward the kitchen. He continued onward, letting the night air allay him. After such a trying, difficult day, he needed a bit of solace.

The gentle breeze dislodged the locks of his hair from its tie but he made no move to right it. Oncoming night sent a dismal mien about the land, bringing with it shadows and the expanse of the star-speckled sky. When he'd calmed enough, he would find Sorsha and relate to her how he'd come to have her daughter on his return. It would take a bit of explaining.

Down the lane near a rocky hillside, a small chapel was made in the hollowed-out earth. A stoned archway led to the quiet place where he'd often reflected on important matters or when he needed the guiding hand of God. But he was surprised to see Sorsha leaving the chapel. She stopped when she noticed him approaching and stood outside the wooden doorway to await him.

"Shaw…"

"Sorsha, love… I am gladdened ye are here because I wanted to speak to ye privately."

"Mamo gave me the key to the chapel and told me that I could use it whenever I wanted to pray. I hope you don't mind that I—"

"Of course not, lass. The chapel is for all within the Mackintosh clan and is not usually kept locked. I am gladdened that ye find it as comforting as I do."

"You do?"

He nodded. "Aye, not many make use of it because the chapel is rather small but I often find peace there. Now tell me, what think ye about your daughter's homecoming?"

Her smile widened and she pressed him back against the door. "I have never been so surprised. How…When did you…How did you get Geoff to release Gillian?"

"It was not too difficult. I told him that we'd married and he spoke of our alliance. He had to know that if he wanted to keep our support, he would have to release Gillian."

"I…do not know what to say and am eternally grateful."

"It is my duty, Sorsha, to protect ye and our daughter." He tilted her head back and set a gentle kiss on her lips. "Aye, the day I wed ye, Gillian became my daughter. I mean to see that she is protected."

"I prayed for so many days that she would be safe until…"

"Ye will tell me now…and I will hear the truth, Sorsha, what happened at Castle Tor, to Rodick, and why Geoff kept your daughter from ye. If I am to protect not only your daughter but ye as well, I must know the truth." He felt her sigh when her body shifted. Shaw pressed her back so he could see her eyes and took hold of both her hands. "There should always be honesty betwixt us."

"You are right. Of course, I shall tell you."

Shaw put his arm around her and pulled her against him. He hoped to comfort her, especially when she peered off and wouldn't look at him.

Her voice came quietly, "On the day of the winter festival, I took Gillian for a day of merriment. On our return, I put her to bed and heard Rodick arguing with someone in his chamber. When I opened the door, I saw Geoff strike him with a dagger. Rodick fell and I tried to get to him to give him aid, but it was too late. He only lasted a moment before he succumbed. Geoff forced me to keep his secret by taking Gillian away. He told me that if I bespoke one word of what happened that night, I would never see my child again. Of course, I never spoke of it to anyone."

"Not even the queen? I know that ye are good friends…"

"Nay, I told no one. I could not tell Margaret and only divulged that my husband had died. She added my name to the marriage list and I'd only found that out when I arrived. Before I left Geoff proposed marriage as a way to keep his brother's murder from becoming known. If not for the king's list, I would have had no choice but to become his wife."

Shaw's eyes burned with anger. The man was a knave, not only because he used a child to gain Sorsha's agreement to keep his vile secret but also because he was going to force her to wed him. If he'd gained his wish, Geoff could have easily thwarted Sorsha by declaring coverture and she'd be unable to testify against him should the sheriff or other lawful entities charge him. Now his entreaties to remind her of her vows to him and the warning not to listen to whatever Gillian told him made sense.

"Shaw, please… Say something."

He held her close and leaned his head against hers. "I make this vow here and now, Sorsha, that ye will never have to contend with that knave. Not only do ye have my protection, but every living, breathing Mackintosh soldier will guard ye and our daughter." He didn't tell her that he was sure Geoff wouldn't give up such a lovely woman as Sorsha or her daughter so easily and he wondered what his cousin would do to win her back.

Would he overtake his clan and try to kill his followers? The threat was there, real, and certain. He needed to make sure his walls, clan, home, and family were secure and guarded against his blackhearted cousin. Shaw would direct his guards to allow no one entrance and ensure that he kept his vow to Sorsha to keep her safe.

CHAPTER THIRTEEN

THERE WAS MUCH to make ready in preparation for the May Day celebration that would take place that day. Sorsha had been up well before sunrise and with the aid of Edra and Enid, the hall was looking quite festive. Fortunately, the children had remained sleeping while she hurried through her tasks. Sorsha smoothed her hand over the tablecloth she'd placed on a serving table near the buttery and admired the fine cloth.

She heard someone approaching and turned to see Clovis standing nearby, shifting shyly from foot to foot. He was confident with Shaw but seemed to feel out of place here in the fief. Still, he cleared his throat and said, "Milady, I am sorry to disturb ye, och the laird left before I could stop him. He went to sanctify the fields with a handful of soldiers."

She smiled at him. "You are not disturbing me, Clovis. Good morn. What does 'sanctify the fields' mean?"

He chuckled. "The priest came early this morn to bless the peat. 'Tis when the head of each family carries burning peat around the fields and crops to bless them. The smoke carries God's blessing and ensures good crops. When the men return, they will put the peat in their hearths to bless their homes and bring good fortune to them."

"Oh, that is lovely. Was there something you needed?" She set a bowl on the table and placed a small cloth inside it. Once

Edra brought the bread, she'd cover it to keep it warm.

Clovis cleared his throat. "Milady Maven has gone to the graves again. Usually, the laird goes to retrieve her but since he's gone…"

"I shall go. Worry not, Clovis." Sorsha heard the patter of footsteps on the stairs. The children were awake! Their sweet faces stared at her as she approached the exit of the keep where Mamo's cloak hung on a peg. "Ah, you finally awakened. Come, you shall eat your morning fare in the kitchen with Edra while I go and retrieve Mamo."

Clovis bowed to her and hurried from the keep.

Sorsha took her daughter's hand and then Luthor's. "Let us find something to fill those bellies of yours." She grabbed her cloak and Mamo's from their pegs and shuffled the children through the doorway into the kitchen. But there was no one inside. Both Edra and Enid were likely seeing to the May Day celebration chores.

It left her in a quandary. She needed to take care of Shaw's grandmother but couldn't leave the children alone in the kitchen. So she lifted Gillian onto a stool and did likewise to Luthor before filling two bowls with pottage and setting a bowl before each of them and bidding them to eat.

As she watched her daughter, Sorsha was saddened. Gillian had always been a quiet child but now she was even more severe. She didn't smile and no mirth shone in her eyes. The lass hadn't yet spoken since her return to her.

Sorsha despaired at what to do about it. Gillian had witnessed her father being killed and Sorsha hadn't been allowed to console her. Then the child had been taken from her and probably left on her own without a tender hand to guide her. Was there a way to bring her daughter back from that traumatic chaos?

Luthor stuck his hand into his bowl of pottage and quickly swiped a handful of it across Gillian's face. He laughed and wiped his hand over his tunic. Sorsha picked up a cloth and tried to clean up the mess, mostly on Gillian's face. Her daughter made no sound or showed any shock.

"Luthor, why…? Why would you do such a thing?"

The lad shrugged his shoulders, picked up a spoon, and dipped it into the bowl, intent on eating whatever remained of his pottage. Sorsha wasn't sure if she should punish him or even what the punishment would be. The last thing she wanted to do was to frighten the lad.

What was obvious was that Gillian paid no attention to the lad. Perhaps he was trying to incite her to speak. If that was so, it was a kindhearted thing to do though his actions weren't very kind at all.

The kitchen door opened and Niahm entered. "Good morn, Milady."

"Please, Niahm, we said we would not be so formal. You are my dear friend now and shall call me Sorsha." She paused, "Right now, I need your favor."

Niahm pressed her long red strands of hair behind her shoulder and smiled. "Of course, I shall be gladdened to help ye."

"Will you watch the children whilst I go and retrieve Shaw's mamo from the graves? Clovis told me that he was unable to get Shaw to do it before he left and he is stuck at the gate on duty."

Niahm nodded but as she peered at the children, her expression crumpled. Before Sorsha knew what was happening, her friend broke down into a mass of tears. Sorsha wasn't sure what she'd said to upset her but the lass was troubled. She hurried to her friend's side and guided her onto a vacant stool.

"Sit and be calm." Sorsha looked about for a clean cloth and found one draped over the side of a bucket of what appeared to be fresh water. She dampened the cloth, then pressed it to her friend's face to wipe away her tears and over the back of her neck. "That should make you feel better. Tell me! What's wrong? Are you ailing? Why are you weeping?"

"The children…" Niahm pressed her hands over her face and continued weeping.

Sorsha set her arm around her to offer comfort. "What about

the children?" She glanced at them but Gillian and Luthor paid no attention to them while they ate their pottage.

"I… How can this be happening? I thought I'd done what was needed, but now…Oh, I cannot be a mother! What am I to do?"

A dawning struck her. "Oho…you are going to *be* a mother."

"That is what the midwife tells me."

She hugged Niahm and pressed her hand over her pretty hair. "I am sorry, Niahm. Have you spoken to Walen?" She knew that he was the child's father.

"No. There is no reason to. He will not marry me."

"How can you be sure if you don't speak to him?"

Her friend sniffled. "I don't know."

Sorsha frowned. "I know you love him and he loves you, doesn't he?"

Niahm shrugged. "He says he does."

"Well then, 'tis easy enough. We shall make sure he marries you…" Sorsha gave her hand a reassuring squeeze. "I am pleased by this and we shall talk more about it. Right now, I must go and get Mamo from the graves. Can you watch the children until I return?" When Niahm nodded, Sorsha turned to the children. "Be behaved and do not give Mistress Niahm any trouble. Finish your morning fare. I shall return quickly."

Sorsha hurried out of the kitchen and practically trotted to the gate; her dash shortened her breath and made her heart pound. She waved to Clovis as she passed. By the time she reached the graves, she was gasping and had to bend over with her hands on her knees from the exertion of running so far. As she did, she noticed that there was a guard trailing her and reasoned that Clovis must have sent him for her protection since she had left the gates.

As she straightened, she scanned the cemetery for the elder woman and spotted her lying on the ground, her long hair spread like a splash of silver against the new green grass covering the graves. With slower steps, Sorsha approached Mamo and knelt next to her. For a moment, she thought she might not be breathing. She touched her lightly on the shoulder and Mamo's eyes fluttered open and Sorsha gasped. Shaw's grandmother appeared briefly confused before she stretched a little and yawned.

"Good morn, Mamo. Here, let us get you warm. 'Tis a chilly morn." Sorsha placed her fur-lined cloak around the old woman's shoulders, noting her frailty. Shaw was right to be concerned; it wasn't good for her to be lying on the cold ground in the night air. "We should get you back to the fief." She helped the lady to rise by gently taking her hands and pulling her upright.

The guardsman stood a good distance from them and couldn't overhear what they said. Sorsha was gladdened because she hoped Mamo would confide in her.

"I...I am sorry to trouble ye, lass. Somehow... Well, I sometimes end my nights here." Mamo appeared embarrassed.

"You did not trouble me at all. Why do you come here? This is such a sad place." Sorsha stuck out her arm. "Hold on to me whilst we walk back."

"This place is dear to my heart. 'Tis where all those I love are resting. They await me."

"I hope you do not plan to join them soon."

Mamo's eyes lowered. "Every day it is my greatest hope, but alas, here I remain."

She clutched the old woman's arm tightly. "And gladdened I am because it would distress Shaw to lose you...and me as well. I have never had a grandmother. Mine passed before I was born."

"I shall be happy to oblige ye, lass, and will be your mamo."

"Mamo, that makes my heart happy. Let us return." She called over her shoulder to the guardsman and said, "Can you take Mamo's arm too. The ground is treacherous here." He did as she asked and held onto Mamo's elbow. As Sorsha traipsed the hilly walk back to the fief, she kept quiet.

"So many are out and about," Mamo said when they reached the gate.

"The festivities are soon to begin. All are excited." Sorsha realized the falsehood she'd spoken then because not all were excited. Gillian was far from jubilant about celebrating May Day. Unlike most children, her daughter had never been fond of festivals. If only her daughter would smile and laugh again. If only she would speak to her.

$\mathcal{S}$

THE FIELDS WERE blessed with the smoke from the peat and the pleas for abundant crops. Many farmers and the families who worked on the land joined the men in celebration by raising their cups to God and in hopeful prosperity. Shaw had left his warm bed and the sweet body of his wife early that morn to attend the duty but he'd wanted to stay put and to perhaps spend more time loving Sorsha. Unfortunately, the important mission called to him and he spent the day preparing for the day's festivities.

Before they sought the boughs to adorn the doorways and window casements of the fair lasses of their clan, there was much to see to. Shaw always delighted in the rituals and meaning of the Beltane festival. He'd always beheld family and the birth of bairns as the foremost important responsibility of his clan. One day, his clan would swell in numbers and would rival any of the clans in the north. At least, that was his aspiration.

Shaw sat beneath a copse of trees whose leaves had yet to sprout and the sun shone through its thick branches. He watched those who continued to walk the field with wads of peat, whipping them to and fro and sending smoke over the dry earth. Soon, crops would flourish and bring them sustenance, food for their horses and other animals, and with hope extra coins to add to their coffers.

Walen approached and sat next to him. He tore into a round-ed loaf of bread and handed him half. "Ye must be hungry."

"Aye. I did not eat before I left this morn. My thanks." He took a bite of the bread and even though it was hard, it tasted good. Shaw washed it down with a chug of ale from a flask he'd retrieved from the satchel that hung by his side. There was only enough to wet his throat and he groused about it. "Bollocks, there's none left."

Trey lingered nearby and joined them. He pressed a cup of ale into his hand. "Laird, here, I brought extra ale. Our clan has not been this gleeful for a long time. This night we will celebrate by dancing around the fires. I look forward to the gaiety."

He chuckled to himself because by then most would have imbibed and the dancing would be rowdy. Shaw lifted his cup. "To ye both for sticking with me and protecting our clan."

They raised their cups and drank deeply.

"Ye know we have yet to select a May Queen. Perhaps there is someone we can encourage to join us in the song of the Goddess?" Shaw's question was pointed at Walen but his comrade groaned under his breath.

"Aye, brother," Trey said with a chuckle. "There is a woman who would make the perfect May Queen and perhaps a Beltane bride?"

Walen scoffed and flapped his hand at them. "What say ye? Cosh, I suspect ye are going to try to get me to admit my feelings for the lass?"

"Do ye not think it is about time ye married? She will not await ye forever, and besides, she is probably the bonniest lass in the Highlands. Ye be a fortunate man to win the heart of that lass." Trey grinned and took his flask, refilling their cups.

"I beg to differ, Trey, for I married the fairest lass in the High-lands," Shaw said and tried to sound outraged but it did not affect his comrades.

"Och, ye did, Laird. I meant the fairest lass besides our lady," Trey quickly supplied.

"Perhaps, Walen, if ye offered to be the May King, Niahm would agree? This night is for coupling with our loves. Will ye not offer her marriage? I fear if ye do not soon, ye will lose her and it would not bode well…" Shaw ceased his speech because he had never pushed his comrade toward marriage before. Still, it was a good thought.

"I have rethought my stance on marriage recently. Niahm is a worthy woman but I am…" Walen took the cup from his brother and drank before continuing, "unsure if I am worthy of her. She is a kindhearted woman and deserves better than me."

Shaw shoved his shoulder. "Of course, ye are worthy of her. She could do no better because I know no more honorable man than ye, Walen. Ye have been my comrade for a long time and always supported me. Now, I give ye my support. I will tell the priest to make himself ready to perform the sacrament."

Walen didn't protest or offer a rebuke. "I suppose, then, I am getting married this night."

They lifted their cups in congratulatory cheer and sipped at their ale.

Shaw laughed and said, "To the May King, may he reign supreme this night."

Trey bellowed with laughter and Walen groaned.

"We should get back so ye can propose to your bride," Trey said and rose.

Shaw enjoyed a leisurely walk back to the fief. He got caught up thinking about what else needed to be done before the bonfires would be lit. Then all would join the revelry.

A sudden blow caused Shaw to land with a thud on the ground and he grunted from the force and groaned as pain throbbed in his shoulder. He shut his eyes briefly but when he opened them, he scoffed at the feeling of cold metal pressed against his throat.

"Damnation, Henny, get the hell off me." Shaw shoved his comrade's chest and Henny fell back a step.

Henny's eyes crinkled with laughter as he pulled back his arm, and re-sheathed his dagger. When he stood, he held out his hand to help him rise. Shaw got to his feet, brushed himself off, and glared at his soldier. Yet he couldn't be irritable with Henny. It wasn't his soldier's fault that he wasn't paying attention this time and had left himself open to an ambush.

"Ye were not ready, Laird." Henny tapped his head. "Something keeping ye unawares?"

"By my faith, Henny, aye, something like that." But Shaw wasn't about to admit to his soldier that he'd let his guard down.

"Ye never know when an evildoer will strike, Laird. Best be ready for attack at all times."

"I did not know on this day of all days that ye would continue your efforts." Shaw moaned and rubbed his shoulder, suspecting that he would feel the ache for the next day or two. "Go on with ye and get back to your duty." Before Henny walked away, he called to him. "And my thanks, Henny, for the reminder."

"Every day, Laird, is the perfect day for the reminder. Beltane or nay..." Henny whistled as he marched off and disappeared beyond the trees.

Shaw continued toward his keep, crossed the bridge, and gave a silent signal to Clovis. Seeing his brethren prepare for the night's festival brought him a sense of pride. His clan delighted in participating in celebrations. They always ate too much, drank to excess, and danced well into the next day.

His happiness for Walen lightened him too and he looked forward to his friend's wedding. That was, until he spotted Sorsha sitting on the wall outside the keep. Her face reflected her grimness with a small pout to her usually bonny lips. He approached her.

"'Tis almost time to light the fires. What are ye about out here by yourself?"

Sorsha rose and embraced him. Her hold of him told him that something wasn't right but until she told him what, he couldn't imagine what troubled her so. Instead of pressing her, he wrapped his arms around her and pulled her close.

After a long moment, she pulled back. "I have had a day."

Shaw motioned to the wall and bade her to sit with him. He made sure there was enough room for her and took her hand. Sorsha sat and kept her gaze on his face. He smiled to hopefully alleviate whatever bothered her.

"I am worried."

"I can tell," he said and bumped her shoulder with his. "Tell me what ye are so worried about? For we are blessed this day and shall celebrate."

"I do not feel like celebrating because…" Sorsha squeezed his hand and nodded. "Well, I shall tell you. Poor Niahm is…*ah*, she told me that she is expecting a bairn. I suspect who the father is but there is no way to persuade him to take her as a wife. What should we do?"

Shaw tilted his head and almost laughed. "*Ah…* Ye see, sweet wife, there is no need to despair because I have it on good authority that Walen plans to propose to Niahm this day. When the fires are lit, the priest will bless their union. All will be well."

"However did you work that miracle?" Her smile was splendid.

"Trey and I forced Walen to admit that he loves Niahm and this is the perfect day to form a marriage union for they'll be blessed by God and our ancestor's Goddess herself."

She clapped her hands and her eyes shone briefly until she lowered her face. "There is something else…"

"Are ye worried about Gillian?"

Sorsha sighed heavily and nodded. "I am. She was always a serious lass even before… Seeing her father murdered has affected her and I was not there to comfort her in her time of need. I fear she will never speak again. How can I help her?"

Shaw pulled her to stand before him and set his hands on her hips. "She will speak when she is ready. Och, I know she must have been distraught because of what she saw and that ye were taken from her. Once she realizes that she is safe and ye are here for her, she will come around. Our daughter will find joy, I make that promise to ye."

"Our daughter? I like the sound of that, Shaw." Sorsha used the back of her finger to wipe away an errant tear.

"Aye, our daughter. When I took her from Tor, I made a vow

that I would be a good father to her, that I would protect her, and that she would find happiness. I meant my promises, Sorsha, and will do everything I can to make them certain."

She pressed her mouth to his and he felt her tremble as he wrapped his arms around her.

"You are a good husband, Shaw, and I am in awe of your goodness."

He chuckled and leaned his forehead against hers. "I am only good because ye are here with me. Ye make me a better man." The honesty of his words somewhat humbled him.

"I'm concerned about Luthor though. I am unsure whether he is trying to befriend Gillian or if he means to torment her. Earlier in the kitchens, he swiped half his pottage on her face."

He tried not to laugh but felt the edges of his mouth tug as he resisted. "He did? Why would the lad do that? I suppose I should have a talk with him about wasting food and being a good example for the lass."

"Perhaps we should allow him to train with the younger lads for a short time each day. That might keep him occupied and out of trouble." Sorsha pressed her hand to his face and smiled.

He leaned into her touch and breathed in her bonny scent. "Now, is there anything else that worries ye?

"Only one more thing… I found your grandmother at the graves again. Clovis told me that you had left before he could tell you that she left the holding early this morn. I worry, Shaw, that she will die there by the graves, alone, cold, and… She is such a good woman."

He took a deep breath at hearing her last worry. "Aye, it concerns me as well. Och, there is naught we can do but to ensure she is recovered each time and returned to the keep."

"I will do my best to keep watch of her, especially when you are attending your duties."

"That is all I can ask, love. Just be sure to take a guard with ye. We know not what Geoff plans or if he is angered that ye are now my wife and not his."

She scrunched her lips at his request. "Clovis sent a guard with me when I fetched Mamo earlier. Geoff will not retaliate, will he?"

Shaw shrugged. "It matters not. Geoff is more concerned with keeping me as an ally rather than a rival for now so we should not be too concerned. Come, let us join in the festivities. We will eat, sing, and dance because I have more to celebrate than I ever have."

Shaw held Sorsha's hand and guided her along. Outside of their home, the children awaited them with Enid by the entrance. His gaze lingered on their wee faces and Shaw was astounded that he was now responsible for them. He'd always held himself accountable for all the members of his clan but with his direct family standing near to him, an extreme sense of protectiveness overtook him.

Sorsha took Gillian's hand and together they walked ahead of him and greeted the other women of the clan. He hung back a little and stopped Luthor from proceeding.

"Lad, Lady Sorsha told me what ye did to Gillian earlier... Why did ye do that?" He knelt in front of the lad and watched his face for a sign of honesty.

Luthor swiped his tunic sleeve across his face. "Laird, I...I was trying to get her to speak. She does not talk. Why does she not?"

He leaned his arm on his bent leg and nodded. "She witnessed something so terrible that she does not wish to speak." Shaw ruffled the lad's hair and smiled. "So ye thought, by doing something rash it would evoke her to respond? Is that it?"

Luthor's head bobbed. "If I make her mad, she might talk."

He had to give credit to the lad because it was a fair idea. "Gillian has had a difficult time, lad, and shall speak when she is ready. Try to be understanding with her."

"Do I gots to be kind, Laird? If I do, she will not speak to me then."

Shaw chuckled and nodded. "Aye, do not worry about the lass. But being kind would gain her friendship and since ye will live here with us, 'tis important."

"More important than getting her to speak?"

He grunted at the lad's question. Maybe he should allow the children to go on as they had and not intervene. Shaw wasn't too knowledgeable about children and why they did the things they did. But Luthor was shrewder than he'd thought.

After a quick supper, the clan gathered near the largest fire. The priest performed a short liturgy and sacrament of marriage for Walen and Niahm and other couples wishing to join in matrimony. All the clan celebrated the unions with cheers and shouts of glee. Shaw kept his gaze on Sorsha and the serene joy in her eyes as she witnessed the weddings with him. He was gladdened too for Walen and hoped his friend found the happiness that he had.

Before long, Sorsha mentioned putting the children to bed and took them inside the keep. The sky darkened until the firelight shone on the faces of his clan. Dancing began and when Sorsha returned, he snatched her in his arms and forced her to skip in line with the others. Her merry laughter was infectious and he found himself laughing too.

The spring rites were the beginning of newfound happiness for them all. Shaw gave his silent appreciation for the blessings and stopped in the center of the dancers to kiss his wife. Whoops and hollers caused him to stop his kiss and the shine in his wife's eyes was well worth the teasing banter from his clansmen.

CHAPTER FOURTEEN

FOR THE PAST sennight, Sorsha had awakened and found Shaw next to her. Many mornings, she was rousted with sweet kisses and delightful morning romps. This morning, she opened her eyes to find her husband slumbering and took more than a moment to gaze at his handsome face, the hardness of his chest, and the waviness of his long, brown hair. How had she been so blessed to be married to such a man?

The bedchamber door burst open and Gillian crossed the room in haste. Sorsha sat up and wondered what the trouble was. Fear widened her daughter's eyes. With her arms spread, she invited Gillian into the bed with her.

"What is wrong? Did you have a bad dream?"

No answer. Sorsha sighed because Gillian still hadn't spoken. She'd given considerable thought as to why her daughter didn't speak or wouldn't. With dread, she wondered if perhaps Gillian feared her. Maybe the lass hadn't seen Geoff strike Rodick but only seen her removing the dagger from him. Did that mean that Gillian thought she'd murdered her father? Lord, she prayed that wasn't so, but until the lass spoke, there was no way of knowing.

A shadow appeared on the floorboard by the open door. She smiled smally suspecting who might be lingering there. "Come, Luthor, and tell me what happened."

Shaw stretched and set an arm over her waist in his reach to touch Gillian's hair.

"Good morn, fair lassies. 'Tis early. What is everyone doing up so early?"

Luthor finally made it to the bedside and peered at the floor. A dawning must've struck her husband when he grunted.

"Oh, I see now… Luthor, did ye do something to frighten Gillian?"

Luthor's head bobbed.

"Come, sit upon the bed and we shall talk about it." Sorsha shifted and placed Gillian between her and Shaw. Luthor crawled onto the bed and sat at the end.

"I did not mean to scare her. Och 'twas just a wee mouse."

Sorsha glanced at Shaw briefly then returned her gaze to Luthor. "A mouse, you say? Where was this wee mouse?"

"I put it in 'er bed. 'Twas just a wee mouse but it would not hurt her. I thought she would yell or something akin but she did not make a sound." Luthor sighed and wouldn't look at either her or Shaw. His wee face remained grim.

Sorsha felt bad for him because he did seem to want to help Gillian. And Shaw had explained what the boy had disclosed about hoping to assist Gillian in speaking.

"I know you were trying to help but scaring her with vermin in her bed is wrong, and ye know that. Ye know, lad, ye must go and find the mouse even if it takes ye all day. Remove it from the chamber and set it free outside. Ye will not be getting any morning fare until ye do so." Shaw sat up, tilted his head at the lad, and pointed at the door. "Go on and we will have a talk later."

"But, Laird, it weren't Squeak's fault. I put him on the bed. I've had Squeaks for a long time. He is only a wee field mouse. If I let him go," Luthor said and sniffled, "I…won't ever see him again. He will run away." The boy paused. "I made a house for him in an old bucket."

Sorsha empathized with the lad. "I think that sounds like a good house for a mouse to live in—as long as you promise not to frighten Gillian with Squeaks again. What do you think, Shaw? Is that not agreeable?"

A quick smile widened her husband's face but he hid it readily enough. "Aye…aye, but if ye find the mouse, ye will still need to be punished for trying to scare the poor lass. I shall tell the stable master to expect ye."

"Can I have my morning fare?" Luthor asked and shimmied to the edge of the bed.

"Aye, after ye find yer mouse. Then report to the stables. Go on," Shaw said.

The lad disappeared quickly but left the bedchamber door open.

Sorsha set Gillian on the floor. "I suppose I should rise and make sure Luthor's mouse has a home and that the children eat a good helping. He'll probably hurry to the stables and forget to eat if I'm not there. I have to wonder if his pranks are more than an attempt to scare Gillian into speaking. After all, lads are always up to mischief."

Shaw shook his head but she saw a flicker of humor shine in his eyes. "I should get up too because I promised to meet Trey and go over the soldier's schedule."

Before he left, Shaw leaned over the bed and kissed her face. Then he pressed a hand on Gillian's hair and smiled. "There is no need to be afeared here, Gillian. This is your home now. I promised that I would not allow anyone to hurt ye. Ye remember that, do ye not? And I always keep my promises."

Gillian made no sounds or movements to acknowledge him. Sorsha's shoulders slumped because eventually, she'd have to do something drastic to get her daughter speaking again.

Shaw washed at the basin, dressed, waved to her, and left in a hurry.

Sorsha took her time and went through her morning routine, taking care to dress warmly since there seemed to be a chill. After she washed, combed her hair, and pulled on the underdress, she selected a woolen overdress that would keep any breeze from making her cold. She tidied up the chamber and pulled at the bed covers, pressing the wrinkles from the edges, and fluffed the pillows.

Gillian stood by the window casement and peered through it. When she called her, Gillian turned and followed her to the children's chamber. There, she readied her daughter for the day, mimicking the tasks she'd just performed for herself.

Sorsha was anxious to get to the great hall to ensure Mamo hadn't gone to the graves overnight. When she reached the large room, Mamo wasn't there. She settled Gillian at the table where she found an assortment of breads and a pot of pottage. It was still warm and smelled delicious. As she set a bowl before her daughter, Luthor capered into the hall. He sat next to Gillian and stole a piece of her bread.

"There is plenty of bread for you both." Sorsha snatched up another piece and set it before Gillian. Then, she spooned a good helping of pottage for Luthor and slid it in front of him. "Eat, both of you. I will return shortly." Before she'd left the hall, Enid strolled in and stopped to pour a vat of ale into the large container by the buttery. "Oh, Enid, I am glad you are here. Will you look after the children for a moment? I need to check on Mamo and make sure she's within the keep. I fear she may have gone to the graves again."

Enid nodded. "I shall, Milady, but usually Clovis tells us when she's left through the gate."

"Oh, well, that is a relief. Perhaps she is here."

Sorsha rejoined the children and as she ate some pottage herself, Mamo shimmied through the threshold. She hurried to get up to assist the woman to the table and pulled a chair out for her. "Good morn, Mamo. I am so glad you are here. Let me get you a bit of food. Are you hungry?"

"Ravenous, lass, and my thanks." Mamo sat opposite Luthor at the table and smiled at him. "I found a wee white mouse outside my bedchamber door, lad. Does he belong to ye?"

Luthor nodded vigorously. "Aye, Milady, that is Squeaks. I

put him into his house! How did he get out?"

"Some mice are very smart." Mamo held out the mouse and Luthor took it from her. He shoved the creature inside his tunic and continued eating his morning meal.

Sorsha smiled at Mamo for her kindness. She suspected that Luthor might be upset if he'd lost his pet. While she finished eating, she spoke to Mamo about the day and their plans. "We should probably get the bedding washed. I shall see if Edra and Enid need help doing the washing. It might warm enough to spend a little time outside."

"I would be pleased to watch the children," Mamo said.

"Luthor will be out of the keep most of the day. He has chores to see to in the stable. But Gillian will be here. Perhaps you can watch her whilst I tend to some things..." She ceased speaking when Shaw entered with an unknown man and woman following him.

"Ah, Sorsha, come and meet my sister Corliss and her husband Idris. They just arrived."

She rose from her seat and approached the woman. Shaw's sister had gleaming, almost black hair, and dark eyes. Corliss didn't resemble Shaw in her looks but she was a stunning woman. Sorsha bowed to her and offered a welcome but the woman passed her by to reach the table.

"Really, Shaw, will ye not offer us refreshment? We have traveled afar and are tired from the journey. We could do with a bite to eat."

Sorsha hurried and grabbed a pitcher of ale from the buttery. She poured them cups and set them before Corliss and her husband. "We are pleased to have you here. Shaw has spoken of your visit. If I can do anything to make your stay more enjoyable—"

Corliss ignored her and gasped as her gaze settled upon the elder woman. "Shaw, shame on ye for not telling me that Mamo was still living. I thought her dead long ago. Mamo, ye are still with us, I see."

Mamo raised a brow and offered no welcome to her grand-daughter. "Aye, why God keeps me here is quite the mystery. But right now I find I could do with some air and shall take the wee lass outside." She stood and took Gillian's hand then the pair of them left the hall.

Sorsha was surprised by Mamo's abrupt departure. Surely she wanted to spend time with her granddaughter, but it was apparent that she wasn't fond of Corliss. Now, Shaw sat next to her as she took a seat at the table and grabbed her hand. He squeezed it lightly as if to give her a silent message—what that was she was uncertain. Sorsha took an empty cup, poured her husband a drink, and handed it to him. He grinned at her and gave a nod of thanks.

"Milady, I am going to the stables now," Luthor said and hopped off the chair. He bowed to her and Shaw.

She almost grinned at the lad's excitement. Most lads liked being in the busy stable. Before he crossed the threshold, she called out, "I shall come and get you before the evening meal."

Shaw watched the boy leave then turned and motioned to his sister. "Corliss, tell us… How long do ye plan to stay?"

Corliss took a sip of her drink and made a face, then set the cup down and gave it a look of distaste, pushing it away from her before she returned her attention to Shaw. "Since Idris and I are now homeless, we hoped to beg for your hospitality."

"There's no need to beg, sister. This shall always be your home," Shaw said. "There is a small chamber available within the keep unless ye want to stay in a cottage. I am sure we can find a vacant one…"

"I prefer to stay within the keep," Corliss said and pressed her hand on her husband's forearm. "Does that suit ye, husband?" The man nodded but said nothing.

Sorsha wondered how close Shaw was to his sister. There seemed to be an easiness between them and he smiled when he offered her a place to stay. Yet Idris had spoken not a word since he'd arrived so Sorsha thought to include him. "And how was the journey, Idris? How far have you traveled?"

Idris, a man whose looks put him in a somewhat lower category than Shaw, shrugged. He appeared thin-bodied, so she took that as if he hadn't wielded weapons much. Not only did he appear lanky, but he had a weak, pointy chin, and his reddish-brown hair barely covered his head.

"My clan resided by the borders, Milady, near Lothian. We were recently ousted by the Cummings clan and until we can recoup what we have lost—"

Corliss interjected, "I wrote to ye, Shaw, and told ye about our unfortunate situation. Our home was sacked and burned. There was naught left and we fled for our lives."

Shaw nodded. "I received your missive, Corliss, but I am unsure why the Cummings would attack your clan. Idris, are ye not on good terms with them? I thought your clan had a treaty of a sort with the Cummings Clan by way of the Chattans?"

"We had, but no longer. Geoff assures me that he will aid me in regaining lands for my clan. When I can do so, my brethren will return to me. Of that, I do not worry."

"How does Geoff plan to retake the lands? Will he offer his army to assist ye in a war?" Shaw's face turned grim with the narrowing of his eyes and a small pout on his lips.

"He assures me that even if I am unable to regain my family's lands, I will have a place to call home. Corliss and I are gladdened ye welcomed us here."

Corliss spoke up then. "Oh, indeed, brother. Geoff was most welcoming as well but I was impatient to get to ye so we only stayed a night."

Sorsha was about to make her excuses to leave and attend her duties when Corliss finally addressed her. "So ye are now the lady of the Mackintoshes?"

Fortunately, Shaw saved her from having to answer the woman. "Indeed, she is. King Alexander offered her as a bride. I am well pleased by it too."

His sister pursed her lips. "I see that ye are. And ye, Lady Mackintosh—"

"Sorsha, please… I hope to become close to you, sister. Shaw is happy at your homecoming."

Corliss made no response either in word or expression about Sorsha's aim to make her feel welcome. "Were those your children? The two wee scamps that just left?"

"The lass is mine. Her name is Gillian and she has recently returned from the Chattan clan." When Corliss looked at her questioningly, Sorsha expounded, "I was previously married to Rodick Chattan. He was Gillian's father. Shaw meantime recently rescued the lad and we took him in. He was alone and—"

Corliss made another sour face and waved at her dismissively. "I detest children. They always get in the way or make a mess of things." Then her lips curled into a smile that didn't reach her eyes. "Ye were married to Rodick? That explains much…If ye ask me, Lady Mackintosh, ye probably would have been better off leaving his child there…with the Chattans."

Sorsha pursed her lips at the woman's haughtiness. She didn't want to dislike Shaw's sister, but any woman who abhorred children wasn't a sort with whom she could be easily friendly. "She is my daughter too. Of course, I wanted her to be with me."

Corliss gave another dismissive wave and, finished with her, turned back toward Shaw. "Ye are still taking in the unfortunates, Shaw? Ye have not changed since we were young. I do not see why ye bother to take in the orphans. Better to let the Church see to them. Do ye not have enough mouths to feed here within *our* clan?"

Shaw frowned, seemingly unwilling to retort to his sister's outlandish claim. But then a light smile set upon his mouth and he nodded. "Oho, aye, we have a good following now and our soldiers' numbers have increased…all by taking in the so-called unfortunates. We are blessed to be able to help others especially children who might otherwise starve."

"Ye always gave out handouts. I suppose Mamo encourages ye to do so? She always complimented ye when ye were younger about your altruism." Corliss took a sip of her ale and blanched again before setting the cup back on the table.

Sorsha rose and couldn't leave the hall fast enough. "I shall go and see where we might put you up while you are here." She didn't await a farewell from Shaw or his crass sister. Idris was even more ungracious with his unrelenting stare.

Sorsha rushed out of the back of the keep and entered the kitchen. She found Mamo and Gillian there, helping Edra by kneading dough. "Ah, there you are. You are behaving?" she asked Gillian. Her daughter dropped the wad of dough that she held and peered at her.

"Oh, indeed she is," Mamo said.

Edra approached and set a small basket of carrots on the table. "I am making rabbit stew for supper, Milady. Will that suit for the evening meal?"

"Sounds delicious. But it appears I need to prepare a bedchamber for Shaw's sister and her husband."

"We will need to clean out a chamber for there are none readied," Edra said. She wiped her hands on an apron that wrapped around her body. "Let us tend to it."

"Can we make certain it is far from my bedchamber?" Sorsha's shoulders tensed after she spoke such words. She wasn't sure if Corliss was liked by the maid. But she was relieved by Edra's response.

"If I had my way, Milady, I'd put her in a cottage beyond the bridge. But och, our laird would not be too pleased by that. He's always cared for his sister, and she can do no wrong in his eyes. He is a good, kind man."

"'Tis the truth," Mamo said. "Unlike my grandson, my granddaughter is self-serving, lass, so protect yourself against her. She shall have ye obeying her every command if ye give in too easily."

Sorsha took the basket of carrots from Edra and began cutting them for the evening meal. The sharp kitchen dagger allowed her to work out some aggression. It seemed Shaw's sister was most discourteous. Until she could glean Shaw's feelings about his sister, Sorsha would be as kind and placating as possible.

CHAPTER FIFTEEN

S HAW'S SISTER HAD been in residence for less than a fortnight and she constantly irritated her. Now, exasperated, Sorsha fled the hall in the hope of calming her ire. She'd allowed the woman to infuriate her to the point that she couldn't remain in the same room with her. Corliss repeatedly mocked the children, ridiculed her choices in caring for them, or corrected her on whatever it was that she thought could be done better. Yet Corliss offered no help in the care of the keep. And her endless requests for her needs had poor Edra running in circles.

Trying to simmer her temper would probably take longer than a walk about the fief. Still, Sorsha tried to remain calm and unaffected by Corliss's chastisement and derision. With some deep breaths and prayers for patience, her anger dissipated and she found herself enjoying the walk.

"Sorsha, there ye are." Shaw approached from behind.

She stopped and waited for him to catch up to her. "I was but getting some air."

"Edra said ye were outside. I thought we could spend a wee bit of time together. We have not had much privacy of late." He took her hand and led her farther away from the keep.

"It has been a trying day and 'tis not even midday. I detest saying this, Shaw, but your sister is unpleasant. She undermines me at every turn and is unkind to the children. I wish she would return to the Chattans. Will she? Can we ask her to?"

Shaw stopped walking and turned to face her. "Corliss means well. She's always been a wee bit overzealous. Maybe she feels threatened by ye, Sorsha. Ye are a hard woman to live up to. I say ye try to be patient with her. Given time, she will befriend ye."

Her shoulders slumped. Sorsha had been more than patient and she doubted with all her heart that Shaw's sister could befriend anyone. Obviously, Shaw cared greatly for her, so she had to bear whatever problems Corliss dealt out. She reasoned that Shaw likely did not see what others saw in his sister—a rude, selfish harridan. He was blinded by his love for her, his only sibling, and besides Mamo, his only direct family. She blew a breath of frustration but didn't continue to berate him about Corliss. Instead, she took his hand and wanted to enjoy being with him even if it was only for a moment.

"The only thing that troubles me is the lack of privacy we have had of late. Come, I know the perfect spot where we can be alone for a time."

On the way toward the gate, Sorsha noticed one of the soldiers lurking by a tree. He seemed to skulk toward them. She remembered the man had attacked Shaw when they first arrived. Henny, she recalled, was fond of ambushing his laird.

"We are being followed," she said, and kept her view ahead.

"I know we are." Shaw turned her and leaned close. His mouth was a scant distance from hers and he smiled. He gave her a quick peck on the lips and then yelled, "I see ye, Henny. Ye should get back to your duties."

His soldier bellowed a laugh and shouted, "Bollocks. Ye are getting better, Laird, at detecting me, aye." Henny marched off and left them.

Sorsha folded her arms around Shaw and pressed her cheek to his tunic. He held her there on the lane and tilted back her head with a gentle hand. She waited for him to kiss her, but his eyes shone with mirth.

"Come, we will seek some privacy where I can snog ye

properly. Many eyes are watching." He clasped her hand and led her to the gate.

Clovis called out. "Milady received a missive, Laird." He scurried forth and presented a sealed parchment to her.

Sorsha thanked him and peered at the message, suspecting that it was from the king's chamberlain. It had been some time since she'd written to Edmund for information about Luthor's parents. She prayed that his news was of a good variety.

But Shaw gently pulled her forward and they ambled over the bridge. Through the woods, they walked and continued for a good distance until they came to a densely wooded area. Shaw held back some of the bushes for her to get through without being caught or scraped by the prickly branches. A clearing appeared and beyond, a loch of pristine beauty shimmered in the afternoon sun.

"Oho, what a beautiful place," she said in awe.

"Aye, my da used to bring me here and we would swim all day."

"'Tis a shame it is not warm enough to swim this day. Will you bring me back when it is? I would love to swim in the loch. Perhaps we can bring the children too?"

"Ye have my promise to and we will invite others too." Shaw neared a thick pine whose lower branches had long since fallen away. Beneath the needled branches, he removed his upper tartan and placed it on the ground. "Come, love, and let us rest here."

Sorsha knelt and then sat facing the water. Shaw took up the space next to her. The solitude of the place relaxed her and all the aggression she'd felt that morning dissipated. How could anyone be ireful or tense at such a beautiful place?

She raised the missive that she still held in her hand and began opening it. Shaw stopped her and he pressed his hand upon hers.

"Do not read it now, Sorsha. Whatever it is can wait. I would rather kiss ye and have ye naked in my arms." Shaw took the missive from her and shoved it beneath the edge of the tartan they sat upon. He gripped his tunic and pulled it over his body until he was free of it.

Sorsha marveled at the sight of his skin, muscles, and the sparse hair on his chest. She leaned close and placed her hand on the hard musculature that covered his heart. His heart raced as much as hers did and she smiled to herself knowing he was just as excited. She scooted closer to him and pressed her body to his side.

"I want nothing more than to be naked in your arms."

He chuckled low and set his mouth on her neck. His lips pressed there and he continued kissing her while he shifted her garments from her shoulders. Sorsha pulled away and hastily removed the layers of her overdress and chemise. The cool breeze brought a shiver over her but she ignored it and lay back.

Shaw discarded his lower tartan and sat next to her. His hooded eyes stayed on hers as he caressed his hand along the length of her bared leg and upward. Excitement surged through her at the thought of being with him.

"I cannot wait to be inside ye," he said with a hoarse voice.

Sorsha pulled him forward and he kissed her, twirling his cool tongue around hers. Shaw withdrew from her and sat back against the tree trunk. He patted his thigh and gave her a wily look as if he was up to mischief. His eyes shone and he nodded.

She sat on his lap with her legs flanking his thighs and set her hands on his shoulders, taking the strands of his hair between her fingers. He was so handsome, strong, and utterly affecting. His hands settled on her waist and he smoothed them around her until they stopped at the base of her back. Sorsha felt his need beneath her bottom and gasped when he yanked her forward.

"Ye have me maddened," he said and pressed another kiss on her lips. Shaw lifted her and she helped him find the way to enter her.

The exquisite sensation of him gliding within her almost sent her reeling. She huffed at the pleasure. With each of his movements, desire surged through her and twinged her womb with the promise of the euphoria she'd now learned to expect from joining with her husband. Sorsha focused on his face and the intensity of his frown. He closed his eyes and gripped her tightly, moving vigorously to pleasure her. She fell against him and moaned as the first twinges of her culmination caused her to tighten her legs.

Shaw held the back of her head with his large hand and pulled her forward. He kissed her fervently and kept up the passionate torment. She fell apart in his arms, rasping, moaning, and calling his name. He joined her a moment later and mimicked her reaction with a groan and by saying her name with a whisper on his lips.

Sorsha clung to him and didn't want the sensations to subside, but as they diminished, she sighed with the delight of it. Shaw kept his arms around her and he leaned his head on her shoulder. His warm breath played over her skin and he seemed content to stay that way. They didn't move for a long moment.

"Ye do me in, lass." Shaw kissed her cheek and he brushed his knuckles along her jaw.

"As you do me. I wish we did not have to return to the keep yet."

"Who says we do? Let us enjoy more time here before we go."

When she moved off Shaw's lap, she reached for her garments. The breeze had picked up slightly and she had grown cold. Quickly, she donned her clothing and waited for him to dress. When he finished, he sat back and didn't seem to be in a rush to hurry back to the fief.

Sorsha reached for the missive beneath the tartan and held it. Whatever news was contained within, she needed to find out. Hopefully, Edmund had found Luthor's parents and they would be freed soon. Better, perhaps they would be reunited with their son. She cracked the seal on the outside of the parchment and unfolded it. Her eyes scanned the words and as she did so, tears sprang unbidden to her eyes.

"What is it, sweetheart?" Shaw moved next to her and tried to take the missive but she pulled it back from him.

"Edmund writes that accounts are being reported that my father's ship left the harbor and struck an embankment. It capsized and no one saw anyone reach the shore. Edmund says the captain is being blamed for his negligence in leaving the harbor when there were apparent rough waters. It is presumed all lives were lost but Edmund says he shall look into it further."

Shaw set his arm around her back. "I am sorry, love. Your father knew the risk of being a merchant and sailing on the waters around the island. Crossing the channel is dangerous even in calm waters. Many ships are lost to its depths."

"I never got to forgive him, my father, for forcing me to marry Rodick. I had hoped to see him again but now that is impossible. I should have told him that I understood why he had accepted the treaty with the Chattans. I just hoped to see my mother again." Sorsha wiped the tears on the rim of her lashes away.

"Ye are so merciful, Sorsha, and I am sure he knew that ye forgave him. Do not despair. I do not like seeing ye weep." He cuddled her cheek with the palm of his hand.

"I shall pray for my family. That wasn't all that Edmund wrote…"

"What is it?" Shaw reached out and took the missive. His eyes scanned the lines Edmund had written. "Luthor's parents have also perished. Oh, this is distressing news, but alas, we will take care of Luthor. He will always have a home with the Mackintoshes."

"It is sad to think that his parents died in prison without knowing what happened to their son. We must honor them and make certain Luthor has a good life."

"We shall." Shaw folded the missive and handed it back to her.

"I was thinking… perhaps we can keep Luthor with us and raise him as our son. He is too wee to be put to training with the other lads. I fear for him and want to keep him with us." Sorsha cared greatly for the lad and it mattered not to her if he was their true son. She would care and love him as if he were.

"If ye wish it then I shall make it so," Shaw said and embraced her. "The only thing that troubles me is how we will break the news to him."

"He will be upset. I wish Gillian spoke. Having another child near his age would be a comfort for him. Still, she won't speak to anyone. I am greatly troubled by it."

Shaw glided his hand over the locks of her hair and nodded. "Aye, as am I. Och, the lass will speak when she is ready. We must have faith that she will and that Luthor will accept us."

He helped her to rise and she grabbed the tartan from the ground. As perfect as the afternoon was with Shaw, it was also disheartening with the news she received from Chamberlain Edmund. Somehow, she had to find a way to protect both her daughter and Luthor. Not only would she see to their safety, but she would love them with all her heart.

CHAPTER SIXTEEN

A DISTURBING NIGHT'S sleep caused Shaw to yawn repeatedly upon leaving his bed that morning. Throughout the night, he couldn't help but be concerned for Luthor's acceptance of their news or Gillian's acceptance of her new family. He'd tossed and turned, envisioning the lad's reaction to hearing of his parents' deaths.

After finding his mamo at the graves earlier and escorting her back to the keep, Shaw ambled around the island. He agreed to meet Sorsha later that evening before the children's bedtime so they could tell Luthor their news. The lad would be sad and there was no way to know how he'd react to the death of his parents. Together, they would break the news gently.

When he reached the training field, he watched some of the men spar with swords and fisticuffs. There were fewer than the usual number of soldiers on the field and he wondered where the rest of them were. Additionally, he didn't see Trey there either. He'd have to have a word with his commander about being absent from his duty, and tell him that he had to set an example for the men.

On his walk back to the keep, he stopped at the stables and visited his warhorse. He hadn't ridden much in the past fortnight. Though he was gladdened he needn't travel because there was much to do at home.

"Laird, I already fed him and filled his trough," the stable master, Jonah, said and pressed back the long strands of his brown hair. The horseman was no older than he was and yet far more muscular from lifting heavy bales of hay and working with the horses.

"Aye? He needs to be exercised soon. I'll take him for a ride later this day or on the morrow," Shaw said absently, more to himself.

"He has been a wee bit ornery stuck in his stall," Jonah grunted. "Och, I can put him in the pen for a while if ye cannot get to 'em."

"My thanks, Jonah, and also for taking Luthor in hand. Is he attending to his chores?"

"He be a good lad, Laird, and is keen to do his duty. I sent him back to the keep a short while ago since he finished mucking out the stalls. The lad could do with a bath for I swear he might've rolled around in the muck and hay." Jonah chuckled. "Och, 'tis just like a wee lad to do so."

Shaw snickered because he'd been the same as a lad, always getting into a wee bit of mischief. He nodded to the stable master and left. There was some time before he needed to meet with Sorsha and so he didn't rush back to the keep. His steps slackened and he greeted his clan's men and women as he passed. Ahead on the lane, he spotted a group of people. Curious as to what the trouble was, Shaw picked up the pace.

In the center of his soldiers, Trey had Idris in a headlock and held him bent over. Soldiers clamored about who was winning the fight. The men grunted in their effort to be free of each other. Trey held a dagger in his hand but Idris prevented him from striking when he twisted his body and jumped back a step or two.

"What is going on here?"

Everyone quieted and Trey shoved Idris's chest and he fell back but scrambled to his feet.

"I asked, what is happening?"

"Laird," Trey said as he returned his dagger to its sheath,

"This man spoke ill of ye and Milady. I heard his affront and challenged him."

"Is this true, Idris?" Shaw stood rigidly and folded his arms over his chest.

His brother-in-law took his time answering and eventually shook his head. "Nay, I know not what this man thought he heard, but I did not speak ill of ye. Why would I, when ye have been gracious enough to welcome me here?"

Shaw motioned the man away. "Go on and return to the keep." He waited for Idris to walk away and then stared hard at his soldiers who got his silent message and returned to the training field. "Trey, halt. I wouldst speak with ye a moment."

Trey turned back and glared. "He speaks falsely, Laird. I heard the man and ye know my hearing is sound."

"Did anyone else hear him speak ill of me?"

Trey shook his head. "Nay, none were close enough. Idris spoke to one of his followers."

"He brought followers?" Shaw was unaware that Idris and Corliss had brought men-at-arms with them. He'd have to ask his sister about it.

"I vow, Laird, that I do not accuse him falsely. Idris said that ye were weak and that our clan could easily be defeated and overtaken. That he would see to it that the breaches were remedied. I do not know what he meant by that but I suppose he thinks to insert himself in helping to guard us. He also said that milady is simple-minded and of no value to ye."

Shaw sighed at his commander's accusation. He wasn't overly fond of Idris but the man was married to his sister. He was family, even if indirectly, and deserved some respect. "Maybe he is right. Maybe I am weak and perhaps our clan could be made stronger."

His soldier scowled with an offended gaze. "Nay, Laird, he is wrong. Ye are not weak and nor is our clan. I asked Idris why he would say such a thing and he offered no excuse. To insult us by saying we can be defeated irked me. He affronted both ye and milady. 'Tis the truth, I wanted to end him."

"Then go on to the field, Trey, and ensure our men are trained properly and are strong enough to defend us. Make them ready for war and leave Idris be. He is my brother-in-law and I cannot have my soldiers threatening him." Shaw normally wouldn't allow such disrespect but he had to be patient with his sister's husband. In time, Idris would understand the Mackintosh men better. At least, that was his hope.

"I would watch your back, Laird, because I trust him not."

"Worry not for me. I do not need to watch my back when I'm on my land. There are nearly one hundred soldiers who see to my protection. Go on, get back to training, Trey."

Trey lowered his head and trudged off toward the field. On his way, he stopped and spoke to Henny, who nodded. Shaw couldn't hear their discussion but from what he could tell, both men adamantly agreed.

At least Henny and Trey were no longer at odds with each other. At one time and for quite a while, Trey had been upset that Henny chose to attack him and the other soldiers. Now, if anything, his commander's dislike for his brother-in-law brought forth a truce betwixt him and Henny.

Shaw had lost track of time and hurried back to the keep. As he traipsed along the hallway to the great hall, he heard Luthor teasing Gillian.

"Ye cannot jump as high as I can. Aye, ye be a wee lass."

His eyes met Sorsha's when he got to the table. She set aside something she was sewing and rose. "I'm gladdened you are finally here. I was about to send someone to find you. Are you ready for our discussion?"

He nodded but didn't say anything. Gillian sat near the hearth on the floor and Luthor skipped around the trestle table. He stuck his tongue out and teased Gillian as he passed by.

"Oh, here is Enid now." Sorsha rounded the table and met the maid halfway. She spoke low and Enid called to Gillian. Then Sorsha moved to stand with Shaw and she grabbed Luthor's hand as he passed. "Lad, we need to speak with you. Go and sit by the hearth." He skipped away and sat on the raised stone that butted the width of the hearth. He peered at them questioningly.

She leaned close to Shaw. "Enid will watch Gillian whilst we have our discussion with Luthor. I shall tell her later what has been decided. And, Shaw, do not push him to accept us. We mustn't cajole him but allow him to consider it. The news will be troubling enough."

"Aye, it will. Och, the lad might be pleased by our offer." He approached the hearth and sat in a vacant chair.

Sorsha moved with him but she took Luthor's hand again and raised him from his spot on the hearthstone. She then sat and settled Luthor on her lap. "Luthor, do you remember that I promised to write to the king's chamberlain to find out what happened to your parents?"

He nodded. "Aye, Milady."

"We heard back from him and I am terribly sorry to tell you that your parents were sickened whilst being imprisoned and they perished." Sorsha set her arm around the lad's back and rubbed him, offering comfort.

Shaw waited for his reaction but the lad scowled and said nothing. "Do ye know what 'perished' means?"

Luthor shook his head but remained silent.

"It means that they died. We are sorry, lad, for your loss." Shaw leaned forward and waited for the lad's reaction.

His wee voice was filled with sadness, "Do ye mean they are in heaven now?"

Sorsha leaned her head against Luthor's. "It does. But they are watching over you from there and I am sure they are happy to see that you are here with us, looking after you. You do like living here, don't you?"

"Aye, Milady. My mama and papa are not coming back, are they?" Tears welled in Luthor's eyes as realization came.

"I am afraid they cannot return to you." Sorsha pressed her hand on his head and sighed. "I know how sad you must be because I too lost my parents. As has Shaw. But we must always hold them in our hearts."

"Lad, ye know that we care about ye. Milady Sorsha hopes that ye will find it acceptable to consider her your mama. But we will give ye time to think about it. Will that suit ye?"

Luthor peered at them and his chin slowly bobbed. He got off Sorsha's lap and faced them. "I do need a new mama and papa. Maybe… Will my mama and papa be ireful if I say aye? Will they think I forgot them?"

Shaw knelt in front of him and set his hand on his shoulder. "Nay, lad, not at all. If anything, they would understand that ye are trying to accept a new family. They would not deem ye forgot them. I am sure of that."

Sorsha wiped at the tears in her eyes. "Your parents would want you cared for and protected. We want to give you a home, Luthor."

Shaw grabbed his small hand and gently squeezed it. "We can be your family if ye want us to be. Ye do not have to answer right now. Take some time to think about it. We will not force ye to stay here or to call us mama or papa."

Luthor's cheeks streamed with trickling tears. He nodded, turned away from them, and left the hall. Shaw followed him to the entrance of the great hall and watched him take the steps to the upper solar. The lad needed to be alone.

Shaw appreciated his need for solitude. Likely Luthor wanted to weep in privacy without being seen as weak.

Sorsha stood next to him and leaned on the opposite side of the doorjamb. "The poor lad. I should go and tend to him."

"Nay, give him a moment or two. He is a growing lad and right now needs a wee bit of time alone." Shaw took her in his arms and embraced her. "Weep not, love. He will accept us. Even if he does not, he shall remain here until he is old enough to care for himself."

"But I want him to want us…" Sorsha pressed her face against his chest.

"We shall have a quiet supper this eve, just the four of us."

Shaw pressed her toward the steps. "Bring the children later to the hall. I will tell Edra to bring the food early so we can spend the evening with them."

"That is a fair idea, Shaw." Sorsha left him and he hastened to the kitchens. On the way, the delicious scent of stew wafted to him. He spotted his sister leaving and she smiled at him as she passed. When he entered the stone building, he could tell Edra was in a foul temper because she stirred the stew briskly, almost sloshing the broth over the edge of the pot. Had Corliss angered Edra? He surmised she had but asked anyway, "Mistress… What troubles ye?"

She gasped and pressed her hands to her chest. "Oh, Laird, ye frightened me. I did not hear ye enter. Naught is troubling me, at least, naught that I will allow. What do ye need?" She bowed to him and smiled.

"Something was troubling ye when I entered. Tell me what it was." Shaw did not like the notion that his maidservant was upset. She worked hard for his household and the last thing he wanted was for someone or something to upset her.

"Honest, Laird, I do not wish to speak of it. 'Tis an unimportant matter. It shall right itself in time. Now, what can I do for ye?"

"Sorsha and I wish to sup with the children earlier this eve. Will ye bring supper soon?"

"I am gladdened to and shall have it brought with haste." She turned back to the large pot that steamed a delicious scent of stew through the kitchen.

Shaw took a deep breath before retreating from the kitchen. He'd hoped that she would tell him why she'd been irked but alas, he wouldn't press Edra. Outside, he walked around the keep in his quest to take in the late afternoon air. Corliss called out to him and he turned to find her on the lane in the front of the keep.

"Sister, there ye are. I have not seen ye all day."

"Shaw, I want a word about your soldiers. They tormented my poor Idris. Idris told me how they attacked him and pulled a dagger on him. They dared to threaten him." Corliss set her hands on her hips and glared. "Your soldiers need to be punished. What do ye intend to do about it?"

He swiped his hand over his face and groaned under his breath. "It was not all my soldiers, only one, and he did not torment or threaten Idris."

"He accused him of deceit and tried to stab him. What I want to know is what ye plan to do about it. Surely ye won't let the man get away with it."

"I spoke at length with the man and he will not bother your husband again. Rest assured."

"Very well, but I am not sure if I am appeased or not. We cannot have our clansmen making idle threats against our family, Shaw, or do ye allow such insolence?"

"Nay, I do not. Now I told ye I handled the situation." Shaw withheld his anger by fisting his hands even though he wanted to lash out about Corliss's husbands actions. Idris needed to find a way to win over the Mackintosh clansmen. "If Idris wishes to discuss the matter further, tell him to come to me and we will talk. I must return to the keep. Sorsha awaits me."

Corliss grabbed his arm to stop him from leaving. "That is another thing, Brother. Your wife… She is not very adept as the mistress of the keep. If ye wish I can assist her. She has her hands full with those children."

Shaw tilted his head at his sister's hostile words. She had spoken with some vehemence in her tone and he liked it not. "Corliss, Sorsha is my wife… She is Lady Mackintosh. She alone has a say over everything to do with the keep and no other. If she asks for your aid, ye will give it. Otherwise, leave her be. And if ye have an issue with my wife, ye will say so now." He allowed her cadence to spur his ire but he hadn't meant to sound angry.

"Nay, I have no issue with her. I only thought to offer my assistance."

"Sorsha was previously married to Rodick Chattan and is more than capable of being the lady of the keep. It would please me if ye tried to befriend her. She has not had an easy time and needs family around her and ye know how much I value family." He yanked his arm from her grasp and made to leave.

Corliss reached out and wrapped her fingers around his arm again, stopping him. "Why does she need family?"

"She recently received the dreadful news that her parents had died."

His sister drew a resigned breath. "I will try, Shaw, to befriend her."

He tugged his arm out of her grip once more. "I must go. This night we plan to have a quiet supper with the children so find your meal elsewhere. The hall is off limits to all." He turned and left his sister standing with her mouth agape at his directive.

Shaw reentered the keep and found Gillian and Luthor sitting at the table. The stew, along with a basket of bread and a bowl full of peas sat in the center. There was also a tray of sweetcakes and a bowl of jellied fruit. Before he took his seat at the table, his gaze shot around the chamber looking for his wife but she wasn't in the hall.

"Where is Milady?" he asked Luthor.

"She returned to the kitchen and said she would come back."

"Ahh… Well then, let us eat." Shaw spooned the stew into their bowls and pushed them toward the children. He took a roll, broke it in half, and handed each of them a piece. "We should eat before it gets cold."

Silence abounded in the hall as they ate. Sorsha still hadn't returned.

As Shaw sat there, he thought about Luthor's plan to entice the lass to speak. He'd tormented her with his silliness but the lad's idea was sound. Shaw chuckled to himself and watched Gillian. She sat with the spoon in her hand and swirled it in the bowl of pottage. He needed to make progress with her soon and so he decided this would be the day that he got her to speak or at least react to him.

Shaw shoved his spoon in his mouth and cleaned the stew

from it. He then dipped the spoon in the bowl of peas and made certain there were a good many on it. With the spoon aimed, he called to Gillian and she raised her eyes. Shaw flicked the spoon's peas at her and they pummeled her body. The wee lass gasped and stared at him as if he'd gone mad.

He continued to incite her response by rolling several more peas across the table at her and she pressed back in her chair, watching him with the beginning of mirth in her eyes. If she wasn't aghast at being pummelled with peas perhaps pottage would serve him better. Shaw dipped his spoon in his pottage bowl and made certain it overflowed with a good helping. He then aimed it and let it loose. A wad of stew hit Gillian in the center of her chest and she shrieked.

"What...? Why...? Oho, Mama is going to be angry," Gillian said with awe.

Shaw grinned at the sound of her winsome voice. Not only was she a bonny lass, but she had the voice of an angel. He found himself lightened at hearing her words.

"Do not worry, lass, I will tell her it was my fault."

Luthor watched them with his mouth ajar. He didn't want to be left out of the melee and he shot a spoonful of pottage at him. Shaw bellowed with laughter. Within a moment, they were flinging pottage at each other and the table was littered with speckled bits of stew.

Gillian's laughter mingled with Luthor's and Shaw chortled at the banter between them.

"What in heaven's name is going on?" Sorsha approached the table and frowned.

"Laird Mackintosh started it, Mama."

Sorsha stared hard at Gillian before she fell to her knees and sobbed. When she caught her breath, she said, "Did my bairn just speak?"

Shaw was delighted to answer her, "Indeed she did."

Through tears and sobs, Sorsha managed to speak, "Thank you. Praise God, he has answered my prayers."

CHAPTER SEVENTEEN

IN THE EARLY morning, Sorsha awakened to a sensual caress over her thigh. She stretched but was immediately pulled back against Shaw's hard body. He pressed his chest to her back and the heat of his skin made her moan. Shaw settled his head by her shoulder and he pressed the strands of her hair back.

He whispered and his warm breath played over her skin, "I cannot resist touching ye." His hand roamed her body, sending pleasurable heat through her. "And kissing ye." His lips pressed on her neck and then her nape.

"If you keep doing that…"

Shaw lifted her leg and pushed his hard erection into her. Sorsha closed her eyes and moaned with pleasure at the sensation of him entering her. His movement was slow and affecting, with desirous thrusts intent to drive her mad. Sorsha held onto the bedding to keep herself from being propelled to the side of the bed. Shaw's fingers gripped her thigh, holding her in the perfect position to keep his momentum. As he continued, Sorsha panted and suspected she would meet her end sooner than he would.

"Do ye know how bonny and alluring ye are?" He pressed his mouth on her neck again and suckled her skin.

The sensation of his lips there coupled with the desire that swarmed her sent her reeling. Her body seemed to weigh more than a crag as she spiraled out of control. Desire wound its way through her body and she could barely breathe. "Sh...*awww, oho.*"

"That's it, love, join me," he said and huffed. Shaw groaned and thrust hard one last time before he too succumbed to his culmination. His moans sounded almost painful but she knew too well that the pinnacle of the climax was both ultimate pleasure and torment.

Sorsha lay back against him, happily enjoying his hold, hard body, and the scent of their lovemaking. Gently, he pulled himself from her and lowered her thigh. His large hand caressed her leg until he reached her waist. His forearm trapped her against him and she pressed her hand to keep it there.

"I hope that you awaken me akin to that every morn," she said with a bit of awe in her voice.

His chuckle vibrated his chest, against her back. "Aye, that can be arranged."

Noise in the hallway came and their bedchamber door thrust open. Sorsha pulled away from Shaw and hastily covered herself. Shaw moaned and rolled onto his back. The children scampered into the room, shouting something unbeknownst to her.

Gillian jumped onto the bed and practically elbowed her stomach. "Mama, he pulled my hair again. So I pushed him and he felled."

"I did not," yelled Luthor. "She pushed me and tried to trip me."

"Is it not too early to be rowing? You have not even eaten your morn fare yet." Sorsha reached to take hold of Luthor's hand. "Go on, both of you. Put your garments on and I shall meet you in the great hall shortly. You will sit quietly and think about how you can be kinder to each other."

The children gazed at her as if they didn't hear her.

"Mama, can we go to the loch, can we?" Gillian continued to spring herself upon the bedding in her excitement. "'Tis hot this day."

Shaw set his hand on Gillian's shoulder to keep her from

springing off the bed. "Mayhap, but ye both need to promise not to fight. I will hear your pledges before we agree to take ye."

The children nodded. Luthor sprinted from the chamber and Gillian crawled from the bed. Her daughter reached the door and turned. "I pledge, Laird, but if he pulls my hair again…"

"If he does, Gilly lass, come and tell me," Shaw said. "I will punish him."

Gillian nodded and then disappeared through the doorway.

Sorsha relaxed back and pressed her eyes. "We need to have several talks with those two."

"Aye?" Shaw said as he threw his legs over the side of the bed. "What about?"

She sighed. "I need to find out what exactly Gillian saw before she was taken away at Tor. And I need to speak to Luthor about his answer…if he will belong to us. Then there is the matter of the two of them constantly haranguing each other."

Shaw chuckled. "'Tis what siblings do, harrang each other. My sister used to torment me when we were young. They will sort it. As to what Gillian saw, she will tell ye in her own time. And Luthor, no matter what he decides, will always be ours." He turned to her and pressed a hand over her hair. "Now get moving, love, 'tis going to be a warm day, and spending it by the loch is a fair idea."

She shifted to leave the bed and grabbed Shaw's discarded tartan to wrap around herself. "I shall have Edra pack us food and we shall stay there all day. But are you not too busy? If you have clan duties…"

"Naught is more important than family. I will go and meet with Trey and Walen. When I return, we shall leave." He ambled to the door but turned back to her, reaching the bed in a quick stride. Shaw set his hands on her hips and pulled her toward him. "My thanks for a good morn." He pecked a kiss on her lips and left.

Sorsha took her time getting ready for the day. She washed, dressed, and tidied up the bedchamber. Though she looked forward to spending the day outside, a pang of guilt came because she should help Edra care for the keep. They had planned to do a thorough cleaning of it. Perhaps she could delay their tasks until the morrow? She'd have to speak to the maidservant and maybe offer her a day of rest. The woman worked too hard as it was.

Her hands pressed the cream cloth of her overdress and she shook the length of skirts to fall at her ankles. After she slipped on the matching leather slippers, she quickly braided her hair and pulled the knots back into a coif. Then it was time to see about the children. She closed the door to their bedchamber and walked spryly down the stairs.

Upon reaching the great hall, she noticed Corliss standing by the hearth with her hand clasping Luthor's arm with force. Gillian stood by, wailing as if she were hurt. An instant sense of protectiveness swarmed her. The heat of her ire reached her face. Sorsha marched to the woman, took hold of Luthor's other arm, and gently pulled him away from the horrid woman.

"What in heaven's name do you think you are doing?" She glared at Corliss, intent on hearing from the woman some sort of apology or explanation.

"This wee heathen almost knocked me down."

"I am certain the lad did not mean to." To Luthor, she said, "Did you apologize to Lady Corliss?" He nodded. Sorsha ruffled his hair and smiled. "It appears that the morning meal will be delayed. Go on and get to the kitchen and we shall eat there. Take Gillian with you. I will come in a moment."

Luthor took Gillian's hand and led her from the hall, both their faces wet with tears.

Sorsha waited until the children were out of hearing distance. "If you ever lay a hand on either of those children again, I shall not be responsible for my actions. I will be akin to a lioness and will protect my children no matter what the cost."

"There is no need, Sorsha, for such protectiveness or your anger. I did not intend to hurt the lad but he is a wily one and I had to hold him still so I could get him to apologize." Corliss passed her and reached the table. She grabbed a cup and held it. "I long to be friends with ye. Will ye not meet me halfway?"

She wanted to scoff at the woman. Friends? Since the day Corliss arrived, she'd been nothing but vindictive and surly. Why would she ever want to befriend her? Still, she was Shaw's sister and he cared for her. Sorsha realized that she must make some effort to keep her appeased.

"If you wish it so, then aye, I would like nothing more than to be friends."

Corliss took a sip of her drink and set her cup down. "That makes me gladdened, Sorsha. Now, I must go and find Idris. He is probably at the training field."

Sorsha didn't wait for her to leave but turned and headed to the kitchen. She crossed the small lane that led to the kitchen doorway which had been left open. When she reached the opening, she couldn't help but listen to the conversation.

"There, there, lass. Lady Corliss did not mean to hurt Luthor. Cease your weeping," Edra said. "Now, there are two bowls of sweetened pottage on the worktable for ye. Go on and eat."

Sorsha was pleased that Gillian had been concerned for Luthor. Perhaps there was hope that they would befriend each other. She wanted them to be close, as dear as siblings.

"Good morn, Edra. 'Tis a beautiful day and shall be warm."

"Oh, Milady, good morn to ye. Aye, the heat already has me short of breath this day."

Sorsha poured herself a heaping amount of pottage. It smelled so good that her stomach rumbled. "Then I propose that we forgo our caring for the keep this day. Shaw wants me and the children to spend the day at the loch with him. I bid you take the day to rest too. We shall see to the cleaning on the morrow."

Edra sat on a nearby stool and fanned herself. "I shall be gladdened to take rest this day. The heat never lasts long. It shall be cooler on the morrow."

Sorsha ate her pottage and then cleaned up the children. She grabbed a basket and set inside various foodstuffs for their picnic:

a loaf of bread covered with white linen cloth, four apples, an empty flask for water, slices of cheese, and a small sack of strawberries. That would hold them over until they return for the late-day meal.

"I shall keep watch over the laird's grandmother whilst ye are gone." Edra rushed to the food shelf and grabbed something. "A chicken for your basket, Milady." She wrapped the cooked chicken in a cloth and added it to the helpings.

"Oh, that shall be delicious. My thanks, Edra. Enjoy the solitude and rest. We shall see you this eve." Sorsha picked up the basket and called to the children. Outside, she walked along with Luthor and Gillian following.

"Will we get to ride horses?" Luthor asked excitedly.

"Nay, I am certain we will walk to the loch. Come along, do not dally." Sorsha picked up her steps and hurried to the gate where she hoped Shaw awaited her.

On her approach, she saw him standing with the watchman. He looked so handsome even from afar. His longish brown locks tussled with the warm breeze, along with the hem of his tartan. He'd rolled up his tunic sleeves which showed the sinewy muscles of his forearms. To think she'd been held within those arms early that morning. Sorsha sighed with happiness.

"Ye look well pleased." Shaw took the basket from her. "Are we ready? What's in here?"

"We are. There's some foodstuff there in case we get hungry."

"Can we swim in the loch?" Gillian asked.

"Of course, ye can, Gilly lass. We shall enjoy the water today." Shaw picked her daughter up and Gillian squealed with laughter. "Let us be off." He set Gillian down and grabbed a large satchel which he set over his shoulder. "I brought some items too for the day."

The walk to the loch took little time. Their excitement to get to the water matched their sprightly steps. Luthor was quiet on the walk and that concerned Sorsha. She wondered what he was thinking about. She wanted to ask, but it was best she allowed him to tell her on his own.

At the loch, Shaw pulled a large thin cover from his satchel and set it upon a shady grassy area beneath the trees. She set the basket of food on it and helped Gillian remove her overdress. Beneath, she had a thin linen underdress which afforded her a little modesty while she bathed in the water.

Shaw and Luthor stripped to their braises and ran into the water. Sorsha collected their garments and folded them, placing them in a pile on the cover. Afterward, she settled on the cover too and slipped off her shoes. As she did so, she watched Gillian, who appeared skeptical about entering the water.

"Do you not want to go in?"

Gillian shook her head. "Not yet, Mama."

"Well then, come and sit with me. We shall talk."

Her daughter sat next to her and watched Luthor and Shaw in the water carousing, splashing each other, and bellowing with laughter.

"I wanted to talk to you about that night, the night you were taken from me. Can you tell me what you saw? You were frightened. I heard you scream."

Gillian peered at her lap and nodded. "Aye, Mama, I was scared. I saw you holding the dagger and I... You stabbed Da. Then someone grabbed me and took me away."

Sorsha's chest tightened at hearing Gillian's recounting. "I promise you, sweetheart, I did not stab your da. I only held the dagger in my hand because I pulled it from him. Your uncle stabbed your da and I entered the chamber at that exact moment. I ran to your da to give him aid but it was too late. So I removed the dagger from him."

"You did not stab him?" Gillian glanced up at her.

"Nay, I certainly did not. Although your da and I were not close, I respected him. The last thing I wanted was to lose him. I am sorry that you had to witness his...ah, that you were taken away. I wept for two whole days because I could not get to you."

Gillian pressed her eye to wipe away a tear that gathered. "I did too, Mama. Are you happy now with Laird Shaw?"

"I am very happy. Are you?" Her daughter shrugged. "Do you know what would make me happier? If you would call Laird Shaw 'Papa'. That would please him mightily. He is a good man and wants to be your father. Will you let him inside your heart as I have in mine?"

"I want to let him into my heart. He makes me laugh." Gillian stood but fell against her and wrapped her arms around Sorsha's neck.

Sorsha wanted to weep at the joy that sprang to her heart. "I have never seen you so mirthful and that makes me happy too. Laird Shaw will protect you, Gillian, and ensure that you are always cared for, but more than that, he will bring you joy and love."

"I feared Da because…" Gillian's words fell away.

"I understand, sweetheart. He was not an easy man and was sometimes frightful. But alas, we are free now to find happiness. There is no reason to fear anyone now." She hugged her daughter close and then set her away. "Not even Laird Shaw's sister. She didn't mean to scare you and Luthor."

"I am not fond—"

Sorsha set her hand on her small daughter's shoulder and caressed her arm with her palm. "You should try to be fond of her, Gillian. She's your da's sister and family. We must be patient with Corliss and allow her to get to know us. Can you do that?"

Gillian nodded.

"Now, go on and enjoy the water."

As soon as Gillian reached the bank, she jumped in and the small waves reached her knees. Shaw grabbed her and whipped her around the surface of the water. Hearing her daughter's sweet laughter made her smile. What a remarkable change to her daughter's demeanor. Perhaps the best thing that happened to them was their change in circumstances. Rodick's death might not have been such an unfortunate happening after all. Immediately, Sorsha pleaded for God to forgive her for such a thought.

Luthor skulked from the water with a pout on his face. "Gillian won't let me have a turn."

Sorsha patted the cover and smiled. "Come sit with me for a short moment. Is the water warm?"

He nodded. "I thought 'bout what you asked, Milady."

"You did? And what is your decision? Will you join our family? I want you as my son, Luthor, but no matter what you decide, I shall still love you."

His eyebrows furrowed slightly but then his frown turned to a smile. "You love me, Milady?"

"Of course I do. I want to take care of you and know that your mama would want me to make sure you are happy." Sorsha kept herself from taking his hand. How badly she wanted to offer sympathy or comfort. "And Laird Shaw would so like to call you son. It is our greatest hope that you accept us."

Luthor swiped his arm across his face. He pulled his knees upward and wrapped his arms around them. "I do, Milady. I want ye as my mama and papa."

Sorsha tried not to let the tears in her eyes fall, but she had to hastily wipe them away. "You do not know how happy I am. The only thing that would please me more is if you would call us Mama and Papa."

"I can...Mama." Luthor rocked on his buttocks and kept his gaze on the water.

"Then let us go and join our family. They look like they are having all the fun." Sorsha pulled him to stand and took his hand. She ran toward the water and he followed. Her toes scrunched in the sandy, rocky bottom, and she gasped at the chill of it. It wasn't too cold, but it was not as warm as she'd thought or hoped it would be.

They played in the water for a time but soon got hungry. After they partook of an early afternoon meal and ate the entire chicken and bread, the children lay back upon the cover, drowsy and lethargic for once.

"Take a wee rest, sweet ones," she said and covered a portion of their bodies with Shaw's tartan.

Luthor lay on his side and called out to Shaw, "Papa, later will ye show me how to fish?"

Shaw's eyes widened slightly when Luthor called him Papa. His grin, though, attested to the fact that he was touched. "Aye, I will, son. Take a wee rest as your mama suggested."

"Papa," Gillian called. "Me too? Will you show me how to fish?"

"Aww, she's just a lass and lassies do not fish," Luthor said.

Shaw chuckled low. "Gilly lass, I will show ye how to fish too. Son, lassies do fish and they can do just about everything we can. I bid ye to remember that."

Luthor nodded. Gillian grinned.

Shaw whittled a stick and tied a string to it. "I am going to see if I can catch a fish or two for supper. Luthor, stay here and protect our family. I will not be long." He marched off toward the water and then continued down the bank.

As Sorsha sat with the children, she cleaned up the remnants of their meal and noticed Luthor's small pout. He wasn't pleased being left behind.

"Mama, will you tell us the story about the mountain and the bun?" Gillian asked. "You have not told it to me in a long time."

"I would love to but how about a new story?"

The children nodded.

Sorsha leaned back with her hands behind her. "I shall tell you a tale that my da used to tell me when I was a young lass. One day, Ant was going to the river to drink. She fell in and was carried along in the stream's current. In the tree nearby, Dove pitied Ant's condition and threw a small bough into the river."

"Oh, nay, does Ant drown?" Luthor asked with awe.

Gillian shushed him. "Don't ask questions."

He bristled. "I can ask questions!"

Sorsha bit back her smile and continued, "Ant swam to the bough and it floated to the shore. Later, Ant saw a man with a fowling piece on a string that he aimed at Dove. The man tried to trick Dove to catch him. To repay Dove for his kindness, Ant stung the man on his foot and he missed his aim. Ant saved his newfound friend Dove."

The children clapped.

"Always remember, my children, that little friends might prove to be great friends," Sorsha finished. She proceeded to tell another story, and then another, making the tales less and less exciting as she saw the children settling down and their eyes growing heavy.

By the time she finished the last tale, Gillian's and Luthor's eyes were closed and they breathed easily. She rose from the cover, approached Shaw, and set her arm around his shoulder. "They are asleep."

"Did ye hear Luthor? He called me papa…and Gilly lass, she called me the same." He leaned his head against hers. "My family…I was blessed, Sorsha, when ye chose me for your husband." He reached for her hair and tucked an errant strand behind her ear. "I never thought I would have wee ones or such a bonny wife."

"It is I who is blessed, Shaw." She lightly kissed his cheek. "There were years when I thought my existence was fated for misery. I always tried to be positive, but then all that happened with Rodick. Then you happened. You have made me so happy."

CHAPTER EIGHTEEN

AS THE DAYS of summer passed, peace had settled amongst his clan. Even his sister seemed more cordial and had befriended Sorsha. He kept busy and trained with his soldiers. Corliss's husband likewise joined the men on the field in the afternoons and took to practice arms. Idris made no further disparaging remarks about their ability to protect the clan, and his clansmen didn't much bother with his brother-in-law. Shaw enjoyed the recent days and spent time with the children and enjoyed the nights with Sorsha.

Soon the long days would grow shorter and the harvest would be upon them. It was a busy time of year with the reaping of the crops, the final shearing of sheep so their fleece would grow in before the cold season came upon them, and making preparations for the long winter.

Shaw stretched and leaned over Sorsha's body. He set a light kiss on her lips and tried not to awaken her but her eyes fluttered open. "Good morn, my bonny wife."

"'Tis morn already?" She moaned. "I am still tired."

He chuckled at her sleepiness. "Ye should try to take more rest this day. Allow Enid to watch the children."

"I shall," she muttered and rolled to her side. She watched him as he readied for the day.

Shaw pulled a tunic over his head and tied the neckline

closed. He then rolled the sleeves and wrapped a tartan around his waist. As he pulled the belt around him, he fastened it and pulled his sword from the floorboard. Once he sheathed it in the belt, he took a deep breath.

"I should go. 'Tis likely Mamo is at the graves. I will fetch her and then I will meet with Trey to go over the day's schedule. There are also the crofters that need to be visited. 'Tis a busy time."

"I can go and get Mamo if you wish," Sorsha said groggily.

"Nay, sweetheart, ye keep sleeping. I'll fetch her. I thought to leave the keep this day because the sentry reported men riding through our northern land."

Sorsha flung her arm out and grabbed hold of his hand. "You will not war, will you?"

He hastily shook his head. "I want to make certain that whoever they were left the area. 'Tis naught to worry about." To reassure her, he pressed another kiss on her lips. "Now, sleep and dream of me."

She closed her eyes and sighed. Shaw grinned to himself. His wife pleased him more than he deserved or ever thought was possible. With quick steps, he left the bedchamber and hurried outside. The air was warm and it hadn't gotten too chilly overnight. Mamo wouldn't need her shawl. As he passed his clansmen, he dipped his chin in greeting but continued.

At the gate, Clovis shouted a greeting. "Laird, fine day. Mistress Maven left a short time ago. She did not spend the night there."

"My thanks, Clovis. I will return shortly." Shaw turned his gaze and searched for Henny, certain his soldier would try to sneak attack him again. The soldier wasn't nearby so Shaw let his guard down. When he crossed the bridge, he ran into Walen who smiled in greeting.

"Where are ye off to, Shaw?"

"I need to retrieve Mamo. She's at the graves again. I will be taking a ride later this morn if ye want to join me. The sentry reported riders passing on our northern border. I want to make sure they are gone."

"Aye, I will ask a few men to join us. It will be good to get away from the keep for a bit." Walen pressed his hands through his unruly blond hair.

"Is your wife perchance giving ye hell?"

"I vow that pregnant women are confounding. One minute she is smiling and full of mirth and the next sour and indignant. I think the woman has gone maddened and I could use a wee bit of time away."

Shaw bellowed a laugh. "Aye, then meet me by the gate."

He continued on and as he approached the small hills that led to the graves, he spotted his grandmother sitting before his grandfather's cross. Shaw didn't speak as he neared in case she was praying but she heard him.

With her gaze fastened on the wooden cross, she said, "I heard ye approach. Come and sit with me."

Shaw knelt and then sat on the sparsely grassed area. "I thought I would find ye asleep again but Clovis said ye had only left."

"When I join your grandda, I want ye to promise to erect a new cross with both our names etched on it." She set small stones around the base of the cross.

"If it pleases ye, Mamo, I will. Come, we should return."

"Ye know, lad, ye are so akin to your grandda. He was a good man and so are ye. I see how ye are with Lady Sorsha and the children. Ye are a sound leader too, fair, and yet tough."

"I try to be," he said and wondered why she was telling him such things. "There is some strife right now concerning land rights that I want to rectify before the harvest comes. Och, I am unsure if I can. Many clans are against the Chattans, Mamo, and I find myself torn in my loyalty to my mother's kin."

She patted his hand. "'Tis because ye seek to honor your mother. Your grandda, Laird Chattan, was an honorable man unlike his sons, your own mother's brothers. They seek to use force to gain what they want instead of bartering. 'Tis the way of the Highlands though. Only the strong survive, I'm afraid."

"If my allies wish to go against the Chattans, I might have to… And then there is the truth that Geoff murdered his brother. He says he had to but to do so…to murder your own blood. What Geoff put Sorsha through and her daughter… It has taken all my will not to go to him, to confront him, and to enact vengeance for my wife and daughter." Shaw hadn't meant to say so much but his words spilled out as if they were a cliffside waterfall.

"My sons have never been agreeable which is why I wanted to reside here with my daughter. Shaw, all men seek vengeance when their loved ones are threatened. But I tell ye this, son, gaining vengeance's reward can be bittersweet."

Shaw rose and held his hand out for his grandmother. She took it and he helped her to rise. "What do ye mean, Mamo?"

"If and when ye seek your vengeance, ye may not like the repercussions." She linked her arm with his and walked slowly beside him. "I shall join my dearest husband soon, Shaw, and I tell ye this only to prepare ye for such. Make sure the cross is changed and I have left a small satchel of items I wish to take with me. 'Tis in my bedchamber in the small trunk beside the hearth."

Shaw didn't want to agree with her because he didn't want her to go to the afterlife. Yet, he had no choice but to nod. Along the rest of the walk, he kept quiet. Mamo gripped his arm a few times when they had to traverse a hilly area. At the bridge, Mamo stopped him and peered at the glistening waters flowing rapidly beneath the wooden structure.

"Ye see, my lad, every path in life has a bridge. The journey is in crossing it, which we all must do. Allow me to do so in peace and be not saddened when I go." She raised her eyes and smiled.

"I want ye to know, Mamo, that I appreciate everything ye have done for me. Ye took care of me when my parents died, raised me to be honorable, and loved me." Shaw set a gentle hand on her shoulder. "If 'tis peace ye seek then ye shall have it."

She nodded and continued. At the gates to the fief, she strolled onward toward the keep. Shaw stood and watched her, certain his Mamo planned to leave him very soon. That dismayed him more than she knew, but he understood her desire to be with his grandda.

"Laird, ye received a missive," Clovis said and jarred him from his thoughts.

He held out his hand and quickly opened the sealed parchment.

SM – We meet with our allied brethren to discuss forthcoming plans. Meet us at the crossing of your land and ours. Yours, AM

AM... He thought for a moment and realized Alan MacPherson had assembled his allies. Although he wasn't in an alliance with him, some of his allies were and so he needed to be mindful of that. Shaw folded the parchment and whistled to Trey who stood down the lane. His commander sprinted toward him and stopped near the watchman's post.

"Laird, what is it? Walen told me ye intend to leave to go in search of interlopers. Do ye wish me to come?"

"Aye, Trey, and we will need more men to go with us. The MacPherson wants to meet and he's called his allies together. We will be gone at least a sennight so pack what we will need. Find Walen and Henny and have them come to me." Shaw left them and walked sprightly toward the keep. He needed to let Sorsha know that he'd be gone for a time.

When he entered, he found her sitting by the dark hearth, sewing a garment. The sight of his sweet wife doing such a chore lightened him. Shaw grinned and ambled forward until he reached her chair. He knelt in front of her and took hold of her sewing. He set it aside on a nearby table and placed his hands on the delicate cheeks of her face.

He kissed her passionately and groaned softly when she responded ardently. Shaw forced himself to pull back. "I am leaving the keep and shall be gone longer than I thought. My allies plan to meet and the discussions may take some time. Och, I want your promise not to worry."

She pressed her hands on his shoulders. "I will not worry."

"I shall leave Walen and Henny here to protect ye, along with a score of soldiers. We'll have the gates closed until my return. That might upset Mamo."

"I shall explain to her why the gates are closed. Do we expect trouble whilst you are gone?"

"There is no reason to believe we would expect trouble, but 'tis better to be prepared."

Sorsha set a light kiss on his mouth and shifted back. "Safe journey and return hastily, Shaw."

"I will, Sorsha." He grabbed a satchel from the peg by the entrance of the keep that he kept there in case he ever needed to make quick travel. Shaw pulled the large strap over his head and hurried to the kitchens. Inside, he rummaged through the shelves and packed some foodstuff for his journey. Mistress Edra entered and after he explained about his departure, she handed him two flasks of ale and an empty one for water.

"Worry not for Milady or the wee ones. I shall watch over them," she said as she walked him to the door.

"My thanks, Mistress. Ye always take good care of us." Shaw bowed to her and left, walking quickly on the lane toward the gate. Walen and Henny approached and stopped him.

Walen said, "Trey told us that we are leaving."

"Aye, except I wish for ye and Henny to watch over my family. Will ye stay?"

His comrade groaned. "I would do as ye bade, Laird, but och ye know that I want to get away for a bit. Can we not have my brother stay? I will take his place."

"I would feel better if ye stayed and kept Sorsha safe for me." Shaw suspected he'd receive some backlash from his comrade. He'd told him earlier that he wanted to get away from his emotional wife. Still, Walen was the fiercest fighter within the Mackintosh clan and he wanted such a man to protect his family.

"I am not pleased, Laird, but of course I obey. Henny and I will ensure Milady and the children are kept safe. I wish ye safe travels but hurry the hell back." Walen gripped Henny's arm and they walked off.

Shaw was about to retreat to the stable to retrieve his horse when Trey came forward holding his warhorse's reins.

He mounted his horse but didn't wait for his soldiers. They'd catch up to him. His horse cantered ahead and he enjoyed the peacefulness of the late summer afternoon. The sun shone in its brilliance, with rays streaking through the leaves of the overhead trees. Shaw often found peace in such a view, on such a ride, but this day, he hoped the meeting didn't hold bad tidings. Then he debated the issue of whether to tell his allies about Geoff's crime of murdering not only his chieftain but his own brother. Such a thing was not condoned in the Highlands. Honor above all held its weight, especially with allied clans.

Shaw decided to wait until the meeting to rationalize whether he should reveal such a dreadful happening to his comrades. Perhaps his allied brethren already found out about Geoff's atrocious deed. If that was the case, then he might have to decide whether to go against his cousin and side with the coalition. Family or not, Shaw would have to side with the alliances.

He slowed his horse to a trot and most of the soldiers caught up to him. Trey remained silent but watchful on the ride. It took them almost half a day to reach the border of his land. By the time they approached the crossing of his land and MacPherson's, the sky had dimmed to dusk. At the bottom of a hill surrounded by large crags, fires lit the fabric of tents that speckled the landscape. It appeared many had shown themselves for the apparently important gathering.

Shaw stopped his horse and dismounted. When Trey jumped from his mount, he handed him the reins. "I will go and find out what's going on. Make camp and have the men be watchful."

Trey nodded and shouted out commands to the soldiers.

He marched off to find MacPherson and passed by many

clans aligned with his: the Mackenzies, the Campbells, and the MacPhails. None of their leaders sat with the men which gave the notion that the meeting was being held without him. Shaw quickened his steps and found the MacPherson men a short distance away. He hurried toward the tent of their leader and was stopped by two guards.

"I am Laird Mackintosh."

As soon as he spoke his name, the guards rushed to pull back the tent opening. He was waved inside and Shaw ducked beneath the overhead flap. Inside, many candles lit the confines. It appeared cozy and calm. No voices were raised in the debate and the conversation was amiable. That was a good thing, Shaw suspected, since he had time to figure out how to dissuade them from attacking the Chattans.

Shaw spotted Alan MacPherson who sat upon a thick cushion at a short-legged table. Supper had been served and all seemed to be enjoying the fare. Most drank and chatted. On his approach, all were silenced and their eyes fell on him.

"Ah, ye decided to join us, Laird Mackintosh." Alan waved him forward. "Come, there is a spot near me. Someone get Laird Mackintosh a trencher and a cup of ale."

Before he sat at the designated place, a servant rushed forward and set a full trencher of food on the table. Then a cup of ale was thrust into his hand. Shaw dipped his chin in thanks to the servants and sat upon the cushion. He folded his legs and sipped at the ale, waiting for Alan to begin his questioning.

When most had finished the meal, Alan used his cup to bang on the table. He cleared his throat and called everyone's attention. "Comrades, we have come together this day to discuss what we are going to do about the Chattans' blatant force and their desire to take over our lands. The Camerons have reported that the Chattans have threatened to build a wall on their land so their damnable sheep might graze upon the fertile grasses that belong to the Camerons."

Voices bellowed objections.

"Now, not only have the Chattans tried to overtake the Cameron land, but they have threatened to encroach on our lands as well. We must put a stop to it. Then there are the rumors that Geoff killed his brother to put his plan of overtaking us into motion. Mackintosh is finally here and we can put the question to him. What say ye, Mackintosh?"

Shaw had just taken a sip of his ale and gingerly set his cup on the table in front of him. He took his time, eyeing each man around the table. Most were allies except for MacPherson and the Frasers, although they weren't allied, they weren't rivals either. There had been no discord betwixt their clans—but that didn't mean he trusted any of the men sitting around the table.

"Well, Mackintosh, did Geoff murder his brother? Do ye keep silent because of your relation to the Chattans? Whose side do ye wish to be on when this war is begun? Ours or your supposed family's?"

The moment was at hand for him to speak the truth. As much as he wanted to protect his mother's family, he had to do the right thing. With a nod, he affirmed their suspicion. "I am related to the Chattans through my mother as well ye know, but she has gone to the hereafter. Her father, my grandda, would have been disappointed by what Geoff has done, not only to his own brother but also to my wife and her daughter. He deserves whatever ye wish to dole out and I declare that I am on your side—the side of righteousness." Shaw swallowed and waited. After a brief moment, a resounding cheer arose.

Alan held up his hand for silence. "I proclaim that it was Geoff who instigated the Cummings' overtaking of the lands given to your sister and her husband, the Dunbars. At one time, those lands belonged to the MacPhersons. The Dunbars had no right to overtake our lands and we must decide how we will proceed."

Voices rose in a clamor of agreement. Some bellowed 'war' and some called for Geoff's death. They were a bloodthirsty lot and full of vengeance. Shaw understood their need for retribution because he too wanted to seek justice for Sorsha and for Gillian, not to mention for his cousin Rodick.

"We will besiege Castle Tor and hold it until that damnable man gives himself up. We, good sirs, shall war with the Chattans at long last," Alan said with his voice full of malice.

Shaw stood. "Before ye all hail off to war, I would remind ye that it is harvest time. Our clans will soon begin harvesting our crops and we need the food to refill our stores for winter. This is not a good time to take up arms. Our crofters and farmers need our assistance. We cannot leave for such a war which undoubtedly could be drawn out. I say we wait until our harvest season is finished. We should set a day to execute this plan."

All watched him with interest and none voiced their objection. Some nodded in agreement.

Alan grumbled. "What ye speak is true, Mackintosh. Aye, we should handle our clan's business before we seek to go off to war. Och, by then though the weather will be cold, and 'tis unusual to take up arms in such weather. The Chattans will not expect to be besieged."

"Ye all want retribution." Shaw glanced around at the men staring at him. Their heads bobbed. "Many wars are fought in the cold season. We will prevail and shall meet a fortnight after the Michaelmas feast. Will that suit all?"

Again, the men bobbed their heads.

"Then 'tis settled. We will go forth in war against the Chattans two weeks after the feast of Saint Michael. All those in favor?" Alan counted the hands raised. He needn't have bothered since all were in agreement.

Shaw retook his spot at the table, finished the hearty meal, and drank more ale. The night pressed on and he wasn't in much of a rush to leave since they wouldn't head home until the morrow. Most had finished eating and some had already left the tent to seek their rest. He hoped to speak to Alan about Geoff's ill deed.

Alan waved off the remaining men at the table. When they

vacated, he spoke low. "I too wanted to speak to ye in private, Mackintosh. I know this must be difficult for ye, going against your mother's family. But crimes were committed and we must seek justice."

"I agree." He poured more ale into Alan's cup and waited for him to say more.

"Can ye tell me what happened? What do ye know about him murdering his brother?"

Shaw hadn't spoken to anyone about what Sorsha had told him. He had to make Alan understand that soon, he alone would seek vengeance against Geoff. "My wife, who was previously married to Rodick Chattan, witnessed Geoff murder him. She walked in on their row and Geoff had stabbed him. She accused him of murder and he had her daughter taken from her with the threat that if she spoke of what happened, she'd never see her daughter again. Then she was imprisoned for months until she was able to gain the aid of Queen Margaret."

"Glory be. So Geoff murders men, holds women captive, and uses children to gain his twisted desires. Aye, he deserves what is coming to him, Mackintosh."

"I will be the one to end his life."

Alan frowned at him and with a shake of his head, said, "His life will be ended, but och, we know not who will inflict his final wound."

Shaw pounded the table with his fist. "It will be me. I will be the one to end his life. I want it known and ye should tell all that side with us that none are to use their blades against him."

"Very well." Alan shook his hand, making good on their accord.

He stood and stepped back from the table. "I am going to seek my rest with my soldiers. On the morrow, we will head out early."

Alan held out his hand and Shaw helped him to rise. "My thanks. These old bones get stiffer the longer I sit. What is the reason ye rush home? We should spend the next day or so planning the besiegement."

"A warm bed and a sweet wife are awaiting me. Och, I can stay a day or two if ye want to go over the strategy." Shaw hadn't considered that the machinations would be planned right then but it probably was best to have a sound plan in place.

Alan chuckled. "I heard the king betrothed ye." He chortled. "But I suspect, ye are not displeased by this. We should all be as fortunate as to have a sweet wife awaiting us and warming our beds."

Shaw regretted speaking of marriage then at Alan's somber words. "I was sorry, Laird MacPherson, when we received word of your wife's death."

Alan set a hand on his shoulder. "Aye, she's been gone nearly two years now. There's not a day that goes by that I do not miss her. Hearing ye speak of your wife reminds me of the love we shared. Ye must hold much love for your wife to want to seek vengeance on her behalf."

Love? Shaw bowed his head but didn't retort to Alan's conjecture. Their discussion forced him to admit something he'd put off for the last months. He'd always been infatuated with Sorsha because of her beauty, kind heartedness, and sweet ways. That infatuation had grown to a love he'd never expected. Aye, he loved his wife.

"If ye want to go, then do so. We will prevail and come up with a sound plan of attack. Perhaps we might even beget peace for us all after Geoff is gone, God willing."

Shaw nodded and hoped Alan's prediction came true. Peace in the Highlands sounded good to him. "Nay, I will stay for a day or two. As ye said, I know the grounds of Castle Tor better than anyone here."

Alan's grin widened. "Good. We shall use your knowledge to our benefit and then I shall see ye at *Braigh Loch Abar* in late October."

CHAPTER NINETEEN

THE SKY BILLOWED with ominous clouds. It would soon rain. Sorsha hurried outside with the children following to beyond the kitchens, where lines hung from poles and where many of the clan hung their garments to dry. She needed to take down the laundry she'd hung earlier that morning. Even if it wasn't completely dry, she wanted to prevent it from getting soaked.

She had spent a bit of time washing Gillian's bedding since she'd had an accident during the night. After retrieving the bedding, she tossed it into a basket and picked it up. Gillian and Luthor ran circles around her, chasing each other in a game.

"Come, we should get inside before the rain falls." She lifted the basket and set it on her hip as she veered around the kitchen. The children in their excitement to be outside ran ahead of her. She smiled at their gaiety. When she rounded the building, Sorsha's eyes widened when she spotted Shaw at the front of the keep. He'd returned.

She quickened her steps to reach him, then dropped the basket and embraced him tightly. With a peck to his cheek, she settled against him. "I am gladdened you are home."

Shaw wrapped his arms around her and prevented her from pulling away. He seemed content to stand there, holding her.

"Papa, can ye teach me arrows this day?" Luthor asked.

"And me too," Gillian said.

"I will if the rain ceases later." Shaw pressed his hands on her back and leaned his head against hers. She heard his inhale of breath and his soft moan. "Lord, I was gone less than a sennight and I missed ye."

"Children, go on inside and find Enid in the hall. Wash your faces and hands for supper will be served soon." She scrunched her eyes with mirth when both Gillian and Luthor grumbled about having to wash. They scampered off and left her alone with Shaw.

"How did your meeting go? You have returned sooner than I thought you would." She peered into his dark gray eyes and saw a strange gaze in them. "What is the matter with you?"

Shaw took hold of her face, gently holding her so she would continue to look at him. "I missed ye, bonny wife. Och, the next time I return from being away, kiss me like this," he said and pressed his mouth against hers.

His kiss sent a swirl of desire through her and she held on to his arms to steady herself. She couldn't help but return the sensual kiss and mimicked the movement of his tongue. Sorsha easily lost herself in the lure of him and the promises his kiss presented. Shaw gave her two light pecks on her lips after he pulled away.

Oblivious to the onlookers, Sorsha continued to grip his arms and grinned. Drops of rain fell and grew in earnest as they stood there. "We should get inside before we get soaked." She stepped back and bent to retrieve the basket.

"Let me," he said and took it from her. "As to my meeting, it wasn't of much importance. Just a few allied clans that wanted to reaffirm our treaties."

"That is good then because I feared you might be called to war." She took the steps inside the keep and he handed her the basket.

"Why would ye think I'd go to war?" Shaw kept her from taking the steps by blocking her.

She shrugged. "Clans are always warring, are they not? I just assumed… Go on and gain your reports. I am sure Walen is awaiting to give you all the details of the happenings whilst you were away."

Shaw chuckled. "Aye and then I will probably go to the loch to wash."

"Do not take too long, supper will be served soon." Sorsha left him and took the steps to the upper floor. Upon entering the children's bedchamber, she set the basket down and immediately smoothed the bedding over the straw-stuffed mattresses. After she got Gillian's bed situated, she tidied the coverings over Luthor's.

She'd dawdled long enough and made haste to get to her chamber. With Shaw's homecoming, she wanted to look her best and needed to change her garments. Sorsha pulled a soft linen underdress over her head. Then, she retrieved a dark green woolen gown woven with a golden intricate pattern around the bodice and sleeves. She knelt by a small chest where she kept some of her belongings and retrieved the gold armband that Shaw had given her at their wedding. As she slipped it over her arm, she smiled to herself, pleased by the reminder of that fateful day.

At her waist, she pulled around a thick brown leather belt and pulled it through the brass loop. Once she finished garbing herself, she quickly fixed her hair and pulled it back with a small leather strap. She fell back upon the bed, pulled off her boots, and replaced them with the soft slippers she only wore while inside the keep.

Sorsha closed the door to the bedchamber and hurried down the stairs. She didn't take the time to notice the sounds coming from the great hall. When she got there, her gaze pivoted around the room. Many were in attendance. Had they come to dine with them?

Someone touched her shoulder from behind and she nearly jumped off the floor. Shaw smiled and pressed his hands on her shoulders.

"I hope ye do not mind, but I invited others to join us at the table this eve. There is a matter that I would put before the clan." Shaw released her and took her hand, drawing her into the hall.

Sorsha stopped by the children who sat at a smaller table beyond the great trestle table. She noted the amount of food on their trenchers. Enid approached and set cups of water before them.

Enid dipped in a small curtsey. "Oh, Milady, I hope ye do not mind but the bairns complained that they were hungry so I filled their trenchers."

"Enid, you are such a help. My thanks. Will you take the children to their bedchamber when they are finished? I have a feeling this eve will become eventful." At the maid's nod, she wondered what announcement Shaw would make and why it concerned the clan.

Before she made off to take her seat at the table, she crossed paths with Niahm who entered and approached. "Good eve, Sorsha."

"And to you, Niahm. My, but that bairn is beginning to show itself. Do you need assistance?" She held out her arm for her friend to take. The girth of her waist had doubled in size in the last month alone.

"Indeed, I am much slower these days. I meant to visit ye but the day passed before I could get out and about." Niahm leaned against her. "Walen is pleased that Laird Shaw has returned. I think he might have been worried whilst the laird was away."

"Well, he has returned and all is well. Perhaps Walen is worried about something else…" Sorsha almost giggled at her thought. Likely the man worried about his wife because Niahm shouldn't be as large as she was. "When are you due to have the bairn again? What has the midwife said?"

Niahm shook her head. "She suspects I should bear the bairn before Yule."

"You have a few months to go then. Perhaps you should get off your feet more often?"

"I wish but mayhap ye are right. I shall try. Enjoy your supper. I am going to sit with Walen so he does not stare at me all evening." Niahm released her and somewhat waddled toward her husband.

Sorsha continued past the long trestle table until she reached the chair next to Shaw's.

"There ye are, Sorsha. We awaited ye before we supped," Maven said.

"Good eve, Mamo. How are you this night? I have not seen you all day." Sorsha began piling her trencher with slices of pork covered in a thick sauce and sprinkled with parsley and spoonfuls of cooked vegetables. She eyed the plums that were coated with a sugary substance. When she was a young lass, her father often brought home sugar from his travels. She was surprised Edra cooked with it because it was a valuable commodity and rarely on hand.

"I was weary this day. These old bones are not meant for cold weather. The seasonal change is upon us, I vow, for soon it shall be cold." Mamo pulled her shawl tightly around her shoulders.

"At least it is raining and not snowing." Sorsha picked up a fat plum and took a bite. Her eyes nearly rolled at the delectable sweetness of the sugar.

Shaw leaned toward her and spoke low. "I thought we could do with a bit of a feast on my return. I take it ye find the plums delicious?"

Sorsha quickly swallowed and nodded. "I have not had sugared plums since I lived at home with my parents." Sadness overcame her with the thought that she wouldn't see them again—they were forever gone.

Voices of varied levels filled the room. As she glanced at the Mackintosh clansmen and women, a peacefulness came over her. She was home and welcomed by his clan. She'd never been so at Tor, except, of course, for Aela's tender treatment. That reminded her that she needed to ask Shaw to help her bring Aela to the Mackintosh holding.

"Lady Sorsha," Corliss called from across the table.

She hadn't noticed Shaw's sister there but offered a greeting. "Lady Corliss, I am gladdened that you have joined us this eve."

"We would not miss a feast. I wondered… Where did you get that armband?"

Sorsha peered at her arm and smiled. "Shaw gifted it to me on the day of our wedding. It was a kind gesture and reminds me of that pleasing day. I thought to wear it to—"

"'Tis crudely made, is it not?" Corliss pursed her lips together and called to Shaw, "Who made that for you, Shaw? Obviously, they were not skilled."

Shaw's brows drew together when he peered at his sister. "I had Ma's old brooch melted down to have it made for Sorsha. The ring of the band symbolizes my unending commitment to her. Why do ye ask?"

"Ma's brooch? I disbelieve ye melted down the brooch. Ma was supposed to give it to me. How could ye?" Corliss folded her arms on the tabletop and glared.

Mamo scoffed. "Och, ye be bent for no reason, lass. Ye know your ma never intended to gift it to ye. The only reason your ma kept it was because of its value in gold. Ye always confessed that ye did not like the brooch. I say good on ye, Shaw, for using it to please Lady Sorsha. That was a fair idea, melting it down to make a cuff for her."

"Ye should have told me that ye wanted it," Shaw said to Corliss.

"Ye never asked and why should I have to ask for a possession of Ma's?" Corliss leaned toward Idris but he spoke low in her ear.

Sorsha was dismayed that she had upset Corliss once again. And just when they were on more friendly terms. She would have to apologize to her privately with the hope that Corliss wouldn't hold it against her.

Idris finished his quiet discussion with Corliss and she nodded. "It matters not…about the brooch, that is. Ma gifted me with other trinkets to remember her by. Lady Sorsha, the cuff does appear beautiful with that gown though."

Sorsha almost choked on the sip of wine she'd taken at what seemed to be a compliment coming from the horrid woman. She nodded but said nothing.

Supper was coming to an end, thankfully. The conversation with Corliss was awkward and she wanted to escape Shaw's sister's watchful eye. Shaw finished his meal and rose. Walen took notice and shouted for all to be quiet. The hall silenced immediately.

"Clan of Mackintosh, in two days hence I will be leaving the fief for a visitation to our crofters and farmers." Shaw took her hand and bade her to rise. "I was given the hand of this bonny woman by the king himself as my bride. My wife, Sorsha, and I will journey to our clan's outlying areas to also give the news that the king has permitted us to keep our tax in the coming year."

A shout of cheer arose.

"We will leave the children here and shall be gone for a sennight or two."

Sorsha kept her expression from showing her displeasure. She didn't want to leave the children but she understood why Shaw wanted to give the news to the crofters in person. Before they left, she had many tasks to see to. Namely, who would watch the children whilst they were away?

"Shaw," Corliss called, and stood. "Idris and I would like to accompany ye and Lady Sorsha on this journey. 'Tis been a long time since I visited the crofters and it might aid my husband when we finally gain the rights to our land back."

"If ye wish to come along, I see no issue with it." Shaw nodded to her.

Sorsha drew a deep breath of discouragement. The only reason she got along with Corliss in the last days was because they hardly ever saw each other. On such a journey, she would have to suffer her company, God forbid, morn, noon, and night.

Corliss and her husband left the hall a short time later. Sorsha noted the hushed, harsh voices between them. They were having a row about something. If anything, she felt sorry for Idris, being married to such a harridan. Still, he was no valiant knight either. The two of them were a match made in Hell with their surly natures.

As she sat by herself, a myriad of items flitted through her mind of things that she needed to tend to the next day.

Even as she trudged up the steps after helping Edra clean up the hall, she yawned and made a mental list. Shaw was quiet on their walk to their chamber. He opened the door for her and she hurried to sit on the bed.

Sorsha removed the gold armband and set it beside her. "I cannot believe Corliss wanted your mother's brooch. You should have given it to her. I feel terrible now…"

"My sister never wanted it. Besides, my ma gave me several of her things to keep. I would not fret about it."

She sighed with weariness and set the brooch on the trunk where she kept her belongings. "I am not fretting about it." Once she finished disrobing, she pulled back the bedcover. Lying back, she closed her eyes and breathed easily.

The bed shifted with Shaw's weight when he sat on the mattress. He yawned and then pressed his body against hers. "I missed ye when I was away."

"You were only gone for three days." She giggled lightly when she felt his lips press her neck. Sorsha reached for him and settled her arm above his waist.

"Three long days, lass. I can see that ye are tired so I will let ye get some sleep. But I promise to awaken ye in the morn and spur your desire."

Sorsha snuggled closer to him. "I like it when you awaken me, as long as you promise not too early." She heard him grunt in response but didn't mind because he was beside her.

She wouldn't admit how much she'd missed him too. With each day, Sorsha was in danger of losing her heart to him. Then she reconsidered her thought. She loved Shaw and always had.

In her bedchamber the next morning, Sorsha readied for the

day. Enid had come to collect the children for their breakfasts and now she finished dressing. As she stood by the window, she gazed at the lane that passed by the fief.

Suddenly, a magpie landed on the stone sill and startled her by chirping noisily. Sorsha jumped back with a gasp. Magpies were thought to bring a bad omen or death. If only one magpie appeared, it was a sure sign that someone would soon die. Sorsha wasn't much for superstition, but birds were often considered mystical creatures. With her hand, she flapped it at the window casement, and thankfully, the magpie flew away.

By the time Sorsha left the holding, clouds grayed the sky and she draped her shawl around her shoulders to ward off the slight breeze. In spite of the chill, there was much activity about the lane. The clan was busy preparing for the harvest. Carts lined the path which would take the harvested fruit and vegetables to the kitchens where they would be readied for storage. Edra would probably be run off her feet all day and so Sorsha headed to the kitchen to help her.

She entered and found the woman sitting on a stool looking somewhat defeated. "Mistress Edra, there you are. Have you seen the children?"

"The children were here but a moment ago but I sent them to fetch straw for me. I have been up before the sun rose this day. My feet are aching and so is my back. I could use your help if ye have the time." Edra moaned and set her hand at her waist.

"Tell me what you need." Sorsha stood beside the table awaiting direction.

"'Tis the day we perform the *sop seile* ritual."

Sorsha poured a cup of warm mead and set it before the elder woman. "This should help ease you. I never heard of such a ritual. What is it?" Although she lived by the border, her family usually followed the English in their practices. Her father had been primarily a merchant with a fleet of ships and most of the rituals he adhered to were those of seafaring. She wondered who would now occupy her father's manor, who would command his fleet of ships, and what would happen to her father's wealth since Edmund had written of his probable death. Hopefully whoever took over her father's business looked out for the men her father had employed and the servants who lived at their manor.

"Oh, Milady, throughout the year straw wisps are collected in buckets and some people add metals like silver or gold to the water. The metals seep into the wisps and when harvest time comes, the men take the wisps and use them to place drops of water onto items needed for good fortune."

"Like what sort of items?"

"'Tis believed that the droplets protect the home and dwellers from nefarious eyes. It is also practiced on horses and their harnesses and rubbed on plows before being sent to the fields when planting begins in the spring. Farmers are a superstitious lot and they think the ritual will bring a good harvest season."

"It is an interesting thing to be sure." She looked at Edra's weary face. "You should stay off your feet for a spell. What do you need me to do?"

"Take that bucket and visit the cottages along the lane. They will give ye the wisps. The wisps will need to be taken to Jonah, the stable master. He shall know what to do with them."

At that moment, Corliss entered the kitchens. "Why is the morning fare late to the table? I've sat there for an eternity."

Sorsha took pity on Edra and spoke up, "Edra has a malady this morn and cannot bring it. If you want a meal, you can fix it yourself."

Corliss muttered something under her breath and turned to face the shelving where the foodstuff was placed. As she went about preparing her morning fare, she ignored them.

Before Sorsha left, she helped Edra rise. "Perhaps it is best that you take to your bed for a little while. You can return later after a rest."

Edra bobbed her head. "Aye, I shall, Milady. I want to check on Lady Maven too."

"We shall see you later, Corliss." Sorsha snatched the bucket that she needed to collect the wisps and guided Edra from the kitchens.

How could the lady hold such disparaged thoughts about her own grandmother? Sorsha thought Mamo's devotion to her husband was kind of romantic, especially in the way she spoke of joining him in the hereafter. Mamo missed her love. Sorsha would miss Shaw if she ever lost him. Maybe she should tell Shaw that she loved him.

She mused about it as Edra ambled inside, and then as she moved down the lane to the last cottage and knocked at the entrance.

A young lass opened the door.

"Good day, I am helping Edra by collecting wisps."

The lass invited her inside. "Milady, we are pleased ye have come. Here," she said, and hastened to the small kitchen area inside the cottage. "We only have one wisp. Da headed to the fields to help with the harvest and Ma was called to help birth a bairn. I am looking after my brother and sister."

"And I am sure you are doing a fair job of it. What is your name?" Sorsha hadn't known that the midwife lived there and so close to the fief, or that she had a daughter who was adept at watching children. She thought Gillian would like the lass. She wasn't old enough to marry but she would make for the perfect lass to look after her daughter when she needed someone other than poor Enid.

"Kathleen, Milady." She curtseyed slightly and hastened to the door.

"It was a pleasure meeting you, Kathleen. Perhaps you can come and have supper with us soon? My daughter would be happy to have another lass to join us."

The sweet face of the freckled lass perked up and she nodded. "I should like that, Milady."

"I shall let you know when." Sorsha crossed the threshold and continued down the lane, knocking at doors and collecting wisps. When she couldn't fit anymore in the bucket, she hurried to the stables to give them to Jonah.

She spotted Shaw helping a man fix a cart down the lane, kneeling next to the wheel. From afar, she greeted him with a wave and a smile. As much as she wished to go over to him, there was no time to waste and she continued to the stable where she found Jonah and set the bucket on the ground.

As she did so, she noticed a horse inside a nearby stall. It was snowy white and quite large. Its mane was long and braided with fashionable ribbons. That gave her the idea that the horse belonged to a woman.

"Mistress Edra had me collect the wisps for you, Jonah," she told the stablemaster. She couldn't help but move closer to the stall and peered over the door. It was a mare. She came to investigate Sorsha. "What a lovely horse." Sorsha reached out to pet its nose.

Jonah bent to retrieve the bucket. "Oh, watch yourself, Milady. She's quite ornery and nips."

"Who does she belong to?" Sorsha withdrew her hand but longed to touch the mare anyway.

"She is Milady Corliss's mare. Corliss does not like anyone touching her animal. Why, she will not even let me feed it or care for it. I keep my distance from it because she oft tries to take a bite of me now and again."

Sorsha wanted to laugh. Of course, Corliss would have such an animal, one as difficult and persnickety as she was. She turned away from the animal. "Do you need more wisps?"

"Nay, Milady, this should do well enough. Ye collected a good many. My thanks. I should be getting back to my duties." He bowed to her before he stepped away.

"Good day then." Sorsha stepped out of the stable and when she saw Shaw still fixing the wagon, she decided to go to him.

"Ye look fetching this day," he told her as she drew closer, and stood. "This is done," he told the farmer, who thanked him. Sorsha waited while he collected his tools.

"I just collected the wisps for Edra. She is run down this day so I thought it best to aid her."

"That's good. I'm sure she appreciated that. You are a good woman. Do ye know how much I want to kiss ye right now?" He swiped his hands together and frowned at the dirt on them. "But I need to clean up first."

Suddenly, they heard Edra's voice and looked to see her practically running down the lane toward them in spite of her aches and pains. "Milady," Edra called, "I cannot find Milady Maven anywhere. I checked her bedchamber, the entire keep, and around the grounds. She is nowhere to be found."

At that moment, Walen and Niahm approached. Walen said, "What is happening?"

"Mamo is missing. We should search for her," Shaw said.

"You are busy getting ready to help with the harvest. I will go in search of her and return her to the keep. Go on." Sorsha turned but Shaw stopped her.

"Sweetheart, I will have Walen go with ye. Let me know when ye find her."

She gave his arm a gentle reassuring squeeze and nodded. "Aye, I shall."

Walen turned back toward the lane and held onto Niahm. "I was accompanying Niahm for a wee bit of air but perhaps she should return to the keep. She might not be up for such a search."

"The walk would be difficult for her," Sorsha said in agreement.

"Do ye two not see me, I am right here," Niahm said teasingly. "Och, ye are right though, I should like to return to our cottage."

As she walked with the couple, Sorsha worried about Shaw's grandmother. It wasn't like her to go missing unless she went to the graves. That would be the first place she would search. When they neared the cottage, Niahm released Walen, gave a wave, and entered their home.

"Are you worried for her…Niahm, I mean?" she asked Walen when they turned onto the lane and headed toward the gate.

"She is mighty large but she says the bairn moves easily. I just pray the bairn is not so large as to cause a difficult birth."

"I am sure she will do her duty when the time comes." Sorsha hoped with all her heart that her friend had an easy labor.

At the gate, the watchman stopped Walen. "Where ye be off to?"

"Milady and I are searching for Milady Maven. Has she passed through the gate?"

Clovis tilted his head to the side and pursed his lips. "I have not seen her this day but it has been a busy morn. Lots of people coming and going."

"We will check the graves. 'Tis likely she has gone there," Sorsha decided.

"I should have kept better watch on the gate, Milady." Clovis whipped his head around and yelled to a guard who bickered with another. "Cease your grumbles, men, and be diligent." He turned back to her. "Should I send men in search about the fief?"

"Nay, we shall check the graves first. If she is not there, then we will need help." Sorsha rushed along. Walen kept up with her and stayed quiet on the walk toward the graves. At the hilly expanse that abutted the Mackintosh burial ground, she slowed her pace.

"Take my arm, Milady, these hills can be dangerous to traipse. I would not want ye to twist your ankle or fall." Walen held out his arm.

As they approached the graves, Walen stopped. "I am certain Milady Maven's husband's grave is yonder," he said and pointed to the left.

Sorsha caught sight of Maven's cloak on the ground. She gasped and sprinted ahead. When she reached Mamo, she knelt beside her and gently touched her shoulder.

"Mamo, 'tis time to awaken. We must return you to the keep." Sorsha shook her a little harder when she didn't respond. Mamo was cold and must've been out there for a while. Sorsha glanced back at Walen. "She will not awaken."

Walen stepped forward and knelt next to her. He pressed his hand near Mamo's nose to check her breathing before turning to look at her. "I think she's gone to the hereafter." He further checked her by pressing his hand on her chest and using his finger to pry her eye open. With a nod, he firmed his lips, proclaiming that Mamo had passed.

Sorsha lowered her chin and tried to stop the tears that welled on her lashes. "My heart aches but at least she has finally rejoined her husband. We shall miss her but she's where she has wanted to be at long last."

Walen set his arm over her shoulder. "Come, Milady, we should return. I shall have some men come with me to collect her. Do ye want to tell the laird or should I?"

She didn't know how to answer his question. "I...I suppose I should tell him. When you return, please bring a cloak to cover her."

"Of course, Milady. Worry not about Maven. We will take care of her." Walen removed his arm from her shoulder and rose. He held out his hand and helped her to rise.

On the return walk to the fief, Sorsha remained quiet. A large lump formed in her throat and she thought that she would probably weep if she tried to speak. How in Heaven's name would she tell Shaw that his mamo passed?

As she neared Shaw, Sorsha dreaded the words she'd say. He appeared happy and jested with the men who helped with the cart. Their banter would have lightened her if not for the fact that she was about to break Shaw's heart. He was laughing as he turned to her but when he saw her face his smile fell. "What's wrong? Have you been crying?" His gaze flew to Walen's somber mien. "Did someone hurt ye? Did something happen? Is Niahm all right? The children?"

She shook her head, on the verge of bawling, but her voice shook when she said, "I'm so sorry Shaw, but I am afraid that Mamo is gone."

"Gone? She has to be here somewhere." He moved his head

back and forth as if he'd spot the elder woman all by himself.

Walen interjected. "Aye, she lies at yonder graves and has entered the hereafter. Maven has finally joined her husband. She died, Shaw."

Sorsha lowered her head and was unable to look at her husband as he pulled her into his embrace and he wrapped her with his strong arms. With a deep sob, she let out her heartache. Fortunately, she regained her composure within a moment and wiped at her eyes.

"I was afraid she would pass... She spoke of nothing but dying in the last months. I shall go and bring her here for the clan will want to say their farewells." Shaw released her and stepped away. "Walen, have two soldiers fetch Father James from the kirk. Mamo would want a clergyman to speak prayers."

Sorsha watched the men depart. She walked almost numbly to the keep and just wanted to hold the children.

CHAPTER TWENTY

T HE DAY THEY were supposed to begin their travel, they laid Mamo to rest. Shaw had risen earlier but couldn't bring himself to leave the bedchamber. Once he did, he'd have to bury his grandmother and say farewell forever. The journey to visit the crofters was put on hold for a time, at least until they'd gotten over the loss.

He stood at the window casement and peered at the somber, gray day. The door opened but he didn't turn to see who had entered. The quiet of the chamber had allayed his sorrow until now and he took a deep breath to keep his voice from shaking.

The soft, familiar sound of Sorsha's footfalls crossed the chamber and stopped when she stood behind him. Shaw didn't want to turn around to face her, certain his mood would dishearten her as much as it had him. She hugged him from behind, placing her hands around his torso and pressing her face against his back.

"You are saddened. So am I. Why are you here alone?"

"I was thinking about Mamo." Shaw turned and kept her from moving away by wrapping his arms around her. "My parents died when I was younger than Luthor. Mamo left her clan to come and care for me and Corliss."

"She was a Chattan?"

He nodded. "Aye, she was married to the laird, my grandfather. He stayed on when his son, Rodick, took control of the clan. She didn't return. When my grandda passed, Mamo had him buried here so she could be close to him. Mamo was the only mother that I ever had or at least remember. She took good care of us and said she'd promised her daughter to look after us if anything ever happened to her."

"Mamo was a good woman."

"I am dismayed to admit that I shall miss her sound advice. Sometimes in the late evening before we sought our sleep, we would meet by the hearth and she would listen to my problems or whatever was troubling me."

Sorsha leaned back and regarded him with her pretty brown eyes. "Shaw, you are not alone. You have me now…and the children, your clan, and your comrades. Many here care for you. You are surrounded by people who love you."

"I know. 'Tis just…hard to accept that she is gone."

"Time will heal our sorrow," she said and clasped his hand. "Are you ready?"

Shaw reached for his grandmother's shawl and the small pouch of items Mamo wanted buried with her, which he had placed on the bed. He would set them with her before she was taken from them.

"We should go. 'Tis time and all await us." Sorsha stepped to a trunk and picked up a bundle of flowers he'd only just noticed. She held them and opened the door.

Shaw followed her, quiet and mournful, down the stairs to the outside. He hadn't much family in his life and losing Mamo hurt deeply. But Sorsha was right, he had her, the children, his comrades, and the clan. He wasn't alone and never would be. He took Sorsha's arm and guided her past the gate where most of the clan who gathered. Many bowed their heads to them as they passed, saying without words their sympathies.

Mamo's body was draped in the finest Mackintosh tartan and had been set upon a board for her to be carried to the graves. The litter was held by Walen, Tray, Clovis, and Jonah, and they slowed their pace when they came upon clansmen and women who wanted to add tokens of farewell to her body.

Sorsha had found some late-blooming aster flowers and picked a good bunch of them to set atop Mamo's grave. She walked beside him and the rest of the clan followed. It was such a glum day with not only their sadness of losing Mamo but the weather seemed to turn. Autumn was bidding them farewell too.

A hearty wind blew at their backs as they progressed over the bridge and small hills before the burial ground. There, his clansmen set down the litter and stood silent in wait for the priest to begin his liturgy. Father James made the sign of the cross and spoke prayers for a good length of time but adrift in his memories of Mamo, he didn't pay attention to them. He noticed Sorsha shift on her feet and he was gladdened that she hadn't brought the children. They would not have been able to withstand standing still and quiet for so long.

Father James sprinkled Mamo's body with holy water and said, "God, we ask ye to receive the deceased into Your loving embrace. We ask that ye allow her entrance into Heaven so that she can rejoin her loving husband. Amen."

When he finished, the priest drew back and stood to the side. Shaw stepped forward to cover Mamo's upper body with her favorite shawl.

Two soldiers placed the newly-etched cross bearing both his grandparents' names as Mamo had requested. Shaw bowed his head in a final farewell and drew Sorsha to retreat with him. The men lowered Mamo into the hole next to his grandfather's grave. Mamo was where she'd wanted to be. He hoped that she was happy in heaven and that she was at long last with his grandda and his parents.

Most left the area after the men began covering the hole. Shaw stood there for a while until Sorsha drew him away by taking his arm.

"Come, Shaw, we should get back to the keep. Edra is putting out a feast so we can celebrate Mamo's incredible life. Many of the clan will attend."

He was astounded. "Did ye plan this?"

"I did and hope you do not mind me taking the liberty. Mamo was important to me and I hardly knew her. I want to hear stories of her life, her kindness, and love."

Shaw leaned toward her and kissed her cheek. "I am pleased that ye thought of that. Mamo would have loved a celebration in her honor."

The walk back to the fief took little time. They entered the keep and he greeted the clansmen and women who lingered in the long hallway that led to the great hall. Sorsha continued to the hall and left him. Music came from the large room and when he entered, he noticed the musicians by the corner. Their music sounded lively with chords meant to get people moving. They played Mamo's favorite tunes.

Shaw mingled with his clan and listened to the wonderful things being said about Mamo. His gaze roved the room until his eyes fell on Sorsha. She sat at the table with Edra and Enid with Gillian on her lap. Lord, she looked lovely, especially at the way she smiled at her bairn. He reached the table and sat in the empty chair next to hers.

His sister and her husband sat on the opposite side of the table a little ways down toward the center. He smiled at his sister and hadn't yet talked to her about losing their grandmother. Shaw wondered if she was sad. Corliss didn't appear so as she spoke and appeared to laugh with her husband.

Sorsha repositioned Gillian on her lap and leaned toward him. "There you are. I lost track of you when we entered. Edra made a feast if you are hungry."

Shaw shook his head. "I could use a drink."

Walen marched forward and set before him a cup. "Laird, 'tis a potent brew. Ye look like ye could use it." He held a cup of his own and raised it high. "To Milady Maven. There has never been nor will there be another woman akin to her."

All those within hearing distance raised their cups and bellowed *ayes*.

Before long, many of his close comrades stood around the table. The conversation turned comical when Walen stood and called for attention and held up his hand for silence.

"I recall when Milady Maven replaced all the ale barrels with water-filled barrels. We all joined Shaw that night for supper and we were intent on getting well soddened with the laird's ale, except when we poured our drinks and drank, most of us spit out the water. She thought she outsmarted us and laughed about it for days after."

Shaw chuckled. He'd been proclaimed the laird right around then and many of the men supported him. Many times, he would invite soldiers and his close comrades to dine with him. But Mamo had said they made too much noise and often reprimanded them.

"I do not know why ye bother speaking of the dead. Lady Maven is gone and there is no sense in bringing up memories that should be put to rest." Idris pushed back his chair and rose.

An instant ire came to him at the man's affront. How dare he disrespect his grandmother? Shaw rose and with his stride long, he reached his brother-in-law in quick time and grabbed hold of his tunic. Before Shaw could stop himself, he'd punched Idris in the face, forcing him to stumble backward.

"What in hell…?" Idris scowled at him and pulled his dagger free. "Ye dare strike me?"

Shouts sounded around him and his clansmen pressed in behind Idris. Shaw disliked the man immensely, but he shouldn't have struck him. He was wrong to do so, but he'd been unable to resist, especially since he'd all but insulted them. Now the moment was rife with tension as his men appeared to want to murder the man and to be honest he was loath to stop them. Still, he needed to try.

"Ye will never speak of my grandmother in such a way. She was worthy of our devotion and we have every right to celebrate her life. If ye disagree, there is the door. Ye can find your way off my land and not return."

His clansmen bobbed their heads and some bumped Idris's body with theirs.

"I meant no offense, Laird Mackintosh…Shaw. 'Tis apparent ye are all distraught and I do not see why ye would cause yourselves further grief by recalling…"

Corliss approached and stood beside her husband. "Shaw, he meant no offense. Are ye not taking his words a wee too much to heart? Idris has had too much to drink this day. I will put him to bed. Come along, Idris. We should go before ye cause more trouble." His sister pressed her husband toward the exit of the hall and they disappeared beyond the threshold.

Shaw rubbed his hand because he'd struck the man with more force than he'd thought. Guilt prevented him from looking at Sorsha or the people who continued to linger in the hall. He retook his seat and slumped back. Idris, he supposed, was due an apology. He shouldn't have been so quick to temper.

He didn't know why, but the longer Idris stayed at the keep, the more he disliked him. The man reminded him of Rodick, Geoff, and most of the Chattans—self-serving. The men of that clan were more boastful and arrogant.

"Shaw…"

He didn't trust the Chattans and now it occurred to him that because Idris was allied with them, he shouldn't trust him either. Yet the man was his sister's husband and family by marriage. Shouldn't he trust his family? Nay, sometimes family was less trustworthy than an enemy. On the morrow, he needed to speak with Idris and clear up the matter but also to scrutinize why he'd come and most importantly when he intended to leave and return to Tor as he'd promised.

"Shaw…" Sorsha stood beside his chair. She leaned close and spoke softly, "I need to put the children to bed. Will you be along soon?"

"I will be a while. Ye go on and get rest."

Sorsha set a consoling hand on his shoulder. "Be sure to come to bed this night and do not get too sotted. You shall be sorry for it on the morrow." She turned away and jostled Gillian on her hip. Gillian's squeal of laughter lightened him and he felt the tugging of his lips.

"I will be along soon," he said to himself. Shaw turned back, picked up his cup, and drank the harsh brew. It did wonders to settle his angst. That and the delightful laughter of a wee minx and his lovely wife.

CHAPTER TWENTY-ONE

IN THE FORTNIGHT since Mamo's laying to rest, Sorsha had tried her best to cheer her husband. He finally seemed to come around and was his old self. Now Sorsha sat in the comfortable chair by the hearth where a good fire blazed. Gillian sat on her lap and Luthor sat on the floor. She cherished the quiet moments spent with Shaw and the children.

"Will ye tell us again about the mountain and the squirrel?" Luthor asked.

"Aye, Mama, tell us about the bun and how smart she was." Gillian giggled.

Sorsha agreed and recited the story again. The children were enthralled by it and she loved the message the story conveyed— that no matter how big or small you were, you were just as important as anyone else.

She regarded Shaw across the great hall. Walen had entered and quietly conversed with him. His comrade handed him a folded parchment. With a wave of his hand, Shaw invited Walen to sit at the table. Shaw opened the missive and his brows lowered as he read it. Whatever the message conveyed wasn't pleasant. He and Walen continued to talk but Sorsha couldn't hear them. A short time later, Walen nodded at whatever Shaw told him. He bowed to her and left the hall.

Shaw stood and approached. "Sweetheart, Walen and I were

just talking about taking the trek to the crofters. If ye do not wish to go, I can take some men with me and be quick about it."

Sorsha lifted Gillian from her lap, setting the child on her feet before she herself stood. The children ran off and chased each other at the other end of the hall. "I thought you wanted me to come along."

"I do," he said.

"Then I shall go." She watched his face as he seemed to consider her request.

"I am supposed to meet with my allies soon so there will be no time to meet with all the crofters. We shall visit only a few and return home. I will send the sentry to convey the tax situation to the others." He nodded as if he'd seemed to come to a reasonable conclusion.

"You did not mention that you needed to meet with your allies again so soon. Is there a reason? Can it not be delayed so that you can visit with your clansmen? I recall you saying that you met to reaffirm alliances. Was there another reason for a gathering so soon?" Sorsha hoped he'd explain that there was no intent to war.

"I, ah…forgot to tell ye that we planned to meet at the end of October. I thought I would be finished visiting the crofters och with Mamo's passing…"

She grabbed his hand and held it. "I understand, Shaw. Was that the message you received, from your allies regarding the meeting? Are they insistent on you joining them?"

Shaw hastily shook his head. "Nay, the message was from Tor but I cannot attend to it right now. I will meet with my allies after the visit to the crofters. They will await me. We shall leave this day in a short time. I would prefer it if ye stayed here."

Sorsha released his hand and stepped back. "There is plenty of light left this day and we can at least journey to the first croft. Perhaps we can fit in more than a few and then you can make the journey to meet with your allies. I still want to come though if you will allow me."

Shaw took hold of her hips and pulled her body toward his. He embraced her tightly and leaned his head against hers. She hoped he didn't disappoint her because she so wanted to go and meet his clan. As the laird's wife, it was important to her.

He drew in a sigh and said, "I shall make ready for the trip and prepare the men. Trey will stay with most of the soldiers to protect the fief. Ye should have Enid stay with the children whilst we are away. We will leave shortly. Meet me at the stables." He kissed her passionately, pulled away, and turned but stopped when his sister and her husband entered the great hall.

"Did I just hear ye say that ye will be leaving? Are ye going to travel to the crofters? Ye said we could come. I really want to go and it would be good for Idris to see how ye deal with your people." Corliss stood before Shaw and waited for him to reply. "Please, Shaw, it is important to me."

"Aye, go then and get ready. We shall leave hastily because I cannot afford a delay in our return." Shaw passed Corliss and left the hall.

Sorsha called to the children. "Come, we are going to the kitchens. You will have your supper there this night." She didn't speak to Corliss and shuffled the children from the hall to the back entrance of the keep. At the kitchen entry, she opened the door and found Edra humming while stirring a heavy pot on the fire in the cooking hearth. Enid sat at the worktable and appeared to be slicing vegetables.

"Good day. Enid, I must travel with Shaw and wondered if you would watch the children for me?" Sorsha glanced at the children and warned, "Do not get too close to that fire. Sit yonder by the shelf." Luthor flinched and turned away from the flames.

"Oh, Milady, I would be pleased to. I shall take them back to the keep and we will play games until 'tis time for supper. Mama has me toiling away here slicing vegetables but I would rather not." Enid chuckled. "Mama, Milady needs me."

"Hmm. Very well, go, lass."

Before Enid collected the children, Sorsha approached them.

She had taken two sweet rolls from the worktable and handed them to the children. "Gillian…Luthor… I am going to leave the keep for a few days. Mistress Enid will take good care of you. You must listen to her and be a good lad and lass." She hugged them gently and pressed her hand on their heads. "Go on. I want to hear nothing but good things on my return."

The children nodded and followed Enid from the kitchen. They seemed to enjoy being with the maid. Perhaps because Enid was fun and often spoiled them with treats. Sorsha didn't like leaving the children, but she needed to support Shaw.

"Ye look like you are about to weep, Milady."

"Leaving them is difficult." She returned to the worktable and stood near Edra.

Sorsha smiled. "Will you pack some food for us? We do not need anything lavish. Some ale, bread, and fruit. I am sure the men will hunt on the journey."

"Aye, I will have one of the soldiers take a sack filled for the laird. I am sure ye must have lots to do to get ready. Safe journey to ye, Milady." Edra slightly curtseyed and dipped as low as her aged body would allow.

"I shall see ye soon." Sorsha left and hurried to her bedchamber. There, she packed garments for herself and Shaw. She added a heavy woolen tartan and grabbed cloaks for them both. Although the day was warm, the nights might grow cold. After she stuffed everything inside a satchel, she practically sprinted to the stables.

When she got there, Shaw stood holding the reins to his horse and another's. "Ye can ride this mare or travel in the cart."

She took hold of the reins and smiled. "I would love to ride on the mare. It has been a while since I rode. How far do we ride this day?" She handed Shaw the satchel filled with their garments and he tied it to his horse's saddle.

"What do ye have in there? 'Tis bulky." He chuckled.

"I packed some garments for us both."

Shaw helped her mount the horse and set his hand on her

thigh. "We will reach the first crofter by early evening. Then we will make camp and set off early on the morrow for the next."

"Did Edra send a sack of food? I asked her too."

He grinned at her. "Aye, lass, she did. My thanks for thinking of it. Och, the soldiers attending us prepared our camp and brought plenty of food. There are two carts full of necessities for our journey." Shaw mounted his horse and led the way to the gate.

When they reached it, there was an assembly of men awaiting them, about ten or so riders. Walen was amongst them, as well as Henny. Trey appeared put out that he wouldn't make the trek with them but stood beside Clovis and assured Shaw that their clan was in safe hands.

They rode out and passed the bridge, the sweeping hills beyond, and then entered a sparse forest of trees. Sorsha was happy to be outside, riding in the cool air of the autumn day. That she got to be with Shaw too lightened her. They needed a little diversion to help them get over missing Mamo.

Corliss and her husband rode at the back of the procession, to her relief. Sorsha didn't want to have to speak with her, certain the horrid woman would have something negative to say, as always. She wanted to enjoy the outing and hoped Shaw did too.

Throughout the afternoon, they rode westerly and only stopped once to rest. The sky was beginning to dim and she hoped they reached their destination soon. Someone from the front of the procession whistled and all came to a stop.

"Is something wrong?" she asked Shaw.

He shook his head. "Nay, we have arrived. This is the croft of Cadger. He produces the most goods of any of our farmers…wool, hay, and wheat." Shaw nudged his horse forward and tilted his head for her to follow.

Sorsha rode between the soldiers who stopped and moved back to make a lane. As they got closer to the crofter's home, her breath ceased in her throat. Before them sat a lovely two-story stone cottage with painted shutters and a short stone wall that surrounded the abode. It was an attractive home and idyllic. She could imagine being the wife welcoming her husband home there after a long day out in the fields. Then she wondered if Cadger was married.

Shaw stopped and dismounted. He hastened to her, set his hands on her waist, and helped her down from her mount. Sorsha shook her feet, trying to alleviate the needles that prickled her and made it impossible to walk.

A burly bald man opened the door to the cottage and bellowed to someone inside. "We have company." He sauntered forward and reached Shaw. "Laird, 'tis good to see ye. I was not expecting your visit but welcome ye."

"Cadge, 'tis good to see ye too. Ye look well. I needed to see ye and hope to make camp in yonder woods overnight." Shaw held her hand. "And I also wanted to introduce ye to my wife. This is Sorsha. Sorsha, this is Cadge."

The man bowed to her. "Milady, welcome. My wife already served supper och ye are welcome to what we have left." Cadge turned and walked toward the cottage.

Shaw continued to hold her hand and gently pulled her forward. "We shall like anything ye have to serve. I could eat a bite or two." Before he entered the cottage, he turned to Walen. "Have the men make camp and erect my tent. We will take our slumber when we return."

Sorsha followed Shaw inside. The cottage was cozy, dimly lit with only a few candles alight and a fire in a small hearth with two chairs situated before it. A curvaceous woman with light hair appeared and carried a tray, completely filled with foodstuffs. There were sweetcakes, jellies, and other breads.

Cadger grabbed a jug from a nearby table and some cups. "Please, take the chairs. Wife, get us some more chairs so we can entertain our laird."

She hastened from the room and returned with one chair. Then she hurried away and came back with another. They all sat now and Shaw picked from the tray. Sorsha ate a large piece of sweetbread which was the most delectable thing she'd ever eaten.

Cadge poured them each a cup of ale. "Milady, this is my wife, Anabelle. Wife, this is the laird's wife, Milady Sorsha. Laird, I am gladdened ye came. We heard about Milady Maven's passing and offer our condolences. But now do ye come with good news or bad?"

Shaw held his cup of ale with both hands. He wore a serious expression on his face. "My thanks, Cadge. It was a difficult time…losing my mamo. 'Tis the truth, I come with good news. I met with the king earlier this year and he offered me the hand of this lovely woman. If I accepted her, I also reaped the benefit of no tax for the year."

"That was an offer I suspect ye had a hard time passing on." Cadge chuckled and Shaw smiled at his clansman's jest.

Sorsha smiled and her cheeks heated a little at their discussion.

Cadge grunted. "I mean who would give up the benefit of no tax? Ye be fortunate, Laird, that the woman was bonny too."

She had to shift her gaze to her lap. Of course, the man would consider the tax ramifications more important than a wife. How foolish was she? But then she wanted to laugh because men were often misguided in their view of women.

"I tell ye, Cadge, I could have passed on the no tax… Lady Sorsha was prize enough and I vow that I could not lose her."

Her heart melted a little at her husband's words. Shaw was the most charming man she'd ever met and he proved it time and again.

"If ye say so, Laird. So why are ye here telling me this?" Cadge asked and his voice grew to a cantankerous tone.

"I want to return the tax that ye previously paid and I will not be collecting further tax for the rest of this year. Use the coins to buy supplies and make repairs to your croft and land. All I ask is that ye send us a good supply of crops and wool." Shaw lifted his cup and took a good chug of his ale.

Cadge was speechless and his brows furrowed. "I cannot

believe what ye speak. That is good news indeed, Laird. Aye, we will certainly put the coin to good use. We shall send ye plenty of goods for your stores." The man struck his knee with the palm of his hand in jubilation. "Do ye hear that, wife? We can repair the plow and mayhap get ye a new spinning wheel."

"The harvest was good?" Shaw asked.

"Aye, the best in the last few years. Och, we had good weather and rain."

"I am gladdened to hear that." Shaw stood. "Well, I thank you for your hospitality. Now we will be off to seek our rest." He stuck out his hand and shook Cadge's. "In the morn, we shall leave early so I might not see ye. I bid ye farewell. Come and visit us at the keep soon."

Cadge and his wife walked them to the door. Sorsha wished them well and followed Shaw toward the encampment that his men had made. There were four large tents in all. The horses were settled and there was a big fire in the center of the tents.

Walen met them when they reached the fire. "Laird, your tent is ready. I will command the men to take to their rest but set two men to sentry duty during the night."

Shaw nodded to him and walked toward a tent. He held the flap for her and she entered. The confines were comfortable with various furs, pillows, and covers set in a makeshift bed. Their belongings were placed in one corner and Shaw's sword stood against the fabric of the tent beside the bedding.

"Let us get some sleep. We will get an early start on the morrow."

She nodded and began undressing. Sorsha left her underdress on and would use it to sleep in. Lifting the top cover, she shifted onto the makeshift bed and moaned when her head hit the pillow. "Lord, it has been a long day."

"Are ye sore?" Shaw asked as he pulled his tunic over his head. He undressed quickly and didn't bother to wear a stitch of clothing for sleep.

"A little." She snuggled against his hard, hot body and

moaned again. It wasn't soreness that caused her to groan but the warmth and strength of his body. She palmed his chest and gently stroked her fingers over the musculature.

"If ye keep that up, I will not be responsible for my actions."

She giggled. "I do not want you to be responsible for your actions."

Shaw chuckled. "Nay? Well then perhaps I deserve a kiss or two?"

"You might." Sorsha shifted her leg over him and straddled his hips. She used her hands to keep herself from falling against him. With her lips slightly pursed, she leaned forward and set a sweet kiss on his lips.

Shaw pulled her against him and she felt the heat of him through her garment. He braced her back and she shifted forward effortlessly sliding her underdress to her waist. She closed her eyes and moaned softly at Shaw's gentle invasion. Shaw eased forward to a sitting position and they rocked together, partners in desire. Sorsha wrapped her arms around his neck and held him tightly as passion completely overtook her.

Their movements increased as if neither of them could meet the other fast enough. Sorsha squealed with pleasure and Shaw grunted. He helped to lift her and she tried to give him room to move. Sorsha tilted forward until she was able to press her breasts against his chest. His hardness entered her swiftly and sent waves of culmination through her entire body. Shaw joined her and climaxed too. His open mouth pressed against her chest and he moaned. The sound of him attaining pleasure made her happy and she took his face in her hands and tilted his head back.

"What you do to me," she said breathlessly. Sorsha set her mouth on his and kissed him with all the passion she could muster. She twirled her tongue with his and kept kissing him until she was forced to take a breath.

"Ye are the bonniest lass," Shaw whispered.

They stayed joined and held each other for a good bit of time. Sorsha's legs twitched and she was sure she would be aching on the morrow, not only because of their vigorous lovemaking but also from the long day's ride. With care, she moved her leg and shifted to sit next to him. Shaw leaned over her and used his fingers to press back the locks of her hair. He placed a kiss on her forehead.

"We should get rest. I warn ye, sweetheart, not to wiggle that bonny bottom against me during the night. I will not be responsible for what I do, for I'll be unable to resist ye if ye do."

Sorsha rolled to her side, closed her eyes, and was content with being held by him. She giggled lightly at his warning and she seriously considered wiggling her bottom just to see if he would own up to his promise. A moment later, she drifted to sleep held by her handsome, passionate, and charming husband.

CHAPTER TWENTY-TWO

Sorsha awakened to light filtering through the tent flap. She sat up and peered at the empty spot next to her. Shaw had risen already and was probably making ready for their journey to the next croft. She didn't want to be the reason for a delay so she crawled from the bedding and hastily pulled on her overdress.

Before she left the tent, she folded the blankets and stacked them in a pile for the men to collect. She grabbed her satchel and now that she was ready, she wanted to go and wash by the stream and perhaps get a bit to eat before they departed.

Outside the tent, she didn't see anyone about until Walen rounded a tree and waved to her.

The man appeared tired and his hair was a tangled mess about his shoulders. "Milady, Cadge's ox got loose last night and the men went in search of it. We will leave when they return. There is some food there, in the satchel," he said, and pointed at the fire. "Help yourself."

Sorsha knelt to rummage through the assortment of fruit and grabbed three plums. That would abate her hunger until they stopped for the midday meal. "Is there a place to wash?"

Walen was about to answer her, but Corliss ambled forward. How the woman appeared so beautiful in the morning, irritated Sorsha, but the woman's lovely black hair fell in untangled waves to her waist. Her blue eyes shone brightly and were stunning. If only she wasn't such a shrew, they might be friends. But then Sorsha almost scoffed aloud at that thought.

"Sorsha, I would like to wash too. There is a river not too far from here. We shall go together. I would probably get lost trying to find my way back." Corliss linked her arm with hers. "We shall return shortly, Walen. Tell Shaw not to worry."

Sorsha had no chance to refuse Corliss's offer and walked along with her. Corliss gave no care that her skirts grazed the ground as they walked. Sorsha tried to hike her skirts up a little to make it easier to walk because with her long legs, Corliss's stride was quicker than hers. As they left the treeline, a stretch of open fields sat before them that led to a craggy area of rocky hills. Beyond the steep hills, she saw the glimmer of water. Near a huge bluff where a boulder sat and shaded the ground before it, Corliss stopped.

"This is a good place to seek nature's call." She ventured forward and squatted beside the boulder.

Sorsha had an urgent need too and for privacy's sake, she used the other side of the boulder. When she finished the chore, she rose and rounded the rock. Corliss awaited her and faced the exquisite view. Beyond the high bluff sat mountainous peaks that seemed to go on forever. The hue of them grayed and some were bluish. The sight mesmerized her because she'd never seen anything so spectacular.

"It is lovely here, is it not? I have never seen such a beautiful view." Sorsha wished she could stay there and gaze with wonderment at it. But there was no time to dawdle. The men likely returned from fetching Cadge's ox by now.

Corliss linked her arm again and eased her forward. "Let us go there," she said and veered around a crevice on the ground. "Take heed. Watch your step."

The woman's concern forced Sorsha to keep her gaze on the ground before her, ensuring that she didn't twist her ankles or misstep. Now, the closer she got to the bluff, the more nervous she became. She wasn't fond of high places and she sensed she'd become dizzy if she got any closer. With a yank to her arm, she dislodged herself from Corliss's hold and stepped back.

"I do not like heights. I shall stay here and await you if you wish to take in the view." Sorsha moved back to the crag and it was the perfect place to sit and await her. "We should head the other way though and seek the stream to wash. I do not wish to be away too long."

"Oh, nay…" Corliss returned to her and pulled her away from the rock. "Come, it is not that high and I do not want to view it by myself. 'Tis bonny and ye will regret missing out. There are waters not too far beyond this point."

Sorsha tightened her hold on Corliss's arm. "Only for a moment then."

Corliss stepped toward the edge and Sorsha's legs shook. Fear lodged its horrible tendrils in every part of her body. Her legs wobbled, her shoulders tensed, and her stomach twisted in a knot that alerted her to the danger she was in. She tried to pull back but Corliss kept hold of her.

"Geoff told me that he had hoped to marry ye and asked ye before ye left for Edinburgh. Ye thwarted him, did ye not? What I wonder is how ye got a message to the queen. Geoff said that ye were good friends. He spoke about his plans and that ye went and ruined it. Do ye know, Sorsha, how disappointed he was?"

"You spoke to Geoff about me?" Sorsha's breath quickened, not only at the thought of being so close to the edge of a drop but also that her sister-in-law had conversations with the knave about her.

"Aye, when I stopped at Tor before coming to Moy, we had a nice visitation. I was surprised to find that ye married Shaw. My brother professed not wanting to marry, and then, here ye are— his attitude greatly changed. I also wonder what ye did to Shaw to change him." Corliss clicked her tongue as if she disapproved of her relationship with her brother. "Ye must be some kind of temptress."

"I had no choice but to accept Shaw. The king put us both

forward for marriage. Shaw and I had met many years ago at the king's castle. We got on then and…" She did not know why she bothered to explain her relationship with Shaw to her. "Our paths crossed again and we were pleased by it. Surely you want Shaw to be happy."

Corliss kept her eyes trained on the view in the distance, her pert nose raised slightly as if she disregarded her. "Not really. I couldn't care less whether he is happy or not. He and I never got on well together. Why should he be happy when I am not?"

"You do not mean that, Corliss. Shaw cares for you. You are the only family he has left."

Corliss scoffed with derision. "He has plenty of cousins who would have stuck by him, but Shaw thought to distance himself from them."

She gripped Corliss's arm tightly and managed to shuffle back a step. "You mean the Chattans."

"Aye, the Chattens. I am so close to getting everything I have ever wanted. There is only one thing that stands in my way—you." She shoved Sorsha and then forcefully pressed her to the edge of the land. "Farewell."

Rocks scuttled on the cliffside. Sorsha cried out and tried to grab hold of Corliss. But then the woman pushed her and her body plummeted over the edge. The descent was long and steep. She screamed with sheer terror then shut her eyes and prayed. At first, she felt dizzy but then a sense of spiraling came. Her stomach knotted and even though she tried to grab hold of something…a stone, grasses, or even a tree root, the land gave way beneath her. She slid downward, her body scraping against the hard rock. Numb to the pain, she thought she would surely die before she reached the bottom.

With a hard thud, Sorsha landed at the base of the summit. Small pebbles and rocks followed her descent, clattering after her. But the sound of the water lapping at the shore brought to her the realization that she had survived.

It was a miracle.

She lay still in case Corliss looked to see if she moved, if she was alive—or dead. Obviously, her sister-in-law had a murderous mission on her mind. Sorsha wouldn't allow her to discover she'd failed in her attempt.

After a bit of time passed, she opened her eyes a mere slit to see Corliss peeking over the edge. She even made a joyful whooping sound as if to celebrate what she saw as her success. Then she pulled her head and shoulders back and disappeared from view.

Sorsha waited a few more moments before she finally began to look around. She lay on a rocky beach of sorts, before the waters of the loch. It was a miracle. Still, Sorsha didn't try to move from where she lay because not only did her head throb, but so too did her leg. Her hands stung too, but nothing appeared to be broken as she wiggled her fingers, then lifted her arms and looked to be sure. She drew a gasp at the sight of the bloody scrapes covering her palms.

Sorsha moaned and wished she hadn't gone off with Corliss. No one knew where she was, or even that she'd gone off with the woman. She'd be left there to die alone, certain her injuries were far too severe for her to make her way back up the hillside. Even if the men searched for her, they wouldn't suspect that she'd fallen over the cliff—or rather, had been pushed.

Why would Corliss want to hurt her? Even as she thought about it, she couldn't discern any reason for Shaw's sister's hatred. Sorsha closed her eyes and listened to the noises around her: birds squawked as they flew nearby, water lightly met the land with a whispered, hissing wash of waves, and the wind that made a light whistle around the bluff—it was almost peaceful. Except for the hammering of her heart and the sound of her own breath, she heard nothing.

CHAPTER TWENTY-THREE

WHEN CADGE'S OX went missing, all were roused and asked to join in the search. Shaw was hard-pressed to reject the offer to aid the farmer. Although he wanted to be on his way, there was no hope for it. He assembled his men and gave the order to spread out to locate the wayward animal.

"How did he get out?" Shaw asked the crofter.

Cadge shrugged. "I do not know, Laird. Last eve, I made sure his pen was closed and put the pin in the latch as I do nightly." The wooden pin was nowhere to be seen now as they viewed the pen and the surrounding ground.

"Why would someone purposely release your ox?" Shaw was baffled by the happenstance. A steer was a sacred and valued property. Men were killed for stealing animals in the Highlands. Surely someone wouldn't risk their life for one ox. "Have ye had any problems with thieves or anyone bent on trouble recently?"

"Nay, Laird, nothing of the sort. Hooligan is my only ox and I take good care of him. I was going to plow the last field this morn and then put him to pasture. He worked hard the past month helping me to harvest the grains."

Shaw walked alongside his crofter. "Worry not, my men and I will help search for him. If he got out, he might not have gotten far."

"Aye, aye… The last time he escaped, he got as far as the

bluff." Cadge grabbed a long rope that hung outside the barn and then another from inside. "We will need these to capture him. Hooligan does not like to be trapped."

They spent a good amount of time searching for the animal. Awakened near dawn, time whittled by and the sun rose higher. So much for getting an early start to the next croft he'd wanted to visit, Shaw thought as he directed his men to search the hills and beyond. Hooligan could be hiding behind one of the higher hillocks.

Finally, they spotted Cadge's ox. An ornery beast, he stood on the butte of a high crag as if he challenged them. His soldiers ran at the steer and tried to rope him but Hooligan wasn't having it. Surrounded by eight men, the ox charged at them. Hooligan's horns were massive and thick, but fortunately for them pointed downward. If they were positioned upward, he and his men ran the risk of being skewered by the beast.

Three men had tried and failed to secure the steer. Hooligan thwarted them easily and practically ran the men over. Overall the animal appeared unamused by their efforts as Shaw's men lay in the dirt and groaned. In contrast, Shaw bellowed with laughter at the easy way the ox had thwarted them. It was as if he were playing a game. Cadge was right when he said his steer didn't like to be trapped.

"Ye cannot run at him. Hooligan is smarter than most oxen. He knows when he is being pursued. Best ye slide forward on light feet," Cadge said, trying to give direction as he shook the bucket of grain he'd secured to tempt the beast to come near.

"Go on, Henny, ye are next." Shaw motioned to his comrade and tilted his head at the ox. "Let us see if ye can catch him. Ye are light on your feet. If ye do, I will bring ye a jug of brew when we return home."

"Do ye mean the good stuff or what Mistress Edra serves us?"

Shaw chortled. "The good stuff. Now, let us see how ye fare. Go on."

Henny held the rope and inspected the knot at the end of the line. If his soldier could get it over the beast's head, then he might have a fair chance at capturing him. Now he ambled forward with slow, light steps. Focused on the food the farmer carried, Hooligan seemed uninterested in Henny, who tossed the rope and missed by a good length.

"Bollocks!" Henny muttered and then ground out a few more expletives.

Hooligan tossed his head, flicked his tail, and pawed the ground.

"Go easy, Henny," Shaw said. "Ye are our last hope. Try again." In truth, he hadn't laughed so hard in ages. His eyes were soaked with tears of mirth as his men had a difficult time trapping one massive, ornery beast.

Henny studied the animal and grunted. "Aye, ye want us to leave ye be? Sorry, ye wee troublesome ox, och your master needs ye. Ye have work to do. Come on now, best ye cooperate." He approached Hooligan from the side. Henny's calm voice seemed to soothe Hooligan.

The steer seemed less threatened now since Henny left a clear path for the ox to escape should he feel trapped. His soldier set a hand on the steer's back and pressed it toward the animal's neck and head.

"There is naught to fear." Hastily, Henny set the rope over the ox's horns and gently pulled it tightly to ensure Hooligan couldn't gain his freedom. "Ye see, all is well. Come, we shall get ye back to your pen." He began walking with Cadge beside him, shaking the bucket enticingly, and Hooligan followed meekly without further trouble.

"I owe ye a jug of brew, Henny. Remind me when we get home," Shaw said and followed the group of men back to camp near Cadge's croft.

As soon as they reached the camp, Shaw hoped to get on the trail to the next croft. It wasn't too far from where they were presently and with luck and some hard travel, they might reach it before nightfall.

On the approach to camp, Henny veered off and led Hooligan to his pen. Shaw traipsed toward his horse and noted all the tents had been packed on the cart. Likewise, the fire had been extinguished and the rest of their belongings were stowed.

From afar, Walen raised his arm and signaled to him, then began to approach. Shaw waited for his friend to reach him. He opened his saddlebag and removed a piece of bread. With the excitement of the morning, he hadn't eaten and was famished.

"Laird, I am gladdened ye returned. Milady went for a walk with your sister earlier and they have not returned."

Shaw swallowed the bread and nodded to him. "Aye? Ye sound a wee bit worried."

"They should have come back by now and have been gone a long time. I was about to set off to find them but heard the men returning. Now that ye are back, I can go and fetch them."

He waved Walen off. "Nay, I will go. See that the rest of the men make ready to leave. I want to get on the lane as soon as I return. Which way did they head?"

Walen pointed to the left. "They said they were going to wash at the river."

Shaw bobbed his head and headed toward the west. An outcropping of trees dropped their leaves overhead as he ambled through a worn lane between the heavy trunks, still chewing his chunk of bread. He kept his eyes trained ahead and focused on where he was headed. He couldn't discern any movement ahead of him as he searched for Sorsha.

Before he left the tree line, something stung him on his back. Shaw turned slightly to find Idris standing behind him. "What goes here?" Then Idris moved and he saw him pulling a blade away. A warm gush—of blood?—flowed and made his garment wet, and the sting grew into a swath of pain over his side and back. He pressed his hand to feel the place from where the pain originated, and grunted.

When he looked at his palm, it was slick and red with his blood. Idris had stabbed him!

His brother-in-law shoved him and Shaw fell to the ground. His head spun from the pain that now reverberated through him. He took quick breaths to try to alleviate it but it did no good. Never had he thought his brother-in-law would attack him.

His training took over his mind and he tried to reach the dagger in the belt loop at his waist. Though the effort brought on more pain and he finally got a hold of it. With the blade held in his hand, he aimed it at Idris.

"Stay still ye bloody bugger," Idris said, kneeling beside him and raising his blade in his fist over Shaw's chest. "'Tis the end."

Shaw flailed his body to try to get away from his brother-in-law, who peered at him with fierce loathing. Though he held his dagger, it slipped in his bloody palm. Unable to get a good grip on the weapon, he struck Idris with his left fist then bent his legs and shoved himself up enough to dislodge the man from atop him while twisting his body to the side at the same time. Idris rolled on the ground face down then pushed himself to his knees. Again he raised his knife and was about to stab Shaw in the chest when suddenly his eyes widened and he made a startled, choked sound.

Before Shaw could make out what happened, Idris pitched forward and fell face-first to the ground. He didn't speak but continued to gurgle and gasp as he convulsed. Shaw's gaze shot from his assailant to the man standing behind him.

Henny gripped his sword, still lodged in Idris's back, and nodded to him. "Ye see, Laird, *that* is why ye should always be aware of who is near. Best to be prepared for an ambush at all times. Ye never know who means to attack ye." Henny yanked his sword free and wiped the blade clean on a dry place on Idris's clothing before setting it down. He then pulled a wad of cloth from the satchel that hung over his shoulder. "Let us get ye bound and back to camp."

At that moment, Walen sprinted up to join them. "What the hell has happened? Laird, are ye hurt? Why is Idris...?" His comrade's eyes shifted from him to Idris, and then to Henny.

"Idris tried to kill me. Henny saved me." Shaw held up his

clean, unbloodied hand for Walen to help him up and tried not to groan when his comrade gently pulled him to standing. "I owe ye more than a jug of brew, Henny. My thanks."

"'Tis my duty, Laird, to protect ye." Henny yanked Shaw's tunic above the wound and proceeded to wrap the thin cloth around his torso. "'Tis a deep wound. Ye will need stitches to bind it. Might take a wee bit of time to heal."

Shaw gave up trying not to groan and pressed the bandage at his waist. He wasn't concerned for himself but for his wife. "I need to find Sorsha. She went to the river with Corliss. Walen…"

"I am on it, Laird," Walen said immediately and sprinted off toward the tree line, disappearing beyond it.

As he waited for his comrade's return, Shaw pondered why Idris had attacked him. What gain would it bring? If he'd died, his clan would have elected a new laird. That certainly wouldn't have been Idris. If anything, Walen or Trey would have been selected by their brethren. Unless Idris had another way to sway his clansmen to let him overtake the clan. Shaw only knew of one way that could happen—*war*.

But Idris had no army with him and his clansmen had fled when the Cummings overtook his fief. That left the man unaided and without the support of arms. Yet he had to have the backing of someone to enact such a daunting, daring plan. Now, worried about Sorsha and overcome by the throbbing in his back, Shaw couldn't reason it through, but he would certainly think more about Idris's plan and what he'd hoped to accomplish.

"Come, Laird. I'll help you." Henny moved to stand beside him. "We'll go to the crofter's house and get you stitched and bandaged."

Shaw put his left arm around his waist and braced himself to feel the pain the movement would bring. But then he spotted Walen running at a breakneck speed through the trees toward them and his heart dropped to his knees. Walen wouldn't be running unless he'd discovered something very bad. He forgot his pain and started toward his soldier and friend.

Indeed, Walen called out as soon as he drew close. "Shaw, 'tis bad… The ladies were not at the river. I searched amongst the grounds and saw something at the base of the cliff. It is…" He paused before speaking. Gathering courage. Shaw felt himself swaying and Henny held him upright. No. It couldn't be.

"Lady Sorsha. She must've fallen."

Sorsha! Shaw wanted to run but with his wound, he could only manage a fast walk. Walen came up to support him on the other side and they seemed to move at the slowest pace ever. His breath hitched the entire way and his heart pounded so much so that he could barely hear anything except a high-pitched noise— along with darkening vision—made him realize he was about to pass out. From the loss of blood or from shock, it mattered not. Sorsha, the love of his life, was…he couldn't even think the word.

Now he gazed over the edge and saw her unmoving body. Everything within him ceased to exist at that moment. He couldn't breathe and suddenly, his heart seemed to still. When he remembered to draw breath, he was able to turn toward his comrades.

"Help me. God willing she lives," he said low. "We need a rope to reach the bottom."

"I will see to it," Henny said. He helped Shaw to sit on the ground before he sprinted away.

"There is no way to reach her quickly if we route around the cliff. It shall take us past nightfall to get to her." Walen knelt at the cliff's edge. "It does not look like the ground here gave way. How in God's name did she fall? Milady is not clumsy, nor is she reckless."

The answer, though horrible to consider, was obvious. Shaw tried to draw a deep breath and failed. "My sister's husband tried to kill me. So someone must have pushed my wife over the edge."

Walen grunted. "She was with Corliss, Laird. Would your sister…?"

When his friend's supposition trailed off, Shaw nodded, as he thought of Corliss's attitude and actions over the past months. Her disdain. Her haughtiness. And though Sorsha had tried not to complain, her apparent hatred of his wife. It may have been Idris who was guilty but he feared not. "Aye, it had to be her. Damn her! It could be no other. Corliss and her husband planned this— to do away with both me and Sorsha."

"Laird!" Henny's voice reached them before he did, even though he ran as if the devil himself chased him. Instead, he was followed by more of Shaw's men. When he reached them, he tossed a good bit of rope to the ground. "I grabbed several ropes, Laird. If we tie them together, we can reach the bottom."

Walen grabbed an end and walked to the nearest tree. "I'll tie this end to the tree to anchor it. Who will rappel the incline?"

Henny tied the rope around his waist. "I shall do it. Walen, take hold of the rope, and slacken it as I go. I am going over the edge of the crag and will go slow."

Walen stood near the edge and as Henny disappeared over the ridge, he loosened a bit of rope moment by moment. Several of his men helped Shaw up to stand beside Walen so he could peer over the edge to watch Henny's progression. He was about halfway down the slope when suddenly Shaw heard a snapping sound.

"Henny!" He, Walen, and his soldiers shouted at the same time. Leaning over the edge, they could only watch in horror as he plummeted and then landed at the bottom not too far from where Sorsha lay.

Shaw breathed heavily in shock at what he'd just witnessed; if not for the men holding him up, he would have collapsed for sure.

"The rope frayed because of the drag," Walen pulled up what rope remained and examined the end. Then he shrugged and began tying it around himself. "I will go."

"'Tis too dangerous, Walen. We should get more aid. I cannot help ye with this wound."

"At least let me get down there. I will signal if Milady and

Henny live by sticking up my thumb. Once I can see to them, ye can send another to get help." Walen didn't wait for him to agree and tied the rope around his waist. "Hold tight."

Shaw's soldiers gripped the rope and wrapped it around their waists and—once they'd wrapped their hands with cloth ripped from their own tunics—their fists. Walen scaled the edge and used his feet to jump little by little down the cliffside. Shaw's heavy breathing intensified his pain, but he kept watch and directed his men to slacken the rope as Walen went along. After what seemed like hours but was probably only a moment, Walen reached the bottom.

He waited for Walen to give him the signal. *Please, God, let them be alive.*

His comrade reached Sorsha first and knelt next to her. He seemed to be assessing her and stuck his thumb up before he shouted, "She breathes." Then he rushed to Henny's side but didn't bother to kneel next to their comrade. Walen kept his head lowered, stuck out his arm, held his thumb down, and shook his head.

A wave of despair rushed over Shaw; Henny had been one of his most trusted and devoted men. It didn't seem right that he'd be dead. He would have been proud to die in service to his laird and his lady, however. Now the clan's war cry rose from his men. *Loch Moigh!*

More of his soldiers arrived from the camp as word of the attacks—and Henny's death—spread, and again and again the war cry arose. The clansmen were saddened by the loss of their comrade, yet enraged about the attack on their laird and lady. "Henny was a good man, an admirable soldier, and will be given the highest honor our clan can give," Shaw told them.

One of the soldiers, Donald, stepped forward. "Laird, our lady will need boards for a litter and for Henny's...body. And more rope."

"One of ye will need to fetch the healer for the laird and Milady. Someone grab the crofter's tools, whatever ye can find.

Let us prepare and make haste."

It wasn't like Donald to take charge of any situation because Henny usually directed him. He'd been a fledgling soldier beneath Henny's guidance and only recently was promoted to a higher-ranking position. Shaw appreciated him stepping forward because, at that moment, he was heartsick, overcome, and feeling weak and dizzy from loss of blood as his wound continued to bleed. He remembered that it was Henny who'd saved his life and who had told him he'd need stitches.

Now Donald knelt beside him. "Laird, what do you command? Who did this to you? What happened to Milady?"

"Idris," he rasped and then realized that Corliss had been the one Sorsha had left camp with, and now she was missing. He had questions to put to her. "Call Gordon. Have him find my sister. Take her into custody for she might be responsible for my wife's injuries. Take her home and put her in the garrison cell. Set the remaining guardsmen to watch her." Fortunately, their fief was just over the ridge and his sister would be secured quickly.

Gordon shouted to Craig and they set out. Both men were well-known trackers and talented scouts. Shaw knew they wouldn't cease their search until they found Corliss.

Cadge arrived, holding a satchel, and the older man shuffled toward him. "Let us see what's what, Laird." He unwrapped the wound and hissed at the sight of it. "It shall be well. I will put some salve on it to keep it from bleeding. Ye need to see the healer though, and at the soonest."

"I'm not leaving Sorsha," he said.

"At least take a wee bit of this to ease your pain." Cadge handed him a small flask and he drank. The crofter helped him to lie back on the grass while he waited, listening to his men moving about and shouting instructions to one another as they worked to rappel Sorsha up from below and to retrieve Henny's body.

He thought about Corliss. Shaw was unsure what he'd say to her. The thought that she betrayed him brought more dismay to his heart. All the times Mamo had spoken truthfully about

Corliss's cruelty made him flinch. He should have listened to his grandmother. Mamo always said Corliss was self-serving, greedy, and was only concerned with her own needs and desires. It had all been accurate.

He shouldn't have trusted his sister, especially around Sorsha. Guilt plagued him briefly as he thought about the suffering Sorsha had endured. But he couldn't hold the blame for long because his wife needed him and he would move heaven and earth to get her help.

Finally, the board that carried her reached the edge, and he painfully got to his feet to move to her. Her eyes were closed but he was relieved to see her chest rising slightly. *Praise God, she hasn't died.* Again he fell to his knees, and for the first time in his life, Shaw wept. He cried with relief, with pain, and with love.

CHAPTER TWENTY-FOUR

IN A DARK shadowy place, as if she floated beneath the depths of the deepest sea, Sorsha heard her name. The voice that called to her was muffled. A man's deep tone penetrated the fog and implored her to awaken. She didn't want to, but then she heard the cries of Gillian and Luthor. She pulled herself toward their voices, bit by bit, until she was able to open her eyes. She blinked. It was bright. But then she focused on her sweet children who stood watching her with tears in their eyes.

"*Shhh.* Do not weep." Sorsha couldn't recall what happened to her and how she'd ended up in her bedchamber. She wondered why the children were crying.

"Mama, are you hurt?" Gillian stared at her unmoving.

Sorsha took stock of her body, testing to see if she could move. Pain thrummed in her head and a more intense pain ached in her back and leg. She reached out to take Gillian's hand and was shocked by the state of her own hand. Scrapes had bloodied her skin and now they were scabbed over.

But the last thing she wanted was the children worrying about her so she retracted her hand and slid it under the blanket that covered her.

"I will be all right, bun. Worry not." But even as Sorsha spoke the words, she didn't hold truth to them. The way she felt and the pain that made her want to moan seemed to thrum through her.

"Where is Shaw…*ah*, your da?"

Luthor shifted forward and touched her forearm. "He is talking with the healer in the hallway."

"Get him, please, and Luthor, take Gillian with you. Watch out for her."

"Aye, Mama, I will." Luthor took Gillian's hand and led her from the chamber.

As Sorsha waited for Shaw, she tried to reason how she'd gotten hurt and how she had returned home. A flash of a memory came to her, that of her falling. Had she fallen from a cliff? Wherever it was, the fall was of a great height.

Shaw stepped into the room and hastened to her. His manner was grim and concern darkened his deep gray eyes. Tears sprang to her own eyes. His joyful gaze was shadowed.

"Sorsha, love…do not move. Stay still. The healer needs ye to remain as still as ye can until he can look ye over." He set a light kiss on her forehead. "God Almighty, I am glad to see ye awake. Ye have been here for almost a sennight."

"What…?" She swallowed the lump in her throat. "I am so parched."

Shaw grabbed a cup that sat on the bedside table. "'Tis only water to wet your throat." He held it to her lips.

She sipped it slowly. "What happened?"

"We shall talk about it later. For now, the healer wants to recheck ye. Ah, here is Louis now. When we got home, he had to set your leg and stitch ye up."

"Does this hurt, Milady?" He inspected her by pressing on her arms and head.

"Nay, Louis. My head hurts a little but not because you pressed on it. What's on my leg? Why can't I move it?"

"Aye, ye probably bumped your head when ye fell and it will take time for it to clear."

"Your leg was broken. I have splinted it after I set it. Ye will have to stay off your leg for a while, Milady. It shall hurt for a time." Louis handed her a drink which tasted a wee bit foul but she gulped down the entire cup. "That should ease your pain, Milady. Rest for that is the best cure for now."

The healer continued his ministrations and when he finished, he clicked his tongue. "'Tis quite remarkable, Milady, that ye did not suffer more significant injuries. From what the laird told me, ye fell a good distance. Until we know for certain that ye did not hurt your insides, ye must stay abed. As to the rest of ye, ye suffered scrapes which I have already covered with a healing balm. It shall take time for ye to heal."

She blinked and tried to keep her eyes open but it became impossible. Finally, Sorsha fell into a deep and dreamless slumber. When she awakened again, her eyes immediately went to Shaw.

He sat in a chair near the window casement with his eyes closed. The shutters were opened and a stream of fresh air tousled a tapestry that sat on the adjacent wall. She watched him and regarded his handsomeness. His hair was pulled back into a tie behind his neck, showing his high cheekbones and straight nose. He hadn't removed the whiskers from his face and dark hair covered his jawline.

She tried to shift her body to sit up but the contraption the healer placed around her leg was heavy. In her effort to reach the side table and the cup that sat upon it, she leaned to her side and moaned but couldn't reach it. It woke Shaw, who moved quickly to her side.

"Ye finally awakened," Shaw said and moved to sit. "How do ye feel?" He handed her the cup.

"I...think I am well enough. Maybe hungry." She drank the water and handed the cup back to Shaw.

Shaw smiled. "Edra has been cooking nonstop awaiting the order to feed ye." He rose and hurried to the door. He opened it and ordered whoever stood outside in the hall, "Tell Mistress Edra that we need a tray of food for Sorsha."

When he returned to her, Sorsha smiled. "Who was outside the door?"

"Luthor. He is mightily concerned for ye and has stood outside our bed chamber door and declared that no other will protect ye. All the clan has been asking for ye as well." Shaw's words quieted.

"Shaw, I wish to sit up. Can you help me?"

He nodded and set his hands beneath her underarms and shifted her upward, careful not to move too quickly or dislodge her leg. "There is much I need to tell ye. But first, ye need to eat."

"I can eat and listen at the same time," she said grumpily. "While we await the food, tell me what happened."

"We were at Cadge's croft, remember?"

She started to shake her head, but that hurt. So she closed her eyes and thought about it. Finally, she recalled the man's face. "Oh, that is right, the crofter. I remember waking up and you were gone. I packed up the tent and Corliss suggested that we go to the river to wash before we began the journey. Oh, Corliss. Is she—"

"What else do ye remember about her, Sorsha? 'Tis important." Shaw sat beside her and took her hand. His thumb played over the back of her hand. He held her gently and peered at her as if he had many questions or awaited an answer that would displease him. "Tell me."

"We were talking and…" Sorsha felt the pull of her brows as she considered that day. "Corliss shoved me and I fell over the cliffside. I remember that I screamed and couldn't believe what she…said. She told me that she…" Sorsha swallowed hard and Shaw handed her the cup of water. She drank deeply, emptying the cup before continuing, "Corliss said that she was close to getting everything she ever wanted and that I was the only thing standing in her way."

"Then she pushed ye?"

Sorsha nodded. "When I was falling, I thought I was going to—"

"Shhh, sweetheart, say naught more." Shaw caressed her hair and smiled lightly. "God answered our prayers…well, *my* prayers. I thought ye were dead and it crushed me."

"How did you get to me? When I was lying there, I looked around to see if there was a way to make it back up the rise but I couldn't see any."

He sighed deeply. "Henny tied a rope around himself but it unraveled and he fell too. Only he did not make it. His injuries took him. We buried him as soon as we returned."

"Oh, Shaw, this distresses me. He died trying to save me." Sorsha pressed her hand on his leg. "I am sorry because 'tis my fault."

"Nay, it was no fault of yours but another's. The rope gave way and Henny fell but Walen was able to make it down the cliff. He stayed with ye whilst we sent for help." He leaned forward and set his head next to hers. "I thought I lost ye."

"Where is Corliss? Did she confess?" Sorsha needed to know where the horrid woman was.

"Corliss is being held by the clan until I have time to deal with her." Shaw pressed his hand on the side of her neck, fondling the curve of her shoulder. "I held such guilt for what happened to ye. I trusted Corliss and did not suspect any discord between us. How wrong I was."

"She is your sister, and of course, you would not think such things. Why would she want to hurt me? What do you think she meant when she said that I was in her way?" Sorsha couldn't reason the woman's motives for wanting to harm her.

"That morn, when I left the tent, we were asked by Cadger to find a missing ox. Most of us went to help the man except for Walen who I left to look after ye and Idris who was eating his morning fare by the fire. I never suspected Idris would try to kill me."

Sorsha gasped at his admission. "What! Idris tried to kill you? When?"

"When I got back to the camp, Walen told me that ye and Corliss went to the river. I bade all to stay there whilst I went to fetch ye. On the way, Idris stabbed me in the back. Henny followed me and he attacked Idris and slew him."

"Oh, gracious, Shaw. How badly were you wounded? Have you mended?" Sorsha took his face in her hands and held him. She peered into his eyes and when he closed them, she sighed.

"'Tis naught to worry over. Louis mended me. I hardly feel it at all now."

"Promise me that you are healed." She implored him with a deep gaze.

"Almost, sweetheart, but soon enough I shall be good. 'Tis beginning to heal. That is why I have waited to meet with Corliss. There is something else I must tell ye and ye might be daunted by it."

She raised his face, feeling the tickle of his whiskers on her palms. "What is it?"

"I must meet with my allies soon…and vowed to at the end of October. 'Tis a matter of importance which is the only reason that I would leave ye now, especially with ye ailing."

Sorsha patted the bedside on the opposite side of her hurt leg. "Come and lie with me." Shaw rounded the bedside and with care, he shifted to position his body as close to hers as he could. She shimmied her bottom so that she lay more on her side and flung her arm over his hard torso.

"Shaw, there is naught you can do to help me improve. But I worry about this so-called meeting you are having with your allies. It will not be dangerous, will it?"

"I will not tell ye a falsehood. It could become dangerous, och I will have many allies with me and my soldiers protecting me. There is no turning back. We must go forth and—"

"Are you warring with another clan?" She pressed herself upward a little to better see his face but he avoided looking at her.

With his eyes lowered, Shaw was quiet for a long moment. "Aye, sweetheart, we are. We war with the Chattans."

Before she could voice her displeasure at hearing his retort, the children ran into the chamber. Shaw reached for Gillian and set her daughter beside her. Luthor stood beside the bed until Shaw too hoisted him onto the bedding. Just seeing the children lightened her mood.

"Mama, are you well now?"

She smiled to appease her sweet lass. "I am well enough but I shall be stuck in this bed for a time. I am in no danger." At least, she hoped that was the truth. Until Louis returned to check her over again, she was uncertain about her condition.

Shaw gently yanked one of her daughter's tresses. "Gilly lass, ye know your mama is going to need tending to and I must leave. Will ye and Luthor make sure your mama has company whilst she convalesces?"

Both children nodded.

Sorsha grabbed Gillian's hand and then Luthor's. "I shall be quite content if you come and join me during the day."

"Will you tell us more stories?" Luthor asked.

"Of course, I shall. Now, go and find Enid for the midday meal."

Once the children left the room, she turned to face Shaw. "Please, tell me why you will war with the Chattans. It is not because of me, is it?"

"Our war with the Chattans is about ye, sweetheart, och it is also about justice. That Geoff used my sister and her husband to try to murder us... Geoff also dispatched his brother in order to overtake several clans' lands hereabouts. The clans want to confront him before he has a chance to call upon his allies. They seek retribution for Rodick, who dealt fairly with them." Shaw sighed and pressed his hand under her chin to raise her face. "My allies have their reasons and I have mine."

"If you come across a maid called Aela, can you send her here?"

Shaw tilted his head as if questioning why.

Sorsha's shoulders tensed in consideration of her maid being amid a war. "Aela went with me to Tor when I first married Rodick. She cared for me and was my mother's maidservant. There is also a lad named Lister who attends her. Rodick made him work in the stables. He too was sent by my mother to care for me after I left my family. They are all I have from home."

"I vow that I shall find them and send them to ye."

She took a soothing breath and nodded. "I just want them safe."

"And all I want is for ye to be safe. 'Tis a miracle ye were not killed." Shaw gave her a light peck of a kiss on her lips. "Now I must go because my allies await me. Try not to worry, Sorsha. I will return when I can."

After he disappeared through the threshold, she wiped away a tear from her eyelash. The thought of Shaw going to war with the Chattans worried her far more than he knew. Her apprehension wouldn't cease until he returned. She prayed that it would be soon.

CHAPTER TWENTY-FIVE

A s SHAW MADE ready to leave for his meeting with his allies, he secured his sword and other weapons he might need. Although he detested the thought of fighting with his cousin, his wife's honor and that of her former husband sat upon his shoulders. He sought vengeance for them both, not to mention poor Gillian who was kept from her mother for months. Fortunately, his allies forced his hand and Shaw wasn't too put out about that.

"There ye be," Walen said as he approached. "Trey has assembled most of the men. There will be a good number of soldiers left for the protection of the fief."

"Good. Ye will stay here too."

Walen's brows furrowed. "Och, Shaw, I would rather go and protect your back. This is a risky venture."

"And I would rather ye stay here and protect my wife. Besides, your woman is heavy with a bairn. Ye should be here for her in case her time comes. Worry not about my back. I shall be surrounded by my soldiers and my allies."

"Very well, och I should remain for Niahm. Still, I wish to seek justice with ye and protect your back on this mission. The Chattans are not to be trusted." Walen retrieved a saddlebag from the ground and handed it to him. "What are ye going to do about Corliss? She is still being held in the cell in the garrison. At least she no longer shouts for her release."

"She will remain there until I am ready to deal with her. 'Tis the truth, I never wanted to hurt a woman in my life…until that day when I found out she pushed Sorsha over the cliff. I seek vengeance for Sorsha, and yet, I know not how to gain it without ending my sister's life."

Walen set his hand on his shoulder. "My friend, all I can say about that is vengeance will gain ye naught but a heart full of regret. On your head, be it if you execute your sister. There are other ways to make her pay besides taking her life."

"Aye, I know that, och, I need more time to consider what I will do." Shaw was completely disheartened at the thought of Corliss's potential demise. Yet his sister had no care about his wife's life when she'd purposely set out to kill her. Now he had to think about how to best go about her punishment. "I must go. Ye will keep watch over Sorsha?"

"Of course, I will. Worry not for her. Edra and the healer will tend to her. By the time ye return, she shall smile at your unsightly face."

Shaw bellowed a laugh at his comrade's banter. "Hopefully, I will return before I am missed." He took the reins of his horse and led it toward the awaiting soldiers. At the gate, he mounted, shouted his clan's war cry '*Loch Moigh*', and led the procession of men toward the crossing. Walen signaled a farewell and commanded the gates to be opened for the men to pass by.

He waited for the men to cross the gate's threshold before he rode through. Shaw tipped his chin to his friend and was grateful that Walen stayed behind. He wouldn't worry about Sorsha so much and knew she was in capable, protective hands.

Along the route to *Braigh Loch Abar*, Inverness's beauty held him spellbound. The elevated land that surrounded the lochs looked as if it met the sky. All seemed still as no leaves fell from the nearly bared trees, no wind fluttered their garments or bushes, and the puffy clouds in the sky appeared motionless. A peacefulness settled within him as if the oncoming war would right the wrongs and bring tranquility to the region. Shaw, regardless of how he felt about his cousin, had to side with his allies. Peace would reign.

His horse reached one of the higher hillocks and as Shaw overlooked the landscape, he noticed the speckle of a large encampment. No pennons or indication of who made camp could be detected, but Shaw was well aware of who had settled there. His allies would not give themselves away too easily by raising their banners. It was best if the Chattans were surprised and remained ignorant of their presence.

He and his men reached the camp and Shaw dismounted. Before he located MacPherson's tent, he was approached by a tall lad. Two of his soldiers hastened forward to intercept him thinking he was a threat. Shaw waved them off and motioned to the lad to come forward. By the look of him, he posed no danger and held no weapon.

He was almost grown to manhood and was as tall as Shaw's shoulders. Yet his face showed no whiskers and his short cropped hair was neither brown nor blond but more of a reddish-streaked mess. He held something in his hand and didn't speak.

"Ye wanted to say something to me? I am listening."

He took a step forward and held out his hand. "I have an urgent message for you."

Shaw took it from him but didn't allow him to scamper away when he turned. "Before I read this message, tell me who ye are."

"I am Lister and you are Laird Mackintosh. My mistress bade me bring you a message from her. I will return to the keep." Lister tried to turn away again and Shaw blocked his path.

"Lister… Ye are acquainted with my wife, Lady Sorsha?"

"Aye, I am. If that be all? My mistress expects my return."

"I see. Well, ye shall be reunited with your lady soon. Await in my tent when my men erect it and I will send Aela to ye." Shaw turned and traipsed toward the MacPherson soldiers.

Beyond them stood the laird's tent. He nodded to the guards and entered to see a meeting in progress. Shaw approached a table where an unfolded parchment spread wide across the wooden top; the other lairds stood around looking at it.

"So, ye finally arrived, Mackintosh," Alan MacPherson said. "What took ye so long? We have awaited ye for a sennight."

"I was unfortunately delayed. Catch me up on the details of the siege." Shaw listened to the men as each interjected and gave their view of how the attack should progress. While he waited for them to come to an agreement, he opened the parchment that Lister had given him and read:

Mackintosh, there is an imminent threat to Lady Sorsha's life. I beseech ye to come at once so I can tell you what I have learned. I fear to put my name to this parchment lest it be intercepted. The lad will tell you who I am. Come at once to the village near Tor. I will be at the baker's stall.

It was left unsigned. Shaw felt the pulling of his brows as he read the lines. What news did the woman have and what threat was made against Sorsha now? He would have to postpone the fray until he met with the woman to find out. There had to be a good enough reason to request a delay and he racked his mind to think of one.

He cleared his throat and called for quiet. "Listen, a moment… I say we await darkness and then we can ambush the Chattans when they least expect it."

Alan MacPherson grumbled. "'Tis not a fair idea, Shaw. Surely they will spot our tents long before we march on to their fief. Their sentry has probably already spotted us. 'Tis too big a risk."

"I need a wee bit of time before we go forth. Maybe we can march on but await until I give the signal to attack. I will hasten back to Tor and will meet ye as soon as I can." Shaw was about to leave when Alan stopped him.

"What is so important that ye must depart?"

"I received a message from someone inside Tor. It must be important and I mean to meet them before we take to arms. Go and get the men readied. I will come as soon as I am able. If ye need to call the men to arms before I return then do so." He wouldn't let the men be in jeopardy because of him. If it were necessary to fight, he wouldn't be the reason they delayed. "I will go and try to make it back before darkness settles on the land and join the attack."

Shaw rushed back to where his men set up their camp. He found his horse tethered with the other horses and quickly got him ready for the trek to the village.

When he mounted his horse, Trey trotted toward him. "Laird, where ye going?"

"I need to go to the village. Get the men ready. Follow Mac-Pherson's soldiers and I shall meet ye there, at Tor." Shaw nudged his horse forward but Trey stepped in front of him.

"At least let me go with ye or take one of the soldiers."

"Nay, I will be quick, Trey. Do your duty and call the men to arms. I will not be long." He didn't wait for his commander's acceptance and rode away.

Night sounds allayed his restless spirit as he rode through the woodland. Shaw kept near the lane but moved covertly lest there be an ambush. Henny's lessons had reminded him that he should be on guard. Although he trusted the message he received was from Aela, he couldn't be certain.

On the approach to the village, Shaw noted the people milling about. It was early evening and most had closed their shops for the day or ended their business in the village. He searched for the baker's cottage and peered at a sign that read *Bakery Goods*. He rode around the building and dismounted at the back. There was an entry there and he decided it would probably be better if he used the back door.

Fortunately, it wasn't locked and he opened the heavy door. Shaw stepped inside and the dark foyer led to the larger area of the bakery. Scents of bread and other goods reminded him that he hadn't eaten and his stomach grumbled.

A tall, thin woman almost bumped into him when he passed through the small hallway. She gasped and set her hands on her chest. Her blue eyes widened in shock at seeing him.

"Apologies, Mistress. I am meeting a woman here by the name of Aela. Is she within?"

The woman nodded and without speaking, pointed to a door.

Shaw listened for the sound of others but heard no one. He approached the door but before he entered, he pulled a dagger from the sheath at his waist. Best be prepared for any eventuality. In a quick motion, he turned the door latch and thrust the door open. The sound of a woman's gasp came but before he could speak to her, he inspected the small chamber. There was one lone worktable within, a large basket of bread loaves, and a small oven to one side. No one else was there and he lessened his guard.

"I am Laird Mackintosh."

"Oh, gracious…" She bowed. "I…I am Aela and sent you the message."

"I received it, Mistress. I bade Lister stay behind and he awaits ye in my tent. My Lady wife Sorsha is safe and well protected at my fief. Now, tell me why ye insisted that I come and what threat do ye speak of?" Shaw's stomach grumbled again at the heavenly scent of the bread but he ignored it.

Aela's brown eyes lowered and she turned away from him. She grabbed a loaf of bread from a basket on the floor and took a knife. "You must be hungry for I hear your stomach bemoaning. Here, eat, and I shall tell you what I overheard."

Shaw leaned against the table and took a slice of the bread. It was delicious and he almost groaned at the taste of it.

"Lady Sorsha left the keep to go to Edinburgh when last I saw her. When she wrote to me, she said that she was safe so I did not worry about her. Then when Geoff received visitors, I served them and overheard their discussion…"

Shaw was intrigued. "Who visited Geoff?" He could guess because he was unaware of Geoff receiving visitors besides his sister. At least, Geoff hadn't mentioned anyone when he'd last seen him.

"'Twas a woman by the name of Corliss and her husband.

Geoff told the man, I, um, cannot name him… That if he wanted to gain lands of his own, he had to take them. Apparently, the man lost his home to another clan. The man agreed and Geoff told him that he could have the Mackintosh fief and lands if he did away with you."

"Ah, so Geoff sought to have Idris slay me. That makes sense. Go on." Shaw's face heated with ire at the realization of his cousin's intention.

Aela nodded. "Oh, aye, that was his name…Idris. Then Geoff said that you had married the woman he intended to wed, Lady Sorsha, and that he was displeased by it. When the woman asked if he wanted Sorsha returned to him, he said nay. Then she asked what he wanted her to do about Lady Sorsha. He told Corliss that he cared not if Sorsha existed and that she would be well rewarded if she found a way to end her. He said Lady Sorsha no longer mattered to him."

Shaw's jaw twitched with more anger. He couldn't believe his cousin ordered a woman to be wounded let alone be slain. Geoff planned to have him murdered and Sorsha as well. That his sister played such a vile part in the blackheart's plan sickened him. He had no choice now but to deal with his sister and banish her.

"Mistress, my wife is safe and protected at our home. She asked me to have ye delivered to her. She worried for ye and wanted me to bring ye home. Lister awaits ye at my camp yonder beyond Tor. Go there and one of my soldiers will take ye to Sorsha."

"Oh, thank heavens. I did not want to return to Tor. I shall go then unless you need anything else from me?" Aela curtseyed to him as he shook his head.

Shaw left the baker's cottage the same way he entered. He mounted his horse and rode for the fray, certain that his brethren were ready to face the threat of Geoff and his evil scheme. The closer he got to Tor, the more he anticipated taking his vengeance.

At the beginning of the lane that led to Tor Castle, his horse slowed and snorted, seemingly alarmed. When Shaw tried to nudge his horse forward, the animal balked, his muscles tensed, and his ears pointed forward.

"Easy there, fellow, easy." Shaw tried to calm his warhorse with a quiet voice, but he too felt trepidation at being on the lane. Rumors abounded that an evil spirit resided within the darkened trees adjacent to the steep incline of the hillocks on either side of the roadway. He wasn't a believer in such things but he had to admit that the area was somewhat unnerving.

Before he reached the end of the lane and the gate, riders sprang out from all directions in front of him. Shaw tried to force his horse back but he was quickly surrounded by Chattan soldiers. His instinct was to take hold of his sword but he had to hold on to his horse or risk falling to the ground and being at the mercy of the enemy.

"Mackintosh, we had hoped to cross paths with ye this night," a man's voice came.

Shaw finally calmed his horse and stared ahead at a man who marched between the soldiers. He recognized him. "Leonard." He tilted his head in greeting and wasn't too wary of the Chattan commander-in-arms. For one thing, Leonard didn't present a formidable attitude, and for another, his voice wasn't harsh and threatening.

"Shaw, I need to speak to ye in private. Follow me." Leonard turned on his heel and walked back toward the castle gate.

When Shaw's feet hit the ground after dismounting, he yanked his sword free of its scabbard. If menace was afoot, he would be prepared. With a spry walk, he hurried after the man. At the gate, Leonard motioned to the guardsmen to vacate their posts. With none near, he waited for Shaw to reach him.

Shaw stopped a wee bit away from him. "What is it ye want to say? I'm afraid that my allies likely surround your fief and mean to attack. If ye intend to hurt me, be prepared for an onslaught. Ye and all your men will be cut down."

Leonard shook his head. "Nay, nay, listen. I heard that Geoff is accused of murdering our laird. Is that true?"

Shaw's shoulders tightened with having to break the atrocious news to the man. "Aye, 'tis the truth. Geoff murdered Rodick which is why my allies surround your walls and want to seek justice."

The commander pressed his hands over his face. "And is it true that he held Milady Sorsha confined within the keep and kept her bairn from her?"

He nodded in answer. "Geoff also sent my sister and her husband to my fief to murder me and Lady Sorsha, but fortunately, we were able to thwart them."

"Gracious, God. I suspected something afoul but for a brother to kill his own…" Leonard shook his head in dismay. "He killed our laird and justice must be sought. We shall aid ye in this quest, Laird Mackintosh. None of the Chattan soldiers will take arms against ye or your allies."

"Tell the men to open the gate. I will seek out Geoff and end this."

Leonard whistled to the men who had vacated the gate and they sprinted forward. After they opened the gate, Shaw marched through. He shouted as loudly as he could to give the signal to his brethren to draw their arms. Before he approached the entrance to the castle, he turned back to Leonard. "Tell my allies what ye have told me. Tell them that I have gone inside."

With that, Shaw marched forward. He yanked the keep's door open and stepped inside. The entry was darkened and no torches were lit on the walls. He moved forward with quiet steps because he didn't want to give a warning to Geoff that he was there. At the great hall, he stopped at the threshold and spotted the man standing beside the trestle table.

Shaw took cautious steps forward. He wasn't sure if Geoff was ready to strike him or if he was unaware that his castle was being besieged. "Geoff."

"Shaw, 'tis gladdened I am to see ye. There are men near my castle walls."

"I know there is. Ye saw them, aye? They come to seek justice." He reached the opposite end of the trestle table and watched his cousin warily, ready for his attack.

"Do ye come to seek justice too?"

Shaw nodded. "Aye, cousin, I do. Why would ye go to such lengths to take the clan from Rodick? He would have allowed ye to rule with him. Ye have much to answer for: the fact that ye imprisoned Sorsha and withheld her child from her, that ye sent my sister to murder her and Idris to slay me..."

"I did no such thing," Geoff bellowed with frustration and rammed his hands through his hair. He paced before the table now with agitation.

"Aye, ye did. Ye murdered Rodick to which Sorsha bore witness... Then ye took her child and kept them apart to gain her accord so she would not tell a soul about what she saw. Ye needed to be rid of us, aye so ye could give my lands to Idris? And so ye sent him to slay me but as ye can see, he was unsuccessful. As to Corliss, she tried to hurt Sorsha but by the grace of God, Sorsha survived. I am sorry to say that ye will not fare as well." Shaw gripped his sword's hilt in anticipation of finally gaining justice for all those whom Geoff had hurt.

Geoff gripped the chair back in front of him and his brows furrowed. "Shaw, cousin, I plead with ye to remember that we are kin and family does not murder family. Ye are my own aunt's son and cannot kill me. I might've murdered Rodick och he deserved it."

"Family does not murder family," he threw back Geoff's words.

"I swear by God that I did not mean to hurt Sorsha. I cared for her. I did not send Corliss or her spineless husband to harm ye. Your sister took matters into her own hands because her inept husband lost his lands. I had naught to do with their actions."

Shaw disbelieved him but perhaps there was a glimmer of truth to his words. Then he remembered what Aela had told him. Nay, the man was guilty. "Regardless, Geoff, ye must pay for the crime of murdering your brother. I cannot hold back your adversaries. The allied clans will not cease their pursuit of justice. Either I slay ye or they… Which is it to be?" Shaw made his way around the table and continued at an unhurried pace while he waited for Geoff's answer.

Geoff stepped away from the table and held out his arms. "I would rather die by ye, an honorable man, than that of a hostile band of ornery Highlanders. Come, send me to the hereafter, Shaw, but let them not destroy my body. I will face the devil himself if need be, och I will be whole."

Shaw was astounded by his cousin's speech. He tensed and before Geoff could react, he shot forward and pierced Geoff's midsection with his blade, exerting his arm and running him clean through. Blood streamed from the edges of his lips, hampering him from making any further speeches. Geoff huffed and kept his eyes trained on him as if he was astounded that he'd followed through on his request. His legs gave out from beneath him and he fell, half-supported against a table leg.

Shaw reached down and pulled his sword free then set it on the table and waited for his cousin to take his last breath.

CHAPTER TWENTY-SIX

S OUNDS OF THUMPING in the hallway gave Sorsha the alert that someone was approaching. She could think of nothing but the war that was taking place at that very moment. Prayers had crossed her lips throughout the morning in hopes that everyone would be safe. She waited with anticipation, hoping that Shaw had returned. When she saw Walen, her shoulders sagged. Then she spotted Niahm and was pleased to see her.

"I brought ye some company and thought ye might need a distraction." Walen supported Niahm as he guided her into the bedchamber.

Sorsha smiled at seeing her friend. "I was rather lonely. My thanks, Walen."

Niahm's movements were slow and when she reached the bed, she shifted to sit. Walen helped to lift her so that her back was to the headboard and then he lifted her feet to settle upon the bed covers.

"Have a good visit, ladies. I will return in a wee bit and must check in with the watch." Walen gave a wave and then disappeared through the doorway.

"I am gladdened you came. How are you?"

Niahm grabbed her hand and held it. "I am ready to have this bairn and I worried about ye. I should be asking how ye are."

Sorsha wrapped her arm with Niahm's and sighed. "My leg

hurts but otherwise, I feel well. 'Tis remarkable that I didn't die in that fall. God was looking out for me."

Her friend nodded vigorously. "Aye, indeed. There are too many people who need ye here. Shaw would have been inconsolable and the children likewise. It would've crushed me as well."

"You are so kind to say so. I am worried about Shaw and the Mackintosh soldiers. They have gone, haven't they?"

Niahm nodded. "Aye, but worry not because they were meeting several other clans. The Chattans could not defeat all of them. They were far outnumbered. Besides, nothing makes a Highlander happier than wielding a sword and fighting for any cause."

"I never saw Shaw look so determined and I feel guilty because if not for me, he would not have a reason to go against his mother's family." Sorsha detested that and prayed somehow that the battle would be finished before it began.

"Oooh," Niahm moaned and dislodged her hand. She pressed her fingers on her lower back.

"What is wrong?" Sorsha shifted sideways to search her friend's eyes and saw the pain in the blueish-green depths.

"My back has been aching for days and 'tis getting worse." Niahm moaned again. "I fear that this bairn might be coming...perhaps this day."

Sorsha gasped and tried to sit up straighter, but the cumbersome brace around her leg prevented her from much movement. "Oh, we should call for help but there is no one to hear us."

Her friend groaned and tried to roll off the side of the bed, but she was stuck and couldn't get her body to cooperate. "I shall go."

Sorsha grinned and pressed a hand on her upper arm. "I do not deem ye can make it out of this bed. Someone will come soon."

"Oh, I remember... Luthor is in the hallway. Aye, Walen gave him a small sack of rounded rocks to play with whilst he stood guard. He told Walen that he would not leave the hall while ye were bedridden." Niahm continued to rub her back, and although she tried not to show her discomfort, small sounds in her throat signaled her distress.

Sorsha called out, "Luthor, lad, come here." She waited for him to show himself and within a moment, he didn't disappoint. His sweet face appeared within the threshold. "Come here, lad." She waved him forward.

Luthor scurried forth. "Aye, Mama."

"I need you to go and find Walen. Tell him Niahm needs him. And then go to the midwife's cottage. It's the last cottage on the lane toward the bridge. Tell her to come quickly. Can you do that?" She had faith in him but he was quite young. Luthor nodded and turned away. "And Luthor?"

"Aye?"

"Hasten. Do not stop anywhere or speak to anyone besides Walen. Find him and send him to us and then go and fetch the midwife. Do not forget." Sorsha watched him slip out the door.

Niahm continued to moan but now she flinched and her body tensed against the bedding.

Sorsha felt helpless to give aid to Niahm. "Luthor is rather young and I hope he does not get distracted. Be calm, my friend, and take easy breaths when the pain comes." She tried to distract her by making idle chatter. "I cannot believe Corliss pushed me off the cliffside. She was not a friendly sort but to be so cruel..."

Niahm gripped her hand and squeezed it. "I believe it. Aye, she was never a friendly lass even when she was...weeeeee." She huffed. "The pains are getting worse. I hope someone comes before this bairn decides to join us."

Sorsha hoped so too because, in her condition, there was little she could do to help. "I pray that is so. It seems your babe is unwilling to wait."

Finally, the sound of someone taking the stairs came along with a loud thumping. Walen rushed into the bedchamber and reached his wife. He peered at her and Sorsha gave him a concerned gaze and a small smile.

"Your bairn is coming. I sent Luthor for the midwife."

A moment later, Edra entered and Sorsha gave a gasp of surprise when she saw who was with her. Aela smiled and approached.

"My Lady, how pleased I am to see you. Edra told me all that happened." Aela took hold of her hand. "I have worried so for you and am gladdened that you appear well."

Niahm groaned and Walen gently helped her to her feet. He wrapped his arm around her waist and when he tried to shift her to the door, Niahm's knees buckled. Walen said, "Come, wife, we shall get ye settled in a chamber here. There is no time to get ye back to our cottage."

Sorsha sniffled. "Shaw found you, Aela?" She wiped at her eyes as happy tears gathered on her lashes at the oncoming birth of the bairn and that Aela had finally returned to her. "I am happy to see you and worried for you too."

"Edra tells me that you took a great fall. I shall look you over but I see your friend there needs urgent help. Let us get her settled for the midwife and I will return." Aela helped to hold Niahm's arm as Walen, with painstakingly slow steps, guided her to the door.

"Niahm, I will pray you have an easy birth. I want to know the minute the baby is born. Someone better come and give me the news." Sorsha lay back, discouraged that she couldn't be there with her friend.

Edra pulled the bed cover over her and poured her a cup of water, adding a powder to it and mixing it with haste. "I came to give ye a wee bit of pain relief, Milady." She pressed the cup into her hands.

Sorsha didn't want to drink it but there was no disobeying the maidservant. She drank a good bit and handed the cup back. Edra set the cup back on the table and pulled the bed cover from over her leg. Thick planks of wood tied with rope held her leg still. Sorsha hadn't yet seen the damage. It seemed to her that the cumbersome cure was more daunting than the pain she endured. The initial agony lessened and her leg didn't hurt overly, but ached now, and only once in a while did a more grueling pain twitch there. Even the tingling in her lower leg and foot had decreased.

"Ye should get some rest, Milady."

"But I do not wish to rest. I will not do so until I hear a word of Niahm…" But sleep she did when a drowsiness came upon her and even though she didn't want to fall asleep, her eyes refused to cooperate and remain open. Sorsha closed her eyes and prayed that her friend had an easy delivery, that Shaw returned soon, and gave thanks for her joy at having Aela there.

GROGGINESS THINNED AS the veil of sleep abated. Sorsha used her tongue to wet her lips and took a deep breath. Her eyes flitted open and she was unsure of the time of day. The window shutters were closed and two candles were lit on the bedside table. She pressed her back a bit to stretch but ceased when it caused her leg to shift. The door opened and someone stuck their head through the threshold. She peered at Aela and smiled.

"Good morn, My Lady." Aela entered and closed the door behind her. The dear woman crossed the chamber and set her healing satchel on the floor next to the bed. "You slept long. That is good because sleep helps us heal."

"Aela, I am so happy you are here."

"As am I. Before I give you a thorough look over, I wanted to tell you that Niahm had a baby boy. She and the babe are doing well."

"Oh, a son. I am so happy for her. Walen must be beyond pleased."

"He sure is and cannot cease telling anyone that will listen what his son looks like, the sound of his little cries, and that he is grateful that his son does not have his mother's red hair."

Sorsha laughed and pressed a tear away at the happiness for

her friend. She couldn't wait to see Niahm's baby and her. "That is the most joyous news."

Aela nodded. "Aye, she did not have too difficult a time. That babe wanted to come quickly. Now, I must say how proud of you I am. Your parents would be too. You married a charming, kind man, and have a lovely family. The Mackintosh clan has been welcoming. You found a place that shines with love."

"I am sorry…" Sorsha set her hand on Aela's thigh when she sat next to her on the bedding.

Aela caressed her face and smiled. "Sorry for what, My Lady?"

"I do not deserve to be called 'My Lady' because I should have protected you and had Shaw go and retrieve you from the Chattans sooner…"

Aela clicked her tongue. "Bah, I was safe enough there at Tor. I was more worried about you than for myself and was gladdened you were able to flee to Edinburgh. 'Twas difficult though, the not knowing what happened to you. When Laird Shaw came to retrieve Gillian, my heart nearly burst with happiness knowing you fared well and that he would reunite you with your daughter."

"Still, Aela, I did not know that Shaw was going to bring Gillian home. If I had, I would have insisted that he bring you and Lister here too. You both have helped me and I care for you like family."

"We understood, My Lady, that you were unable to at the time. If you had done so, it could have spurred Geoff's wrath and we bided our time there. Now, no guilt for either of us. We are all safe and amongst a devoted clan."

"What did I ever do to deserve you?" Sorsha smiled at her winsome friend pleased beyond words to be reunited with her.

CHAPTER TWENTY-SEVEN

J UST AS DAWN broke over the horizon in the distance, Shaw sat
upon his horse gazing at his land. *Home at last.* It had taken days
to remedy the situation at Tor and to make certain that his
mother's clan was well settled with a new laird. The clan bickered
about who would best lead their clan, and finally, most of the
elders and soldiers agreed that Leonard would make the best
laird. It took coercion on his part to get Leonard to agree to
accept. Now that their commander was put in charge, Shaw
hoped there would be no further strife between them.

Home. He was never so pleased to see the bridge and gate to
his fief. Many times, he thought about Sorsha and prayed that she
would begin healing. He would go to her soon enough but there
was one matter that he needed to handle before he could seek his
wife.

He waved to Clovis as he and his followers rode past the gate.
When he dismounted, Trey approached and took the reins of his
horse.

"I shall have someone tend to your horse, Laird." Trey turned
and whistled to a young soldier who hurried forth to do his
bidding. "I suspect ye want to tend to that task ye've been putting
off?"

Shaw nodded to his comrade. "Aye, but first we will find
Walen. I want ye both there when I question her." He marched

onward to find his friend, intent to have support when he spoke to Corliss. Before he reached the barracks, Walen rounded the building and came from the direction of the tower fief.

Walen held out his hand and greeted him with a smile. "'Tis good to have ye back. I have news aplenty if ye wish to hear it now…or it can wait."

Shaw stopped walking ahead and turned to him. "Is Sorsha well?"

"Oh, aye, she is healing. Her attendant Mistress Aela is seeing to her. From what Louis tells me the woman is irksome but och I think there is a bit of rivalry betwixt them. He says she seems to know what she is about so I am pleased to report Milady mends."

"That is a great relief." Shaw started to walk on when Walen pulled him back with his hand to his bicep.

"I also wanted to tell ye that I have a son, a handsome lad, who thank God above, appears more akin to me than his mother. I would not want to have a red-haired lad with a temper." Walen chortled with laughter.

Shaw embraced his longtime comrade and pounded his back. "Congratulations, my friend. I cannot wait to see him. Have you named him yet?"

"We shall when the clergyman comes, och I was thinking of naming him Samuel." Walen's gaze fixed on him until he shook his head. "Unless ye want to use that name for your son."

Shaw was taken aback. "Ye want to name him after my da?"

"Aye, I do. Laird Samuel was a good man and raised a fine son, a man who now leads us with good grace and with firm guidance."

He was astounded by his friend's kind words. "My da would be pleased by your honoring him. Aye, the name Samuel it is then. Now, I ask ye and Trey," he said with a nod to Walen's brother, "to come with me. I must speak to Corliss and could use the support."

Both brothers followed him inside the barracks. They made their way past the many bunks where the men slept, past the areas where the garrison was kept until they reached the steep steps that took them below. Down beneath the barracks, several cells were made to house those who committed crimes. The cells were hardly used to hold any of the Mackintosh clan and only a few enemies had ever been confined there.

As Shaw approached the cell where his sister was kept, he drew in a resigned breath as he motioned to the soldier who guarded Corliss. The man stepped back and retreated.

Regardless of how much he detested what he was about to do, Shaw had to continue. Corliss must've heard their approach and stood by the iron bars, clutching them. He stood before her and glanced back at his brethren who remained ready to support him. Walen and Trey stood only a few steps behind him.

"Shaw…ye finally came. The soldier told me that ye put me here. Why have ye kept me here in this filthy cell?" Her voice betrayed her indignation.

"Ye know well why. Corliss, that ye are my sister sickens me."

She scowled hard with hatred in her eyes. "Why do ye not enlighten me then because I do not deserve this horrid treatment? What have I done? Ye condemn me without giving me a reason…"

"Mamo always said ye were a selfish lass, and by God, she was right. That ye tried to have me harmed and my wife… I must tell ye that your husband no longer breathes. Aye, for my clansman killed him. He deserved to die and so do ye for what ye have done."

She stepped back from the bars. "What exactly have I done?"

"Ye pushed my sweet wife off a damned cliff. Aye, do not bother to deny it for she well remembers every word ye spoke before ye did the vile deed. And then one of my closest comrades fell to his death trying to rescue Sorsha. Your husband tried to murder me but fortunately, he was unsuccessful."

"Your claims have no merit."

"The hell they do not. I will hear no falsehoods from ye lass and know the truth of the matter. Geoff told me that he did not ask ye to harm us and that ye took matters into your own hands but I disbelieved him. Ye conspired with him, did ye not? Aye, ye wanted your husband to become laird here and thought by overtaking me that he could do so as your husband." Shaw's breath hitched by the time he finished his tirade. "I vow, lass, I have never wanted to kill a woman before. But och if I got my bare hands around your neck, I could squeeze the life from ye without remorse. Ye deserve no less than to join your husband in hell."

Her voice came in a whisper, "It was the only way, Shaw… Ye knew that our lands were destroyed by the Cummings and we had nowhere to go. Our only hope was to return here to my family's land. It was Idris who suggested that we usurp ye. I swear, Shaw, that I did not want to harm ye or your wife." She sobbed and clung to the bars. "Please, I beg ye to forgive me. What will ye do? Will ye murder me as ye claimed to want?"

"Nay, lass, we Mackintoshes do not murder women regardless of their sins. We shall have ye returned to your husband's people, the Dunbars. Ye will not set foot upon Mackintosh land again for if ye do, I will give the order that ye be cut down. Do ye understand?"

She nodded but said nothing.

"Ye are a disappointment to our clan. Our parents would have been distraught to know the lengths ye went to for your own selfish wants. I wish never to see ye again. Ye are dead to me lass." Shaw turned and walked away from the cell, heavy-hearted, full of anger, and yet still, sad at the loss of his only sibling.

When he reached the outside, he turned to Walen and Trey who followed him. "Have a regiment of soldiers take her to the Dunbars and have them relate my orders that she is not to return to our lands."

His comrades agreed with nods but said nothing. Their gazes held pity for what his sister had done. Shaw walked away with his gaze lowered, toward the fief, and was only intent on seeing his wife. When he entered the keep, he took a glimpse of the great hall and saw Gillian and Luthor with Mistress Edra and Enid. Aela was there too, along with the lad, Lister. Their mood seemed merry and he smiled.

Shaw took the steps two at a time and reached his bedchamber. Before he pushed the door handle, he took a calming breath and wanted to be eased before he saw Sorsha. After a few more inhales, he shook away his trepidation and pushed the door open.

He stood and watched Sorsha's unmoving body for a moment then closed the door quietly in case she was sleeping. When he turned back to the bed, he found her watching him.

Before she could utter one word, he rushed forward and set his lips on hers. Shaw kept his mouth against hers and pressed his hands against her cheeks. When he drew back, he kept his eyes fixed on hers and smiled. "By my faith, sweetheart, I could not get back to ye quick enough."

"I worried…"

He gave her lips another light peck. "Aye, I suspected ye would. All is well now."

She patted the other side of the bed and shifted onto her hip. "Come, lie beside me."

Shaw rounded the bed and sat on the bedding. "I do not want to hurt ye."

"You won't. There is plenty of room and I have missed you." Sorsha grabbed his hand and pulled him toward her.

He eased onto the bed and faced her. "God, it gladdens me to see ye doing so well. I was unsure how ye fared and… I worried that ye would be taken from me."

"Before you say anything, I want to thank you for sending Aela. You kept your promise."

"Aye, she sent me a message and I directed her here. She seemed to want to come. Walen tells me that she aided in your recovery?" Shaw caressed the length of her hair and studied her face for any sign of pain.

"She helped a good deal. Louis had my leg bound by a tree

but Aela said it needn't be so holdfast, and she fixed me up. How did your war go? I prayed that not many would be hurt or died. They were not, were they?" She set her head back on the pillow and eyed him.

Shaw pressed his hands over his face and groaned. "'Tis the truth, not one man perished... Well except for one. The Chattan soldiers gave themselves up before we could take arms against them. They were mightily displeased with Geoff and practically handed their laird over on a trencher. I spoke to Geoff at length, and well, he realized that the alliance would take his life."

"Did they?"

Shaw didn't want to hide anything from her and so he told the truth. "Nay, I did. He asked me to and so I...put my sword in him. I wish that I did not have to take his life, och he caused us much grief and his own end. Ye need not worry about him further, sweetheart. He cannot hurt us anymore."

"What of the Chattans?"

"That is what took me overlong. We placed a new laird before I was able to leave. The alliance wanted the matter settled before any of us left the area. All agreed that Leonard was the only man to lead them."

Sorsha nodded. "Leonard is a good man. I am glad to hear that."

Shaw couldn't cease touching her and ran his hand along her arm, her torso, back to her face and hair. He was pleased that she hadn't succumbed to her injuries because he would've been lost without her. "I will not abide by interference from the Chattans going forward. Though they are my mother's kin, they have my allegiance as long as they do not cross me."

"You sound so serious, husband." Sorsha leaned against him and set a kiss on his face.

"I am serious." Shaw shifted his body closer to hers, delighted to be next to her. "Sorsha, I waited for what seemed like a lifetime for ye and I only want ye to be happy."

"That is all I want too, for you to be happy. I have loved you for so long that I cannot recall a time when I did not."

He grinned. "I love ye with all my heart."

"I am ready, Shaw…"

He took hold of her hand and couldn't cease his grin. With the pad of his thumb, he stroked it over the top of her hand and was content to linger there for the rest of the night. "Ready for what?"

"I am ready to have more children."

He chuckled but then sobered. "Aye, I would like nothing better than to hold my bairn, a wee one that ye shall give me. But och, ye need to heal first, love, and then we can get started on it. Honestly, I cannot wait to be with ye again."

She shoved his arm in jest. "I do not mean right now but aye, when I am healed. We shall have a bairn… I cannot wait either and hope to give Niahm's son a lifelong comrade."

"Our children will be blessed with their friends and family. We shall see to it." Shaw lay his head on her shoulder and closed his eyes. Contentment came to him with the dreams of their future, a new beginning filled with happiness, friends, family, love, and solace.

EPILOGUE

Castle Moy, Eilean Nan Clach
Inverness, Highlands Scotland
Autumn 1261

SHAW STOOD BESIDE the entrance to the main hall and watched his wife settle into a chair by the hearth. Around her, the children listened intently as she told them a story about a mountain and a squirrel. He smiled to himself because he'd heard her tell the tale countless times. Still, the children listened as if they heard it for the first time.

He had just returned from going over the soldiers' training regimen and ensuring duties were tended to by the watch. Seeing Sorsha surrounded by their kin, reminded him of his grandmother. How Mamo would have loved to be there, to hold Gillian and Luthor. Likewise, his father's namesake, Samuel, who waddled around with his unsure steps. The wee lad was remarkable in his appearance with his light hair and Walen's face.

When Luthor spotted him, he sprinted from beside his mother and hurried toward him. "Papa, can I go and train with the lads this day? Ye promised…"

His pleading look wore Shaw down and he nodded. "Aye, go and find Trey. He will put ye in with a group of fledglings. Listen well and learn. For God's sake, do not get yourself injured. Your mama will never forgive me."

Luthor's grin widened on his face. "I will not get hurt, Papa."

Then he ran through the hall's entrance to the outside before Shaw could change his mind.

"There you are," Sorsha said and rose from her seat.

Gillian took hold of Samuel's wee hand and guided him back to Niahm who sat at the trestle table speaking with Edra and Aela. Sorsha's gaze lingered on Samuel for a moment before it shifted to him. Shaw grinned, for he knew well what she was thinking…that perhaps by early next summer, they might have a wee son of their own. That night, he planned to give the news of their expected bairn to the clan.

Gillian crossed the hall to get to Kathleen, a lass who Sorsha employed as a nurse for their daughter. She picked up a stuffed doll that Enid had made for her and sat next to the chair Sorsha vacated. She and Kathleen whispered and giggled together. It brought him such happiness to see the lass playing and being carefree. She had changed much since she arrived at the Mackintosh fief.

Clovis entered with Enid holding onto his arm. His gate watchman had recently married the lass and they were still in wedded bliss. Shaw chuckled to himself because he too, even after all this time, was still in wedded bliss himself. He was thoroughly contented with being married to Sorsha.

"Laird," Clovis said as he approached. "The king's man, his chamberlain, Edmund, is at the gate and wishes to be bid entry. Should we allow him inside the gate?"

"Edmund is here?" Shaw felt the pull of his brows as he wondered why Alexander's man traveled from Edinburgh to see him. "Of course, allow him entry."

Clovis left Enid with her mother and rushed out of the keep.

Shaw approached Edra and stopped next to the table. "Mistress, will ye have Cook prepare a good meal for we have guests? I should like to have a wee celebration this night."

"Of course, Laird. I shall see to it at once." Edra and Enid left the hall.

Aela sat with Kathleen and Gillian by the hearth.

Sorsha walked toward him with a slight hitch to her gait. Sometimes, when she walked on her leg a little too much, she limped.

"Sit ye down, wife, because I can tell ye are hurting."

She walked in a slow gait until she reached him. "Just a little."

Shaw pulled out a chair at the table for her and then one for himself. They sat and he poured them each a cup of ale. "I told Edra to have a feast prepared for this eve."

She smiled and nodded. "Did I hear Clovis say that Edmund is here?"

"Aye, he is letting him through the gates now. Strange, because I can think of no reason why Edmund would come all this way. I hope nothing happened to Alexander or Margaret or that he means to call all to arms against Norway. I did not deem he'd do so this soon."

Sorsha folded her hands on her lap and peered at them. "Lord, I hope that is not why he comes."

Steps came from the hallway and Shaw rose from his seat. When Edmund entered, he approached and greeted him. "Chamberlain Edmund, this is a surprise visit. What do ye here?"

Edmund lumbered past him to the table and sat in his vacated seat. "Lady Mackintosh, 'tis good to see you. You look well. Are you still pleased with your marriage to Laird Mackintosh? If not, I can have our king remedy that for you." He grinned teasingly.

"I am more than pleased, sir. How are you? You have traveled a great distance. I hope you do not bring bad tidings," Sorsha said.

Shaw reached the table and took the seat on the opposite side of the table. He poured Edmund a cup of ale and set it before the man.

Edmund immediately snatched the cup from the table and drank. When he finished, he gave them a look of dismay. "I am afraid my news is not good."

"Is Margaret all right? She fared well birthing the baby?" Sorsha asked.

"Indeed. She is well and gave our sire a daughter at the end of last winter. 'Tis rumored that Alexander might betroth his daughter to Haakon's son but as yet has not made a decision. It could be years afore he gives her hand."

"I am pleased though for Margaret, and that she is well. Please, forgive me for being forward, Edmund, but what is your news?" Sorsha sat forward and her eyes seemed to send a pleading urgency.

Shaw suspected that his wife was impatient because the man wouldn't have come all the way to the Highlands for a simple visit and he'd said his news wasn't good.

"My news is for you, Lady Mackintosh. You received the news of your parents' presumed deaths?"

"I did. My thanks for sending me the news. I am sure it was a difficult task to send such a disparaging message."

He bobbed his head. "I kept my missive short at the time because I was unaware of the facts and until I could confirm the truth of the matter... I'm sorry to say that your parents indeed perished in the sea. Your father, mother, and his brother Ottuel traveled with King Henry's heir William Adelin aboard the White Ship. They unwisely left the harbor against sound advice and the ship capsized and sank near an embankment. 'Tis stated by witnesses that all drowned and none could be saved because the channel was quite rough. You have the king's condolences, My Lady."

Sorsha's gaze fell to her lap and when she looked up, she had a sadness in her eyes. "I am sorry to hear that so many died. Who will be my father's heir be? He has a vast shipping business and earldom."

Edmund drew a heavy breath. "That is being decided by the king himself. There is only one male heir, your cousin Ranulph, your father's nephew. If your husband objects to running your father's business then it shall be passed on."

Sorsha turned her face to him. "What say you, Shaw? Do you want to be in the shipping business?"

"Hell, no. I am pleased enough with my lot in life here in the Highlands and being laird to my clan. Besides, I know naught about shipping. Give it to my wife's cousin."

"I will convey your rejection to Alexander on my return. There is another matter though and that is the trunks of coins that were left to My Lady by her father and mother. I was told to deliver them to her at the soonest." Edmund called out and his attendants marched forward, carrying trunks of various sizes into the hall. "These are filled with coins. Your father wanted you to have what he deemed to be your dowry and since he did not have to provide one when Laird Chattan agreed that there be no recompense. 'Twas unlike him but for some reason, Rodick professed that he did not want to take coins from your father. Lord Richard, your da, wanted the trunks sent to you upon his death."

Sorsha's eyes widened but she said nothing until he cleared his throat. Shaw stood and was astounded by his wife's father's gesture. Such wealth would never be rejected. He disbelieved his good fortune. Not only had he won the hand of the loveliest lass in the land, a woman whose tender heart rendered him completely enthralled, but she brought him wealth beyond his wildest dreams.

"I wonder why Rodick refused her dowry. That was unlike him but then his brother Geoff stated that his brother was weak and gullible."

"I am told that Lord Richard and Laird Rodick had a verbal agreement that if ever Rodick needed his aid or ships to travel upon he would provide him with such." Edmund refilled his cup and drank again.

"I do not know what to say…" Shaw's eyes roamed from trunk to trunk, ten in all likely filled with enough coins to see his clan through many a winter.

"Say you accept," Edmund said.

"Of course I do…that is if Sorsha accepts too."

Her shoulders rose with a sigh but then came the slight

movement of her chin as she nodded. "I feel horrible because I cursed my parents for forcing me to leave my home and demanding I marry Rodick."

"There is one trunk that is from your dear mother, My Lady. She wrote a note to go with it." Edmund handed her the parchment.

Sorsha took it from him and opened it. She read aloud:

Dearest Daughter, if you are reading this missive that means that I am gone. I want you to know that I despaired the day you were taken from me. However, I could not rebuke your father's will when he bade you to marry the Chattan laird. Know that I held you in my heart for all my days. I pray that you have found a happy life and that you have borne your own children, to give you the joys that you had brought to me. I give you everything I cherish. ~Your devoted mother, Lucia, House of d'Avranches

Aela rose from her seat across the hall and watched them. Her hand rested on her chest and she appeared to have shimmery eyes.

Edmund pushed a small trunk across the table. "She wanted you to have this trunk but I fear there is no key to open it. Perhaps your husband can have his blacksmith open it for you."

Aela gasped. "Sorsha, here," she said and pulled a key that hung on a golden-woven rope from around her neck. "Your mother told me to hold on to this for you and to give it to you when the time was right. I suspect that she knew that one day you would receive the trunk."

Sorsha held out her hand and peered at the key. She placed it inside the ornate plate where the lock was held within and turned it. A click sounded. Sorsha turned and glanced at him.

Shaw approached to stand beside her. "Go on, sweetheart, open it."

She pressed the lid open and her eyes widened. Inside were jewels and trinkets that her mother had collected throughout her life. There was a small piece of parchment. Sorsha held it and read: *Within are the memories of my life. Some belonged to your grandmother. Keep these treasures in the family and I hope one day you give them to your daughter. LD*

Tears gathered in Sorsha's eyes and Shaw set his arm around her to offer comfort. She leaned against him and wiped at her eyes, unspeaking and full of distress. Gently, her fingers perused the objects within the trunk.

"Well, now that task is handled, I can be on my way," Edmund said.

"Has the king decided what he shall do about his quest to expand our lands? Has he declared war against Norway yet? I am beholden to send him soldiers when that time comes," Shaw said readily.

"The king and queen returned to Scotland in early spring to get back to their royal duties. I am certain Alexander will eventually go ahead with his plans but as yet he has not spoken of the matter." Edmund rose from his seat and stood next to Sorsha.

"Chamberlain Edmund, I invite you to join us for a feast this night. Rest a day or so before you head back out." Shaw put forth his words as a directive rather than an invitation.

Edmund rejected his offer by shaking his somewhat flabby chin. "I am afraid I cannot stay for entertainment, Laird Mackintosh. I have other news that I must deliver here in the Highlands. I must travel to Buchanan land. God help me."

"What news do you take to the Buchanans?" Shaw asked. "I hope it is not unpleasant."

"I can only divulge my news to Lady Eva, I'm afraid. Nay, I must go to her at once. She will be distraught to learn what I must tell her. That is if I make it past the ornery Buchanan sentry to deliver it."

Shaw understood. Not many confronted the Buchanan soldiers. Though the Mackintosh soldiers were fierce, the Buchanans were practically barbaric in their fighting tactics. They allowed no one to pass through on their lands, even their allies. He commiserated with poor Edmund because his task was of a most difficult nature.

"I shall go. I bid you both my wishes for good health and I shall tell Alexander how pleased you both are with your marriage. He will be gratified to hear such. Pray for me that the Buchanans welcome me." Edmund bowed to them and hastened from the hall with his attendants following.

Shaw helped Sorsha to a chair and lowered her into it. "Are you all right, Sorsha? The news ye received was most troubling. I am sorry to hear what happened to your parents and they are really gone. I had hoped the report was false."

She sniffled back her tears and nodded. "I am well but sad to know they are really gone too. There is only one thing that consoles me, Shaw, and that is I am now here…with my family, with the people I love, with my charming husband, and the Mackintosh Clan."

"Aye, but, sweetheart, we are the fortunate ones." A smile widened on her lips and he leaned back admiring her bonny face. "What are ye smiling about?"

"I just remembered… On the day that Rodick died, Gillian and I were at the Yule festival in Blarmacfoldach. We visited a fortune teller and for once, the seer spoke true." She looked far off and laughed.

"Why what did the seer say?"

"She said that something dreadful would happen to me that day and it did…Rodick died. She also said that I would be reunited with someone from my past—you. I thought that I was destined for hardships for the remainder of my days, but I only hoped for prosperity." Sorsha raised her eyes to his. "I think our lives are destined for goodness going forward." With a press to her stomach, her eyes shone with love.

Shaw leaned toward her and placed a gentle kiss on her face. The Mackintosh Clan would thrive, not only from the wealth they received from Sorsha's family but with the love that would endure for a lifetime. Prosperity would be theirs.

The End

About the Author

Read a Scottish or Medieval Historical Romance book by Kara Griffin and transport yourself to the mystical enchanting realms of the Scottish Highlands and Medieval Britain. Stories of noble swoon-worthy warriors and strong but sweet heroines will have you rooting for them as they encounter dastardly villains, political upheaval, and family dysfunction. Be romanced with sweeping tales of love and honor.

Kara Griffin has always had a vivid imagination and has been an avid romance reader since her early years. Inspired by her grandfather's heritage, she loves all things Scottish. From the captivating land to the ancient mysticism, all inspire her to write tales that make you sigh. With heroes, heroines, villains, and romance, there's always a Happily-Ever-After in her stories.

When Kara is not writing, she enjoys family life with her husband of 34 years, daughters, and five grandchildren. Living in the Pinelands of New Jersey, she spends a lot of time at a nearby lake, the Jersey Shore, and wooded areas of the Pine Barrons. She and her family are huge sports fans and cheer on the teams of the city of Philadelphia.

Website – karagrif66.wixsite.com/authorkaragriffin
Facebook – facebook.com/AuthorKaraGriffin
BookBub – bookbub.com/authors/kara-griffin
Amazon – amazon.com/stores/Kara-
Griffin/author/B006ZCH4PG
Goodreads – goodreads.com/author/show/1428371.Kara_Griffin
IG – authorkaragriffin

www.ingramcontent.com/pod-product-compliance
Lightning Source LLC
Chambersburg PA
CBHW071245300726
48975CB00002B/554